BTR 10/18

KT-220-053

‎9030 00006 2194 4

How to Fall in Love Again

AMANDA PROWSE is the author of nineteen novels including the number 1 bestsellers *What Have I Done?*, *Perfect Daughter* and *My Husband's Wife*. Her books have sold millions of copies worldwide, and she is published in dozens of languages.

Amanda lives in the West Country with her husband and two sons.

www.amandaprowse.com

ALSO BY AMANDA PROWSE

Novels

Poppy Day
What Have I Done?
Clover's Child
A Little Love
Will You Remember Me?
Christmas For One
A Mother's Story
Perfect Daughter
Three-and-a-Half Heartbeats
The Second Chance Café
Another Love
My Husband's Wife
I Won't Be Home for Christmas
The Food of Love
The Idea of You
The Art of Hiding
Anna
Theo

Short Stories

Something Quite Beautiful
The Game
A Christmas Wish
Ten Pound Ticket
Imogen's Baby
Miss Potterton's Birthday Tea

How to Fall in Love Again

Kitty's Story

Amanda Prowse

HEAD
of ZEUS

LONDON BOROUGH OF WANDSWORTH

9030 00006 2194 4	
Askews & Holts	11-Oct-2018
AF	£11.99
	WW18011282

First published in the UK in 2018 by Head of Zeus Ltd

Copyright © Amanda Prowse, 2018

The moral right of Amanda Prowse to be identified as the author
of this work has been asserted in accordance with the
Copyright, Designs and Patents Act of 1988.

All rights reserved. No part of this publication may be
reproduced, stored in a retrieval system, or transmitted in any form
or by any means, electronic, mechanical, photocopying, recording,
or otherwise, without the prior permission of both the copyright
owner and the above publisher of this book.

This is a work of fiction. All characters, organizations,
and events portrayed in this novel are either products of
the author's imagination or are used fictitiously.

9 7 5 3 1 2 4 6 8

A catalogue record for this book is available from
the British Library.

ISBN (FTP): 9781788542159
ISBN (E): 9781788542135

Typeset by Adrian McLaughlin

Printed and bound in Great Britain by
CPI Group (UK) Ltd, Croydon CR0 4YY

Head of Zeus Ltd
First Floor East
5–8 Hardwick Street
London EC1R 4RG

WWW.HEADOFZEUS.COM

This book is for Laura Palmer, "Hand in hand we danced, scattering magic in our wake and that magic lies on the paths we all walk, just waiting for discovery..." ajwp with love.

One

1974

'Kitty,' her mother called from the stable yard, 'come back here right now! You are not to go near that pony again today. I've told you twice!'

'But why can't I go with you and the boys?' Kitty stomped her little riding boot on the cobbles and stuck out her bottom lip.

'Because.'

'That's not an answer!' Kitty bellowed, hitting the leg of her jodhpurs with her crop.

'Well, it's all the answer you're going to get, my little love. Now go into the house and scrub up and ask Marjorie for some tea and sandwiches. We won't be too long.'

'But, Mum, Marjorie smells of dog and even though you say you won't be too long, I know you will. It's not fair! I ride better than Ruraigh, just ask Daddy, and Hamish is a crybaby. And I never cry!'

Her mother rubbed her brow, the soft leather of her riding glove squeaking across her fair, freckled skin. 'For the love of God, Kitty, why do you have to question everything! Why can't you for once just do as I ask, just *once*?'

Kitty shrugged inside her Fair Isle sweater and wondered the same thing. She knew her mum, always keen to be doing something, was constantly saying, 'To sit idle is a waste of a day, a waste of a life, and who wants that?' Not Kitty, that was for sure. Her fidgety nature meant she completely understood her mum's need to be on her way, but her mum appeared to have forgotten how much Kitty hated having her wings clipped. And it felt horrible.

She might have only been seven years old, but Kitty knew that her compulsion to query everything was not something her six classmates shared. She had overhead Miss Drummond saying to the priest, 'That young Kitty Montrose, she has wings on her feet and the devil on her tongue – it's a full-time job trying to coax her into staying in her chair!' This description had filled Kitty with happiness, though she suspected the other girls in her class would have been upset in her place. With wings on her feet, she now knew she could outrun Ruraigh and Hamish, her cousins, no matter that they were a whole one and two years older than her. They might have known words she didn't, occasionally teaching her the odd one, but she wasn't going to let them beat her at everything, no way.

'I'm meeting everyone on the ridge – we're going for a hack, and I'm already late.' Her mother sighed. 'We want to catch the last of the light.'

'Please, Mum! I love riding up there,' she whined.

'Well, you shouldn't love riding up there, it's way too steep for your pony, and the weather comes in quickly. It's not safe.'

'If it's not safe for me, how come it's safe for you?'

'Because I'm a grown-up. And remind me, why am I still here having this conversation?' Her mum walked forward, leading the tall horse.

'But Daddy said I was a natural,' Kitty said in desperation.

'Your dad's an idiot!'

Kitty knew her mum didn't really think he was an idiot. She watched the two of them after supper each evening, sitting in the library while she played in front of the fire. Her dad would rub her mum's toes as they drank cocoa or whisky and giggled, sometimes whispering when they thought she couldn't hear.

She stuck her chin out and pulled her most endearing face. 'Please, Mumma!'

Fenella Montrose ignored her pouting daughter, stepped up onto the mounting block and swung her leg over the muscled back of Ballachulish Boy. 'Go and find Marjorie. I shan't tell you again, you wee scamp!' she shouted, but with a flash of love in her eyes and the twitch of a smile around her mouth. She gathered Balla's reins loosely, making the lightest contact between her hands and the bit, then clicked her tongue against the roof of her mouth and gently squeezed his girth with her lower legs. Horse and rider walked serenely out of the yard.

A ball of rage swirled in Kitty's tummy as her cheeks turned pink.

'Kitty? Kitty, hen?' Marjorie called from the deep front porch of their vast grey house, Darraghfield. 'There's soup, sandwiches and cake when you're ready!'

Late afternoon was Kitty's favourite time of day. As the sky turned purple, softening the outlines of the deep glens and rolling Highland hills around them, the lights of the main house would come on one by one, reminding her of an advent calendar with each little window opening to reveal a secret.

'Kitty! Kitty!' their housekeeper called, her tone becoming more exasperated.

Using the shadows, the little girl wove her way across the cobbles, darting this way and that to stay hidden, looking back over her shoulder until she felt the scratchy straw of Flynn's bedding underfoot.

'Sshhhh! Flynn, we're on a secret mission.' She held her finger up to her lips and told her pony not to make a sound. 'We're going to follow Mummy and her friends out and come home before them and they will never know we've been gone. Don't worry about Marjorie, she can watch *Crossroads* in peace in the kitchen.'

With her two red plaits bouncing up and down, Kitty trotted Flynn across the cobbles, out of the yard and along the lane. She looked up at the darkening sky and breathed in the late-afternoon air, which was heavy with moisture and the sweet scent of moss. With a wide smile of satisfaction, she walked her pony across the field; clumps of tall thistles and lichen-covered rocks littered the wet grass, making the going a little tough along the sharp incline. Bending forward, she patted her pony's flank with the flat of her palm. 'You're such a good boy, Flynn! I love you.'

At the top of the field they broke into a canter and it was only when Kitty looked back down the sweep of the bank towards the house that her smile faded. It was further away than she'd anticipated and suddenly the path wasn't where she thought it would be. She'd forgotten that this side of the ridge fell into darkness first, as the sun dropped behind the towering conifers along the summit.

'It's okay, Flynn. Don't be scared, boy. We'll just go down very slowly and go home – we'll be back on the lane before you know it. I think it's too late and too dark for a baby pony like you to be out all on your own.'

Kitty's heart was beating loudly and droplets of sweat had broken out above her lip. Her hands felt clammy against the reins and in the half-light the trees and hedgerows harboured the sinister shapes of monsters and ghouls. The two of them went forward with caution; Flynn's steps were hesitant, and Kitty's breath came in short bursts.

'Don't be scared, Flynn!' She swallowed. 'It's only the dark and we're nearly home. We'll get you settled and I'll go and watch TV with Marjorie in the—'

Kitty didn't see the large red hind and her baby feeding on the lower slope of the field, but Flynn did. He whinnied, bucked and raised his two front legs, skittish on the slippery bank, before throwing Kitty down hard.

It was a shock to view the world from such an odd angle when only seconds before all had been well. She screamed as she tumbled. A pain in her arm drew all her attention as she lay on the grass, finding it hard to catch her breath. Flynn, now free of his rider, raced off as fast as his little legs would take him, in the opposite direction of the house. She heard his canter fade into silence.

Kitty cried loudly, glad at first that no one was around to hear. Then she fell into some kind of sleep, the soft moss and grass as her mattress, the damp earth soaking her clothing and the crescent moon peeking at her from behind the dark bruise of dusk.

'Kitty!'

The call was faint to start with. She thought she might be dreaming, but the uncomfortable ache to her body told her she was awake. Slowly opening her eyes, she tried to sit up, but the pain in her arm and shoulder made moving impossible.

'Kitty!'

It was louder this time, closer, and then came beams of light, swinging up and down the field from powerful torches. She raised her good arm and flexed her fingers as best she could before replying quietly, 'Here,' and then again, louder, 'Here!'

'Kitty!' There was an almost hysterical edge to her mother's voice. 'Oh, sweet Lord above!'

She closed her eyes and heard the flat, heavy thud of footsteps running across the ground to where she lay, accompanied by shouts and the metallic jangle of lanterns and torches. Her body softened a little. They'd found her.

'Oh, darling! Oh, my baby!' Her mother sobbed. 'Are you hurt?'

'No,' she managed. Even in her dazed state she knew to lie so as not to make her mother any more anxious.

'Now, Kitty Montrose, what have you been up to?' Her dad's soft, calm tone made her smile, despite her discomfort. His big bald head, and hands as wide as pans came into view as he crouched down beside her. Just knowing he was there made everything feel a whole lot better.

'I wanted to ride with everyone up on the ridge, and...' Her face scrunched up as the left side of her body throbbed.

'There now.' He smoothed her wispy fringe from her clammy forehead. 'You need to breathe and try and relax your muscles, and remember that you're a warrior, like your mum.'

Kitty nodded. She never forgot. *A warrior, like my mum.* It made her special. Strong.

'Let's get you inside and warmed up.' Her dad bent down and Ruraigh swung the torch over her form.

As the beam of light fell across her left arm, her mother screamed. 'Oh my God! Her arm! Stephen, will you look at her arm!' Then came the sound of Hamish being sick into the grass.

'Don't look down, Kitty.' Her dad leant in close and spoke firmly, yet calmly. 'Keep your eyes on my face and we'll get you to the hospital and they can patch you up and you'll be good to go.'

She could hear the fear in his voice, and despite being told not to look, he had piqued her curiosity. She lowered her eyes and stared at her arm. It looked odd to say the least – it was broken, clearly, and stuck out from her body, twisted at a very awkward angle. It was scary to see something so familiar so bent out of shape and, strangely, once she'd seen it, it hurt even more. 'Fuckaduck!' she screamed, before giving in to tears of fear.

Despite the dire circumstances, Ruraigh laughed and Kitty wondered what was so funny about the word that he and Hamish had taught her only yesterday.

Moving Home

Kitty let her eyes rove across the mountain of sealed boxes stacked neatly along the back wall of the landing, their contents summarised in scrawls of thick black marker-pen. More still were lined up in the bedroom, with others dotted around the kitchen. Every room of the four-storey Victorian terrace in Blackheath, London had been dismantled; the fittings and fixtures had been plucked off walls and gathered from shelves, cloaked in bubblewrap and secreted away inside the cardboard boxes, ready to emerge in their quite different new home. It felt odd, packing up a lifetime of memories. She hadn't banked on it being so emotive, but with each new box filled she felt swamped by recollections. Some of her happiest times had been spent in this house, playing with the kids when they were little, on the sitting-room rug that now stood, rolled and bound with tape, waiting in a corner. And she'd had some of her saddest times here too, curled up in the chair in the sitting room, waiting for the next big showdown, crying silently and wondering how she'd got it all so wrong.

Kitty had no idea she had so much stuff.

Lots of it belonged to the kids, admittedly. She had unwittingly become the custodian of the crap they didn't want in their own homes. Everything from ski gear to boxes of books, camping equipment and even a spare rabbit hutch – God only knew where that had come from! Not that she minded, not really. Having their things around her allowed her to believe at some level that they still lived there, and that in itself was a comfort.

Moving house, however, was a good chance for a clear-out. It forced her to investigate long-abandoned corners and dusty cupboards that bulged, mostly with rubbish. It was surprising that after years of taking up precious space in her home, the value of certain things was no more than the fact of their having been around for a long time. She sent the clutter to the tip without too much consideration. At least where they were moving to was big, with plenty of storage. Although, last she'd heard, certain individuals already had their eye on several of the outbuildings, which would apparently be perfect for a woodworking studio, a workshop and a potting shed, if she remembered correctly. She smiled at the image of them set up and cosy in a family home; the giddy swirl in her stomach was that of a teenager and not a fifty-two-year-old woman. She rather liked it.

It was early morning. Sophie, who had popped in as promised to help with the lifting, called down through the open loft hatch. Kitty was grateful for her stopping by.

'Are you ready, Mum? This is getting heavy.'

Kitty stretched up her arms and steadied herself against the aluminium ladder, which felt none too secure. 'Yes, drop it! The anticipation is killing me!'

'Here it comes.'

Kitty braced herself and gathered the sturdy plastic box into her arms, which were still strong, muscled. Sport, and swimming in particular, had proved to be the kindest thing she'd done to her body over the years.

'What's in it?' Sophie called from within the dusty confines of the loft.

'Give me a chance! Good Lord, are you this impatient with your pupils?' She laughed, trying to imagine her daughter in her role as teacher, a department head, no less.

'I am, actually – they're all petrified of me.' Sophie laughed.

'Poor them.' Kitty smiled with pride.

She lugged the box across the narrow landing and heaved it onto her bed, before pulling it open and showering the duvet with dust. As she peered inside, her heart fluttered and she felt a whoosh of excitement in her chest. She looked up at her daughter, who now stood in the doorway of the bedroom. 'Oh, Soph! Oh, how lovely! These are my old photographs. Mainly from when I was little, and a few from school, I seem to remember.'

'Ooh, marvellous – snapshots from debauched parties and your misspent youth, I hope?' Sophie rubbed her hands together and flopped down on the bed next to her mother.

'Hardly!' Kitty laughed. 'More likely me in the swimming pool or playing Scrabble with your grandad – that kind of thing.'

She ran her fingers over the collection of images, some dog-eared and others sporting the sticky ring of a carelessly placed glass of squash. Some were in black and white, others had gone sepia-toned where the colours had faded. But every one of them took her back to a particular place in time; she could recall the decor, the time of year, even the scent of summer grass or winter fires.

'I know you all snap away now on your phones quite frivolously, but in those days photographs were only taken by a sturdy camera and they felt quite important. They were printed and some even got framed and made it onto the mantelpiece, and they were always hung on to; they were precious things. Not like now when you have thousands of them sitting on that tiny screen and you delete them willy-nilly.'

'Yes, but we get to choose the best pictures, edit them, even, so we wouldn't end up with something like this!' Sophie held up a picture of Kitty as a small child in a hand-knitted Arran jumper. Her hair stuck up at odd angles and her eyes were half-closed. The whole image was blurry. It was less than attractive.

'True! But I like the authenticity of it. That's exactly what I was like – a bit boisterous, too fidgety to sit still for a camera and always wearing jumpers like that. I was probably eager to get to my pony or to run off somewhere.'

She delved into the box and pulled out another image of her with her head close to the beautiful broad forehead of a pony.

'Oh, Sophie!' She sighed, turning the image outwards so her daughter could see. They both laughed. 'Will you look at that! That is a look of pure love!'

She had written on the back: *Kitty Dalkeith Montrose aged nine and a half with Flynn.*

'I love how I've given my full name lest there be any doubt!' She peered more closely at the picture. 'You can't see it here, as my arm is hidden, but I had just come out of hospital. I remember being desperate to get back to Darraghfield. I think this was after the fifth operation on my arm. I hated being away from home, the food was terrible and there was a very strict ward sister who put the fear of God into me, put the fear of God into all of us! She was revered throughout St Bride's – you remember St Bride's, don't you? The local cottage hospital up there.'

'The one where Nana went sometimes...?'

Kitty nodded quickly and continued. 'Your nana and grandad would come and visit me for an hour every night. That was all they were allowed. They'd take a painted green metal chair from a stack by the door, just the one, mind, as per Sister's rules, and take turns sitting on it. And they'd try and make me laugh, cheer me up, right up until the five-minute warning bell for the end of visiting time, and then your nana would sob. She cried so easily...' Kitty paused, close to tears herself now, at the memory of her mother.

'She'd weep and go on about how I might have been killed that night, when I was seven, but I always thought she was exaggerating. I do know I hurt my arm so badly that it took six operations over about four years to get it to this.' She held out her arm, which was far from straight, far from perfectly fixed.

'Funnily enough, the thing that bothered me most was that I'd been promised a shotgun for my tenth birthday and I was so looking forward to it, but I knew that with my wonky arm I wouldn't be able to shoot straight. The idea of not being as good a shot as Ruraigh and Hamish... God, that was more than I could bear. They teased me so much.'

'Even then?' Sophie smiled.

'Yes, even then.' Kitty shook her head and was surprised by how maudlin she felt. 'Just talking about the hospital takes me back to that room – I can smell the antiseptic in the air and remember the layout of the ward.' She ran her hand over the bone that was permanently bent. 'I've been told that if I'd been taken to a bigger hospital, with specialist surgeons and all that, you'd never be able to tell I'd hurt my arm.'

'Instead you were probably sawn open by a rank amateur at the cottage hospital who was over the moon to be dealing with something other than frostbitten fingers, haemorrhoids and babies with croup.'

'Probably something like that.' She smiled.

'I rather like your wonky arm, Mum. It's just another thing that makes you unique.'

'Oh God, Sophie, is that the kind of cliché you offer your students?'

'Only the shit ones who need a bit of bolstering.'

'You are funny.'

'I've got to go.' Sophie glanced at her watch, then back at her mum. 'Do you know, I've never seen you this happy. It's wonderful.'

Kitty looked up at her. She was overjoyed that her daughter approved of this new beginning. 'Thank you, Soph. I love you.'

'Love you too. Don't bother coming down, I'll see myself out. I expect you'll sit here for some time working your way through those.' She nodded towards the box of photos.

Kitty pressed the one of her and Flynn to her chest. 'I wish I had time, but this old house isn't going to pack itself up.'

'Will you miss it, Mum?'

Kitty took a second or two to formulate her response. 'I will miss the happy memories that I have of you and Olly being little, and I'll miss Blackheath's lovely shops!' She smiled, briefly. 'But I think I'm overdue this change and it will be good to live free of all the ghosts that lurk in the drawers and cling to the curtains.'

'But you don't regret *everything*, do you? I mean, you can't, it's too much of your life.'

'Oh, Soph, not only do I have so much to feel thankful for, but I try to regret nothing. It feels pointless. I do wish I'd had more courage at times. I wish I'd listened to my instincts. But regrets...? Not really.'

Two

'And where are you off to, if I might ask?' Marjorie said as she wiped the grill pan dry after its scrubbing.

Kitty looked down at her flat, fourteen-year-old's chest, her skinny, purplish chicken legs and her sorry-looking bathing suit, turned grey from having been thrown into the wash with the navy towels. She bit the inside of her cheek, remembering what her mum had said about being sarcastic and how it was most unappealing. 'I was going to go for a quick swim.' She nodded in the direction of the pool, beyond the side garden and behind the hedge, as she draped the large, rough-textured beach towel over her shoulder.

The one good thing to come out of the riding accident back when she was younger was the advice from the doctor at St Bride's. After the second or third failed operation on her wonky arm, he'd suggested she take up swimming to help with dexterity, muscle tone and all the rest. And Kitty had loved the idea straightaway. Seven years on and swimming had become an important part of her life. Something no one could deny her, not even Ruraigh and Hamish.

'A quick swim?' Marjorie did this, repeated nearly everything she said, which irritated her. Her dad had explained that Marjorie was no spring chicken and was probably doing so to ensure she had heard correctly. No matter, it still grated.

'The sun's out.' As if proof were needed, Kitty pointed to the light flooding through the wide sash window and onto the worn wooden countertop, highlighting the bleach marks left by Marjorie's overzealous scouring. 'I don't want to miss it.'

Having lived all her life in the notoriously unpredictable climate of the Scottish Highlands, Kitty was well used to it being summery in the morning and wintry by the afternoon, or vice versa, and she wasn't about to give up on this glorious window of opportunity. It was Easter and the weather was unseasonably good.

'Patrick has cleaned the pool out and I've been waiting for a dip. I shan't be too long.'

'Waiting for a dip? They'll be here any minute! I'd advise that rather than messing about, you go and wash your face and clean your teeth.'

'Wash my face and clean my teeth?' Maybe this repetition thing was infectious. 'I don't see why I have to, it's only Hamish and Ruraigh and I know for a fact they don't clean their teeth when they're going to see me! They hardly spoke to me last time they were home.' She toyed with the edge of the towel and pouted in the indignant way that only a fourteen-year-old girl could.

It had been a hard thing for her to accept that in the four years since her two cousins, brothers by any other name, had started at the prestigious Vaizey College, hundreds of miles away in southern England, they had stopped including her as much, if at all. Each trip back to Darraghfield had seen a slow but undeniable erosion of their closeness. Gone was the rough and tumble of their playful holidays, and no longer was she confident of being able to make them laugh or challenge them to a kick-about. It was as if they no longer found her good company, and she wondered what about her could have changed so much. 'Oh no, not Kitty!' she overheard Ruraigh moan when Hamish had suggested inviting her for a muck-about on the river. 'She'll only slow us down!' Her cheeks had flamed with anger and her eyes had sprouted tears. Suddenly she'd found herself relegated to the status of a baby. She also heard Ruraigh remark to Hamish that she was 'the most boring girl in the world', and that hurt.

The changes were subtle at first; they began asking Patrick the gardener's sons to make up a four with them for tennis, Monopoly or golf, even though she and Isla, her friend in the village, would have happily stepped up to the plate. They made private jokes about people and places she had never heard of: 'Aye, Twitcher! Twitcher!' they bellowed, before rolling around on the sofa. She sat, excluded and awkward, staring at the TV and trying not to care, wondering who or what Twitcher was and why it was so funny.

Their bodies had changed too, the soft pouches of boyhood replaced by hard muscles and wiry hair. When they'd arrived at Darraghfield for the summer holidays after their first year at Vaizey, she'd thought they looked yucky. She was nearly twelve, but at thirteen and fourteen, they were like alien creatures. Their voices had altered too, becoming deeper, with less of a crackly edge, and their vowels had got more rounded, the burr of their Highland heritage much less distinct. Words like 'grass' and 'bath' were elongated in a way that made them sound like royalty or the presenters on the BBC.

'Stinky old school, stinky old boys!' had been her conclusion when they'd finally left for the start of the autumn term.

'What's that?' her dad had asked over the top of his newspaper.

'I said, "Stinky old school and stinky old boys!"' she repeated with clarity and passion, lifting the teaspoon with its smudge of tea residue and smacking the top of her boiled egg with force.

Her dad had placed the paper on the breakfast table and given a half-smile. 'It's not easy being Ruraigh and Hamish. Their mum and dad are far away—'

'Yes, India.' Kitty was happy to show her knowledge and did so with a tone as dismissive as she could muster, hoping to indicate that she couldn't care less. So what if her stupid uncle was in the stupid army and they lived a stupid amount of miles away. Why did that make it okay for the boys to leave her out? She could play Monopoly as well as Patrick's boys. Fact.

'That's right – India. And that's why Darraghfield has always been their home, and that means you, Mum and I are very important to them.'

She sighed, wondering how he hadn't noticed their rejection of her and if he had, why he wasn't bothered by it.

'And here's the thing, Kitty – when you get older, things change, your mind and body grow so that you can absorb everything you see and everything you do. That doesn't mean you forget what you already know or who you already love, but it does mean that things that seemed so very important in your childhood get a wee bit diluted.'

I don't want to get diluted! I want to stay as I am.

'D'y'understand?' her dad asked earnestly.

She nodded even though she didn't. Not really.

In some ways, Kitty felt differently about her cousins now that she was fourteen – or at least about teenage boys in general. She and Isla gawped and giggled at the pictures of David Essex and John Travolta in the copy of *Jackie* maga-zine they bought every week from the village shop. They gossiped about what their first kiss would be like and which of the boys in the village they'd choose if they had to. Kitty secretly suspected that Isla had a bit of a thing for Ruraigh, but nothing had been said yet, much to her relief.

Marjorie placed the grill pan in the top oven and shooed the dishcloth in Kitty's direction, sighing affectionately and bringing her back to the discussion at hand. 'It shouldn't matter who is coming to the house, you shouldn't want to greet anyone with mud on your cheek or anything less than sparkling teeth!'

'Ah, well, the mud will be taken care of in the pool.' Kitty wondered if this qualified as sarcastic or practical. It was hard to tell.

Marjorie pushed the tight sleeves of her blouse up over her wide, white arms. 'Tell you what, let's compromise. You go and clean your teeth, and I agree, a quick dip will take care of the mud on your cheek, but you are not to dawdle in there – a short swim, then back up here for changing.'

'Thank you, Marjorie!' she yelled as she darted along the hallway to the downstairs bathroom, adjacent to the boot room.

She raced past the two suits of armour that stood like the shells of soldiers at the bottom of the wide, sweeping stair-case, and out of habit she patted the huge tapestries that lined the corridor as she whizzed by – patting them helped stop the dust from gathering, her mum always said. They were ancient, possibly from a similar period to the pikes crossed on the wall above them, talismans from significant battles fought by the Dalkeith Montrose family back in the day.

Darraghfield was pretty grand, but Kitty, having spent every day of her fourteen years there, knew no different and so never gave it a thought. The Dalkeith Montrose family had lived there for three hundred years, and some of the people in the gilt-framed portraits on the stairs, hallways and half-landings did look a bit like her dad. It was her dad who now ran Darraghfield and its estate, making sure the salmon-rich rivers and grouse shoots were well managed and kept the family's wealth steady. Despite its history and size, the house itself was homely: in the reception rooms, the furniture was rounded and worn, with thick wool blankets over the arms and rugs brought back from travels far afield on the slate floors. Everywhere carried the residual smell of real fires.

In the bathroom, Kitty grabbed at the toothpaste tube and squeezed it, stuck out her tongue, licked a blob off the end, then swiped her hand across her mouth. Job done.

'What are you up to in there, Kitty Montrose?' Her mum leant on the doorframe, smiling at her.

Kitty was pleased to see her as these days her mum was more often than not upstairs. 'I've just cleaned my teeth.' She twisted her jaw defiantly.

'Uh-huh.' Her mum widened her eyes, not letting on if she was aware of the lie or not. 'And you are off for a swim? As if I need to ask.'

Kitty nodded, looking at her smart, beautiful mum, who knew better than Marjorie what her outfit meant.

'Can I plait your hair? It'll stop it getting so knotty in the water, my little mermaid.'

'Sure.' Kitty followed her to the stairs and sat on one of the lower steps. Her mum sat a little higher, with her silk night-gown and robe flowing over her knees and down the wooden stairs. Without a brush or comb, her mum raked her long fingers through Kitty's wild mane of curly red hair, smoothed it from her scalp and unpicked the knots. It felt so special to have her mum tending her hair so lovingly, and she enjoyed the snug feeling of sitting against her legs with the caress of soft silk on her arms. This was the version of her mum she loved best, the one who did these nice things for her, unhurried and interested, in close proximity.

'My mumma used to do this for me each morning and I loved it. When I first met Daddy, I used to get him to brush my hair for me. He thought I was odd, but I loved that feeling, Kitty, of someone looking after my hair while I sat with my eyes closed and let my thoughts wander...'

Kitty closed her eyes and did just that, as her mum nimbly divided her hair into two bunches and twisted them into fat plaits that sat either side of her head, close to her scalp. She fastened the ends with two elastic hairbands recovered from her robe pocket.

'There.' Her mum leant forward and kissed Kitty on the forehead. 'You'll do.'

'Thank you.' She stood and turned to face her mum on the stairs. 'I love you, Mum.'

Her mum's face broke into a wide, adoring smile. 'And I love you too, so much.'

'You can come and watch me if you like?' She pointed towards the garden.

'Oh...' Her mum shook her head, a little crease of worry at the top of her nose, as she gripped the neck of her nightgown. 'I think I might just go back up to bed.'

Kitty nodded and swallowed the lump of disappointment in her throat. Her mum slowly stood and began her climb back up the stairs; the effort it took, it could have been a mountain.

Kitty ran into the boot room and slipped on her flip-flops, which were a tad too small, this now apparent from the way the backs bit uncomfortably under her heels. Shutting the stable-door of the boot room behind her, she sprinted down the gravel path, leapt over the shrub border, raced across the patch of grass and made her way through the narrow gap in the laurel hedge.

The hedge was the screen around her special place, providing shelter and privacy for Darraghfield's beautiful Italianate-style heated swimming pool, a fancy addition for the third wife of her great-great-grandfather. Throwing her towel onto one of the wicker steamer chairs, she paused, taking in the perfect sunny vista as she stood on the edge with her long, pale toes curled around the curved lip of the tiles. The sunlight danced on the surface as it shifted in the breeze and the Roman steps at the far end wobbled, distorted in their watery home.

Kitty bent her knees and angled her back just as her dad had shown her. With her head tucked, arms level with her ears and hands reaching out, she leapt and pushed herself forward, feeling the immediate thrill of breaking the surface as the water rippled from her form. Working quickly, she propelled herself forward, hands slightly cupped, waggling her feet, moving at speed until her fingertips touched the opposite wall. She flipped around awkwardly, lacking the grace of swimmers who had the knack, and headed back, feeling the delicious tensing of her muscles against the resistance of the water.

Eight, maybe ten lengths later and her breath came fast. She trod water and wriggled her finger first in one ear and then the other, then smoothed the droplets from her face with her wrinkled palm. She felt both peaceful and very much alive. The sun warmed her freckled skin and all was right with her world.

I could stay like this forever… My happy place.

She lay on her back in a semi-doze as the water lapped at her ears. Lying like this turned the world into a quiet place, a refuge of sorts. It had been lovely to see her mum up and about earlier and she was grateful for the touch of her fingers on her scalp. It was a reminder of how things used to be. She let her eyes wander to the slate roof of Darraghfield, picturing her mum ensconced in the beautiful turret room, curled up, as she often was, looking small in the middle of the big bed and wanting to do nothing more than sleep. Dad said she was 'very tired'. Marjorie said she was 'under the weather'. Neither explanation came close to answering the many questions that flew around Kitty's head. It was as if life exhausted her mum and nothing interested her, not even the tiny bird skull Kitty had found next to the path up by the stables. She'd rushed eagerly up the many fights of stairs and along the hallways, cradling the tiny, delicate thing in her palms, but not even this remarkable discovery had been enough to draw her mum from her sadness.

It wasn't a surprise, not really. Kitty knew that if her mum wasn't interested in her once-beloved horse, it was most unlikely that a little bird skull was going to prove a hit. The handsome Ballachulish Boy was groomed and fed but rarely ridden. He too took on the drop-headed melancholy that seemed to be spreading over the estate like a malaise. And then he was gone. It had been a dark day when she and her dad had watched him being goaded reluctantly into a trailer, tears prickling their eyes. 'He deserves better' was all the explanation her dad could offer.

Kitty executed a forward roll in the pool, as if resetting her thoughts. Then she reassumed her floating position.

Peaceful. Thinking now of nothing…

Just as the light arrived dappled through the leaves of the laurel hedge, so sound was diluted, reaching her ears differently. Kitty closed her eyes and let her arms bob by her sides, and there she stayed, happily floating on the water with the spring sun on her skin and the muted burble of birdsong in the distance. She heard the faint echo of a car door slamming and pictured her cousins alighting with bags, sports paraphernalia and a desperate need of the bathroom, as her dad slapped them on the back and wrapped them in brief, tight hugs. Just the image of her dad close by made her feel safe.

She had no idea how long she stayed like that – minutes, an hour? Her hold on time was skewed, so lost was she to the water. But then, quite unexpectedly, she sensed a change to the shape of her world.

A dark shadow loomed between Kitty and the sunshine.

Slowly she opened her eyes to see a man standing on the poolside. He stood with his hands in his pockets, shirtsleeves rolled above the elbow. She blinked and realised it wasn't a man but a boy; a little older than her, but a boy nonetheless. Embarrassment made her right herself in the water. Ashamed that he'd seen her in a state of complete abandonment, her blush flared.

She stared at the floppy-haired outline of him and the shape of his face, a face that would become very familiar but which was not yet known to her. It was as if the universe knew that to reveal him to her completely might be more than her teenage heart could bear. Far better this gradual revelation of the body, the name, the life that would become so entwined with her own.

Kitty quite forgot she was wearing the ugly swimming costume that was baggy in places, worn thin on the bottom and discoloured to a dull grey. Truth was, she could barely think straight.

'Angus!' Ruraigh's voice called and the boy turned slowly and was gone.

Kitty watched him walk through the gap in the hedge, then lay back in the water. But she was no longer at peace. She was in fact agitated. Thoughts crowded her mind – what might be for supper, how long would it take for her toes to turn to prunes, and when would she grow boobs – and each one of them was topped and tailed by the image of a slender boy called Angus.

'So that's a fine Scottish name you've got.' Kitty's dad smiled at the boy over the dinner table as her cousins heaped peas and buttered new potatoes onto their plates, dwarfing the slabs of poached wild salmon that they'd been served.

'Yes, but that's about where my Scottishness ends, I'm sorry to say.'

'Can you believe that, Uncle Stephen? There were Ruraigh and I picking him for our rugby team, thinking we were kindred spirits and that he'd know the game, guessing we might have friends in common, and all the time he was from the New Forest, masquerading as a Scot with a name given to him by his grandfather!'

'Was your grandfather Scottish?' Kitty's dad asked with thinly disguised hope.

'I'm afraid not. Ruraigh is right – I'm a fake. My grandfather served with an Angus in the war and that was how I got my name.'

Stephen Montrose shook his head. 'Well, we shall make a Scot of you yet.'

'No wonder we kept losing at rugby – he couldn't kick straight if you glued the ball to his foot!' Hamish rolled his eyes.

The boys laughed, Angus blushed, raising his hands in

defeat, and her dad chortled in the way she loved, with creases at the side of his eyes and his mouth wide open. This was how he used to laugh, on the sofa in the days when her mum had managed to keep her illness at bay. Or at least when Kitty had been less aware of it; if she really thought about it, the signs had always been there.

She felt torn, hating the male camaraderie and her exclusion from it, but pleased her dad was laughing. When he was like this, his happy mood lifted everyone, made everything seem possible. Gone was the stilted conversation around the table, when everyone ate too quickly, in a hurry to be elsewhere, and gone too were the worried glances at the dark shadows beneath eyes in want of sleep. The knot of unease in her stomach miraculously unwound, leaving her with a void that she filled with hope. It was nice to get a break from the anxiety.

She wished it could always be this way.

'Well, if it's a kicker you're wanting, you could do a lot worse than Kitty, isn't that right?' Her dad waved his laden fork in her direction. 'Been training her since she was knee-high.'

'Not much call for kicking in a swimming pool!' Hamish nudged his brother and they laughed. 'Got them gills yet, Kitty?'

For the first time, she wondered if she too had changed. Maybe her cousins were not solely to blame for their gradual estrangement. Ordinarily she would have stood and thrown a spud at Hamish or shouted out loud that she'd seen him close to tears when they watched *Kramer Vs Kramer* – she had a store of insults ready for occasions such as this. But today the words stopped on her tongue and her cheeks reddened. She was aware only of Angus's presence and how she might appear to him if she let her rage get the better of her.

She was still trying to think of an appropriate response when Angus leant forward, his elbows on the table, his white shirtsleeves rolled up to reveal bronzed forearms peppered with fair hair.

'I thought a strong kick was exactly what's needed to propel you through the water?'

He didn't look at her, didn't address her directly, but she knew that he spoke in her defence and it felt wonderful! Fireworks of happiness danced in her stomach, along with something else – a tingling, a churn of longing that was as new as it was scary. As if on autopilot, and to mask her confusion, she did what came naturally, picked up a spud and lobbed it – scoring a direct hit at Angus. Immediately, she ran from the room, tears gathering.

Twenty minutes later, Kitty sat with her jeans rolled up and her feet dangling in the water. The pool lights were on and the bright turquoise space seemed to glow in the evening darkness. She heard the rustle of the hedge and whipped round to see who or what might be disturbing her moment.

'It's only me.' Angus spoke as he approached and Kitty's heart leapt into her throat. He padded around the tiles and came to sit next to her, so close she could smell the tang of his end-of-day sweat and the whiff of supper and nerves on his breath. She stared ahead, hoping that her heart didn't sound as loud to him as it did in her ears, thinking it would be a most bizarre thing for him to hear. He slipped out of his Docksides and rolled up his jeans before sitting down next to her, only a reach away, then placed his feet in the water next to hers.

'I'm sorry about your shirt,' she whispered, still mortified at the memory of the buttery spud landing squarely on his chest.

'It doesn't matter. It'll wash. Your dad said Marjorie might have a go at it tomorrow.'

She nodded, thankful for Marjorie, who just might save the day. 'I wasn't aiming for you.'

'As I said, no harm done.'

She kicked out in the water and watched the ripple spread.

'I think there's so much more to a swimming pool than a place to swim,' he began.

She turned her head to the left. He had her interest – although he could have been reading aloud from the phone book and she would have been drawn.

'What d'you mean?'

Angus took a deep breath through his nostrils and spoke softly. 'When you get into a pool alone, it has a special kind of feel about it. You almost become one with the water.'

'Yes!' She nodded. *Exactly.* This boy might be a friend of her cousins, but he understood.

'It always feels like the biggest win if you arrive at a pool and there's no one else in it. I think you swim at a different level – it's impossible not to, with that whole body of water there just for you. Doubly so if the pool is outside.'

'I've only ever swum here and in the sea.'

'Which do you prefer?' He looked at her now. She noticed the way his hazel eyes meandered all over her face, as if committing her to memory, learning her, and she liked it.

'Here. It's my spot.'

'Yes, I saw you here when we first arrived...' He let this linger.

She smiled and nodded at the memory of that moment, which had managed to set the tone, hijacking her day.

'The pool at Vaizey isn't up to much. It's big but not pretty, and they keep it on the cool side. And there's something quite revolting about a school pool that has a hundred or so unwashed boys' bodies in it each and every day.' He laughed. 'One of the lifeguards once told me I wouldn't believe the things they found lurking at the bottom!' He pulled a face.

'Urgh, no thanks!' She felt a little sickened by the thought.

'Well, you'll have to get used to it or find somewhere else to swim, and that's not easy in rural Dorset.'

Kitty turned her body to face him. '*I'm* not going to Vaizey! No way! Why would you think that?' She shook her head at the absurdity of his suggestion.

'Oh, I don't know. My mistake. I... I thought...'

'There you are, Angus!' Ruraigh called from the gap in the hedge. 'Fancy knockout snooker in the games room?'

'Sure.' He stood and stamped his wet feet on the tiles, gathering up his Docksides and holding them in his outstretched fingers as he walked off.

Kitty stared at the imprint of his wet feet on the ground next to her. She watched them dry and fade, wondering if he'd been hinting that *he* might like her to attend Vaizey... But surely not – he was sixteen and she was pale and boyish with a wonky arm and no boobs and, according to her cousins, the most boring girl in the world.

Over the rest of the Easter holidays, Kitty tried to engineer ways to be alone with Angus; she wasn't trying to be devious, she was simply keen to study him without anyone else around. Once or twice she caught him at the tail end of breakfast. Ruraigh and Hamish always wolfed down their eggs and toast at breakneck speed, unwilling to waste a moment of the day. Such was their impatience, they'd abandon Angus, who ate in the same manner with which he undertook any task, with precision and consideration. He would sit alone at the table in the morning room with a slice of Marjorie's homemade bread raised to his chest, the crust of which was always thick, hard and slightly burnt, delicious with a generous curl of salted Scottish butter.

One time Kitty walked nonchalantly into the room to look out of the window, as if assessing the weather. On another occasion she opened the drawer of the mahogany sideboard, searching for goodness knows what in a place that she knew contained only faded playing cards and her dad's ancient solitaire board with some of the little white pegs missing. These activities were a red herring; her sole purpose was to be near him, to look at him, gathering images that she would store in the evolving montage in her brain. Tiny details held unfathomable fascination for her: the way his long fringe flopped over one eye when he leant forward; the square shape of his fingertips when they flattened on a surface; the barely audible 'T' sound he made before he laughed, and how if something wasn't that funny to him, he omitted the laugh altogether and just uttered the little 'T'. Kitty collected up all of these snippets and built Angus in her mind, layer by layer, filling in the gaps with her wishes and desires about what a boy, no, what a *boyfriend* should be.

Today she'd been pretending to look for the morning newspaper.

'Where are you off to?' he asked from the table.

She looked down at her jodhpurs and riding jacket. *What is it with people?*

'I'm taking my pony Flynn out for a hack. He's getting on a bit and I need to keep his joints moving or he seizes up.'

Angus seemed less than interested.

'Do you ride?'

Please say yes... She pictured the two of them cantering along the ridge as day broke, watching the warm sun soften the brittle spikes of the conifers that loomed large on the snow-capped hilltops.

'God, no!' He laughed and she heard the echo of that little 'T'.

'Have you ever tried?' she pushed, unable to accept that someone was willing to miss out on the most fabulous experience the world had to offer. After swimming, of course.

'Yes, once or twice. Not really my thing.' He dusted the crumbs from his hands and reached for a napkin. 'Plus I've seen your pony. Don't think he'd take too kindly to having to ferry me around.'

'He's stronger than he looks.' She leapt to her beloved Flynn's defence. 'You should have seen my mum's horse, he was a beauty.' Kitty smiled at the image of her mum in her riding habit astride the impressive Balla Boy, who used to do her bidding at no more than a click of her tongue or a flick of the reins. 'But he's been sent to a yard somewhere near Hawick. He needed a lot of looking after.'

'I guess with your mum being depressed, that was hard – too much for her.'

Depressed. She stared at him. It was as if a thunderbolt had been fired into Kitty's chest. That was the first time she'd heard the word associated with her mum. She knew almost nothing about depression, but she instinctively sensed Angus might be right. Her stomach bunched with equal measures of sadness and anger. How come Angus knew about her mum's illness, which meant Ruraigh and Hamish did too, and yet she didn't?

Tears welled and colour bloomed on her cheeks – entirely regrettable in front of Angus. She drew herself up tall, turned on her heel, and without another word marched out of the door, along the hall and across the back yard. Without knocking on the door of the former stable that had long ago been converted into the estate office, she turned the handle and walked in. Her dad was on the phone. He winked at her and pointed at the leather chair positioned on the other side of the wide mahogany desk, which was cluttered with piles of paper and faded, dog-eared files. While he continued his conversation, she sat and stared at the tartan carpet, until her eyes felt a little fuzzy.

'Yes, yes, of course, Malcolm, that sounds good. Will you call Dezzy for me about next week's fishing permits and lodge accommodation?' Her dad nodded, as if Malcolm on the other end could see him. 'You're a pal. Speak soon.' He put the phone down and clapped loudly. 'Well, how lovely, a visitor!' He beamed. 'Although in future please remember that the only thing better than a visitor is a visitor bearing tea.'

Kitty declined to comment, in no mood for his banter, not right now.

He failed to take the hint. 'And if memory serves correctly, you usually only come down here when you either want something or I am in trouble. So, which is it?' Her dad smiled and sat forward, knitting his knuckles together on the desk.

'It's both.' She picked at a loose thread on her sand-coloured joddies.

Stephen Montrose let out a loud laugh that sent ripples of love around the walls. She wished he wasn't being so upbeat, not when the topic was anything but.

'Is Mum depressed?' She sucked in her cheeks, disliking the feel of the word in her mouth.

Her dad sat back in the chair, his soft expression

disappearing. He rubbed his eyes and face, as if suddenly over-come with fatigue. 'Who said that to you?' he asked quietly.

'Angus, but I know he will have heard it from the boys.' Whip-smart and in tune, she held his gaze, daring him to lie to her.

He nodded and let out a deep sigh. 'I suppose I've been waiting to speak to you about it, or, more accurately, putting it off.' He inhaled and continued, his voice barely more than a whisper. 'Your mum... Your mum is very poorly. A lot of people say, "Oh, I'm a bit depressed," but what they really mean is fed-up or angry or tired, and that's very different.' He paused again and looked skywards, in the way that he always did when considering his words. 'What your mum has is much more than being a bit fed-up. It's called severe clinical depression and it isn't a trivial thing.'

Kitty racked her brain, instantly trying to think of the times in her life when she had seen her mum with her head back, laughing. Happy. 'She did my hair the other day and she seemed fine – she wasn't dressed or anything, but she smiled at me.'

Her dad nodded. 'She has days, moments when she is good.'

'What about a nice holiday, or a day at the beach, or we could go up to Kilan Pasture and pick her some wildflowers?' Kitty suggested.

Her dad continued, with a quiet, sad smile. 'I wish it were that simple, darling. I wish there was a place or an event or a distraction that might bring her happiness, but it's nothing she can snap out of, it's not like a mood. It's as if your mum has been plunged into darkness and no matter where she is, what lies ahead, how good things are or how much we love her, it doesn't bring her any joy. Nothing does.'

'Not even me?' Kitty's voice was small.

Her dad sniffed and pulled his handkerchief from his cor-
duroys before blowing his nose loudly. 'Well, Kitty, never
doubt how much she loves you, how much she loves us. But
this should surely show you how terrible this depression is,
because you... you are all the joy in the world, and so if your
mum is unable to take part in that, to enjoy you, it must
surely be because part of her brain is a bit broken.'

'How did it get broken?' She thought about falling from her
pony and her arm snapping – was that possible with a brain?

Her dad shook his head. 'We don't know. But it did and it's
just like breaking a limb...' She looked up, wondering if he
had read her thoughts. 'Or having a disease of any other kind.
But the difficulty with having a broken brain is that other
people can't see what's wrong and that makes it hard for them
to understand it.'

She nodded because she too found it hard to understand.
'Can't they just fix it?' She inadvertently looked at the kink
in her wonky arm and flexed her fingers, thinking of all the
operations and recuperations at St Bride's.

'Well...' Again his voice was crackly with emotion. 'She
has spoken to a lot of doctors and they've given her medicine,
and sometimes she feels a bit better, a bit brighter, but most
of the time she doesn't. It's like someone has switched off her
happiness.'

Kitty looked out of the window as it started to rain, and
considered the facts. The thought of someone switching
off your happiness was one of the saddest things she could
imagine. 'How long will her brain be broken for? How long
until they can switch her happiness back on?' She pictured
turning off the video recorder in the TV room and counting
to ten in the hope that when she turned it back on it would
work just fine.

'Those are good questions.' He swallowed and rubbed his beard, she could tell that, like her, he could not wait for that day. 'It's like part of Mum has gone away and all we can do is wait for it to come back to us. Hope and pray that it comes back to us.' He squared his shoulders. 'But the truth is, we don't know where it's gone and therefore we don't know if it's a short or long journey. It might have gone round the corner or it might have gone to Timbuktu.'

It was Kitty's turn to sigh; this was not the answer she'd been hoping for.

'Her brain might never get fixed, or it might only get a *bit* fixed or it might get completely better.' He raised his palms. 'And that's another thing about this terrible illness – no one knows. No one can give me certainty, facts or timelines, only what they think.'

'Like guessing?'

'Yes. Exactly like guessing.'

'Can you… can you catch it, Dad?' Her eyes flickered with the guilt of being concerned for her own health at a time like this.

Her dad tucked in his lips and shook his head vigorously from side to side, seemingly unable to verbalise his response. She saw tears now sitting in little pools in his eyes.

'I think it's a proper shit disease,' she offered.

'Aye, Kitty, it is. Proper shit.' He smiled at her warmly. 'Would you like me to come out with you? I can saddle up Benson and—'

'No, thanks.' She stood. 'I'd rather go out on my own.'

Kitty saddled up her horse in silence and rode Flynn hard along the path that ran adjacent to the wide river at the bottom of the glen. 'Oi, Kitty!' Ruraigh called out from the bowl of the river as she flew past. She barely glanced in his direction, aware of him standing in the water, waders pulled high, casting his rod back and forth with a flourish that he hoped might tempt supper. She knew Marjorie was hoping for a haul of fat fish. Hamish lay sprawled on the grassy bank with a cigarette held high. She suspected Angus had stayed up at Darraghfield, and who could blame him if it meant not having to spend the day with those two idiots.

'Good boy, Flynn!' She spoke into his mane. His ears pricked up and with her head bent low, the two tripped with confidence along the stony path. As they rounded the curve in the river, her breath stuttered in her throat. She discovered that Angus had not stayed up at Darraghfield but was in fact standing all alone in the shallow fringes of the river, kicking up the sediment with his wellington boots and skimming flat stones over the surface of the water. His jeans were tucked into his boots and his jersey and shirtsleeves were pulled low on his wrists to ward off the worst of the cold breeze that was known to gather speed along the riverbed.

In a single action she pulled Flynn to a stop and jumped down, almost running into the water. With her heart pounding, she stood in front of the boy who had invaded her dreams and unsettled her equilibrium from the moment he arrived. This new knowledge about her mum had shaken her, frightened her, and she instinctively thought that contact with Angus might somehow help her.

'Kitty!' He looked a little surprised to see her. 'Hello.'

'Do you want to kiss me then?' she asked, with her hands on her hips and a tremble to her limbs.

He raised his eyebrows and an amused if slightly confused smile crossed his lips. 'Do I want to? I'm not sure,' he answered rhetorically, looking up the river to see if the other boys could see them.

Without giving him a chance to consider her proposition further, Kitty stood on her tiptoes and pressed her closed mouth against his, abandoning herself to the moment. Her worry over her mother's ill health flew from her mind, to be replaced with a deep, joyous longing that filled her gut and spread along her limbs like fire along kindling. She pulled away and looked at the flushed face of Angus, who smiled and drew her to him once again – into his arms and into his life.

When the others were around, Kitty and Angus did their best to be discreet, snatching sweet, chaste kisses on flushed cheeks whenever they could, and joining sweaty palms to hold hands when no one was looking. As the end of the holidays drew near, and with it the time to say goodbye, Kitty was surprised at how sad and listless she felt. She couldn't concentrate on anything, couldn't even summon the enthusiasm to go out on Flynn. Tears came at the slightest provocation from Ruraigh or Hamish, and she had an almost continual sinking feeling in her stomach. She and Angus said a private goodbye in the games room the night before he left, swapping notes and promising to write, but as she lay in her bed that night she started to panic. Was what she was feeling the beginning of depression? Supposing her dad was wrong and it was catching after all? She didn't want her happiness flying off to Timbuktu, didn't want to float around in her pyjamas with the faraway look of her mum and unwashed hair sticking to her scalp.

Next morning, Patrick swung the Land Rover and its three teenage passengers out of the yard and she and her dad waved until it was out of sight.

'So, you quite like this Angus fellow?' her dad asked as they both stared into the distance.

Her embarrassment flared and her mouth went dry. 'He's okay, I s'pose,' she managed, burying images of the two of them entwined, lips locked – the very last thing she wanted to imagine in front of her dad.

'Well, that's well and good, but be careful – I know how sixteen-year-old boys think—'

'Da-ad!' she interrupted, with a yell and a dig to his ribs with her elbow.

'Jesus, Kitty, I'm ancient and I still think like a sixteen-year-old boy!'

The two laughed, standing on the gravel until their giggles stopped and the place felt eerily quiet.

'You're going to miss them.' He ruffled her hair and she tutted, angered by such a babyish gesture. She was nearly fifteen, and what's more, she was a teenager who'd been *kissed*, actually kissed, by a boy, and that changed everything.

She nodded. *Miss them? Yes, I will...*

'Well, don't fret, Kitty.' He smiled at her, pulling her close. 'You might be seeing them sooner than you think.'

She noted the way he shifted on his feet and how his Adam's apple bobbed up and down in a large swallow. 'What do you mean?' She looked up at the big man who didn't know how to lie to her.

'I've been thinking, maybe *you* might like Vaizey College?'

Kitty gave a loud snort of laughter. 'Give over! Don't be daft, Dad! As if I'd ever leave you and Mum.' She looked up at the turret that housed her parents' bedroom. 'As if I'd ever stay anywhere other than Darraghfield!'

Moving Home

Kitty made her way downstairs and into the narrow kitchen, where she flicked the switch on her coffee maker for her second cup of the morning, putting the capsule into the fancy little machine that was now indispensable. She opened the cutlery drawer, now much depleted as she'd already made a start on packing up the kitchen. Two sets of knives, forks and spoons rattled around, the sight of which made her feel a little lonely. She had a flashback to happy evenings hosting dinner parties for up to twenty of their friends squashed around the table, elbows tucked in, plates smeared with gravy, the constantly refilled wine glasses catching the light from the chandelier overhead.

She closed the drawer, picked up the small vanity case that Sophie had brought down from the loft earlier and set it on the kitchen table. As she popped the tarnished brass lock, she gazed at the contents, momentarily frozen with the memories they evoked. She hadn't expected to cry, but the discovery of what lay on top sent a wave of sad recollection coursing through her. She reached in and gently lifted out her mum's hairbrush, its back beautifully worked in silver and mother-of-pearl. Turning it over in her palm, she ran her fingertips through the fine boar's-hair bristles, touching the long, dark hairs that still sat entwined about their base.

Part of her mum.

Kitty couldn't stop the sob that found its way along her throat and left her mouth as a loud cry. She pictured that morning in her childhood when she'd sat on the staircase in Darraghfield as her mum plaited her hair. The day she met Angus for the first time. She allowed herself to dwell briefly on that fourteen-year-old innocence, that momentous Easter holidays when adulthood had loomed so suddenly and from such different directions it left her almost breathless.

Now, nearly forty years on, Kitty wondered how she might do things differently if she had the chance to rewind time. If only her mum had been well that day, if only she had taken up Kitty's invitation to come and sit by the pool, had counselled her confused, naive, headstrong daughter to take it slowly, to not to be swept off her feet by the first boy who come along and seemed to show an interest...

Too many ifs. Kitty reminded herself sternly of what she'd said to Sophie earlier about not having regrets. The coffee machine gave off its drone to let her know her coffee was ready. Sniffing up her tears, she wiped her eyes on her sleeve and went to grab her little espresso cup.

Three

It had been a relatively successful morning or at least one that had passed without major incident. Matron had kicked her out of bed at six thirty sharp, even though she'd insisted she didn't want breakfast and didn't need a shower. Rather than protest, she decided to think like a warrior and 'crack on', as Marjorie would say. So she painted on a smile and she cracked on. The desire to vomit had all but faded and she'd been pleased to spot Hamish through one of the classroom doors as she wandered the corridors. She managed to get through chemistry without revealing the true extent of the gaps in her knowledge, realising that her education on the subject to date had been rather rudimentary. It turned out Isla was right: Miss Drummond was a bit shit. History had been a blast; the Second World War and its aftermath was a topic that she and her dad had chatted about on numerous occasions in front of the fire, and she was grateful that the lingering memory of those conversations allowed her to bluff her way through the lesson.

Her nerves bit at the oddest moments, like when she was trying to find someone to sit with at lunchtime. It was as she realised she was yet to make a single friend that her sadness threatened to engulf her. It still felt surreal: here she was at

Vaizey College, just a couple of weeks after she'd stood in the drive at Darraghfield and waved off Ruraigh, Hamish and Angus. It had all happened very fast, and she'd not really had time to process what it meant and how she felt about it. In fact it hadn't even felt real until the point when she'd said goodbye to Marjorie.

It was Marjorie who'd accompanied her down on the sleeper train, and Marjorie who'd organised everything before she left, mending and ironing her clothes, packing them into her dad's old trunk and making sure it was securely stashed in the guard's van for the journey south. Kitty had understood that her parents couldn't make the trip to Vaizey with her, but that didn't make it any better. Her mum had barely left her room for days and her dad never spent a night away from her when she was in that state. Though Kitty wished they could have come and said goodbye and helped get her settled, she was aware of the irony – if her mum had been capable of travelling all the way down to Dorset on the train, then Kitty wouldn't be coming to the stupid school in the first place. Not that she blamed her mum; she knew Mum wouldn't have chosen her illness in a million years. Kitty could sense how scary it was for her, and she still couldn't stop worrying that she might catch it herself. What if Vaizey made her brain broken and sent her happiness to Timbuktu too?

Poor Marjorie. Kitty had held on to her coat as they stood hugging in the corridor and begged her not to leave. Marjorie had cried, patting Kitty on the back with hands that had made her a million sandwiches and washed her clothes a thousand times. Kitty buried her face in her chest and hoped she knew how grateful she was for everything.

She fished out the handkerchief Marjorie had embroidered for her, dabbed at her eyes and dug deep to find a smile, determined to put a brave face on things. She walked into the quadrangle and felt an instant lift to her spirits when she spied her idiot cousins walking towards her. Ruraigh gave her a brief hug for the first time ever and Hamish stood close and with a hand on her shoulder whispered, 'It's all going to be okay, you know that, don't you?'

She nodded, even though she didn't know any such thing. But standing next to them, people who knew her, her kin, who knew about her life away from Vaizey College, well, it made her feel a wee bit better.

It was at the end of lunch that she caught sight of Angus across the dining hall. Her heart raced, but her head buzzed with self-doubt. Would he ignore her now that she was in his world, a world in which he was very much established – captain of the 1st XI, no less – and she was the new girl from way out in the sticks? Maybe he already had a girlfriend at school, one of the cool, sophisticated fifth-formers that were clustering around him. As Kitty listened to the assured way the other girls spoke, she hated the sinking feeling of inadequacy in her gut. Everyone looked and sounded much cleverer than her. They all seemed to know where they were going, and she didn't have a clue. She felt like a salmon trying to swim against the current. If she'd had the option, she would have curled up and hid, just like her mum in her bedroom in the turret.

But then Angus turned round and smiled at her, and Kitty's spirits soared. Her stomach bunched with joy, just as it had at Darraghfield, and she was overcome with the desire to kiss him again, everything else forgotten. It was all she could think about.

*

In the afternoon, Mr Reeves, the rather odd, portly tutor with a gravy stain on his shirtfront, chaperoned her to an empty classroom and then abandoned her. He'd appeared most put out by her arrival, reminding her of Marjorie when she got in a tizz, as if she were a late and unexpected arrival for dinner and he was going to have to upset the seating arrangements and lay another place.

'Come on, Kitty, you're nearly one day down,' she whispered to herself as she sat there waiting for something to happen, wiping the nervous sweat from her palms on her school skirt. 'You can do this.'

She became aware of someone to her left. Turning her head, she saw a boy hovering in the doorway, leaning on the frame. He stared at her until he realised she was returning his stare and looked away. Kitty noted the hunch to his shoulders, which were a little rounded, as if he was trying to hide, trying to fold himself away. She knew how he felt. He had a nice face, handsome, framed by dark curly hair, and yet his manner was that of someone in a semi-permanent state of apology. Very different from the confident swagger she'd seen in other Vaizey College boys. And it was unusual that he was alone; she'd noticed that the boys tended to travel in packs, be it a rugby clique or an academic group. And probably because of this, she felt an immediate bond with him.

He approached hesitantly, glancing nervously around the room as if he'd been warned that a trap might be sprung at any moment; the fall guy, forced to walk beneath the carefully balanced bucket.

Kitty thought it curious that of all the empty seats in the classroom, he pulled out the one next to hers and took up position alongside her at the two-person desk. It was a little awkward. She saw him swallow and understood that he might be too shy to introduce himself. She took it upon herself to break the ice.

'Hi there, I'm Kitty.' She smiled warmly and waved at him, even though they were close enough to speak.

He gave a small, nervy nod. 'I'm Theo.' He sat down and stared at her face, apparently having lost some of his earlier reticence.

'Well, you're going to have to help me out here, Theo. You know when a girl is a million miles from home and is smiling as though she has it all figured out but is actually just very scared, wondering how to fit in at a new school this late in the term?' She dipped her eyes, her voice sincere.

'Uh-huh.'

'Well, I am that girl.' She laughed softly and leant in closer, laying her fingers briefly on his arm. She felt him flinch beneath her touch.

Don't be afraid. It's okay... He reminded her a little of her mum – scared of the world and not sure of his place in it. The boy, Theo, clearly had no idea how attractive he was or how endearing his unassuming nature was.

Kitty continued, whispering now. 'Actually, that's not strictly true. I'm a warrior like my mum and that means I can get through just about anything.' She sat back in the chair and rested her hand on the desktop. 'Mr Reeves told me to sit here and then left me all alone. He seemed a bit odd.'

'I guess.' Theo nodded. 'And people fear people who are odd, weird. They think they're toxic, contagious.' He blinked.

'I suppose we do.' She gave a small laugh. 'I was going to give it five more minutes,' she said, 'and then run and hide somewhere, but then you turned up. You just might be my knight in shining armour.'

He beamed now. 'I'm not usually this early. I was working

in the library...' He let this trail, as if there was significance there that he was unwilling to share. 'It's a coincidence, really. Out of all the people that might have turned up early... I'm a Montgomery, so you must be...?'

'Oh! Oh, I see!' She smiled when she caught his thread. 'I'm a Montrose. So that explains the seating.'

They both laughed.

'I think I can get through this, Mr Montgomery, with you by my side. What was your first name again?'

'My name's Theodore, but everyone calls me Theo.'

She twisted her head to look at him. 'Theodore? Let me guess... after Mr Roosevelt? I must confess, I can't think of any other Theodores right now!'

'Actually, no.' His face broke into a wry smile, 'I was named after Theobald's House. My father was a Theobald's boy and my grandfather too, in fact all the men in our family came here, but I think my mother drew the line at Theobald and so Theodore was the compromise.'

'That's crazy!' She put her hand to her cheek. 'So your family are, like, Vaizey College through and through?'

'I guess.' He shrugged. 'I sometimes wish I was named after Roosevelt instead. It would be easier and quicker to explain.'

'And is that a Rudyard Kipling novel I see in your bag?' she peered at the green cloth spine.

'His poetry actually. For prep.'

'We have a lot of it in the library at home, you must know some of it already?' Her eyes blazed with enthusiasm.

The look he gave her made her heart lurch. His hesitation coupled with the flush of embarrassment to his cheeks. 'I'm afraid not. I haven't really read any yet.'

Kitty feared she was making him uncomfortable and smiled broadly. 'Well, why would you? My boyfriend is the same.'

How delicious that word sounded. *Boyfriend!* 'He only reads comics, if you can believe that!' She shook her head and reached for her textbook.

'You have a boyfriend?' he asked, sounding shocked and almost disapproving.

Her frisson of joy disappeared as fast as it had arrived and the self-doubt returned. Did he not see her as suitable girlfriend material? Her face coloured. 'Yes.' She nodded. 'My cousins are already here at Vaizey – Ruraigh and Hamish Montrose…'

Theo nodded and she was glad to have the connection. 'They always bring their friends home for the holidays, and he's one of their gang, so we kind of met a while ago. He's a fifth-former,' she said with pride. 'Angus Thompson – do you know him?'

Theo nodded again, but, strangely for a Vaizey boy, did not go on to share the many ways in which they were connected or recount times when their paths had crossed, as seemed to be the norm for Vaizey pupils, at least as far as her cousins and Angus were concerned. They were also going on about the importance of family connections stretching way back.

'Are you sporty?' she asked.

He shook his head. 'Not really. Are you?' He swallowed, reminding her of a boy in her primary school who, as the youngest of six, always felt that what he had to say was of little interest and so hurried to get to the point, sparing the detail, allowing the silence to return.

'Swimming, that's my thing. I love to swim. My dad always says that one day I'm going to develop gills behind my ears!' There was something about him that made her want to confide in him, made her think he might understand how lonely she felt, on her first day away from home. 'I'm finding being here harder than I can say,' she said quietly.

'I understand that,' he replied.

'My mum and dad are my best friends really. God, I know how naff that sounds, but they are. We do so much together and I would rather be with them than do anything else. Do you know what I mean?'

But he simply nodded at that, obviously didn't feel ready to share whatever was going on in his home life. She smiled again at the boy who she could tell, even after one short chat, sat outside the pack, on the edge of the circle, was different. And she liked him all the more for it. Theodore Montgomery… it was such a grand name for a boy who seemed anything but.

The moment the bell rang at the end of class, he gathered up his books and left quickly, as if trying to avoid the crowds, as if trying to avoid people. Again, her thoughts turned to her mum, scurrying off to the sanctuary of her bedroom, and her heart lurched for the both of them.

'What do you know about Theodore Montgomery?' she asked Lulu, a girl in her dorm, as darkness fell on the day.

'Theo?' Lulu looked skywards as if trying to place him. 'He's one of the background boys – you know, not popular, hardly ever see him, never goes out. A bit weird, really. Gives me the creeps.'

'Why does he give you the creeps?' She felt a flash of indignation on his behalf. 'I thought he seemed quite sweet. Interesting.'

Lulu shrugged. 'I dunno – just one of those guys who will look at you but never talk to you. Odd. By all accounts, his parents are *mega* loaded. They've got a mansion in London and property and stuff, sports cars, and his mum's very pretty and dead trendy. I've seen her.'

I wonder what everyone would say about my mum, my house... Kitty fell quiet. Up at Darraghfield, no one discussed money or status; it just didn't interest her or her friends in the village. But at Vaizey it seemed that a family's wealth was openly talked about, and that the size of their house and what car they drove was important. She couldn't say that it made her feel comfortable.

She gathered all the information about her new friend and stored it away, thinking again of her own family situation. She knew what it felt like not to be able to face people. Poor Theo, her knight in shining armour.

She would be his friend or at least she would try. There was something about him, a feeling that had lodged itself in her breast, in the way some things did.

It was Theo who found her crying one day a few weeks later on the cricket pitch.

'What... what's the matter?' He approached cautiously, looking left to right as if checking the coast was clear and it was safe to approach.

'Oh! Hi, Theo. It's nothing, just ignore me, I'm being silly.'

'But you're crying,' he pointed out, as if to suggest that nothing silly would have prompted that kind of reaction.

His kindness melted her resolve. 'My pony died,' she began.

'That's awful.' Theo held her gaze, speaking without guile.

'His name was Flynn, and I loved him, I really did. My dad found him... in the stable a week ago... and it was too late to get help – he'd just died.' Her voice wobbled, but Theo was looking so sympathetic, she carried on. Angus hadn't really got it when she'd told him, so she'd decided not to go into it with him or anyone else. 'I'm okay if I don't think about him too much, but sometimes I forget he's dead.' She looked up with an embarrassed little smile. 'Just now I was thinking about going home for the holidays and about how great it would be to see Flynn, and then... I remembered what had happened.' She swiped at her teary eyes. 'And it was like I'd just heard the news all over again.' She raised her arms and let them fall to her sides.

Theo seemed at a loss as to what to say. He looked out towards the hedgerows and took his time formulating his response. 'I don't think there is anything I can say, Kitty, to make you miss Flynn any less, but I do think he was lucky to have you. I bet a lot of people have animals in their lives and don't care for them half as much as you do.' His voice dropped to little more than a whisper. 'I can't imagine anyone loving me so much that they would miss me like you're missing your pony right now, so he was very lucky, wasn't he?'

'I guess he was.' She sniffed, smiling up at her kind friend. His words made her heart flex. She hated the fact that someone as lovely as Theo did not consider themselves loved. She watched him walk across the school field, heading for the groundsman's crooked cottage, and decided to seek solace in the one place that might cheer her up: the school pool.

Angus had been right – it was pretty grim. The grout between the tiles was grey and thin, some of the tiles were chipped, and it was odd being indoors, beneath the low, timber-clad ceiling. But any pool was better than no pool, so Kitty pulled on her swimming hat, curled her long toes over the edge of the board and dived in. As she lost herself in the watery world of fractured light and distant echoes, her thoughts cleared and her heart-rate steadied. She pounded up and down, working through the aches of her muscles until her body felt soft with fatigue. She forgot her worries, her sadness and even her grief for her boy Flynn – swimming made her forget most things. At one with the dip and swell of each stroke, she imagined she was in her beloved pool at Darraghfield. She became so lost in the moment that when she came up for air at the end of her swim, the breath caught in her throat and she gasped to find herself not in the beautiful Italianate pool built by her great-great grandfather but there in the slightly grubby, over-chlorinated pool at Vaizey College.

Her mind was full of Theo for the rest of the day; she thought about him as she lay in her dorm, waiting for sleep, and she hoped that one day someone might love him as much as she'd loved Flynn, because he was kind and lovely and he deserved it.

The term passed quickly and with so much to learn about the Vaizey routine, timetables, her boarding house and after-school activities, she was usually exhausted by the end of the day. In between all the official school commitments there was the challenge of stealing time with Angus. Their favourite spot was the little copse of fir trees beyond the cricket pitch. If Angus didn't have cricket practice or wasn't hanging out with his friends, they'd snatch twenty minutes there together in the early evenings, after prep and before supper, exchanging news, holding hands, kissing under the trees in the twilight. With all that, and being so busy with schoolwork, Kitty managed to put her longing for Darraghfield to the back of her mind. She was careful not to give in to her yearning for home; she knew that was a rabbit hole from which there would be no escape. So she painted on a smile and she cracked on.

The rules at Vaizey College were many and varied, not least governing contact with home. All she got was one meagre phone call home each Thursday evening, hardly sufficient but all the more precious as a result. She knew that her dad sat waiting in the estate office, his hand hovering over the phone, ready to pick up immediately and ensure he didn't waste a second of their monitored chat time. He took calls from Ruraigh and Hamish over in Tatum's House too, but the times were staggered to allow for that.

Kitty could always tell from her dad's tone of voice that his emotions ran high, so she did her best to paint the most positive picture she could. She knew not to ask after her mum as there was never any news, no change, and to go over the dire, stagnant situation made them both sadder than they could bear. It also felt like a waste of their treasured minutes, which ticked by all too quickly. Instead, he would tell her about any deer that had come to visit in the lower paddock, they'd reminisce about Flynn together, and he'd talk about Marjorie, telling her how she fussed over him and continued to run the house with rigorous governance. Kitty closed her eyes when they spoke, picturing herself sitting opposite him in the leather chair on the other side of the desk, where the tartan carpet hurt her eyes and the log burner roared on a winter's night, making short work of the chopped wood that was always neatly stacked either side of the fireplace.

This particular call was coming to a close and she felt her heart drop.

'So, Kitty,' her dad began, 'it's not long till the summer holidays. Patrick's getting the pool ready and I might have a wee surprise for you.' He laughed.

'You know I hate surprises! Tell me now!' she begged, feeling an instant lift to her spirits along with the maddening crackle of energy, wondering what his secret might be.

'Uh-uh, you'll just have to wait.'

Matron tapped her watch. That was it, time up.

'Time to go, Dad. Love you. Bye!'

'Bye, my darlin'. Mum and I love you too, so very much. Never forget it.'

I never could, Daddy...

Kitty lay in her bed with her stomach bunched in anticipation. It was always the same on a Thursday night. Part of the joy of her weekly call was in the recalling of all that her dad had said. Tonight felt extra special. His parting words with the mention of her mum had sent a beat of joy through her. Her mind whirred with all the wonderful possibilities of what her surprise might be, and then it occurred to her – her mum was better! They had fixed the broken part of her brain! Her happiness had come back from Timbuktu! What else could it be?

Turning her face into the pillow, she beat her feet on the mattress with excitement. Her mum was better! This was the very best thing imaginable. Oh, the things they would do together! Her mum could borrow her dad's horse and they'd hack up along the ridge, or they could jump in the car and make their way to the beach like they used to on a bright sunny day, running up and down on the white sand before eating one of Marjorie's delicious picnics by the water, then sitting under a thick blanket on the damp sand and watching the red, red sunset.

'You all right there, Kitty? You sound like you're squealing,' one of her roommates called from the other side of the room. This caused a ripple of laughter through the dorm.

'I'm more than all right.' She beamed into the darkness, knowing that life was about to get a whole lot better now that her mum had returned from the place far, far away.

Moving Home

Kitty finished her coffee and rinsed the cup, placing it on the draining board. She picked up her phone and fired off a text to her son, Olly.

> Good morning! Day started well. House already looking like a storage depot, but getting there. If I collapse under a mountain of boxes, please use your key and come rescue me. In which case, please feed the cat. X

Smiling, she placed her mum's hairbrush back into the vanity case and thought it might be time for her shower. She trod the stairs and reached into her bedroom to grab her dressing gown from the hook on the back of her door. Her phone buzzed in her pocket; a response:

> We have a cat?!

She laughed. He was funny.

The cardboard box sitting at the back of the door was in the way, Kitty kicked it with her foot and as the flap moved, she was drawn to the navy corner of a book that she had not seen for some time. She gathered it into her hands like a precious thing and sat on the corner of the bed, running her fingers over the gold embossed words 'Vaizey College Year Book 1981' She chuckled, as she flicked through the pages, each picture, phrase, comment or joke a reminder that took her right back to that place and time. She laughed at the group shots of her peers with backcombed fringes, the pushed up sleeves, narrow ties and skirts rolled above the knee, an insight into how they tried and failed to modify their rather dull bottle green uniform. There were faces and names she had not considered for some time, years even. She turned the page and her heart jumped in her chest at the sight of a young, blonde man in full cricket whites with a bat slung over his shoulder and a wide smile. *Angus*... it was sometimes possible for her to forget how very handsome he was and the way it had made her feel to be in his company, her desperate adoration of him and the way she craved the feeling of his mouth on hers. She read the print below the image: 'Angus Thompson. Tatum's House. Captain of the Cricket 1st XI.' She noted the way the other boys looked at him with something close to hero worship and realised he was only a couple of years younger than Olly was now. This was scary at two levels, firstly she remembered how grown up they felt when they were in fact mere pups and secondly how fast she had rocketed into adulthood. She hoped that things for Olly would move more slowly, that he'd have more time to live a little, to enjoy himself. Not that he seemed to be having any difficulty in that department. Someone had taken a biro to the year book page and scrawled 'scholarship boy!' in ink with an arrow pointed towards Angus. Kitty closed the book. It was a sharp reminder of the nature and hierarchy of Vaizey and that Angus' route into its hallowed corridors, not from family money or the old boy network, but because he was a grammar school boy who was smart and who worked hard. This, as then, the thing she admired about him the most.

Four

The boys had been quiet since they'd got on the train for the penultimate leg of their journey. She too dozed a little, watched the weather from the window and read from her copy of *The Secret Diary of Adrian Mole Aged 13¾*, laughing at the antics of the hapless boy and his strange family. He made her think of Theo, who'd told her he was off on a family holiday somewhere; it might have been the south of France, she couldn't quite remember, but she hoped he'd have a wonderful summer in the sunshine with his father and his apparently very glamorous mum.

A bubble of excitement grew in her stomach as the train crossed the border; just to be back in her beloved Scotland felt like a reward. Home! Her first term at Vaizey actually hadn't been too bad, all things considered, but she couldn't wait to see her mum and dad, and Darraghfield, of course. She pressed her nose to the window and smiled, despite the rain. She had big plans for the holidays: to spend as much time as possible with her mum, and to swim every single day in a pool without a grotty, stained ceiling and with no one else to upset the rhythm of her strokes. A whole ten weeks! It felt like a lifetime, stretching out before her like an endless path of happiness and laughter. She was still not convinced that

Vaizey College was the right place for her to be, but the joy of coming home after so many weeks away made it almost worth it. And who knew, with her mum now better, maybe they wouldn't send her back? The thought sent a frisson of happiness right through her. She was so happy, she felt like clapping and whooping!

'What are you clapping for, you strange child?' Ruraigh sighed and Hamish laughed.

She stared at them, unaware that she had actually clapped. *Darraghfield. Home...*

The moment the taxi pulled into the driveway, she shot out of the back seat, not caring how or even if her trunk was unloaded from the boot. Leaving the boys to heft the bags and thank the driver, she raced through the front door, skidding to a halt in the kitchen, where Marjorie was scrubbing the hot plate on the Aga.

'Marjorie!' She ran over to her, wrapping her arms as best she could around her stout middle.

'Well, I never! What an entrance.' Marjorie tutted her dis-approval at such an exhibition even as her widening smile gave out quite a different message. 'It sure is good to see you, hen.'

Neither mentioned the last time they'd seen each other, locked together in that desperate hug in the corridor at Vaizey.

She gave Kitty a small squeeze before almost pushing her away with a nervous shove.

'Where's Dad?' Kitty grabbed a warm cookie from the plate in the middle of the table and pushed the whole thing into her mouth, immediately reaching for a second as a deluge of crumbs tumbled down her jersey.

'He's away down at the village with Patrick, getting the messages. We weren't sure what time you'd be back.' Marjorie took in Kitty's scowl. 'Don't look so fed up, he'll not be long. And you can stop cramming those cookies – I've a nice piece of roast beef in the oven and at this rate you'll not be wanting your tea.' She winked.

'I always want my tea!' Kitty reminded her, already looking forward to a supper at the kitchen table. 'I'll go up and see Mum.'

Marjorie looked up briskly. 'Why not wait for your dad?'

'No, it's okay. He might be ages and I've really missed her and I know she's missed me.'

'Kitty! Kitty!' Marjorie called after her, but as was often the case with Kitty, who had fire in her belly and wings on her heels, it was too late. She was already racing along the hallway and bounding up the back stairs to the main landing and then on to the turret rooms and her parents' bedroom. She ran her fingers through her straggly hair and smiled as she gripped the brass door handle and slowly turned it.

Kitty could not have properly explained what she was expecting, but it would have included the waft of her mum's floral scent, so liberally applied that it clung to her clothes, her mum's arms flung wide around her, and a thousand kisses dotted all over her face to make up for all the ones they'd missed. And this would be accompanied by a burbled out-pouring of love: '*Oh, how I love you, how I've missed you! You look so tall/gorgeous/grown-up! Let's go for a walk – no, let's go dancing! Let's go sit in front of the fire and you can tell me everything. I want to hear all about life at Vaizey, and boys! Are you still sweet on Angus? Is he your boyfriend?*'

But this was nothing like that. Not even close.

The room smelt bad. So bad that Kitty's nose wrinkled at the sour, unpleasantly malty mixture of bad breath, wind and body odour, all tinged with something vaguely medicinal. The air felt greasy on her lips, and with the windows tightly shut and the heavy curtains drawn, there was not even the faintest breeze to stir the atmosphere or dilute the horrible fug.

'Stephen?' The small, crackly voice came from the mattress.

Kitty stepped forward slowly and whispered into the half-light, her eyes now adjusted and able to make out her mum's tiny, wizened frame. She was swathed in a flannelette nightie that had once sat snugly on sturdy hips and rounded breasts but now hung off bones stretched over with thin skin. Her body looked like it was sick of living.

'No, Mum.' She tried not to let her shock overwhelm her. 'It's me. It's Kitty.' She swallowed.

'Kitty! Oh Kitty!' Her mum leant on one stick-thin arm and heaved herself into a sitting position, wriggling up on the bed until her back rested on the plump pillow mountain. She reached out her arms and her face crumpled as if she was crying, but there were no tears. Her mouth hung open in a dark hole. 'Come and sit here,' she eventually managed, patting the space next to her.

Kitty hated that she instinctively felt reluctant to get any closer to her beloved mum. *My mum!* 'Shall I... shall I open the window?'

'No! Don't do that.' Fenella Montrose held her hands out and spoke forcefully, as if her daughter had suggested something monstrous. 'I can't have them open, in case they're looking at me! And they might be, right now!' She pulled her nightgown closed at her throat. 'They watch me, Kitty. They watch me all the time,' she whispered, a stricken expression on her face.

Kitty looked from her mum to the velvet curtains that hid the outside world. Words faltered in her mouth and she wished she'd done as Marjorie had suggested and waited for her dad. She finally took up the spot next to her, trying to ignore the smell of her unwashed body and the sight of her thick hair, once soft and shiny, now clinging to her head in an oily cap, the ends wisped and curled, the rest hanging in ropey knots around her shoulders.

She looked like a madwoman.

Kitty swallowed the thought. *She's not mad, just struggling. Severe clinical depression, a broken brain, that's what it is.*

Her mum gripped her hand with desperation and it was then that the tears began to trickle down her sallow cheeks. 'It's been so long since I saw you, my baby girl.'

'Just a few weeks, Mum—'

'No,' her mum interrupted, shaking her lollypop head on her weak neck, 'not weeks, years and years. They took you from me.'

'I...' Kitty didn't know what to say. She could never have imagined feeling afraid of the woman she loved, but she did.

'You need to stop your dad! He's trying to send me away.' Her mum bowed her head and collapsed against the pillows. 'He sent Balla Boy away, and then you, and now he's trying to send me away too – I know he is. I have to try and keep alert! I can't let it happen. I can't leave Darraghfield.'

'He wouldn't do that, Mum. He loves you,' Kitty offered weakly. She would never have imagined he'd send her to Vaizey, but he had.

'And that woman... Marjorie!' Her mum spoke with narrowed eyes and a face twisted with hatred. 'She's trying to poison me! I can't eat anything she's touched because she will kill me, Kitty. She will!' She sat forward and grabbed at Kitty's shoulders, her gaze wandering and her mouth slack. The exertion seemed to exhaust her and her eyes closed, as she sank back into the pillows.

Kitty cooed and smiled as best she could. Backing out of the room, she raced down to the kitchen.

Marjorie spun round at the sound of her footsteps. 'Kitty! I told you—'

Kitty didn't hear the rest of her scolding. Bent double, she vomited onto the flagstones, watching as the cookie-riddled splatter crept across the kitchen floor.

'Oh, dear God!' Marjorie rushed forward and gathered her long red hair in her hands, out of the way.

'What's going on here?'

Her dad came in via the back door and Kitty glanced up briefly, so glad to see him, incapacitated though she was by her sickness. She felt bereft. The world she'd been excitedly picturing while she was away at school no longer existed. Her mum was still in Timbuktu or somewhere much, much further...

'She might have rushed a cookie or two when she got in,' Marjorie offered by way of explanation.

'Ah, that'll have done it.' Her dad placed the bag of groceries on the table and palmed small circles on her back.

Kitty stared at the pool of vomit on the floor in front of her, unwilling and unable to say that it wasn't the cookies that had made her sick, it was the sight and smell of her mum and the flame of naked fear that her bizarre words had fanned.

'I'm so glad you're home!' her dad whispered. 'And look, there's someone here who's very keen to meet you.'

Kitty raised her eyes. A ball of fluff was poking out from inside her dad's wax jacket – a wee collie pup.

'This young fella is Champ. I've told him all about you.'

She smiled thinly at the cute dog panting in her dad's arms. It would have been the loveliest surprise had she not been expecting something far, far more.

*

Kitty envied Ruraigh and Hamish their ability to simply pick up where they had left off the last time they were home. It was as if the environment flexed to accommodate them rather than the other way around. She watched, fascinated, as they literally grabbed the snooker cues from where they'd placed them in the rack on the wall and continued with their game. Their bedrooms were pretty soon covered with the paraphernalia that accompanied them wherever they went – rugby balls, tennis racquets, gym shoes, shorts, dirty laundry, clean laundry and the odd textbook, there for show more than anything useful. She knew that no school assignment was going to get in the way of their summer schedule.

It was only two days in and already she found it harder to be home than she could have imagined. Darraghfield was the place she loved. The long and winding driveway, the neat garden encircled by seemingly endless moorland, and the gothic flint architecture, capped turrets, deep, stone-mullioned windows and moss-covered quoins were all she had ever known, and yet now, no matter where she was on the estate, she could only picture her mum cloistered in the darkened room, reeking of desperation and quite lost. Kitty's eyes were continually drawn to that side of the house as if she expected her mum to be peeking out, keeping watch. She'd already visited her twice since that first time, sitting on the side of the bed while her mum slept, guilty at how relieved she was at being spared more intense interaction. Even when she wasn't in her mum's room, she found it hard to properly relax and almost impossible to eat; her mum's illness had upset the balance of the house as well as her own constitution.

Now she sat on the flat rock at the top of the field with her knees hunched into her chest, looking down over the valley below, breathing in the smell of damp, mossy earth and taking in the majestic view, enjoying nothing more than the sound of the wind whistling through the tall trees and skimming the water as it swept up the glen.

The maniacal roar of quad bikes fast approaching shattered the peace. She gritted her teeth with irritation. The over-revved engines and obvious speed told her it was her cousins driving and not her dad and Patrick, who preferred to potter.

'Wosamatta, Kitty? Missing lover-boy?' Ruraigh called as he hurtled past on the quad.

She shook her head and ignored him, her expression sullen. The boys saw her fling with their friend as a great source of amusement; she'd heard them ribbing Angus at school and had liked the way he'd taken it in his stride and made no attempt to deny it. It made her feel a bit wanted and that was nice.

Hamish came soon after, standing on the pedals and trying to make the bike lift on the bumps.

Idiot.

'Away and straighten yer face!' he yelled, laughing as he went.

She stuck two fingers up. The boys only howled their laughter louder. A few minutes passed and then she heard her dad's unmistakable whistle, no doubt trying to coax the energetic, inquisitive Champ to order.

'There you are!' He let out a deep breath and loosened his scarf about his neck. 'I've been looking all over for you, thought you might be in the pool.'

'I was, earlier.' She spoke softly.

'So much for summer, eh? This weather is cold.' He sidled up and sat next to her on the rock, rubbing his hands together before forming them into a little cage into which he blew warm air.

'I kind of like it like this,' she confessed.

'Me too. You seem…' He paused, and she knew he would have been waiting, seeking out the moment to chat, and apparently this was it. 'You seem quiet.'

'I feel quiet.' A shiver ran through her at this truth.

'Aye.' He let the air settle between them. 'Marjorie said you went to see Mum when you arrived and she feared it was that that might have upset your tum.'

She nodded, resting her chin on her knees and running the flat of her palm over the lichen-covered rock, liking the feel of the small shards and jags on the cool rock beneath her fingertips.

'What did you think?'

Kitty shrugged, unable to accurately explain to her dad just how horrible she'd found it, her words unspoken out of loyalty and embarrassment.

'I know it's not easy…' he began. 'I'm a grown-up, Kitty, and even I've found it…' Again he paused, seeming to search for the right tone and phrases. 'Living under the same roof as your mum's illness is like living with a huge, dark monster of which I'm quite afraid. And as if that wasn't bad enough, I pretend I can't see it! I don't talk about it, don't mention it. And yet there it is, hovering at the table when we eat, looking over our shoulders while we clean our teeth at night and even sitting at the bottom of our bed, staring at me while I make my twice nightly visit to the bathroom.'

She looked up at him, grateful for his eloquence. 'That's how I feel, Dad, like it's everywhere, and like I don't want to look at it. It makes me feel scared.'

'It makes me feel scared too.' He placed his elbows on his

knees and leant forward. From this angle she was able to study his wide, square back.

'It's not just the weather that makes me feel cold.' He sighed. 'Your mum used to be sunny, noisy! Always singing or humming or calling out, and that brought warmth to our home, but now Darraghfield is chilly, and the mountain we have to climb seems insurmountable and joy has fled from every room.'

'Don't say that, Dad! It'll get better.' She hoped this wasn't a lie.

He nodded vigorously, as if this might make it more plausible. There was a beat while neither of them spoke; the breeze whistled and brought with it the faint scent of heather. Her dad looked back at her. 'Here's the thing: I don't know how to acknowledge this monster, I don't know what to say to it. Should I stand tall and confront it like the unwanted intruder it is?'

She stared at him, knowing no answer was required.

'I think about that every minute of every day. But what if the monster retaliates, gets mad, roars louder than me? How would I cope then? I'm already weary from living with it for so long.'

Kitty nodded. He looked weary. And she got the feeling he was glad of someone to talk to about it.

'Everything I used to consider routine has been disturbed or destroyed. To continue to ignore the monster feels like the easiest option, but I must admit that does little for my confidence or my belief that I can steer our family ship through these rocky waters.'

Her cousins' boisterous shouts drifted back to them from the path down to the river.

'I always thought I could plot a route through anything

that might come our way, always had a calm horizon within sight, but I hadn't reckoned on the strength of this adversary. And I am tired of it, Kitty, so very tired.'

'What can we do to help her, Dad?' she said in a small voice. 'We have to do something.'

She'd never seen her dad like this before, almost admitting defeat. His eyes were red pools of sadness.

'I… I have never been more afraid of anyone or anything in my whole life.'

'It's still Mum! It's still her!' Kitty said imploringly.

'I know. Oh, I know, and I still love her now like I've loved her always.' He swallowed and at his words she felt her pulse settle a little with relief. 'But this illness, this monster has got its claws into the person I love the most. It has wrapped her in its arms and sits with her perched on its lap while it whispers in her ear.'

'She can't help it, she—'

'I know, Kitty! I know she can't help it!' She knew he would regret raising his voice, a rare thing and a clue as to what simmered beneath. 'But sometimes it feels like a tug-of-war between me and the monster, the prize being the person I love – your mum.' He drew breath. 'And I cannot honestly say who will win.'

'I think, Dad, that no matter how hard it is for us living with the monster, for Mum it must be much, much worse.' She stared at her dad, who gave a small suggestion of a smile.

'You're right, of course, my smart girl.'

'And remember, Dad, Mum is a warrior.'

He blinked as he stared at the horizon, and, again, Kitty hoped this was not a lie.

★

Her birthday came and went, a non-event really, on a grey, rainy day and not how she had envisaged celebrating turning fifteen. Marjorie had wrapped up a pair of hand-knitted socks and made a carrot cake. Kitty went through the motions, but for whose sake she wasn't sure. Her mum fidgeted at the table, eyeing their housekeeper with suspicion, her body language screaming that she was desperate to flee. In truth, Kitty almost preferred it when she was ensconced in her room. It meant the rest of them could at least relax a little, pretend.

It had been three days since she'd last stood outside her mum's bedroom door, her sweaty, nervous palm resting on the door handle, drawn inside out of duty rather than desire. Cautiously she twisted the knob and peeked through the tiniest of gaps. Her mum sat in the middle of her bed, crying quietly. Her dad, sitting slightly to one side, held her tight, her greasy hair spilling down over his shirtfront. 'It's okay, Fenella. It's okay, my darling. I'm right here, I am right here...' he cooed, rocking her softly, as if dealing with a baby.

Kitty quickly and quietly closed the door, feeling the familiar icy sadness at the sight of her mother's distress, but also something else, a twinge of embarrassment at having witnessed the tender moment between her parents. It felt very different to when she used to watch them chatting, whispering on the sofa, back when her mum would sip at her glass of single malt and giggle like a girl; back when there'd been light behind her eyes instead of fear; back when she was a warrior and Kitty had hoped to grow up to be just like her. That had been her dream. She couldn't remember when the prospect of turning out like her mum had become a nightmare.

It was a week later that Angus arrived. Until she saw him, her stomach remained knotted, and fretful thoughts disturbed her sleep; the idea that he might have had a change of heart, might have kissed another girl on his family trip to Cornwall, was horrible and persistent. She was sure there'd be plenty of admirers among the families with whom they had holidayed 'forever', and her feelings of inadequacy sat by her side like a shadow. She didn't know how she would cope without his affection, especially at school, where having an older boyfriend, and a good-looking one at that, marked her out, had become her thing. It was a shield of sorts, a shield that kept the bullies at bay and was something to be proud of. She might not have been able to chitchat to her mother during the Thursday night phone calls or receive long letters from her full of questions and witticisms, but Angus Thompson, captain of the 1st XI was her boyfriend and that was enough to set her apart.

For the first time ever, Kitty pored over articles on how to be beautiful. She'd begun taking an interest in her appearance and was spending far longer than was healthy pondering her many non-existent flaws. *I wish I had bigger boobs. I wish I had boobs of any size! I've got massive thighs – what can I do about that? My skin's so pale, I wish I had one of those Californian tans, and as for all my freckles… Urgh…*

The night before he was due to arrive, she conditioned her wild red hair, then gripped the disposable razor and with a grimace swept it over her shins and calves. The fair, downy hair went down the plughole, leaving her skin with a womanly sheen not dissimilar to the pictures in the magazines. Her armpits and groin were given similar treatment. She liked the way it felt, this new, shiny, squeaky, hair-free skin. Grown-up. It was one of a thousand moments when she wished she could ask her mum for advice or at least share news of this momentous occasion; it would have made the old Fenella chuckle with delight.

Angus smiled as he walked into the hallway the next day, his sports bag slung over his shoulder, flicking his long fringe. His presence alone dispelled her anxiety. She might have only just turned fifteen, but she was old enough to know that had there been some other shinier girl in Looe to hold his attention over the summer, he would not have hotfooted it all the way up to the Highlands to see her, no matter how good the banter between him and her cousins. The way he held her gaze and the knowing look they exchanged told her they were still a couple. There was something that flowed between the two of them; if she'd had the words, she might have described it as a longing. His skin had been toasted brown by the Cornish sun and he looked handsome!

Kitty swallowed the flames of happiness that flickered inside her – Angus could have anyone, so why her? He grabbed her hand and pulled her into the games room, kissing her roughly as he pushed her up against the wall with a sense of urgency that made her heart race and her legs go weak. A strange tingly feeling started in her stomach and radiated throughout her body; she didn't know what it was, but she knew she wanted more of it.

'Did you miss me?' he asked, his white teeth coming in close once more, to nip at her bottom lip.

'I did,' she admitted, her voice hoarse with lust. 'I was worried you might meet someone in Cornwall.' She laughed nervously, hoping for a swift rebuttal.

Instead, he placed his hand under her hair and cupped the back of her neck, holding her fast. 'As if, Kitty!'

Just hearing her name on his lips sent a jolt of pleasure through her. But then came the sound of her cousins' feet thundering down the stairs; their cue to spring apart.

''Bout bloody time!' Ruraigh punched Angus on his upper

arm. 'We've got bait warming in the sun but didn't want to leave before you arrived. Grab your waders!'

Hamish pumped his hand in the grown-up manner that she'd seen rehearsed at school a thousand times.

Kitty slunk down on the wide sofa and grabbed a book from the shelf; it didn't matter which book, she had no intention of reading it, but she needed the prop, something to steady her shaking hands and calm her flustered pulse, as she caught her breath.

'SeeyoulaterKitty,' Ruraigh called as the back of his head and the back of his raised palm disappeared from the room. Despite the lack of an invite, she was irritatingly glad that he had acknowledged her at all.

Angus followed his friend but turned briefly in the doorway, keen to loiter, as if they had unfinished business. It was no more than seconds, but the look he gave her was so intense that Kitty's stomach shrank.

Her appetite over supper was non-existent, partly in anticipation of what might lie ahead for her and Angus, but also, much to her shame, because her mum had joined them at the table and preoccupation with her strange behaviour killed Kitty's appetite. Her mum sat quietly, an ethereal presence that seemed quite unaware of the conversations happening around her; she just sat there pushing the steamed vegetables around her plate and nibbling no more than a tiny cube of venison before politely making her excuses and slipping from the table and the room like a ghost.

As if choreographed, shoulders collectively sank around the table as she exited. Kitty tried not to notice the way the boys looked at one another, wide-eyed and aware, their silent exchanges speaking volumes. She was embarrassed, upset and furious on her mum's behalf. Her dad did his best to change tack and she loved him for it. He clapped his big, cupped hands loudly to draw their attention and ready them for one of his tales. This time it was the one about the badger the size of a man that he swore he found sitting in the leather chair behind his desk in the estate office.

'All he was missing was a wee pair of round gold-rimmed spectacles and a natty waistcoat with a fob watch.' He wheezed his laughter. 'And he looked up at me and we both paused and I swear in my head he said, "Can I help you?"'

She had heard it before, of course, but it was no less funny for that. She loved him for his theatre and more so for recognising the need for it.

Stephen's diversion worked, to a point. After supper, Kitty and the boys gravitated to the library. Hamish was fixated on burning things in the roaring fire, his focus and analysis of the task in hand worthy of any good scientific experiment. He held a crisp packet on tongs into the flames and watched intently as it shrivelled and gave off a steady noxious stink. This was followed by an old playing-card box, found under the sofa and riddled with dust. It actually fizzed in the flames, emitting a momentary green glow. She knew it was a sign of their boredom that they were all equally rapt by his exploits, quietly watching from the sofas or, in her case, from the ancient Indian leather pouffe with a tired-out Champ slumbering across her legs.

They might have all been staring at the fire, but she was aware of the current, a silent crackle of communication that flared between her and Angus on the other side of the room. It was a little after eleven that he stood and said his goodnights before loping up the wide sweep of the stairs. She knew this was her cue and counted down the minutes she considered to be a prudent interval, not wanting to cause suspicion. She even managed to execute a perfect fake yawn. Sleep, however, was far from her mind as her body pulsed with excitement.

Thankfully, her cousins had turned their attention to back-gammon and now sat at the card table, illicitly sharing one of their uncle's cigars, puffing like enthusiastic amateurs as they studied the wooden chips.

Kitty knew every dark corner of Darraghfield: which stairs creaked, what picture would swing from the wall to reveal a safe, and which doors led to narrow corridors or secret passages. She knew which window frames not to poke because the damp wood was too far gone to be patched up with paint and would leave a fingertip-shaped hole, and she could direct visitors to warm corners inside old pine wardrobes where folded motheaten blankets made the best hiding spots ever. Yes, Kitty knew the house back to front and inside out, and yet tonight, as she padded barefoot along the dark ships'-timber flooring, she felt as if she was venturing nowhere she'd been before.

Slowly she turned the handle of the spare room in the east wing, then closed it behind her. Angus was already under the blankets and for this she was grateful, not sure she could have coped with anything less surreptitious than simply sneaking into the bed alongside him. The low-wattage bulb nestling behind the faded tassels of the lamp on the writing desk sent dark shadows leaping up the floral-wallpapered walls. The light was dim and she was glad about that too.

Kitty pulled back the blankets and stared at Angus's legs; unlike hers, they were covered in fine down, turned blonde in places. She noted the line on his thighs where his shorts had blocked his dark tan from taking hold in the Cornish sun and above which the skin remained pale. He turned onto his side, and with a heady sense of inevitability she slipped against him, holding her hands up above her head like a child in need of assistance as he peeled her T-shirt from her body and pushed her shorts down with his long toes.

She had discussed what sex might be like with Isla, her friend from the village, and had listened with interest to the late-night chats between the girls in her dorm, but now, as she lay there after the event, she felt very little. In fact, she felt less than very little; she felt... nothing.

With something close to disappointment and an unsatis-fied ache, Kitty looked at her bundle of clothes that lay in a heap by the foot of the bed and wondered if she could restore them without waking Angus, who was now sound asleep beside her.

Underwhelming though that first sex was, that summer changed everything. Kitty felt different. Not that she could talk to anyone about it. The girls in her dorm, her new friends, all had long-standing plans, Isla was working over on Mull at her aunt's B & B, and her mum, the one person she wanted to confide in, was lost to her. Her cousins, even if they had been the type of boys she could have chatted to about such matters, still kept her at arm's length socially, and even though she and Angus walked hand in hand, she still felt like the unwanted younger sibling tagging along and trying to fit in.

Kitty found it hard to sleep, her mind full of questions. What she and Angus engaged in felt like the most natural thing in the world, and yet, although she would never say so to another living soul, the more they did it, the less of a big deal it seemed. Eventually it reached the point where it held about as much mystery and excitement as kissing; it was just sex, that was all. It was both predictable and quick and left her wondering what all the fuss was about. That struck her as a bit of a shame. When sex had been unchartered waters, the idea of doing it had been exciting; thinking about what it might be like had taken up a lot of her thoughts, but now that they had done it seventeen times, it was very much 'just sex'. And if Kitty were being honest, she rather missed the mystery and thrill that had once surrounded it.

She used to think that when she had sex for the first time she would learn some great secret, something that all non-virgins knew and kept to themselves, something that bound them all in the non-virgins club. But there was nothing. No big reveal, no secret, no code... Her expectations had definitely been higher. She didn't feel sexy – she didn't feel anything. And afterwards she felt happy that once again they'd got away with it without being caught, and happy that he loved her. This she felt certain of because surely if he didn't love her, he wouldn't have sex with her, would he?

'So, back to school, eh? Where did those weeks go?' Her dad smiled at her, as he crept into her room and, as had become usual of late, she looked away, embarrassed by the knowledge she now possessed, worried that he might be able to read her non-virgin state on her face.

'I'll be back for exeat and it'll soon be Christmas,' she mumbled as she packed fresh notebooks and pristine fountain pens into her bag.

'Christmas? Good Lord, Kitty, I haven't given up thoughts of summer yet. I'm clinging to the prospect of some autumn sunshine, so please don't make me start thinking about Christmas.'

'I love Christmas.' Her smile broke wide at this truth. It was the time of year when Darraghfield came into its own. Fires roared in every grate and Marjorie went to town preparing vast amounts of food. Kitty loved the leftovers best, wolfing down slices of cold turkey, peeling hunks of baked ham from the bone with greasy fingers and placing them on rips of freshly baked bread, then slathering everything with dollops of Marjorie's homemade chutneys and pickles, which would be lined up on the table in ribbon-wrapped jars. Her mum dressed the hall and staircases with garlands of pine heavy with cones and interspersed with bows of Montrose tartan, a fiddly job, but the end result was always beautiful and much admired by everyone who came to the festive drinks party. Those parties nearly always ended in an impromptu ceilidh, with the dancing finishing in the early hours. It had turned into a tradition that, weather permitting, as dawn broke, everyone would sway arm in arm on the brow of the front lawn to watch the skies turn lavender-coloured as the sun rose over the glen.

'Do you think Mum might be feeling a bit better by Christmas?' she asked, pausing her packing for a moment, her voice quiet.

Her dad walked over and crushed her to him in an unexpected hug. He spoke into her hair and there was desperation in his voice. 'We're doing all right, aren't we? We can do this, Kitty – I have to think we can!'

She swallowed to quash the nerves that were making her stomach churn; the prospect of leaving him alone was not a happy one. 'We can, Dad.' She nodded against his chest and closed her eyes, sending her wishes up into the ether, hoping they might reach the cloistered bedroom in the turret. 'We will all be fine, Dad, just fine.'

Kitty didn't want to leave Darraghfield, didn't want to leave her mum and dad and Marjorie, but it wasn't as if she had any choice, and at some level she knew it was easier for all concerned if she was away at school; one less thing for them all to worry about.

As soon as the taxi pulled into the car park at the front of Vaizey College, Hamish and Ruraigh grabbed their bags from the boot and ran eagerly towards the dorms and the friends they had missed, leaving her on the back seat, forgotten.

As she stared up at the imposing façade with a sinking feeling in her gut, she saw Theo walking across the quadrangle with his suitcase under his arm. His trousers were a little high on his ankle after his summer away, and his blazer was tight across his back. He was sporting a deep, envy-inducing tan and had clearly grown quite a lot, his physique now something that drew her attention, along with his handsome face. She felt a warm glow at the prospect of catching up with him, knowing that if she could talk to anyone about her strange summer, it would be him. She tapped on the window of the cab, but with his head low and his stride determined, he didn't hear her.

'Thank you!' She smiled at the driver and grabbed her overnight suitcase from the boot, lifting it against her hip and tilting forwards as she walked, keen to try and catch up with Theo. The three trunks were being forwarded separately. She made her way across the car park and by the time she got to the quad, there was a small group of boys standing in the middle and quite a lot of noise – calling out, yelling. She wondered if it was some kind of sport being played, highly illegal within the quad walls. Kitty stopped in her tracks and dropped her heavy case to the ground. Her heart raced and her breathing came in fast bursts as she recognised Wilson and his friends and saw Theo with his fingers curled into his palms.

Wilson was bouncing on the balls of his feet with his fists raised, and with horror Kitty realised that he and Theo were fighting! Judging by the look on Theo's face and the red stain on his cheek, he'd already been hit. She raised her hand to her mouth, unsure whether to cry out or simply cry. Knowing how private and acutely sensitive Theo was, she stepped back into the shadow of one of the quad pillars and dragged her bag with her. From this hiding place, she watched, unseen, as events unfolded.

'Too scared to hit me, faggot?' she heard Wilson shout as he rocked his head from side to side and jabbed a couple of mock blows. The third, however, landed on Theo's left eye socket. And this was when Kitty started crying for real; seeing her friend hurt was more than she could bear.

Theo held a cupped palm over his face and Wilson's idiot pals skittered about like excitable pups, whooping and hollering as they cheered their leader on. 'Poof!' Dinesh yelled. Kitty had never hated anyone more.

Theo tried to stand up straight, but Wilson's next blow caught him on the side of the head.

'What sort of bloke doesn't fight back? What the fuck is wrong with you?' Wilson spat. 'Is it like the homo code?'

In the heat of the moment, she became aware of someone running into view and then she saw Wilson's head jerk sideways as something struck him on the side of the face with force.

'What the fuck?' Wilson yelled, in a high-pitched voice that told her he was hurt, embarrassed, and she was glad.

It was only when Kitty looked away from Wilson that she realised that the person who'd hit him was none other than old Mr Porter, the groundsman at Vaizey, someone she knew

Theo was very fond of. Wilson said something Kitty couldn't hear and Mr Porter slapped him again. Blood trickled over his chin and down his shirtfront and he remained kneeling, shocked and subdued by Mr Porter's intervention, as was Kitty.

'What is going on here?' Mr Beckett, the scary housemaster of Theobald's House, yelled across the quad.

Kitty knew it was time to leave. She grabbed her bag and walked the long way round to her house. Her heart pounded in her chest and her tears flowed. Theo, her sweet, calm, kind friend… Even the idea of him fighting with someone was crazy – the boy who didn't say boo to a goose; the boy who once built a small envelope for a ladybird to crawl into before carefully placing it on the outside window so it wouldn't be hurt. But she wouldn't have blamed him if he had fought back. She knew he got taunted and called a poof quite a bit. She sometimes wondered if he might be gay, if that might explain why he didn't have a girlfriend at Vaizey despite being so handsome and lovely to be around. But he'd never said anything to her and she would never ask.

She didn't want Theo to ever know that she had witnessed his beating, didn't want him to feel the shame. An image came into her mind of her dad resting on the edge of the mattress with her mum in his arms as he rocked her gently, cooing, 'It's okay, Fenella. It's okay, my darling. I'm right here,' speaking softly, as if he was dealing with a baby. Right now, as she walked slowly to her dorm with tears running down her face, Kitty understood the need to take someone you cared about into your arms, especially when they were vulnerable and hurt. She understood the desire to try and make things better, even if you knew you couldn't.

Moving Home

Kitty towel-dried her hair and pulled a soft navy V-necked jersey over her shirt. She felt fully refreshed after her shower and flicked on the radio before gathering the pile of leaflets and newspapers by the side of the bed. She decided to sort them into the trash or the recycling, part of her great clean-up, pack-up day. She smiled as the strains of Fat Larry's Band 'Zoom' wafted from the speaker, taking her back to the summer of 1983 and the night of the leavers' ball. As a fifth former, Kitty was not allowed to attend, no matter that her boyfriend was inside the main hall where laughter and music floated from the open windows. She had crawled along the garden wall to avoid detection and now sat beneath the window with her ear cocked, trying to hear any clues that might help her understand what was going on inside. She pictured Angus looking fine in his dinner jacket and the swarm of sparkly blonde girls gathered around him, all trying to usurp her. She hated the insecurity that plagued her. After all, if she found it hard to cope with him attending the leavers' ball without her, how on earth would she cope when he took up his place at Birmingham University?

'Kitty?'

She spun around to see Theo, standing on the path with his hands in his pockets.

'What are you doing here, Theo?' she whispered, wary of giving away her position.

'What am I doing?' he laughed. 'I have snuck out and I'm going for a walk and it's not me who is hiding in the shadows beneath the window. Do you want me to give you a leg up so you can see inside?' He nodded towards the high window.

'No! Shhhh! Stop talking so loudly, if we get discovered we are in so much trouble.'

Theo crossed the grass and slunk down by her side. 'Are you spying on Angus?'

'Trying to.' She confessed. As 'Zoom' seemed to rise in volume, wrapping them in a sweet cocoon.

Theo turned to face her. 'You know, Kitty, you really have nothing to worry about. Angus I am sure knows that he is very lucky to have you and he would be crazy to do anything to jeopardise that.'

'Thank you for saying that, Sweet Theo.' She ran her fingertips over his arm and felt him tremble beneath her touch. He jumped up as if scalded and straightened his blazer. 'We should dance!' he proclaimed.

Laughing at this uncharacteristic display of confidence, Kitty stood and put her hand inside his, as he placed his other hand on her waist. The two waltzed inexpertly with clumsy steps along the path. Kitty laughed, dizzy in the moment of abandonment and quite giddy at the sensation of joy that filled her up and there they twirled, in the dark, on the path with Fat Larry booming out into the night air.

'So long ago.' Kitty sighed at how quickly the years had been erased.

Five

Kitty pressed her face close to the keypad and punched in the door code for Angus's halls of residence, a rather uninspiring concrete block on the edge of the campus. The grey clouds overhead, threatening rain, did nothing to enhance its attractiveness. Despite the lack of electronic whirr that usually preceded entry, she tried the door anyway, pulling and then pushing the door handle, but it was stuck fast.

'Damn,' she muttered, aware that she was not supposed to be on campus without visiting permission, should not have been trying to gain access to the building without a resident present and should definitely not be in possession of the entry code. There was of course the possibility that her nervous haste had caused an error, so she tried again, slowly this time, pushing each number and pausing before trying the door again. Nothing. At least now that was one rule she wasn't breaking, as she appeared *not* to have the code.

Standing back, she placed her hand sideways on her forehead to shield the sun and peered up at Angus's window, wondering whether or not to risk throwing a stone at it to get his attention. She instantly decided not to – knowing her luck, the stone would break the window and she'd have to face the wrath of the infamous warden. It was impossible from that angle to tell if Angus was in or out, so she continued to stand a while, pondering what to do.

As she did so, Maxine, a girl who lived along the corridor from Angus, loped up the path, earphones plugged into her Walkman, singing the recent Mr Mister hit quietly to herself. Kitty hated the song; it was all about broken wings and learning to flying again, and it always reminded her of her mum's illness. She lived in fear of her mum's wings having suffered permanent damage and getting more broken every time she went through one of her bad periods. Each time her mum's mind wandered, it seemed to take her further away; this made coming back to normality even harder, with more and more ground to recover. Kitty worried that one day she might not bother, that she might simply stay high above the clouds, drifting for eternity.

Maxine smiled and waved and unhooked her earphones. 'Oh hi! You're Angus's friend.'

'Yes.' Kitty swallowed, glad that Maxine had remembered her but feeling so inadequate standing next to this cool, nonchalant girl that she felt compelled to set her straight on their relationship status. 'His girlfriend, actually.' She smiled.

A flicker of surprise crossed Maxine's brow, and Kitty's confidence crumbled. *I know, I know… Why would someone as gorgeous as Angus pick someone like me?* If she'd had the nerve, she would have rammed the point home and told Maxine that they'd been going out since she was fourteen, having sex since she was fifteen… *That's four years we've been together! Four whole years.* Instead, she just stood there with a nervous smile on her face.

Maxine nodded and spoke quickly. 'Well, I can let you in, of course. I've no idea where he is.'

Kitty gratefully followed her inside, walking up the cold

concrete stairs behind her, trying not to focus on her rounded hips and shapely bum. How she hated her own flat, boyish frame.

Don't be daft, Kitty. It's you he has sex with. You he loves.

It was a relief to find the door to his room unlocked. She crept inside, hating feeling so exposed as she trespassed in the corridor. One quick glance was enough to confirm that Angus was elsewhere. Flopping down on his immaculately made bed, she inhaled the strong scent of his favourite cologne, Armani Pour Homme, which clung to the bed linen, relishing the prospect of their reunion. They didn't get to see each other very often, with her being at college in London and him at university here in Birmingham. Her eyes swept over the neat desk, where pens and pencils sat in a grey mesh pot and lever-arch files were lined up uniformly on the single shelf; even his T-shirts were folded with precision and placed in order of colour on top of the linen hamper in the corner. She smiled at the evidence of his tidiness obsession. It was quite the opposite of how she liked to live, surrounded by the soft comfort of clutter. Having been raised among the cosy disorder of Darraghfield, she couldn't imagine doing things any other way.

A large cork board covered a chunk of the free wall and on it her boyfriend had pinned his timetable, a couple of pamphlets, one of which detailed the sports hall opening hours, and a notice about a proposed ski trip in the new year. The rest of the space was filled with photographs, neatly and evenly spaced, of course, with colour-co-ordinated thumbtacks holding each corner. The goofy faces of Hamish and Ruraigh grinned at her from behind the large salmon that rested against their upturned palms. That had been quite a day. The one photograph of her he had selected showed her deep in concentration, curled into the wide armchair in the library at home and caught from the side unawares while she pored over a book with her finger in her mouth, her hair falling across her face. It was in black and white and she liked it; she looked older somehow, and a bit aloof, both of which she saw as desirable traits.

She knew Angus had lectures today, but he was expecting her anyway. She decided to be bold and, shedding her clothes, she slipped between the crisp white sheets on his narrow bed, her intention being to maintain a sultry pose ready for when he returned. Instead, she fell asleep and was first aware of his presence when he bent down and gently kissed her forehead.

'Hello, you!' He laughed his greeting.

Kitty smiled at her boyfriend and peeled back the duvet to reveal her naked form. After any time apart like this, she always found it hard to relax until they'd had sex. It was as if the anticipation of doing it sat between them like an obstacle, making conversation stilted, unnatural.

'Well, it's a bloody good job I didn't bring the lads back here!' He snickered, ridding himself of his trainers, jeans and rugby shirt with haste and diving onto the mattress.

She loved the warm feeling of his arms around her. 'I've missed you,' she whispered.

'And I missed you,' he replied, before kissing her roughly and pushing her back onto the pillows.

It was as Angus slept that Kitty turned over in the narrow space and found her attention caught by something. She pushed away the copy of *The Grapes of Wrath* that sat on the nightstand and saw a cassette tape. Carefully, she reached over and held it up to her face, reading: *Mixtape by TP*. Turning it over, she studied the list of songs that had been painstakingly written in neat, tiny script: *Level 42 'Something About*

You', Animotion 'Obsession', Fine Young Cannibals 'Johnny Come Home', Tears for Fears 'Shout...'

'What are you doing?' Angus asked suddenly, his eyes wide, making her start. His accusatory tone made it seem as if she'd been discovered snooping, which sparked a rumble of disquiet in her gut.

'I... I found this.' She sat up, holding the tape in the air with one hand and the duvet over her chest with the other. With her thoughts running wild, she instinctively felt the need to hide part of herself.

'It's got some good songs,' he offered nonchalantly, before lying flat on his back with his arms forming a bony triangular pillow behind his head.

'Good songs?' She hated the distrustful rise to her voice. 'Who is TP?'

Angus twisted his head to look at her, his brows knitted in confusion, her attitude clearly surprising to him. 'It's Thomas on my course. He's a proper muso and I'm rubbish with all that stuff – that's what seven years of boarding school does to you.' He chuckled. 'While I was running around the playing fields at Vaizey trying to keep up with Ruraigh, he was hitting the clubs of Manchester. He knows so much about music, keeps trying to drag me to all these alternative gay clubs – he's gay, obviously. You should have a listen. Honestly, Kitty, some of it's really good.'

She felt the instant spread of embarrassment over her neck and chest. 'Oh God! No!' She slapped her palm against her forehead. 'I'm a jealous girlfriend! Angus, no! I never wanted to be one of those! And yet here I am with my heart racing and I feel like crying over a bloody tape!'

Angus laughed and reached for her wrist, pulling her down towards him. 'I love that you're a bit jealous. It means you care.

But trust me, Kitty, if some other girl had given me a mixtape, I would hardly have left it there for you to see, would I?'

'I know! I know!' She bit her lip, embarrassed. 'I *do* care, but I don't want to be *that* person! God, I was even looking at Maxine earlier, wishing I had her boobs and her hips.'

'Are you kidding me?' He laughed. 'There is no need, Kitty. We are strong, you and I. We've got history.'

Taking solace from his words, she placed the tape back on the nightstand and picked at a thread on the duvet. 'Yes, we have.' She loved that he was sophisticated and urbane, loved that he was so different from her outdoorsy cousins. It made her feel special, cool. Imagine getting Ruraigh or Hamish onto the dance floor at a gay club! The very idea made her smile. 'But I find it hard with you being up here at uni and me down in London. I just wish I could see you more.'

'I know. Me too. But we have to trust each other. As far as I'm concerned, that's an absolute given, and there's no grey area – we either do or we don't, that's it.' He held up his hands.

She bit her lip, hating the question that formed on her mouth. 'I do trust you, I think. I want to, certainly,' she mumbled. 'But can I ask you one question and I promise I won't ever ask it again.'

Angus sighed, and she could tell by his expression he'd hoped the topic was closed. 'Of course.' He coughed and sat up; the two now faced each other.

'Have you slept with other girls? Or even come close to it? Truthfully, Angus.' She cursed the quiver of tears.

He gripped the top of her arms and stared into her eyes. 'I swear to you, Kitty Dalkeith Montrose, that I have not.'

Relief flooded through her and she fell into him. 'I'm sorry.'

'There's no need for sorry, but you don't have to ask and you don't have to worry.' He kissed her nose.

'Even though we've been together so long now,' she whispered into his chest, 'I guess... I still can't quite believe that someone like you wants to be with someone like me.' Kitty knew that a small part of her would always feel like the girl Ruraigh and Hamish thought was boring, the daughter her mum chose to hide from, and the girl her adoring dad had nonetheless sent away to Vaizey College.

Angus gave a wry laugh. 'It's me that's the lucky one! I think that every day.'

'I might believe you one day,' she mumbled through her smile.

Angus looked up towards the corner of the room, as if this was where the answer to her insecurity might lie. Carefully, he pulled back the duvet and crept from the end of the bed. She watched, wondering where he was off to, as he walked around to the side of the bed and dropped down onto the floor. She laid her head on the pillow so their faces were level and he smoothed the hair from her face, toying with the ends.

'Let's get married.'

'What?' She giggled, needing to have it repeated to make sure she hadn't imagined or misheard his words.

This time he spoke slowly. 'We should get married, Kitty. Not immediately, but when you finish your course. In two or three years. Let's agree to it and then you'll know for certain that no matter how far apart we are, you are mine and we have a future together. Not just any future, but a wonderful future!'

'Are you being serious right now?' she asked hoarsely, her throat tight with emotion.

'I've never been more serious about anything in my whole life.'

'Oh my God, Angus! I would love to marry you!'

He leant forward and kissed her sweetly, and her heart soared.

'Where would we get married?' she asked, already getting wrapped up in the detail, already starting to believe that this might actually be real.

'I was thinking somewhere quiet, a registry office maybe…' He let this trail and she tried not to let the disappointment show in her face. Angus laughed loudly. 'As if! Oh, Kitty, your face…! No, my darling, there's only one place – Darraghfield, of course.'

It was this small detail, his understanding of just how much it would mean to her to get married at home, which caused her tears to break their banks. *Darraghfield… Of course, that would be perfect.* She allowed a picture to form in her mind of her dad in his kilt, Ruraigh and Hamish raising a toast, and her mum smiling on her special day. Maybe she could even decorate the stairs and bannisters with garlands like she used to for Christmas. It would look spectacular. Only someone who truly loved her would know how important it was for her to marry at her family home.

'I love you so much, Angus.' She grabbed him and pulled him close, covering his face with kisses and holding on to him tightly, as if he was the anchor that gave her strength, stability.

'How lucky am I?' He kissed her again.

'I shall be Mrs Thompson.'

'You will.' He beamed. 'We shall live in London and I'll work in the City and we'll have a swimming pool for you to swim in every day and I will make you happy! I promise, Kitty, I will make you happy.'

She nodded, more than certain of this fact.

The next day she took the train back to London with a movie rolling in her mind of her wedding day. She had to stop herself shouting out in excitement, suspecting that everyone else in the carriage thought she was just an ordinary girl, but she wasn't, she was a girl that a boy like Angus Thompson wanted to marry! The knowledge that she was engaged, even if only informally, was far from scary – quite the opposite, in fact. She felt settled, as if she could finally exhale and relax, knowing that Angus wanted her for always. It felt wonderful.

'Mrs Thompson...' she muttered under her breath, before pulling out her jotter and pen and practising her signature – *K Thompson. Kitty Dalkeith Thompson. Mrs Angus Thompson* – over and over again. It was an odd thing, but at that moment she remembered being at school and sitting next to Theo one day in class and writing *Kitty Dalkeith Montrose Montgomery* in the back of her file, just to see what it might look like. Funny she should think of it now.

As the taxi bumped along the lane, Kitty glanced across the back seat at Angus. He, as ever, was neat and unflustered and looked fresh and composed. 'I don't think anything ever ruffles you,' she said. 'You're always calm.'

'On the outside, maybe.' He grinned. 'But, trust me, the prospect of breaking the news to big Stephen that I'm going to make an honest woman of his only daughter... well, I can assure you, that's playing all kinds of tricks with my stomach.' He pulled a sicky face.

'You don't have to worry – he already loves you, and all he'll be concerned about is that you love me.'

'And I do.' He nodded.

'You don't say it.'

'What?'

Kitty licked her lips and chose her words carefully. The last thing she wanted was to be arriving at Darraghfield with the fog of a row hanging around them. 'You tell me I am loved, but you never say, "I love you" – not those three little words.'

Angus shifted in his seat. 'I don't see the difference.' He lifted his chin and looked out of the window, and her heart raced. She had expected him to immediately say it back to her or at least deny that he never said it. His cool dismissal caused a small void to form in the base of her stomach; she hoped she could fill it before they waltzed up the aisle together.

As the taxi rounded the bend and her family home came into sight, her face broke into a smile. She reached into her handbag to pay the driver. Angus patted her arm. 'Just a mo,' she replied, mildly irritated. Whatever it was he wanted could surely wait.

'Kitty!'

Again she ignored him, ferreting inside the cavernous soft leather pouch for her purse. 'Just a sec, please, Angus! You can see I'm trying to pay the man.'

'For the love of God...' He raised his voice. 'Will you just look up!'

She regretted the actual huff that came through her nose as she turned her head towards the front lawn.

Her breath caught in her throat and her tears pooled instantly. 'Oh!' she managed, swiping her tears from her cheeks and smiling through her jumble of thoughts.

She's come home! The monster has gone away, and my mumma has come home.

Fenella Montrose was standing on the grass in jeans, wellington boots and an old sweatshirt that Kitty thought she'd thrown out years ago. Her hair was neat, clean and pulled into a loose ponytail, and she was bending forward with a wide rake in her hand, pulling bundles of shiny copper-coloured leaves into fat parcels before depositing them into the waiting wheelbarrow. There were only a few seconds before her mum spotted them, but Kitty quickly took in the glow to her mum's rounded cheeks and the contours of her bust, which had all but returned. Most heartening was how fast she was moving; gone was the floating grey spectre of a woman who was barely present. The thing that brought Kitty the most joy was her mum's expression; the fear had disappeared from behind her eyes, the wrinkles of distress and confusion on her brow had smoothed, and she smiled as she worked, as if all was right with her world.

Kitty stepped from the cab and made her way slowly around the car and towards her mum. Fenella laid down her rake and the two women stared at each other, each revelling in the familiar image of the person they loved and the person they had missed so very much. Fenella broke into a little trot and wrapped her girl in her arms, holding her tightly; gone was the fragility that meant Kitty held back, instead she felt the wonderful shape of her mum against her chest.

It was some seconds before Kitty spoke the words that, unrehearsed, came naturally. 'I've missed you.'

The sound of her mum's quiet sob was enough to trigger her own.

'I've missed you too. And I've missed me and I've missed Daddy. I've missed a lot.'

Kitty pulled away, still happy to look at her mum in her returned state. 'But you are feeling better?' She hardly dared ask.

Fenella nodded. 'I am. I don't really know why, but a few weeks ago I just woke up feeling different. I didn't want Dad to tell you, in case it was a false dawn – there've been a couple – but here I am today! Not a hundred per cent, but miles away from where I was.' She smiled.

Timbuktu – a long, long way away.

'Now, how about a cup of tea? Marjorie has made cake of course.' Her mum half covered her mouth and spoke sideways. 'She might not remember where she left it, but she definitely made one.' Fenella pulled a face. 'Come on, Angus, bring the bag!'

Kitty was happy to let her mum direct proceedings, her assertiveness reminiscent of the mum she'd known as a child. The two linked arms and made their way inside.

The house looked the same but felt different, or maybe it was simply reflecting the happiness of its inhabitants. Even Champ had a new waggle to his tail and extra mischievousness in his scamper. Marjorie seemed a little conflicted by the reappearance of her employer in the kitchen, which until a couple of weeks ago had been solely her domain. Kitty understood that it couldn't have been easy: Marjorie had been the object of her mum's paranoia for no good reason and now there they were, standing side by side at the sink. It was her dad, however, who fascinated Kitty. He looked younger. He looked happy. He stared at his wife continually, with a smile hovering on his lips. He monitored her every move, pulling out chairs, placing down cups and removing potential obstacles, as though she were a visiting queen made of glass and he was responsible for keeping her intact. His expression was one of disbelief, as if he was afraid that if he looked away, she might disappear altogether.

'Your journalism course sounds wonderful,' her mum called over her shoulder as she poured tea. 'I picture you like a modern-day Lois Lane, running everywhere with your notepad, hunting out a scoop!'

They all laughed – *this* was the old Fenella.

'It is wonderful, but I'm not quite at the Lois Lane scoop-hunting level yet.' She smiled at this image of herself. 'You know I've always loved writing, but learning how to make everything succinct yet informative, which is the difference, I guess, between producing prose and producing copy – I'm really enjoying that.'

'You always used to write diaries!' her mum remembered.

'I did, and I still do, actually, but not as frequently. I only write down the really important stuff. I read some of them recently – they're quite dull!'

'Oh, I'm sure – you have the dullest life!' her mum joked, before instantly looking soulful, as if aware that large parts of her Kitty's life had been marred by her own illness. That was not something Fenella would want diarised; it would make less than pleasant reading and she knew would have been even harder for her child to write down.

'So, Angus...' Stephen patted him on the back, changing the subject, as was his skill. 'Kitty tells me you have a job lined up after graduation?'

'Yes, in the City. Derivatives.'

'Good. Good. Splendid.' Her dad nodded and she could tell by his lack of further enquiry that, like her, he didn't have a clue what that actually meant. 'And have you seen the boys?' He was always eager to hear any snippets about the nephews he loved as his own.

'Yes, Hamish and I met for a beer before the match at Twickenham. He was on good form, but then, as tradition dictates, he went to sit with the Blues and I stayed with the Whites.'

Stephen laughed loudly and banged the tabletop. Champ pricked up his ears. 'Shame on you, Angus! We'll make a Scot of you yet.'

'And I'm happy to report that both boys are going to be in

France at the same time as me in the new year for a ski trip. We're off to Val d'Isère.'

'Oh, smashing!' Her dad seemed glad to hear they were doing nice things; she suspected he lived vicariously through the hijinks of the boys.

'Would you like to come too, Stephen?' Angus asked with a steady voice.

'Skiing? In France? With you boys?' Her dad looked towards his wife, and Kitty could see that no matter how flattered he might have been by the invitation, the thought of leaving her was inconceivable. 'If it was the Cairngorms, I might be tempted, but all the way over to France…? I think I'll have to pass and wait to hear what shenanigans you all get up to when you get back; I doubt I could keep up with you young bucks, but thanks for asking me.'

'It's more than just a ski trip, actually.' Angus coughed.

Kitty felt the flutter of nerves, unsure of what might come next but knowing where he was heading.

'It's to celebrate our engagement.' He beamed. 'At least, I hope that'll be the case – if you give your blessing for me to marry Kitty. If not, it'll be a rather drunken holiday to commiserate!'

'Really?' Her dad grinned.

Angus nodded, a little sheepish.

'Kitty! Oh my word!' Her mum abandoned the tea-making and rushed over to embrace her daughter before moving along the table and holding her future son-in-law in a tight squeeze. It warmed Kitty's heart to see her fiancé's head squashed against her mum's cheek – a lovely, unabashed act of closeness.

'I don't think it's my blessing you need, son. It's Kitty's,' her dad said while reaching for the handkerchief secreted in his trouser pocket. 'Are you happy, Kitty?' he asked with a warble to his voice.

She nodded and looked at her parents a little shyly. It was such a grown-up thing. 'Yes, Dad, I'm really happy.'

He reached across the table and shook Angus's hand warmly in both of his, seemingly at a loss for words.

'Do you have a ring?' her mum asked.

Kitty shook her head. 'Not yet.' She saw the knowing look exchanged between her parents. 'Angus wants me to have his grandmother's ring, so we'll collect it when we go to his parents'.'

'Have you not met them yet?' Fenella asked.

'Not yet.' She swallowed. 'I'm nervous.' She had to admit it was odd that after four years together she still hadn't been introduced to Angus's mum and dad. Early on, she'd tried to press him on the subject, wanting to find out more about his childhood, but he wouldn't be drawn. He was dutiful when it came to phoning them every week, but to Kitty their conversations sounded stilted and overly polite, and she soon gave up listening in.

'And I told you there's no need,' Angus chipped in, his eyes twinkling at Kitty. 'What's not to love about you?'

Stephen smiled at the boy who was clearly echoing his own thoughts.

'I think a cream dress might be nice.' Kitty shrugged her shoulders with excitement. 'I'd like a full skirt and puffy sleeves.'

The sound of sniffling came from the range. 'Cream? What a suggestion! You'll be wanting white, surely!'

Kitty jumped up and went to hug Marjorie. 'Or maybe white, yes,' she said in a conciliatory tone.

'Oh, ignore me – you usually do! I mean, if you had ever

listened to me, you wouldn't be walking around with one wonky arm, would you now? Instead of gallivantin' off, you'd have had a quiet night in front of the telly with a round of toast on your lap and that would have been that. But instead we ended up in the hospital!'

'Oh, Marjorie!' Fenella called out affectionately as they all remembered that terrible night more than ten years back.

'And of course, Marjorie, it wouldn't be my weddin' without you making ma cake.'

'Your wedding cake?' she asked with a tremble to her lip.

'Well, who else would I ask?' She kissed the old woman on her florid cheek.

'I'm not sure how well it'll travel...' Marjorie let this hang.

Both Kitty's parents seemed to hold their breath, waiting to hear where their daughter had chosen to celebrate her big day.

'It'll only need to go to the barn – I'm getting married here, of course!'

Kitty would never forget her mum's expression, which lit up her face as she beamed with happiness. Her dad wept openly, suddenly quite overcome with emotion, and Marjorie seemed to grow a couple of feet in height, proud beyond words that it was she who'd been asked to make the cake.

Kitty had got back from Darraghfield a few days ago and had invited Ruraigh round to her London digs to have a catch-up and fill him in on the good news about her mum. He sat back on her bed and laughed. 'All this shite in your room! How can you stand it?' He prodded a stack of magazines piled haphazardly on the desk that sat at the foot of her bed.

'It's not shite, it's my stuff.'

'Yes, but do you *need* so much stuff?'

'Apparently I do, or it wouldn't be here, would it?' She cast her eyes over the disarray of make-up and bottles of lotions, potions and scent. Her counter was littered with textbooks, notebooks, her trusty Olivetti typewriter and tens of cassettes with a unique array of music ranging from Depeche Mode and Barclay James Harvest to Guns N' Roses.

'Kitty, I live in a one-bed flat and I have less than half the junk you've crammed into this room.' Ruraigh laughed.

'I've told you, it's not junk!' She turned and closed her eyes in mock disgust at her annoying cousin. In truth, though, she was happy at the new closeness that had taken hold since they'd all left school. She enjoyed his company, even if they didn't get to see each so much now they were all doing different things. 'So, where are you taking me? Somewhere nice, I hope?' She hunched her shoulders with excitement as she slid her arms into the cardigan she'd retrieved from the floor, shaking out the creases and dust before putting it on.

'No, somewhere cheap.'

'God, Ruraigh, you're so tight! Let's go get a fancy dinner – steak and chips!' she yelled.

'No way! I'm saving. A kebab will do you just fine.'

'What are you saving for?'

'I'm saving for fancy dinners with girls who are not my cousin. And for my future.'

Kitty roared her laughter – he had a point. 'Your future? What are you, middle-aged?'

'No, but I need a buffer. You never know, do you? It's not like I can call up my dad and ask for help.' He shook his head and she sighed, this their mutual acknowledgement at just how useless his parents had proved to be over the years.

'Have you heard from them?' She was unsure where his parents were currently stationed.

'I got a postcard from Mum last week. Hong Kong.'

'Nice.' She saw the flicker of upset on her cousin's face, aware that no matter how old he got, it must still hurt to know that he and his brother came second or third in the pecking order – after a glamorous overseas job and a fancy social life. 'You can always call Dad if you need anything – you know that.'

'I do.' He smiled fondly at the mention of his uncle and surrogate father.

'Anyway, won't you be taking over Darraghfield when you're old enough?'

'Really? Won't that be you?' He looked at her quizzically.

She shrugged, suddenly aware that she couldn't picture Angus at Darraghfield, not for any period longer than a holiday. She gave a brief smile. 'I think I might have a different future... So, what do you think of our news?' It was more than a little irritating that it had fallen to her to raise the subject.

'You mean the engagement?' He blinked.

'Yes! Of course that!' She tutted. 'What else?'

He looked up at her and hesitated. 'I suppose good... Yes, good – if it's what you want.'

Kitty had been about to drag a brush through her hair, still knotty from her swim earlier at the public baths. In her eagerness to dive in, she'd forgotten to braid it, but now she paused and turned to face her cousin. 'Is that it, Ruraigh? Is that all you can say?' She swallowed the emotion that gathered at the back of her throat, a combination of anger and bitter, bitter disappointment. 'Angus is your friend and I'm your cousin and I would have thought you'd be over the moon!'

'I...' He moved his mouth, words failing him.

'No, don't bother trying to make good now! What is it with you?'

'I'm happy if you're happy, Kitty. I just...'

'You just what?' she yelled, facing him with her arms folded across her chest.

'I don't know...'

'Well, I don't know either! God, to think we've all been trying to work out the best part you and Hamish can play at the wedding, and right now I don't even know if I want you there. How can you be that indifferent?' Her tears sprang at the unthinkable possibility that the boys she so loved might not be in attendance.

Ruraigh sat forward on the bed. 'It just all seems a bit rushed.'

She laughed. 'You are kidding? I've known him since I was fourteen! I've practically grown up with him, and unlike you and Hamish, he never treated me like an unwanted guest, he never sidelined me for Patrick's sons or, worse, ignored me!'

'Kitty, you're my cousin! And we were kids...' He stood up and hovered awkwardly by the bed. 'I suppose it's just that I'm used to you and Angus being friends, part of a gang, and the thought of you setting up home together—'

'For God's sake, Ruraigh! What are you trying to say, that I'm not mature or sophisticated enough to be his wife? God, what is it with you lot, always trying to make me feel small...' She turned to face him, incensed now but also suddenly worried. 'Has Angus said something to you? Has he, Ruraigh? Or to Hamish? Is there someone...' She gulped, made herself be brave. 'If you've got something to tell me, either spit it out or get the fuck out of here!'

'I... I don't know anything.' He spoke with his shoulders raised and his palms upturned. 'I just... Angus is a top bloke, but...'

'But what?' she roared.

'He hangs around with a weird crowd these days. That Thomas Paderfield, I don't like the cut of his jib. I hardly get to see Angus any more—'

Kitty was properly livid now. 'God, Ruraigh, I expected better of you – though Christ knows why. What, you're jealous of Angus's new friends? Worried he might have grown out of all that schoolboy bravado and be maturing into someone a bit more sensitive?' Her heart raced. She'd probably gone too far with that. But what the hell, Ruraigh had it coming.

Ruraigh blanched and looked taken aback. 'I... I don't know. It's probably nothing.'

'Christ, Ruraigh, you can cause a hell of a lot of damage with your "probably nothing" rumours.'

'I don't want to fall out with you, Kitty.' He spoke softly.

'Well, maybe that decision isn't yours to make!'

Ruraigh sighed. 'Let's just go out for supper and we can—'

'Supper?' She interrupted him. 'You must be kidding! I wouldn't go out for supper with you if I was starving!'

'Don't be like that.'

Kitty stepped over a pile of dirty laundry on the floor and opened the door to her room; she stood back, waiting for her cousin to leave.

'Really? You're throwing me out?' he asked with his hands on his hips and disbelief in his voice.

'Goodbye, Ruraigh. I'll tell Angus your congratulations card is in the post!'

He walked slowly past her. She tried to slam the door after him, but it caught on a stray slipper and stuck fast on the carpet. In frustration and sadness, she threw herself face down on her mattress and sobbed. A part of her was genuinely nervous, and she knew that was why she'd reacted so badly. Did Ruraigh really know something she didn't? Were all Angus's protestations about her being the only one actually just him being his usual smooth, charming self? She didn't much like Thomas and his crowd either, truth be told; they made her feel a bit of a country bumpkin. Was there someone in that crowd that Angus found more interesting, more sophisticated? Someone who had a proper suit in her wardrobe and knew exactly what derivatives were?

She sat up, blew her nose and wiped her eyes. She walked barefoot down to the communal entrance hall where the public telephone lived and was thankful to find it free. She dialled the number of the phone in Angus's halls of residence and waited for the pips before putting in her ten-pence piece.

A male voice answered. 'Hello?'

'Hi, could you please get Angus in Room 22 D. If he's not there, could you leave a note to call Kitty – he has the number.'

'Sure, hang on.'

It was an inconvenient but well-honed system and all students were well rehearsed in it. Kitty gripped the phone to her face and could hear the laughter of people walking past at Angus's end, the creak of the front door and the slam of it closing.

Eventually a voice came on the line. 'Kitty?'

'Oh, Angus!' she sobbed, big fat tears making it difficult to speak. 'I'm so glad you're there.'

'Hey, what's up? Don't cry.'

'We… we are okay, aren't we? You do want to get married? You do love me?' she managed through fractured breaths.

'Of course I do.' He kept his voice low. 'There's no need to cry. We're strong, you and I, remember? Now who or what—'

The phone beeped and went dead. Her money had run out. She hung up and waited to see if Angus would return her call. He didn't. He probably didn't have any ten-pence pieces either.

No matter. His words of reassurance had done the trick, and with restored lightness of spirit, she decided to go and grab one of the girls from her corridor and head out in search of that kebab.

It was three weeks later that Kitty set off with Angus to meet his parents. Despite reminding herself that this was a happy occasion and that her own parents had received the news of their engagement with enthusiasm, she was still petrified.

Please like me! Please like me!

She looked out from the back seat of the taxi and exhaled through bloated cheeks. 'I feel a bit sick.'

He laughed. 'You need to calm down. I've already told you, they're nice people, ordinary people, and they're very much looking forward to meeting you.'

'I think I might actually be sick,' she repeated, winding down the back window and taking in lungfuls of air as she tried to clear her head.

Kitty stared out at the place where Angus had grown up. It was quite unlike anywhere she'd been before: a newish estate with houses that all looked exactly the same apart from their cars and their garden ornaments. Her stomach was in knots and Angus, seemingly in direct response to her pale complexion, continued to repeat, 'Don't worry, they will love you!', but it didn't really help.

The houses reminded her of Monopoly hotels, being all of a regular shape and quite close together. They were large, square red-brick boxes with fake white pillars holding up the porches, and all the front doors were painted black. It was very orderly, with neat patches of lawn and the bushes shaped into orbs; even the climbing plants were contained, pinned to trellises. It was so different to Darraghfield, which featured barely a single straight edge and where nature ran wild, inveigling its way over brickwork and between fence posts.

They walked up the short front path hand in hand and Angus rang the bell. Leaving her no further time to panic, the door opened and she was staring into the faces of her future in-laws.

His mum and dad were a surprise. She had seen a couple of photographs taken on holiday showing his parents laughing on the back of a boat, and there were those rather formal phone conversations she'd overheard, but these people were very different from how she'd envisaged them. Angus's mother was small and nervy with her hands tucked inside her cardigan sleeves. She was without make-up and Kitty cursed the blush and mascara she had applied on the train.

Kitty rather awkwardly lowered her arms which she had raised slightly, fully expecting a hug, as her future mother-in-law reached out her hand and said, 'Hello, dear, call me Lynne.' Her smile was fleeting and Kitty noted the thin set of her mouth, which turned down at the edges; it gave her an air of meanness, made her look miserable. His dad was, like Angus, a neat man with close-cropped grey hair and gold-rimmed glasses; he shook hands with her and with Angus. *Shook hands with his son!* Kitty couldn't help but picture her dad greeting Ruraigh and Hamish after any time apart, enveloping them in his wide-armed hug, holding them fast until long after they tried to wriggle free.

The house was quiet – again, quite different from Darraghfield, where, even if there was no music playing, no burble from the radio and no one singing or shouting, the building emitted its own distinctive noises. The Aga, the heart of the house, pulsed like a living thing and the ancient beams and floorboards creaked and cracked as the temperature varied from day to night. Rickety boilers and radiators rumbled and gurgled, real fires crackled and spat, and the wind whistled along corridors, moving curtains and lifting the pages of books. Outside, birds squawked and sheep bleated, and dogs barked at both. Despite Darraghfield's size and remoteness, life hummed all around and it was nearly impossible to feel afraid or lonely. Here, however, inside the square, double-glazed home, the quiet almost had weight.

The four walked into the sitting room and took up seats on two identical red velvet sofas which faced each other. There was a formality to the whole exchange that she had not expected. She studied the two people sitting opposite and tried and failed to see Angus in either of them. Where he was confident, they seemed shy, reluctant. She let her eyes roam the walls of the lounge, noting how empty it was and how clean, clinical almost. A very large picture of Angus in his Vaizey uniform hung above the fireplace inside a heavy gold frame. Lynne followed her eyes, 'That was a day, I can tell you, when we got the letter of acceptance from Vaizey.' She nodded at the portrait. 'It still seems unbelievable that our boy went there, quite something and God willing it will have set him on the right path for life.'

'Yes, God willing.' His dad echoed and for the first time Kitty noticed the crucifix propped against the fireplace.

She shivered, as she nodded and wished the place were a little warmer. Although, and Kitty would never have said this to Angus, she suspected that the house would feel a little cold even with the heating on.

'I thought we'd have supper about fiveish?' his mum said, quietly.

'Lovely.' Kitty beamed. 'Thank you.'

'No point in making a pot of tea so close to our meal,' Lynne stated thinly.

Kitty, who was dying for a cup of tea, glanced at her watch. It was three thirty and she could have fitted in at least three cups between now and five – if they'd been in Marjorie's kitchen, they'd have been compelled to have a cuppa as soon as they arrived whether they wanted one or not and no doubt a slab of cake too. She wondered how they would fill the next two hours. Her stomach bunched with a cold feeling of dread.

'I expect that taxi from the station was expensive.' Lynne addressed Angus.

'Not too bad.' He smiled and drummed his fingers on his thighs.

'They've changed the one-way system in the car park there,' his dad added. 'Now you have to come out of the lower entrance and go across the traffic to come up onto the high street, it's ridiculous.'

'Sounds it.' Angus nodded.

Kitty couldn't stand it any longer. 'We're so excited about getting married!' She bounced on the seat and felt the eyes of all three on her, as if her energy was at best misplaced or at worst embarrassing.

'And Angus says you want to do it at your parents' place?'

'Yes!' She swallowed her disappointment at her future mother-in-law's lack of enthusiasm or congratulations, wondering in jest if she was in cahoots with Ruraigh.

'It sounds very expensive – not only a big do, but having to travel all the way up to Scotland.' She made the little 'T' sound that preceded her snorty laugh and for the first time Kitty saw the resemblance between Lynne and her son. It was bewildering to Kitty that she made the whole event sound more like a chore than a celebration.

'My mum and dad are happy to pay for everything. I'm their only daughter and they have spare rooms and would really love you to stay with them.'

Angus's parents exchanged a look, which she found hard to read. Her blood ran cool nonetheless. There was a moment or two of awkward silence during which Angus coughed. His dad spoke eventually.

'I suppose you want Grandma's ring?' he asked with an air of reluctance, as he stood, walked over to the faux fireplace and plucked a small blue velvet box off the mantelpiece.

Kitty had pictured many times what it might be like when Angus finally put the ring on her finger. She'd imagined the theatricality of it: the two of them alone in front of a fire, his heartfelt words of love, toasting the occasion with something fizzy, and her weeping at the beauty of it all. The reality was very different. Angus's dad sniffed, lifted out the thin gold band with its surprisingly plain, flower-shaped cluster of red garnets and handed it to Kitty. She nervously placed it on her own finger and her heart sank. *It's not about the ring, it's about the meaning behind it, and I love this man and he loves me!* She smiled at her fiancé, who leant over and kissed her cheek.

'They nearly buried her in that.' Angus's dad nodded at her hand. 'We had a right old job to wrestle it off her finger – rigor mortis, you know – but we got there in the end and it's a good job we did, eh?'

Kitty stared at the ring and not for the first time that day swallowed her desire to throw up.

After a quiet dinner, she and Angus caught the train back to London. He leant his head on her shoulder and dozed, while she stared at the ring on her finger and thought about the strange afternoon they had spent. His mum had served roast beef on the dot of five. And after a rather long Grace, solemnly given by his dad, and just as Kitty had been about to put a piece of beef into her mouth, Lynne had informed the table how expensive it was, which for Kitty sucked all the flavour out of it before she'd even tasted it. She turned and kissed Angus's sleepy head, as if this might combat her negative thoughts about his parents. She knew that when she thought back to this day, all she would picture was his mum's obsession with money and Tupperware. It had fascinated Kitty, the way Lynne had a Tupperware box for everything. She'd scraped the leftover food into one, but she also had Tupperware boxes with coins in, Tupperware boxes full of rubber bands... You name it and she had a plastic box for it! She could see why Angus was so neat, boxing away every aspect of his life to keep things orderly.

The train picked up speed as Kitty thought about how different the Thompsons were from her mum and dad. His parents' rather cold formality had shone a light onto some of her fiancé's quirks and for that she was grateful. It had given her insight into his stiff, religious upbringing; no wonder he so loved the relaxed life of Darraghfield. She decided it could only be a good thing for her to learn to be neater and also to maybe think about money a bit more. Like her parents, she was never extravagant, but she also had never had to think about money. It was only by stepping away from Darraghfield that she could see how lucky she'd been.

'I think I can make your mum and dad love me. I think I can break through their shells – I shall try very hard,' she whispered into Angus's hair, safe in the knowledge that he was fast asleep. She looked again at the garnet ring on her finger, which she decided to soak in gin when she got home, hoping that it might disinfect it a little. The thought that it had been prised from a dead woman's finger made her shiver.

Failing that she could at least have a big swig from the bottle, a thought she welcomed at the end of this rather extraordinary day.

Moving Home

Kitty turned the radio down. The box of photographs sitting on top of her duvet caught her eye. One in particular, which she recognised from no more than the glimpse of a blue, blue sky, captured by her dad's steady hand. She sat on the bed and pulled the picture from the box, gently wiping the dust from it with her fingertips. It had been taken during her engagement on a trip home, a long time ago. She remembered the exact moment: her dad calling from the grass, knees bent, jacket splayed, camera raised. 'Say "cheese"!' he'd called and they'd done just that, heads together, laughing into the lens with the sun shining down on them and a wide smile lighting up her face.

Kitty remembered the feeling of happiness that had filled her right up, her joy not only at a lovely day spent with those she loved, but at all the wonderful things they had to look forward to. She lifted the photographs from the box and placed that one at the bottom, covering it over with the others.

'Yes, it's true,' she said into the ether, recalling her conversation with Sophie earlier, 'I do wish I'd had more courage at times. I wish I had listened to my instincts...'

She made her way down the stairs. The morning sun shone through the rear French windows and Kitty decided to make a list of all the jobs she needed to get done today, otherwise she would see time disappearing and night falling, leaving her behind schedule. As she reached into her handbag for her notepad and favourite list pen, the phone in the kitchen rang.

She looked around her. With the walls stripped of pictures, she felt a little forlorn, like the room had lost its soul. She pictured cooking the kids' tea when they came in from school and popping their little plates laden with fish fingers, chips and peas on the table while they burbled about their day. She sighed at the memory.

'Mum?'

'Hello, darling.' She smiled, as she always did at the sound of her daughter's voice, no matter that she'd seen her only a short time ago.

'Just checking to see how you're getting on.'

'Oh, that's sweet. Fine, thanks. What are you up to?'

'Greg's just cooking brunch, aren't you, darling?' This, Kitty knew, was intended to let her know that she couldn't talk freely.

'I see!' Kitty laughed. 'I hope you've got some antacid in the bathroom cabinet.'

Sophie chuckled.

'God knows, I love the boy...' Kitty grinned. 'And I love how he loves you, but in the wee small hours I sometimes get a flashback to his grapefruit, orange and fish surprise. And the surprise is that even though the whole horrible event happened well over a year ago, I could still throw up at the memory.'

'Uh-huh! Oh, I know what you mean!' Sophie answered disingenuously. Greg was obviously still within earshot.

'I still can't believe he didn't think it would be a problem leaving a scoop of prawns and two whacking great cod fillets in his hot rucksack all day and then cooking them that night.' Kitty swallowed. 'It still makes me queasy!'

Sophie roared her laughter and changed the subject. 'I told Greg you would probably still be looking at photographs and dawdling.

I predicted you would be curled on your bed not realising that an hour or so had slipped by, or that you'd be in the kitchen foraging for coffee.'

'And you would be right.' She smiled. 'I was just looking at a photo of Angus and me, my dad took it up at Darraghfield.'

'How did that feel?'

'Odd, I suppose.'

'Did you look happy? Young? I bet you were lovely.' Kitty could tell Sophie was smiling.

'Of course I did! I was a baby – we all look lovely when we're that young, the curse being that we don't realise it until we look back, and then it's too late.'

'Well, aren't we jolly this morning!' Sophie laughed.

'You're right. Sorry, darling. How's my gorgeous granddaughter?'

'Roseanna's great, Mum. But listen, I don't want you to sit there feeling all melancholy and reflective – this is a happy time for you, remember? Good things are happening! Really good things!'

Kitty laughed, still stunned by the bubble of excited anticipation in her gut. 'I do remember, and you know I am fine, truly. But it is strange, packing up the house. There are a lot of memories that I'd swept under rugs and shut away in drawers, so I'm bound to be a bit reflective.'

'Okay, I'll leave you to it. But don't forget you need to get packing, there's not long until the move.'

Kitty shook her head, this role reversal the biggest indicator that she was getting old, even if, at fifty-two, she felt younger than she had in years. That was what happiness did.

'Speak tomorrow, and enjoy your brunch!'

'Oh, Mum, my God! He's just gone back into the kitchen, so I'm whispering. You should see what he's prepared – I'm trying to be brave, but it's an egg with some sort of garlic sauce and he's had yoghurt sitting by the radiator for an hour!'

Kitty's stomach bunched. 'Wash it down with strong tea, darling, and mop it up with bread – my two top tips.'

They both giggled as they ended the call. She sat back and thought about the secrets held within a marriage. Sophie unwilling to tell her spouse about his horrendous cooking and she and Angus, nothing so frivolous of course, but secrets nonetheless...

Six

Two and a half years was an unusually long engagement, but Kitty didn't mind about that. She enjoyed the sense of security it gave her, happy that they were now living together in London, and no longer felt the need to know precisely where Angus was or who he was with on the evenings he went for a drink after work. Besides, it meant she could finish her course before they actually got married. It was almost time now: she just had her final assignment to submit and then she could concentrate on how she and Isla should wear their hair, whether to set up the reception in the main hall rather than the barn, as the weather could not be guaranteed, what centrepieces to have for the tables – she was thinking greenery with blue thistles and wild flowers – and the thousand other chores on her to-do list.

In truth, the whole wedding thing made her nervous. Not the day itself or even the many details still to be decided – she was of the mind that none of that really mattered – but the prospect of spending the rest of her life as Mrs Angus Thompson. She loved him that much she knew, but the heady, heart-fluttering passion that she'd read about…? What they had was far from that. It was instead cosy companionship, a warm feeling, a reassuring sense that she'd been chosen, that Angus wanting to marry her conferred on her a special status.

She'd made cryptic mention of her concerns to Tizz, Ruraigh's girlfriend, one afternoon when they'd gone out for coffee together, but Tizz had just laughed and said that most people who were about to get hitched wondered whether there might be something better out there. '"What if" moments are good, positive!' Tizz said. 'Because without questioning, without doubting, how can you know if you're making the right decision?'

Kitty took a long slurp of her cappuccino, having nothing to add.

'At the end of the day, you settle for what you have,' Tizz continued, 'as that's what's on offer.' She'd gone a bit hesitant then, had busied herself stirring the sugar into her coffee, before asking, 'Do you not think, Kitty, that as a wannabe writer you might be more prone than many to having romantic, fanciful notions about relationships? Notions that are never going to match up to the reality. When it comes down to it, bodice-ripping and endless gifts of chocolates and flowers are all very well, but it's the ability to sit down and talk that matters, don't you agree?'

Kitty had nodded, and she knew Tizz spoke the truth. But the occasional bit of bodice-ripping would have been nice… At twenty-one, she expected to be having the best sex ever! And she wasn't. There was nothing wrong as such in their relationship, nothing she could pinpoint, it was just a feeling, a tiny sliver of doubt, fuelled by Angus's aloof nature and the many hours he spent at work or out with Thomas and the rest of his gang, while she stared at the TV catching up on *The Bill*.

She often pondered on Tizz's comment about being able

to sit down and talk about things. Angus could be quite cool when it came to discussing emotional subjects, including her mother's illness, and there were times when she found herself wishing he was more open and supportive. Having now spent time in the company of his parents, she knew where this came from. This morning had been a particularly upsetting example. She'd been reading a letter from her dad at the breakfast table, and the way he'd mentioned her mum – *I know Mum would want me to send you all her love* – without lying but also without spelling out that she was clearly having a bad episode, had made Kitty sob into her cereal. Angus hadn't reacted to her tears at all, had simply looked up at her and then back at his newspaper, which had made Kitty both sad and furious. She had pointedly not returned his goodbye kiss when he set off for the Tube, and had purposely not shared with him the details of her day ahead.

Now, two hours later, Kitty put her negative thoughts about Angus to the back of her mind. She had just handed in her last assignment and had the rest of the day to herself. She ambled down the street, loving the feel of the warm autumn sun on her bare midriff, a rare day when being in London felt like a novelty. It was sometimes hard to retain her enthusiasm for life in the capital when the rain-streaked concrete and soaked tarmac only seemed to highlight the gloom, but sunshine made all the difference. That and the fact that she planned to go to the big pool in Camden for a swim later. Angus had promised her that they'd be able to afford a house with its own pool in London one day soon, but for now she made do with the public baths in Camden; it was about as far from the laurel hedge at Darraghfield as it was possible to get, but she still relished every opportunity to be in the water.

She stopped at a newsagent's window to read the small ads,

wondering if she might offer her services as a dog-walker and whether that could be a salve for the things she missed about Darraghfield – the animals, the outdoor life, being surrounded by nature. How she missed the place. In her more fanciful moments, she wished she could fast-forward to a time when she and Angus would move home and she would be able to swim in her own pool every single day. She wondered what Angus would say about her doing dog-walking. He wouldn't get it, he'd say they didn't need the money and that she'd be better off concentrating on the wedding; he wouldn't understand that it was about more than just a measly hourly rate.

She was drawn to the sound of a bell, a café door opening, and felt the need for a restorative coffee. As she was wondering whether to bother or whether she'd simply make her way home, she turned her head, and there, standing on the pavement seemingly deep in thought, was none other than Theo Montgomery!

'Oh my God! Theo? Theo!' Fuelled by excitement, she yelled much louder than was necessary.

He did a double-take and seemed a little abashed, but, like her, also delighted. 'Oh my God! Kitty!' He beamed. 'No way!'

She rushed forward, dropping her bag and file on the pavement. Jumping up, she threw her arms around his neck. It was wonderful to see him, her old school friend and confidant, and today of all days, when she was pining for her family, it gave her a warm feeling of belonging.

'What are you doing here?' she asked as she pulled away, taking in his handsome face and his broad-shouldered physique.

'Just on my way to uni.' He pointed up the road.

'Oh God, it's *so* great to see you!' She bobbed her knees,

giddy, excited, as if in the presence of Theo it was permissible to revert to her teenage self. 'Do you want to grab a coffee? Have you got time? I don't want to keep you.' She pointed over her shoulder with her thumb to the café along the street.

'Now?' He checked his watch as if weighing up the consequences of being late for wherever he was headed.

'Yes, now!' She laughed.

'Yep, of course, great!'

She fell into step beside him. It was a strange thing: she was twenty-one, at the end of her course, living with her fiancé and about to be married, yet at that precise moment, walking along the street with Theo by her side, she felt like she was fourteen again and just as clumsy. Even her natural walking pace lost its rhythm and she feared she might stumble if she didn't concentrate. She kept turning her head to take him in. He was taller, broader, slimmer than when she'd last seen him, but still with the handsome face and thick dark curly hair she loved.

'I'm at college, not far from here.' She nodded into the distance.

'And you're studying journalism, right?'

She wondered how he knew that – probably from one of the Old Vaizey Boys. 'Yep.' She nodded. 'Don't know if that's what I'll do finally, but I'm enjoying it, so...'

'You're a long way from the Highlands.'

'I know.' She looked down. 'And I miss it so much. There are days when I have to stop myself throwing everything I own into a suitcase, jumping on a train, climbing into my walking boots and racing up a mountain to gulp down lungfuls of that beautiful clean air!' She closed her eyes briefly.

And I miss my mum and dad. I miss them so badly, it hurts. I sometimes wish I could wind back the clock and be a child

again, running barefoot without a care in the world and my
mum and dad close by...

'Running up a mountain or going for a swim.' He smiled.

'Oh, Theo, you remembered! Yes, I still love to swim.' Kitty
beamed.

As they queued for their drinks, she studied his clothes:
a crumpled pink shirt that was in need of an iron, and slim
jeans that fitted snugly over his long, muscular legs. She swallowed the frisson of attraction that flared in her gut. *Don't be*
ridiculous, Kitty, this is Theo! Your friend! And you are about
to get married!

She gathered the creamy, chocolate-sprinkled cappuccino
from the counter and made her way to a vacant booth along
the laminate-clad wall. Theo followed with his can of 7up.

'It is so good to see you, Theo.' She studied his face and
found his blush under her scrutiny most endearing. 'You
look...'

'I look what?'

'You look lovely.'

'Lovely? I'd prefer something a bit more rugged,' he quipped,
tensing his arms into a he-man pose before sipping from the
can.

'Nope.' She shook her head. 'It doesn't work like that. You
don't get to choose the words in my head and that's it: you
look lovely to me.'

There was a second or two of silence while her words settled over them like glitter. They held each other's gaze without embarrassment, as if their shared history allowed for this
intimacy.

'I've often thought I might bump into you, and I've kept
a lookout for you, but you never go to any of the reunion
events at Vaizey, do you?'

'No. I have absolutely no desire to go back.'

'But you should. They're good fun and it's nice to catch up with people.'

He sat up tall in the seat and she caught the flash of hurt in his eyes. It saddened her, the memory of his fight with the school bully on that fateful day, after which he'd become even quieter and more withdrawn.

'Only hell or high water would drag me back there,' he offered, finally and firmly.

Kitty changed the topic. 'I always liked sitting next to you,' she said. 'I liked it very much. I remember how whenever Mr Reeves said something risqué or stupid we'd look at each other – that little glance that meant we both got it!' She threw her head back and laughed loudly and without restraint in a way that she hadn't for a long time.

'He was so dull.'

'He was *so* dull!' She laughed again and he joined in.

'Shall we get some cake? I'm starving.' She liked how at ease she was with him. He had after all seen her crying in her school uniform, and humiliated on the hockey pitch. And he'd helped her with her homework. 'Just one bit, we can share.'

The two sat in the booth with a slab of Victoria sandwich between them and two forks, jousting for the best bits of the disappointingly dry sponge. It was for Kitty the nicest hour and a half she'd spent in a very long time, one of those rare occasions when there was absolutely nowhere else she wanted to be. It was as if the real world had slipped away and she was once again a kid, free from the responsibility of adulthood, free from her fears as to what her future as Mrs Angus Thompson might hold.

'So, Theodore,' she asked sternly, 'have you learnt any of Mr Kipling's poetry yet?' She dipped her chin and looked at him through her strawberry-blonde lashes, expecting him to laugh loudly and punch her arm. What came next floored them both.

Theo carefully laid his fork on the tabletop and took a swig of his lemonade. He stared into her eyes and began.

'This is from "The Gypsy Trail".' He coughed. 'By Rudyard Kipling.

'The wild hawk to the wind-swept sky,
The deer to the wholesome wold,
And the heart of a man to the heart of a maid,
As it was in the days of old.

'The heart of a man to the heart of a maid –
Light of my tents, be fleet.
Morning waits at the end of the world,
And the world is all at our feet!'

Kitty pushed the cake plate away from her and knitted her hands on the tabletop. Her eyes glazed over with emotion, and so did Theo's. It was a moment to be cherished.

She looked down into her lap and her voice when it came was hushed. 'That's beautiful.'

'You are beautiful. The *most* beautiful. I have always thought so. Always.'

Tears started falling unbidden down Kitty's cheeks. There was such sincerity and sensitivity in Theo's compliment. The way he looked at her was something she would never forget. He made her feel special; special just for being her. It was the way he'd always looked at her, even at school, but right now it felt different, more intense, somehow. More serious. Her whole body trembled, and the tears continued to flow.

'Please don't cry! I'm sorry if I made you sad.'

'I'm not crying because of you, I'm crying because I've got so much going on that sometimes I can't think straight.' Kitty sniffed and looked up at him, unwilling to bring Angus into the conversation or talk about being upset with him that morning, and not wanting to spoil the mood by talking about her mum's fragile health.

Theo placed his hand over hers. 'Oh, Kitty, I'm sorry to hear that. Do you want to go and get something to drink that isn't coffee?'

Kitty nodded and managed a smile.

The pub was quiet, but their boozing was frenzied: whisky shots followed pints of beer, and by early afternoon they were more than tipsy. Kitty felt fearless; it had been an age since she'd let go like this and the more she drank, the more she liked it.

Theo suddenly reached for her hand, pulled her to him and kissed her firmly on the mouth. She might have been part sloshed, but that kiss was definitely in the bodice-ripping category. Her stomach fluttered at the hint of what else they might experience together. At a deep, visceral level, Kitty wanted more of it.

They pulled apart and stood inches from each other, as if no words were needed. Theo reached for his bag and coat and Kitty downed the last of her drink before picking up her file. Hand in hand, with Theo leading the way, they part ran, part walked to his flat in Belsize Park. They kissed on the stairs and again in the hallway. With intoxicating flames of pure pleasure leaping in her gut, Kitty was entirely caught up in the moment. By the time Theo opened his front door, she was pulling at his shirt, yanking it free from the waistband of his jeans.

'If you knew the minutes, hours, days, weeks I have dreamt of this moment, Miss Montrose...' He kissed her hungrily, guiding her to his bedroom.

'You are my knight in shining armour, remember?' Kitty slurred, hooking her hands around the back of his neck and inhaling the scent of this boy, now man, who had been in her life for so long and was now presented to her in this most unexpected and wonderful way. It was as if scales had fallen from her eyes.

Kitty woke but kept her eyes closed, lying still for a moment or two, letting her brain and stomach settle. There was a split second when she didn't know where she was. She pushed out her toes and they touched a leg – Theo's leg. Instantly she recalled where she was and what had happened. The image of Angus swam into her mind and bile rose in her throat, partly out of guilt and partly because of the booze that still sloshed through her veins. She froze, breathless at the realisation of what she'd done.

Shit! Shit! Shit! Oh my God, Kitty, what were you thinking? How could you?

She opened her eyes slowly and smiled nervously. And there it was again, that look in his eyes that conveyed so much more than vague words ever could. It was a look of love. A look of hope. Kitty felt a stab of guilt at the fact that she had no doubt, and without any right or forethought, encouraged both.

'Oh God, Theo!' She placed her hand over her eyes, as if the lamplight offended. 'What time is it?'

'Nearly seven.' He yawned.

'In the evening?' She sat up straight. *No!* How had that happened? She had to be somewhere. She had to be home!

'Yes, in the evening!' He laughed, as if it was amusing, as if they were starting out. The kind of laugh that in another life, at another time, would have led to more lazy kissing and then a lazy evening...

'Shit! Oh Shit!' Kitty flung back the duvet and, unabashed by her nakedness, felt around on the floor for her hastily discarded clothing.

'It's not that late – I thought we might get some supper?' He moved the pillow beneath his head to get comfy.

The gentle confidence in his voice made it even worse. Her heart thumped at the horribleness of what she was about to do. She hated herself for it, hated that she was going to let him down and hurt him, hated that she was going to tarnish how he saw her, possibly fatally, and forever fracture their friendship.

'Supper?' She stopped ferreting on the floor and glanced at him, stricken. 'Theo...' She chose her tone deliberately, wincing at the devastated expression that had crept across his handsome face. She could tell that he was readying himself for words he instinctively knew he did not want to hear. His shoulders rounded and his chin dropped and she felt grubby.

She gulped and looked mournfully into her lap. She so wanted to tell him how wonderful he had made her feel, how exciting their union had been, so unlike everything she'd known before, and how if things had been different...

Her skin prickled at the memory of his kiss along her décolletage, the slow, unhurried pace with which he'd touched her; there'd been no rush, no bitter tang of disappointment, no being left wanting. It had been complete, beautiful, and she'd felt strangely present in a way she never had before. She had no idea sex could be like this. It had been quite, quite beautiful.

But things were not different. Angus was at home waiting for her and she had chosen the flower arrangements for the top table, the hymns for the service...

She blinked suddenly, whipping her head as if returning to consciousness. An image of Angus on one knee leapt into her mind. She thought about the garnet ring sitting on her bedside table, removed on her swimming days to ensure she didn't lose it in the pool. She curled the knickers in her palm as she shook her hair from her face. Then she glanced up.

Come on, Kitty, you're a warrior, like Mum.

'I'm getting married.'

It was the only way she could say it – quickly and without dressing it up. Her words cleaved open the quiet tenderness between them, peeling the beauty from the day, leaving them both raw and embarrassed. She felt horribly exposed.

Theo looked at her and for a second was that same fourteen-year-old boy all over again, the boy with a permanent air of disappointment, the boy who'd tried to hide from life, the boy who'd sat in the classroom and confessed to not knowing any of Kipling's poetry.

'You're...?'

'I'm getting married,' she repeated, a little louder this time. She swallowed the tears that threatened.

I'm so sorry, lovely Theo. I have often thought of you and I suspect I always will. You are so special to me...

'To Angus?'

'Yes, of course to Angus!' she snapped. She sighed. 'Sorry, but who else?' She stepped into her pants and bent down to retrieve her bra.

Theo looked away, and she wished she wasn't naked, hurrying now into her pants.

'Who else indeed.' He ran his palm over his stubbly chin.

'I feel...' she began. 'I feel a little... uncertain,' she mumbled as she fastened her bra.

'Well, I guess that's something for you to discuss with your... fiancé.' The word sounded sour on his tongue. He sat up against the wall and watched her dress, his breath coming in starts, as if there was something he desperately wanted to say.

'I have to go. I'm late.' She shook her head, flustered, mortified, awkward. Finally, she slipped into her trainers and made for the door.

She looked back over her shoulder, committing the sight of him to memory. 'Goodbye, Theo.' She bit her lip and her expression softened. 'Today was lovely.'

'Lovely?' He wrinkled his nose and sounded nonplussed.

'Well, it was for me.'

More than you will ever know, Theo. The first for me in so many ways, and even though I know I've messed up, I am so, so glad that it was with you.

Angus had cooked supper and as Kitty prepared to tuck into the hot, fresh pasta, she picked the moment to come clean about her day, not wanting to make her meeting any more clandestine than it needed to be. She decided to give him some but not all of the facts, thinking that this might assuage a little bit of the guilt that filled her right up. The very thought of how she had betrayed him made her feel sick to her stomach.

'You're so late, I was getting worried,' he said as he lifted his wine glass. 'And you smell like a bloody brewery!'

'I had a couple of drinks at lunchtime. I bumped into Theo Montgomery – he was in my year at school, d'you remember him?' She forked the food into her mouth and kept her eyes on the table.

Angus paused, now grating the hunk of parmesan over his plate. 'Vaguely. A quiet chap, oddball, bit of a squirt, parents are loaded.'

'He's not an oddball actually.' She was incensed on Theo's behalf. 'He's really nice, a friend. I met him on my first day at Vaizey and he was always very kind to me.'

'Well, of course he was.' Angus snorted. 'He was a little twerp and you were hot! Still are hot!'

'Hot? Well, thanks!'

'Anyway, darling, enough about your friend Theo Montgomery. I have a surprise for you – something I hope you'll love.'

Kitty ran her hand over her collarbone, where the memory of Theo's illicit kisses lingered, and looked up distractedly at Angus. 'A surprise…?'

Angus did this sometimes, came home with something lovely, quite out of the blue – a glamorous pair of shoes, a ticket to a film premiere. She forced herself to focus on the present, pleased to be reminded of Angus's generosity and thoughtfulness. There were many reasons why she wanted to be married to him, and his spontaneous gestures of affection were part of that.

Angus grinned. 'Yes! I've booked a table for eight of us tomorrow night at that new Italian place, The River Café. I remembered you saying how you'd love to go there, so I made a few calls, phoned up our usual gang and—'

Kitty could barely reply through the choking swell of tears and guilt. 'Oh, Angus, that's lovely of you. How sweet you are.'

Kitty went to bed early, leaving Angus dozing in front of the television. She lay motionless, staring at the ceiling, replaying the strange and lovely events of the day, feeling by turns excited, sad, guilty and energised. She had done wrong by

Angus, she was in no doubt about that. But it was a one-off, fuelled by alcohol, and a bit of a last hurrah before she settled down for good. After all, Angus was the only person she'd ever slept with. So it probably wasn't that surprising that she'd had a wobble, a 'what if' moment. She could practically hear Tizz's voice in her head, telling her exactly that. '"*What if" moments are good, positive! Because without questioning, without doubting, how can you know if you're making the right decision?*'

She smiled at the image of her wise, pragmatic friend and turned her face into the pillow. Tizz was on the button, as usual.

Marrying Angus is the right decision, one hundred per cent. I will marry Angus and everything will be okay. It will. Everything will be okay.

Moving Home

Kitty finished her list and made a start on the dresser in the hall, gathering the detritus that had gathered in the bits-and-bobs drawer: old packets of mints, elastic bands, taxi flyers, pizza coupons and even half a tennis ball. She opened the big black bin liner and lobbed the lot into it.

Sophie's words played in her head. The girl was right; this was a time for happiness – good, good things were happening! She bunched up the bin liner and grabbed her mobile, pressing the number on speed dial.

'Hello, you! ... No, nothing's wrong. Just wanted a chat. ... I am surrounded by boxes, which are making me itch to get moving. Truth be told, I think this bit between deciding to go and actually going is the hardest part. I feel a little in limbo. But that said, instead of sorting and packing and making any kind of progress, I've spent the laziest of mornings, idling over photographs, doing the easiest chores and drinking coffee! And that's why I'm calling – I need a bit of reassurance.' She took a deep breath.

'Cold feet?' She laughed loudly and cradled the phone to her face. 'No, never. Nothing like that. I just I just wanted to hear your voice...'

Seven

'So, which do you think – the tartan sash or the veil? I think it would be too much to have both, as one draws attention from the other. Especially if your bouquet is, as you say, trailing, it might all be a bit too clashy.'

Kitty stared at the shop assistant, trying to feel the same level of enthusiasm for the task in hand. 'I don't really mind. Whatever you think.'

'You don't mind? That's not an option! It can't be up to me! You *have* to mind. It's important! This is 1988 not 1888, and you are a young woman in control of your destiny. We even have a woman prime minister, you know!' The assistant winked. 'You can choose whatever pleases you!'

'Is it really that important?'

'Yes! Of course.' The woman sucked her teeth and peered at Kitty from behind the horn-rimmed glasses that sat forward on her nose. 'The way you look on your wedding day will be captured by the photographer and that image will sit on a dusty shelf for the rest of your life. Right now, at this very moment, you have the chance to determine whether you look at that picture every day and think, "Ooh, good choice, glad I went for the sash!" Or whether you curse at the sight of it and wish you'd gone for the more virginal veil. As I said, it is important.'

'Excuse me.' Suddenly and without too much warning, Kitty gathered up the skirts of her wedding gown and ran towards the back of the shop. Realising she wasn't going to make it to the bathroom, she grabbed the umbrella stand that stood by the back door and bent her head into it, vomiting noisily as the room swayed around her.

The woman followed and stood behind her. The two were silent for a beat while Kitty spat, wiped her mouth and straightened, leaning on the doorframe for support.

'We can always let the waistband out at a later date, if that is required?' She folded her arms and stared at her knowingly.

Kitty left the doctor's surgery and walked home with a feeling of dread in her stomach. She closed her eyes, wishing, praying, and still digesting what the doctor had confirmed. She was nearly ten weeks pregnant and would be getting married in another eight.

Pregnant! A baby! What the hell am I going to do? What am I going to say to Angus?

Kitty knew that she'd been at her most fertile when she'd slept with Theo. They'd had sex without protection, drunk and idiotically neglectful, living in the moment without heed of the consequences. By the time she and Angus had got round to having sex, it was in her safe time and, as ever, they'd used a sturdy condom and spermicide, just in case. There was very little doubt in her mind that this was Theo Montgomery's baby. She closed her eyes and tried to calm her racing heart. Her mouth was dry and wave upon wave of sickness lapped at her gut. She was too shocked for tears, too afraid to think straight.

Maybe I can keep it a secret? Maybe I can let Angus think it's his child and he might never find out.

She pictured Angus's fair hair and slight frame compared to the muscled, swarthy Theo, whose hair was almost black and whose eyes were dark. The two men were polar opposites, and with her fair colouring there was no way she could conceal the physical truth, even if the idea wasn't morally repugnant.

You have to tell him the truth. You have to! It wouldn't be fair. Give him the facts and let him make the decision. Oh my God.

For someone who rarely prayed, she certainly reached out to God, knowing that what she needed right then was indeed a bloody miracle.

Her thoughts raged. How was she going to tell him? What was she going to say? What would his pious parents think? She tried to imagine the exchange, saw him calling off the wedding and throwing her out of the flat they shared. Her stomach bunched and again sickness filled her mouth. She bent forward over the kerb, resting on a bin as she was sick over a drain.

'Hair of the dog, love! Best thing!' a man called from a passing white van. He and his passenger chuckled.

Somehow, she managed to make it home without a repeat performance. The phone in the hallway was ringing as she let herself in.

'Hello, darling!' Her dad's cheery tone was almost more than she could stand.

'Hi, Dad.'

'Hey now, what's up? Are you crying?' he asked softly.

She swallowed and placed her hand on her stomach. 'A bit.'

'Well, whatever it is, I'm sure there's no need for tears. Some pre-wedding jitters maybe?'

'Maybe,' she managed.

There was a beat or two of silence while her dad let her sob.

'I hate to hear you so sad, Kitty. Has Angus upset you? Because if he has…'

She took a morsel of comfort from his rising, angry tone, knowing he would always leap to her defence if necessary. 'No, he's fine. It's…'

'It's what, darling?' he coaxed. 'You know what Marjorie says: a problem shared is a problem halved. What can I do to make it better?'

'Nothing, Dad. Not this time.'

'Goodness me, it sounds fatal! What is it, Kitty?'

'I haven't told anyone, but…' She wiped the back of her hand over her nose and eyes. 'Oh, Dad…'

'Kitty Montrose, you are scaring me now.' He spoke a little sternly. 'Do I have to saddle up the Land Rover and drive all the way down to London or are you going to talk to me? Come on, darling, nothing is that bad.'

'I think… I think I might be pregnant.'

She heard her father's sharp intake of breath and closed her eyes, feeling the blush spread across her face. It was hard enough to be confessing to her adored dad that she'd even had sex, though he was well aware that she and Angus were living together. This was definitely not the time to be telling him the full story. She'd already decided to tell no one but Angus about Theo, thinking of the other proverb that Marjorie was fond of – 'Least said, soonest mended.' No matter what the outcome, it would mean that Angus could save face, be in control. She owed him that much, and more besides. She pictured Theo propping his head against the pillow on his bed. *I thought we might get some supper…?*

'Wow, Kitty.' Her dad took another deep breath. 'I don't know what to say.'

Me either, Dad. Me either.

'What does Angus think?'

'I haven't told him yet. I'm going to tell him tonight. I don't want anyone to know.'

'Well, no point until it's confirmed.'

She felt the slip of tears over her cheek.

Her dad coughed. 'I always think of you as my little girl – you always will be – and so this is going to take a bit of getting used to. But it might be wonderful. In fact, no "might" – it will be wonderful!' She could tell by the shape of his words that he was smiling.

'I know,' she whispered. 'It might.'

'Are you well, Kitty? Do you need anything at all?'

'No, Dad.'

'I'm glad you can talk to me. It means the world. And you know, Kitty, there are many journeys that end somewhere glorious, but they don't always start that way. Try to look towards the future. This might not be the timing you would have hoped for, but it's a gift nonetheless. Having you has been the single best thing that happened to your mum and me.'

Kitty bowed her head and let her tears fall; she was having trouble seeing beyond the end of the evening, let alone the future. 'I don't want you to tell anyone, not until I know what's what.' This was as clear as she could make it without giving specifics.

'I understand. It's your news to tell, not mine. Plus Mum has been a little quiet – nothing to worry about, but I don't want to overload her.'

'Is she okay?' Kitty felt the leap of fear in her throat. The worry over her mum's mental health was never any less than a heartbeat away.

'She is. I'm keeping an eye on her, you know...'

'I do.'

He cleared his throat again. 'I love you, Kitty Montrose. Always have, always will and I am proud of you. You know that, don't you?' His voice cracked.

She nodded. 'I love you too, Dad.'

A few hours later, she heard Angus tread the stairs of the flat and pause in the hallway, no doubt to hang up his coat and deposit his keys on the half-moon table that housed the telephone and a wire tray for post.

'Kitty?'

'In here,' she called, from the tiny sitting room where she sat with her legs curled beneath her in the glow of the table lamp.

He rushed in and flopped down onto the other end of the sofa, leaning back on the cushions and stretching his legs out in front of him as he loosened his tie. 'Am I glad this day is over! I've been speaking to arseholes all day who don't want to listen... Anyway, enough of work. What do you fancy for supper? Shall we cook something? Or would you like noodles – I don't mind picking them up?' He twisted his head to look at her. 'Oh God, what's the matter? Have you been crying?' He sat up and turned to face her.

She nodded.

'What's up?'

'I... I need to talk to you, Angus—'

'Talk away!' he said, interrupting her. 'Nothing's worth tears, though – we have so much to look forward to.' He patted her leg. 'I got the engraved cufflinks back today for Ruraigh, Hamish and both dads, and they look brilliant.'

'I can't talk about that right now. I... need you to listen to me, Angus. I need you to let me talk and concentrate… and then we can discuss it, but… but if you interrupt me, I might not ever finish, okay?' Nerves caused the words to stutter in her throat and she fought the desire to vomit.

'You're scaring me a bit, to be honest.' He gave a small, nervous laugh.

'Please, Angus, can you just let me talk?'

He nodded and folded his arms across his chest, as if this might help contain any errant words that might emerge.

'I went to the doctor's today…'

Angus's eyes widened.

'It's okay, I'm not ill, not really, but I am pregnant.' She whispered this and held his gaze.

The colour drained from his cheeks. 'Jesus!' He placed his hand over his mouth and breathed through his fingers. 'Pregnant? Are you sure?'

'Yes.' She nodded.

'But… but we've always been so careful! Fuck!' He leant forward and rested his elbows on his knees.

Kitty stared at him and tried to quash the feeling of disappointment in her gut. She knew there was more to be said, more words, facts and admissions that would cut him deeper, damage them further, but at some level she had hoped for a show of love from him, something that might make her feel like a baby would be welcomed into their lives. A wonderful thing.

'I can't believe it!' He shook his head. 'Jesus! How far are you?'

'Ten weeks.'

He exhaled through bloated cheeks and looked skywards. 'Ten weeks,' he repeated. 'Shit!'

'Angus…' She twisted her body until she could easily reach

him and placed her hands on his arm. 'Angus...' She swallowed. 'There's something else.'

'Not fucking twins?' He half laughed, his eyes like saucers.

She shook her head. 'No. No joking. I need to tell you.'

'What?' he urged, looking up at her, his face still pale and with beads of sweat on his top lip.

'I did something terrible, something that I am ashamed of and something that I need to tell you, but I don't know how. I'm scared, really scared of how you'll react, but I know that I owe you the truth, and what you decide to do with that truth is up to you. I will understand and respect your decision, no matter what it is.' Her tears came in gulping sobs and she struggled to get the words out.

'Jesus, Kitty...' He was almost breathless. 'Just tell me! What else?'

It was now three weeks since that night and things were understandably still strained. Kitty walked softly around the flat, trying to be quiet and make herself invisible. Angus did the opposite, slamming doors and thumping countertops, as if his mission was to create noise and mayhem, as if trying outwardly to match the turmoil that raged inside. She would never forget the way he had laughed in the immediate aftermath of her confession, as if it were a horrible joke.

'You are fucking kidding me, right?'

He had looked at her searchingly, like he was waiting for the punchline and she noted the slight tilt to his nose and the curl to his top lip, as if he was disgusted by her. It made her feel dirty. There was no discussion, no plans shared about dealing with the pregnancy. She didn't know if the wedding was on or off; she didn't know much. She lived in limbo, crying into her pillow each night, alone while Angus drowned his sorrows with Thomas and the boys, and she woke each day dogged by morning sickness that made her feel utterly miserable. What should have been the happiest time in her life turned out to be one of the very worst. Not that she had anyone to blame but herself.

What did you expect, Kitty? What did you really, honestly expect?

She and her dad talked a few times on the phone, but usually one of them was not in a position to chat, with either Angus, her mother or Marjorie lurking in the background. It made their conversations stilted, awkward and coded. She clung to his earlier observation that there were many journeys that ended somewhere glorious even when they hadn't started that way. It helped.

She kept replaying the moment Angus had walked from the room in silence, his reaction unreadable, his fingers balled into white-knuckled fists, leaving her curled and miserable on the sofa to ponder her options. Time and again she imagined throwing her clothes into a weekend bag and jumping on the train home. The thought didn't scare her; in fact, in the face of her loneliness, the idea of sitting in the library with her parents and Champ as a fire crackled in the grate and her belly grew was far from unpleasant.

Angus's silent treatment, noisy crashing around and indifference towards her made her feel lost, alone and afraid. She talked to her baby at night, apologising for its less than auspicious start and promising that things would get better. The small kernel of life blossoming inside her was the single thing that brought her flashes of joy. She might or might not be getting married, Angus might no longer want her, and from the way her dad had mentioned her mum's tiredness, it might even be that her mother's mental health was once again on the slide, but as she laid her palm on her stomach in the dark of night, she felt the pulse of life and smiled.

My baby, my child, my little one... The baby I made with Theo, my friend.

And then one afternoon, just after she'd managed to stall the caterers, who'd called to confirm numbers for the evening reception, Angus arrived home with what could best be described as a spring in his step. His upright posture, sprightly demeanour and wide smile were almost as unnerving as the latent anger that had simmered over the last few weeks. This was altogether less predictable and therefore more chilling. A shiver ran through her.

'Okay.' He pulled out a chair at the kitchen table and sat opposite her. 'This is how I see it.'

She joined her knuckles on the tabletop to steady their tremble while she awaited her fate.

'This has damaged us, but I love you.' He said this matter-of-factly, but it was no less reassuring for that.

Tears pricked Kitty's eyes. 'I love you too.' Her voice was hoarse with relief. 'I do, Angus. I love you too.'

'We're young, but we work well together. We've always worked, Kitty.' He gave a tight-lipped smile.

'We do.'

'You messed up.'

'I know. I know!' She nodded. 'And I'm so sorry. I am so, so sorry!'

'I've thought about it day and night, I've sought advice from Thomas and others...'

Kitty was glad he'd been able to confide in his friends. She wished that she'd had her own confidante over the last few weeks.

'And I don't want to throw away what we have, Kitty. I've weighed up the pros and cons, looked at how we live and how we want to live. And this situation is not insurmountable. At least I don't think it is.'

She nodded, willing to say and do just about anything to preserve the future for herself and her child. It felt like she was being given a second chance and she was overwhelmed with gratitude.

'I mean, Christ, which of us is without a secret part of our soul!' He sighed.

She nodded again, not sure what he meant but in no position to enquire further.

'I have conditions.' He drummed the table.

'Of course.'

'I don't know if it needs stating, but if you so much at look at another man, that will be it. Literally. It's not about the sex so much as the lying, the deceit. I don't want to live like that. I can't.'

'I don't want to live like that either!'

'If it happened again, we'd be divorced before you'd finished mumbling a confession. I can give you the benefit of the doubt, Kitty, but I won't be made a fool of.'

'I wouldn't do that to you, Angus. It was one mistake, one stupid, drunken—'

'All right!' He raised his palm. 'We don't need to go over it again. I want you to have nothing to do with Montgomery. Nothing at all. That's a given.'

'I promise.'

'I also think it only fair that we tell the child. The thought of having this hanging over us, of us continually waiting and wondering if and when it might be revealed, would feel like a sentence, and the idea of him or her growing up duped and suspicious is even worse. Everyone needs a clear identity. It's important. So if we are going to do this, we do it openly and then it won't be an issue. We head it off. There's no need to go completely public, but within our immediate family circle there should be no shame. No secrets.'

Kitty looked up at Angus with gratitude. He was displaying more maturity, sense and forgiveness than she had any right to expect. That he was so concerned for the child's welfare was quite overwhelming.

'No shame. No secrets.' She allowed herself the beginnings of a smile. 'Thank you, Angus. It will all be okay, won't it?'

'Yes.' He nodded and placed his hand over the back of hers. 'It will all be okay.'

The following morning, Kitty sat at the table in the kitchen and tapped the fountain pen on her cheek. It was a hard letter to write, the hardest. But she had to do it. Wanted to. Angus was giving her the chance of stability and Kitty knew from looking at her own parents' situation that forgiveness and stability were the things that got you through the darkest of hours. She carried with her the fear that one day her sadness might slip over a line and become something else entirely; that she might end up like her mum. It would be the stead-fast, predictable life she had with Angus that would get her through that. She flipped open the top sheet of the Basildon Bond notepad and gripped the pen, liking the flourish of blue ink on the paper.

My dearest friend, Theo.

She scratched through and tore off the sheet, starting again.

~~Oh , Theo, this is a hard, hard letter for me to write.~~

And again.

~~Theo, I am so scared, so nervous, but feel I owe you at least this.~~

Finally, she settled into the writing and tried not to over-think the words. With a racing heart, she watched the fountain pen dance across the page.

Hello Theo,

I hope you're still at this flat. I have thought long and hard about whether to write and what to write, so here goes.

It was an unexpectedly joyful day when I last saw you. It was a day of escape and I want you to know that I have never done anything similar before or since. I hope you believe me when I tell you that it was special for me. I know how that reads and we both know that alcohol was the catalyst, but there are very few people on earth I trust in the way I trust you, Theo.

Theo, oh Theo…

I'm pregnant.

I can only imagine what it's like for you to read these words. Perhaps it feels the same as it did for me when I found out.

I thought you deserved to know. It is yours. I want to keep this baby and I'm still figuring out how to make it all work. The one thing I do know is that this is not the path for us, for you and me. We are not those people. I'm marrying Angus soon, in a few weeks, and he is aware. It's been horrendously difficult for us both. For this reason, I think it only fair that we have no further contact. If our paths should ever cross, please respect my wish for us to never mention this. I beg you, Theo.

This is the only way I can build a life. Please.
   I say goodbye now.
   Your friend,
   Kitty X

She placed her head in her hands and sobbed, picturing the handsome, sensitive man who had recited poetry to her across the tabletop and who had taken her on the most delicious physical journey. But she didn't really know Theo; their history wasn't enough to justify throwing away the chance of happiness that she had with Angus, who had done something quite wonderful and forgiven her.

Kitty dried her eyes and placed her hand on her stomach. It was time to put thoughts of Theo Montgomery out of her head and concentrate on making a success of her life with the man she had been with since she was young.

That was it: no shame, no secrets.

'So, are you nervous?' Hamish asked as he pulled the Land Rover off the motorway.

Coincidentally, Kitty felt a rush of butterflies. 'I don't know.'

He laughed. 'How can you not know?'

She turned in her seat to face her cousin, who had kindly offered to drive her up to Darraghfield from London. They were well practised at travelling this route, as ever stopping only a couple of times for coffee and food and to take a quick nap in their seats. Angus was driving up separately, with Thomas, his best man, and Ruraigh was going up by train with Tizz, for which Kitty was thankful. The rift between her and Ruraigh, though healed on the surface, had left a deep scar that needed more time to knit. He was as cool about the wedding as he had been over their engagement and it maddened her. Gone was the easiness between them and in its place a new wariness, invisible to others but glaringly obvious to her. It bothered her that her dad might get wind of it; he had enough on his plate and would be hurt to think they were anything other than the best of friends.

She looked over at Hamish. 'I don't know if what I'm feeling is wedding nerves or general excitement or morning sickness. I keep thinking of all those people looking at me and I feel a bit sick about that, and I'm worried about Mum, of course...' She knew she didn't need to elaborate. It was, however, a wonderful relief to have her pregnancy out in the open, to be able to discuss it without fear or embarrassment. She had told them all that the baby was Theo's, with the final message being that if she and Angus could handle the fact with grace and tact, then so could they. As Angus had predicted, once everyone knew, the whole situation felt far easier to bear.

She'd still found it difficult to tell her father, though, embarrassed to have to inform him that the daughter he adored had well and truly fallen off her pedestal. Despite the challenges in their own marriage, she knew that her parents would never so much as contemplate being unfaithful; it was just something they would never do. But when it came to it, her dad had been characteristically generous and non-judgemental, talking only about how he couldn't wait to meet his grandchild and what a super mum Kitty would be, helping her to navigate the situation in the way he knew how. Kitty had never loved him more.

Angus's mum, however, had not taken it well. Angus had broken the news over the phone, and Kitty had listened through the kitchen wall. 'Who cares what Reverend Smithson thinks, Mum?' he'd said tersely into the handset. 'It's none of his business anyway.' Kitty's face had flushed a deep red; though Angus rarely saw his parents, he was touchingly concerned about making them proud of him, and now she'd been responsible for tarnishing their son's image. There wasn't Tupperware box big enough to contain that sort of faux pas.

Hamish kept his eyes on the road but gave a small nod. 'Well, you will look just fine, and Fenella is doing great. Uncle Stephen will be right by her side and he'll not let her struggle, wedding or no wedding. As for that baby, it doesn't know that today or tomorrow is different to any other, so you can just let him be.'

'Or her.' She smiled and rubbed the small, welcome roundness to her belly. She and Angus were steady. They both agreed that this baby when it arrived would be loved and would love them in return and that was all that mattered. She was so thankful, ignoring the uncomfortable thought that niggled at her in the early hours, that she was somehow beholden to her fiancé, that his benevolence might come at a cost.

'I reckon it's a boy.' Hamish grinned. 'I have big plans afoot for a miniature rugby kit. With enough coaching, we could end up with a future Gavin Hastings on our hands.'

She laughed, happy that her cousin was taking such an interest in her child. 'I do love Angus.' She felt a wave of something close to relief that this day was happening at all.

'Well, that's a good job!' He chuckled.

'I love him, but I don't know how well I know him – does that make any sense? Even after all this time. Sometimes—'

'Sometimes what?'

'I don't know... I suppose sometimes I feel a bit like he's holding back, and I don't want him to, I want him to be himself completely with me.'

Hamish took his time answering. 'Well, even though you've been a couple for ever, you've only been together as grown-ups for a wee while and I guess you're both still getting to know yourselves as well as each other. But that's okay, Kitty. The three of you will all grow up together. You have all the time in the world to get to know each other. As a couple, you've already had to face more challenges than most.' He glanced at her stomach. 'And I have known you my whole life and I know that he can only discover how great you are.'

'Jesus Christ, Hamish, what is wrong with you? This isn't another tearful moment, is it?' She shrieked her laughter, hiding the emotion that flared within.

'I cried once! Once! And who didn't cry at *Kramer Vs Kramer*? Are you ever going to let me forget it?'

'No, probably not. I love you, even if you are a big softy.'

Hamish tutted and looked out at the road ahead. He punched the radio on and the strains of 'Cracklin' Rosie' filled the car. Far better they sing along than give in to that emotional, mushy stuff they were so bad at.

The house and grounds looked beautiful, lovelier than she had ever seen them. Patrick and her dad had worked hard and the gardens were as neat as a pin. The large terracotta planters, usually studded with the twigs of dead plants, were overflowing with variegated ivy and specially imported bright red geraniums. The front gates and iron fencing of Darraghfield had been give a new coat of glossy black paint and every window sparkled. Even the gravel had been raked and picked free of weeds.

Champ raced out to meet the car, barking his greeting.

'Hello, boy! Hello, you!' Kitty bent down on her haunches and let the dog sniff her hair as she petted his muzzle. 'I bet you are wondering what all this fuss is about!'

'Hamish!' She looked up in time to see her dad wrap his beloved nephew in a warm hug. 'Good journey, son?'

'Not bad. She spoke the whole way – I've got earache!' He jerked his head in her direction.

'Let me look at you.' Her dad walked forward and gave a small shake of his head. 'My baby is having a baby. How is that even possible?'

'I don't know, Dad.' Instinctively she placed her hand on her bump.

'You look wonderful.' He reached forward and kissed her tenderly on the forehead. She knew this was a gesture of understanding, an acceptance of her situation, and she was grateful for it.

'Where's Mum?' She looked over her dad's shoulder, half expecting her to pop up. She remembered coming up with Angus when they'd first got engaged and her mum standing in the garden, bossing everyone around. Kitty had loved it.

'She went for a wee rest after lunch. We'll give her a shout in a bit. She's dying to see you.' He winked, trying for jovial, but Kitty caught the slight twitch to his left eye. He never could lie to her.

'Oh, here she is!' Marjorie ambled from the house, moving her arms as if she was running, even though her feet were doing little more than a shuffle. It made them all chuckle.

'Oh, a baby! A baby!' Marjorie reached into her pinny pocket for her handkerchief and blotted her nose and eyes. 'It's amazin'!'

'Thank you, Marjorie.'

'And don't you let anyone be telling you that you are putting the cart before the horse. I mean, your wedding was booked and this baby will be born in wedlock. That should be well enough for those to whom these things matter.'

Her dad rolled his eyes and Kitty's thoughts turned to Angus's pinched-faced mother to whom these things mattered a lot.

'Can I see my cake?' Kitty rubbed her hands together, excited.

Marjorie took her by the hand and led her into the hallway and through to the dining room.

'Oh my goodness! Oh wow!' Kitty stared at the three-tiered monstrosity that listed to the left. It was covered with mismatched blobs of icing that made for a lumpy surface. 'Marjorie!' she said enthusiastically, stalling for time, trying to think how to phrase the necessary in the most genuine way possible. 'You made this? For me?'

'I did.' She nodded proudly. 'With royal icing that was a bugger to work with, and all the fruit has been properly steeped in whisky. Do you like it?' She looked at Kitty expectantly.

'Marjorie, I have never loved a cake more!' That was the truth.

Marjorie's smile spoke volumes. 'I knew you would. All we are missing is the wee bride and groom to put on the top, which Patrick has ordered for me and he assures me they will be here by nightfall.'

'If they don't turn up, I'll get the modelling clay out,' Kitty offered.

'Now that's not a bad idea! I think we might still have some of your old Play-Doh around somewhere.'

They both folded with laughter.

'I've been digging a lot of your baby stuff out for the bairn.' Marjorie was a little misty eyed.

'That means the world to me.' Kitty calmed and caught her breath. 'How's Mum doing?'

Marjorie averted her gaze. 'Oh, you know, hen... good days and bad.'

'And how is she today?'

'Not good.'

'And yesterday?' she whispered.

'Not good.'

'How about the day before that?'

Marjorie shook her head and reached for her hand, which she took into both of her own. 'Don't let anything spoil your sunshine.'

'I'll try, Marjorie. And thank you for our beautiful cake. I do love you.'

'Och, away with you. I need to crack on!' she mumbled as she reached for the hanky in her pocket and dabbed at her eyes.

With all those staying overnight ensconced in the library, where whisky flowed and the noise levels rose in direct proportion to the amount consumed, Kitty decided to sneak out. She rummaged in her old chest of drawers until her hands fell upon a rather raggedy swimming costume with enough slack in the old elastic to accommodate the swell of her bump and her growing boobs.

Having grabbed a towel, she slipped her feet into a spare pair of wellingtons from the boot room, fastened her dressing gown and made her way to her beloved pool.

It was a beautiful evening, with the unseasonably warm wind making the leaves dance overhead. The pool lights were on and as Kitty placed her towel and dressing gown on top of her wellington boots by the side of the water, she felt very much at peace. Forgoing her dive, she slipped into the water and felt the familiar shudder of pleasure ripple along her skin. With a sudden appetite to cover ground, she began her lengths, concentrating on finding her breathing rhythm, exhaling with her face in the water and taking a full, deep, sharp inhalation each time her face lifted under the arc of her left arm. She ploughed through the water, length after length, her thoughts clearing and her whole body feeling properly alive. With her breath coming fast and having done thirty-odd lengths, she lay back in the water and let it lap over her ears. All she could hear were the murmurs from her watery world and the loud beating of her heart.

She stretched on the surface, wiggling her toes even though she couldn't see them. At that angle, and looking straight ahead, her bump obscured just about everything. She loved it. She placed her hand on the safe pouch where her baby nestled. If it was a girl, they would call her Sophie; if it was a boy, Oliver. They had decided on Montgomery Thompson. She was still unsure if this was a brave or stupid decision, but if, as agreed, they were going to be open with the child, then this name would acknowledge its heritage and should help it feel like it belonged, strengthening its identity. Angus hadn't flinched at the idea. He was still calm and appeasing, and in response, Kitty was quiet and grateful.

They had stopped having sex a while ago. Angus had said he was worried about hurting her or hurting the baby and even though she had tried to reassure him that if they were gentle it would be fine, he was adamant. Kitty ran her hand over her body and wondered if the real reason was, as she suspected, that her swelling form repulsed him in some way – whether because she was pregnant or because of how it had happened, she wasn't sure. Either way, she didn't feel very good about herself, even though she understood. When she raised it with him in the most delicate way possible, he assured her it would be business as usual once the baby arrived. She truly hoped so.

She felt lonely, missing the way sex bound the two of them,

reminded them that they were facing the world together. This lack of physical contact made their home feel cold. She tried not to think about that afternoon with Theo, which physically had been so much more. Her body tingled at the memory of his touch, the unhurried ease with which she had been lost to him. It played in her head like a symphony and in her more fanciful moments she was quite unsurprised that something so perfect had produced this little miracle.

Kitty righted herself in the water and shook her head, wiping her face. This was not good enough! She should not be thinking about Theo on the night before her wedding – not on any night! It was unfair on Angus; kind, forgiving Angus, who was working hard, recently promoted and doing his best to build a wonderful life for the three of them. Life with Angus would be steady and calm, and this she knew was where happiness lay.

It was as she dried her skin and stepped into the wellingtons that she became aware of someone coming through the hedge.

'Mum!' She ran forward in the cumbersome footwear and into her mum's arms.

'My darling girl. Oh you look wonderful!' Her mum breathed into her damp hair, kissing her scalp. 'Big day for you tomorrow, for us all.'

Kitty pulled back to look at her pale face with its dark half-moons of worry sitting beneath sunken eyes. 'Mum, if it's too much for you…'

'I'm fine. And no matter what, I'll be there, darling, because I am here.' She touched her fingers to her daughter's chest. 'And it will be the same for you with your child. Whether I am standing by your side or miles away, I am always here.'

'Yes.' Kitty could do nothing to stop her tears. 'You are, Mum. Always.'

Her mum slipped back through the laurel hedge like a spectre, almost as if she had never even been there.

Kitty knew she should be getting an early night, but with all the guests now either asleep or in the kitchen tucking into Marjorie's pork pie and chutney, she decided to sit in the library for a bit, with Champ sprawled across her lap and the fire crackling. Not that it was cold, but she wanted the comfort and distraction of the flames. She stroked Champ's silky ears and thought about her mum, reassured now, after their brief chat by the pool.

She yawned and was finally thinking of calling it a night. Isla was coming early in the morning to help with her hair and make-up, and she knew the boys' drinking around the kitchen table might go on until the early hours. Champ nestled appreciatively against her bump. Suddenly the door swung open and Angus came into the room.

She sat up straight, causing Champ to leap up. It was a shock to see that Angus had been crying. His nose was running and his eyes were puffy and red. He was a man of cool emotions and she'd never seen him like that before. Her heart raced, and she could only assume that this level of distress was because he'd decided to call off the wedding. Ridiculously, her first thought was, *Oh no, Marjorie's cake! What a waste!*

He sank down onto the rug and placed his head on her lap. Kitty ran her fingers through his hair. 'What's up, darling? What on earth is wrong?' she asked with a warble to her voice, waiting.

'I do love you, Kitty, and I want to marry you. I want you to make me the man I need to be.'

She felt a flood of relief and kissed his head, guessing that the reality of marriage and fatherhood was hitting home on this night before the big day.

'Oh, Angus! You are going to be a fine husband and a wonderful father! You are! We will do it together.'

He nodded and gripped her arms, and they sat like that for a while with the fire leaping and the logs hissing. And Kitty saw the image of Theo fade. This level of concern, this dedication to their future no matter how rocky the start, this was what marriage was all about.

Moving Home

Kitty pulled the cardboard box from the cupboard under the stairs and knelt on the floor to open it, ignoring the slight creak to her knees. She smiled at the rather dusty collection of Sylvanian Families characters – mice in pinnies, rabbits in dungarees and dogs in frocks. She lifted them out and was instantly taken right back to when Sophie was three.

'Mummy! Mum! I need you here now!'

Sophie did that: she called out, hollering fit to burst, until Kitty went running to see what the emergency was. It was usually a matter of life-altering importance for her three-year-old, like she couldn't find the bed for her Sylvanian Families rabbit or she had a lolly stick, formerly attached to an actual lolly, stuck in her hair, or she had switched on the television but *The Raggy Dolls* wasn't on and she needed her mum to fix the scheduling.

'What's up, Sophie?'

'I finished!' She held up the small round melamine plate featuring Babar the Elephant in his green suit and tiny gold crown.

'Oh, well done!' Her daughter responded well to praise, even if it was only to acknowledge the fact that she had devoured a whole slice of cheese on toast cut into squares.

'I want Daddy!' Sophie had asked suddenly and just like that the moment had seemed right to Kitty.

'He is on his way home, darling and you know, you are a very lucky little girl.' Sophie had stared at her. 'You are very lucky because most little girls only have one daddy, but you, you are so special that you get two!'

'Two daddies?' Sophie had asked with a little wrinkle of confusion on her button nose.

'Yes!' Kitty grabbed a daddy rabbit and a daddy squirrel and a baby hedgehog. She placed the unlikely trio on the table and pointed at them. 'There are all kinds of families, Soph. And you have me, your mumma and you have Angus daddy and there is this other daddy,' she touched her finger to the rather portly looking rabbit, 'you have Theo daddy too and even though you haven't met him and you might not for a very long time, he is your dad too!'

'Is he going to put me to bed?' Sophie took the daddy rabbit into her pudgy little palm.

'No. Daddy will put you to bed, just like he always does.'

'Will daddy Theo get me a present?'

Kitty laughed, knowing it was typical of her child to be thinking along these lines. 'I don't think so and you might not meet him until you are much older, but I know him very well and I can tell you that he is,' she paused, trying to control the catch to her voice, 'he is really lovely.'

Kitty cradled the small animals to her chest and enjoyed the wave of nostalgia that came over her. That day lived in her memory. She had dreaded having to tell Sophie and yet it happened easily, naturally and this was how it had always been. Not that she had time to sit and procrastinate any longer – the day was marching on and she had scarcely made a dent in her list. She popped the creatures back inside the box and moved it to one of the stacks by the front door. She went back to the cupboard and placed her hand on the wooden floor. Reaching for another box, she felt the dust and dirt with her fingertips and the sensation took her back to another day, when her heart had begun to splinter. Those fragments had lodged in her mind, so much so that with just this touch to the floor of the cupboard, it took all of her strength not to sob.

Eight

1996

Kitty ran her hand over her daughter's dark curly hair as they sat together in the square kitchen at the back of the Georgian terraced house where they now lived in Blackheath, southeast London. Angus's promotion when Sophie was a toddler had meant they were able to take on the hefty mortgage. It had been a thrill, putting the key in the black front door of what she'd felt would be their forever house. The sitting and dining rooms had been knocked through by the previous owner, creating a vast open-plan living space with glorious floor-to-ceiling windows at each end. Light flooded first one half and then the other as the day progressed. Kitty loved to watch the sun dapple the wooden floor and rarely felt the need to look at the clock on the mantel, knowing exactly where she was in the day by the way the light fell. It was just one of the magic secrets of the storybook house.

Two matching fireplaces sat along the outer wall and bookshelves nestled in the alcoves on either side. An old dining table and six heavy chairs with ball-and-claw feet, which her parents had consigned to their basement, had made their way down the motorway in the back of a cow trailer and now dominated the dining area, the burnished mahogany having been given a new lease of life. Kitty was more than happy to have part of her beloved Darraghfield around her every day. Angus had drawn the line at her suggestion of oil paintings and ornate mirrors, which she thought might have worked very well. He favoured lighter watercolour seascapes, which she had to admit looked elegant against the blue-grey painted panels. She had reluctantly rewrapped the antiques and left them in the basement with the other treasures.

Keeping the house running smoothly and looking after Sophie and Angus were pretty much Kitty's entire world. That and swimming. Three times a week she took herself off to the pool in nearby Greenwich, relishing the chance to float and dream. Things with Angus were stable and comfortable, but he worked hard, came home late and quite often seemed a bit remote. It was her adorable, effervescent daughter who brought the fun into her life, but now that Sophie had turned eight and was well established at junior school, Kitty had taken a part-time job in a local art gallery. It was good to have something else to think about.

'Can I make a cake?'

'Urgh.' Kitty pulled a face; the mess her daughter created when cooking turned a simple cake-making exercise into an hour of post-cookery deep-cleaning.

'Pleeeese, Mum! I want to make one for Dad!'

'All right, Soph. I'll get your apron, otherwise your uniform will be covered.'

Kitty made her way to the large cupboard under the stairs, where alongside boxes of toys and books there were tennis racquets, walking sticks, wellington boots and trainers lined up on the floor. Coats, hats and scarves hung on the sturdy coat-rack on the wall and the Hoover lived next to the ironing board, long broom and dustpan and brush. Kitty lifted her daughter's apron, dislodging Angus's heavy coat as she did so. It fell to the ground. Various business cards, receipts and a handful of change clattered onto the polished wooden floor.

'Shit!' Kitty cursed.

'I heard that!' Sophie reprimanded from the kitchen.

It was as Kitty straightened up and prepared to shove the bundle back into the coat pocket that her eye was drawn to a shiny red card that seemed to stand out from the others and a receipt. Pulsing in her palm, it invited her to look further.

'The Anvil, 88 Tooley Street, London Bridge,' she read under her breath. She raised the card to her face and studied the image of a moustachioed man in a peaked leather cap with a large cigar clamped between his teeth. She fingered the receipt, for two beers and two tequilas, and the date, a Tuesday evening, the week before last.

'Come on, Mum!' Sophie called out impatiently.

Kitty painted on a smile and restored the items to her husband's pocket, trying to ignore the dull feeling of mistrust in her gut. But she couldn't forget it; her mind kept returning to the ostentatious card and the niggling sense that something wasn't quite right. Finally she remembered: that Tuesday had been parents' evening at Sophie's school and Angus had been all set to come. But at the last minute he'd phoned from work, saying he had to go for a drink with an important client. She'd thought nothing of it – his job was demanding and being social was part of it. He was often out late. But a gay club…?

Some three hours later, Angus arrived home and strolled into the kitchen.

'Dad!' Sophie yelled. She pointed at the plate which proudly displayed her rather flat creation, 'I made you this! Carrot cake!'

'Wow, Soph!' He bent down and kissed her face. 'That looks marvellous. Is it really for me?'

Sophie smiled. 'Yep, I wanted to do a practice, we are making one at school next week.'

'Well, how wonderful, thank you, darling.' He winked at his wife over Sophie's head. Kitty felt her heart lift; he really was the very best dad.

'Pasta?' she lifted the saucepan and carried it to the sink to drain.

'Ooh yes, lovely. And a glass of red if there's one going.' He took a seat next to Sophie who was already enjoying her supper. 'So how was school?'

'Bit shit.'

'Sophie!'

'Oi!'

Both she and Angus shouted in unison.

'Mum said it earlier.' Sophie loaded up her fork with pasta.

Kitty poured the aromatic ragu, which had been simmering for hours, over the twists of pasta and ladled a healthy portion into a shallow bowl for her husband.

'Well, Mum can say it if she wants, you on the other hand...' He smiled at his wife. 'This looks lovely. Thank you, Kitty.' She smiled thinly, took a slug of wine and sat at the table.

'Are you okay?' he asked, studying her face.

'I'm fine,' she offered curtly, jerking her head towards their daughter, the code for 'We'll discuss this when she's asleep'.

Angus nodded and tucked into his supper. The atmosphere in the room changed, charged now with unspoken anticipation and a certain wariness on both their parts. It turned the delicious ragu into something quite flavourless and the pasta stuck like paste to the roof of Kitty's mouth.

With Sophie finally packed off to bed, Kitty stacked the

dishwasher and turned off the light before making her way into the sitting room. Angus was watching the news, sitting on the sofa with his stockinged feet resting on the edge of the coffee table.

'So what's up?' He wasted no time in getting to the point, as was his way.

She sat in the chair by the fireplace and curled her feet under her as she took a deep breath. 'I found something today and it's kind of bothered me.'

He made the little 'T' sound and gave a small laugh. The noise she had once found so endearing irritated her tonight. 'Sounds ominous!' He swallowed. 'Come on, Kitty, talk to me!'

'It was a business card in your coat pocket.'

'What business card?' He wrinkled his nose, his eyes never leaving her face, his expression open, the look of a man who had nothing to hide, and she felt the flare of embarrassment at any awkwardness that she might be about to cause.

'It was red, a bit... I don't know, homoerotic.' She gave a little laugh, embarrassed by her choice of words. 'It was for a place called the Anvil, in London Bridge.'

'And...?' Angus looked at her levelly.

'You said you were out with clients that night – it was Sophie's parents' evening, remember? I can't believe you took them to... a gay club. Did you?'

This time there was a momentary hesitation before Angus replied, enough for Kitty to notice. 'Jesus Christ, this feels like an inquisition. I *did* go out with clients, like I told you. But then... it was too late for the parents' evening, so Thomas and I dropped in at the Anvil. Bit sleazy actually, but we went for a couple of drinks.' He shrugged.

She stared at him, wondering how to continue her questioning in the manner she had prepped. She hadn't expected him to be so appeasing. Bloody Thomas Paderfield. He might be Angus's best mate, but in all the years she'd known him, Kitty hadn't warmed to him. There was something fake about him, just like Ruraigh had said.

'Thomas just happened to be in the neighbourhood, did he? And you didn't think to tell me?'

Angus snorted. 'Because it wasn't important. What's got into you?'

'I don't like the secrecy, Angus. It's like you've got something to hide. When I found the card…' She faltered, not entirely sure what it was that had caused her such unease, and unable to articulate right now how it had made her stomach flip.

'*Found* the card!' He swung his legs off the table and sat forward. 'Found it? Have you any idea how that sounds? The fact that you went rifling through my pockets is a bit worrying – is that where we're at? What next, combing through the bank statements, having me followed?'

'No! Of course not. Don't be ridiculous! And I didn't go rifling through your pockets. I was fetching Sophie's apron and knocked your coat and it fell onto the floor.'

He raised his eyebrows, clearly doubting her explanation, which incensed her.

'If you say so, Kitty, but you seem pretty riled…'

'I am not riled!' she shouted. 'I just can't see why—'

'Why what?' Angus looked her full in the face, challenging her to come out with it.

Kitty took a deep breath. 'Why you'd go to a gay club and then lie to me about it.'

Angus shook his head. 'For God's sake, Kitty! I didn't lie about it! It was just a non-event! I've known Thomas since we were eighteen. He was my best man, for Christ's sake. He's my best friend. Give me a break.'

Kitty gulped down her angry tears and tried to calm down. She might not like Thomas, but, really, what was she achieving here? 'I'm sorry, Angus, I—'

'You should be. It's pissed me off! I work my arse off all day and come home to a cold shoulder and a guessing game over supper.' He stared at her.

Kitty felt the beginnings of a headache and rubbed her temples. 'I'm sorry. I don't know what's up with me. Can we forget the whole thing?'

Angus stood and undid the top button of his shirt, loosening his tie. 'Sure we can. I'm off to have a shower.' He made his way to the door, then stopped and looked back over his shoulder, his hand resting on the frame. 'It's a bit rich, isn't it, Kitty? You were the one that couldn't keep your knickers on and I'm the one being made to feel guilty.'

As Angus trod the stairs, more tears gathered at the back of Kitty's throat. This was by no means the first time he'd used her infidelity as a weapon against her; he sometimes brought it up when he badly needed to win an argument or as a way of deflecting her criticism of something he'd done. It always had the same effect on Kitty, pulling the rug from under her feet and leaving her feeling vulnerable and afraid.

She sniffed and wiped her eyes with the back of her hand, wishing she could turn the clock back, wishing she could go back and not mention the bloody business card. In fact, if she had the ability to turn back time, she would go back to the day she met Theo on the pavement and she'd smile politely and immediately make her way home – without going to the pub, let alone going back to his flat.

No, no, no! Don't think that! You wouldn't have Sophie!

The very idea was unthinkable. She loved her daughter beyond measure; loved her exactly how she was and for exactly who she was, and that was all down to that one glorious, life-changing, memory-making afternoon.

It was now the weekend and the air had long since cleared. Angus and Kitty were sitting side by side in the back of a cab. 'How late do you think this thing will go on?'

Kitty tutted and smiled at her husband. 'Ruraigh and Tizz have finally got engaged! It's supposed to be a celebration, not a chore!'

'I know, but Sundays are so precious, and a barbecue, as you know, can last an hour or a whole day if you put your back into it. And it's such a long way.'

'It's Chiswick, not the Highlands, and he's my cousin and one of your best friends. So please try and be happy. After all, we've got no Sophie to worry about for once. How often does that happen – a whole night to ourselves! So we can drink and dance till dawn if the fancy takes us.'

'I expect Sophie and Bonnie will be doing the same thing.' He chuckled.

'God, I hope not! Sleepovers might have got a bit more exciting since we were kids, but they are only eight! Mind you, it won't be long, Sophie's getting so grown-up.'

'Tell me about it. I put the Mini Pops CD on in the car and she rolled her eyes and said, "Oh Dad, can we have the Spice Girls instead?" I had to look into the back seat just to check there hadn't been some inexplicable time-shift and there wasn't a teenager sitting behind me!'

Kitty threaded her arm through his and rested her head on his shoulder. 'I love you.'

Angus kissed the top of her head by way of reply.

The Victorian terrace in Chiswick was bursting with people.

Music and laughter filled the air and it was a reminder to Kitty that not all of their peers were married with kids; some were still living the carefree life of the mature student or the new professional. Not that she would have swapped her life for anything, but a day like this away from the routine of child-care, school runs and cooking supper was a treat. Uni friends, work colleagues and Old Vaizians populated the rooms and spilled out into the garden, where a rather grubby-looking oil-drum barbecue was turning out the very best food. She wolfed down decent servings of mouthwatering chicken drum-sticks in a sticky honey glaze and near-charred bangers, the perfect foundation for numerous cold beers and three white-wine spritzers.

Hamish rushed over with his new girlfriend Flo and lifted Kitty off her feet. 'So, another wedding at Darraghfield!' He smiled at her as she concentrated on not toppling over and, more importantly, keeping her plastic wine goblet upright.

'And what about you two? You could do a double-wedding! That would be ace!' Booze removed all filters from Kitty's mouth.

Flo squawked. 'Did he tell you to say that?' She nudged her beau in the ribs. 'He can't understand why I am happy *not* to get married. I mean, good luck to Ruraigh and Tizz and all that, but I just don't get it. I don't feel the need to put on the frock and announce to the world that I love this man. I don't even believe in God. It would feel hypocritical.'

'I hear ya!' Kitty raised her glass in her wobbly, drunken hand.

'Did you hear, Kitty, that Theo is engaged?'

The words, casually offered, felt like rocks being smashed into her gut. They left her winded, but she kept her smile in place. 'I didn't hear that. Congratulations to Theo!' She lifted her drink in the spirit of the occasion. 'Good for him.' Her heart twisted with a strange mix of feelings and she recalled his words, spoken so long ago, at school, when he'd comforted her over the death of Flynn. *'I can't imagine anyone loving me so much that they would miss me like you're missing your pony right now.'*

'Her name is Anna, apparently, and he's pretty smitten,' Hamish added.

Anna... Take care of his heart, Anna – it's a good one, a true one and one I could quite happily have claimed for my own. Again, Kitty recalled the feel of Theo's kiss on her collarbone that day they'd made Sophie.

Hamish was already onto the next subject. Casting a theatrical glance at Flo, he asked her, 'And did I hear correctly, that you love this man?' He pointed his finger at his own chest and grinned at his girlfriend.

'I do,' Flo replied, with a striking softness to her tone that Kitty found quite moving. 'I love you.'

Hamish leant over and kissed his girl.

'For God's sake, get a room!' Ruraigh yelled as he gripped his brother in a headlock.

Kitty roared her laughter and recalled the two of them as kids, wrestling on the front lawn at Darraghfield, the rough-housing only ending when her dad pulled them apart or one of them started crying.

'You two...!' She smiled at them affectionately.

Hamish and Flo went to dance and she faced Ruraigh, raising her glass. 'Congratulations, Ruraigh. I love Tizz, absolutely love her and I wish you both every bit of love and luck in the world. Not that you're going to need it – you're wonderful together.'

'Thank you.' He nodded.

She watched his colour rise, confident that he'd noted the overly effusive wording of her toast, intended to remind him of his lukewarm response to her own engagement, all that time ago in her college room.

There was a beat or two of silence while both looked at each other, as if aware that this was the time to put to bed the awkwardness that had simmered between them ever since.

'You hurt me.' She spoke plainly.

'I never meant to hurt you, Kitty. Not for the world.' He looked at his feet.

His apology caused her tears to pool – easy enough, as they'd been threatening since she'd found out about Theo and his Anna. But hearing her cousin's words of remorse made her realise how much she'd longed for them.

'It always mattered to me what you thought.' She glanced up at him, tried to catch his eye. 'I wanted to be just like you and Hamish, I wanted to make you proud and I was so excited to be marrying one of your friends. I thought you might have picked Angus for me and I couldn't wait to see your face light up when I told you he'd proposed.' She looked at the floor, reflecting on the depth of her feelings, surprised how raw she felt still. 'I guess I was waiting for that look you used to give me when I'd done good. Like the time we went clay-pigeon shooting – d'you remember? – and you and Hamish dropped out when the competition got too fierce, but I went all the way and came second to Patrick's son. I beat you both!'

'Yes, you did.' He smiled, shaking his head. 'You always had to beat us.'

'Or at least keep up. That was enough for me.'

Ruraigh took a step towards his cousin. 'Did you ever think, Kitty, that I was only looking out for you, trying to protect you? Did you ever think that? That's what big brothers do!

But, Christ, your reaction made it impossible for me to even talk to you. There was so much—' He stopped talking and took a deep breath.

'So much what? Go on!' She punched his arm.

'So much I wanted to say to you. But hey, it looks like it's all turned out just fine, and that's that.'

She held his gaze and felt the tremble to her bottom lip and the twist in her gut. 'It's not perfect,' she whispered.

'Nothing's perfect.'

'I guess.' She pictured her parents on the sofa in the library, giggling and sipping whisky, before the monster came to live with them, before her mum's mind got a bit broken. 'Tell me, Ruraigh. Please. I need to know what it is with you!'

He looked over his shoulder, as if checking that Angus wasn't within hearing distance, then spoke into her ear. 'There might have been rumours – rumours that I paid no heed to.'

'Right.' She waited for him to continue.

'And that Thomas Paderfield... As I told you at the time, I've never liked the cut of his jib.' He paused.

'What do you mean?' She blinked away the image of the garish red card. *The Anvil.*

Ruraigh rubbed his hand over his stubble and took a long pull on his beer bottle. 'He and Angus were arguing the night before your wedding and... there was something about it I didn't like.'

Kitty pictured her fiancé coming into the library and remembered how distressed he'd been. *'I want you to make me the man I need to be.'*

'Tell me, Ruraigh. I need to hear it.'

Ruraigh flushed red, stammered a bit, then said, 'I might have misheard, got the wrong end of the stick, but Thomas seemed to be talking about... about Angus having to make a choice. And how…' He stared at his feet, scratched his stubble again. 'How… that choice was between him and you.'

Kitty's heart was hammering so fast she could barely breathe, let alone reply to Ruraigh's bombshell. Images of Angus and bloody Thomas Paderfield swam into her head. The red card. The mixtape. The long nights out drinking. Was there a whole other story behind Angus's remoteness, a story she hadn't even contemplated? The friends he never invited home. The puffy eyes before the wedding. She staggered backwards, and Ruraigh caught her, held her close.

'You have options, you know, Kitty,' he whispered into her hair. 'There isn't a deal made that can't be broken.'

Kitty was still fumbling for a reply when Tizz burst into the room. 'There you are! Come on, you two, come and dance in the kitchen!'

'You bet.' Ruraigh squeezed Kitty tightly, and she felt the estrangement of the last few years slip away. 'You're a warrior, like your mum,' he said quietly before being led away by Tizz.

'You're quiet.' Angus knocked his knee against hers as the cab wound its way home through the darkness. It felt strange to be out past midnight.

'Just tired,' she lied, thinking about Ruraigh's words and also about Theo's news.

'It was a bloody good party! You were right – it was good to have a drink and a dance, and we should definitely do it more often.' He gripped her hand.

She stared at their joined knuckles on the back seat and replayed the conversation with Ruraigh over and over in her head, slicing and dicing the exchange to extract every single drop of meaning from it.

'*There isn't a deal made that can't be broken.*' It occurred to her that Ruraigh might have inadvertently used precisely the right word. Had she done a deal with Angus, albeit one that she wasn't aware of? Could it be that he had forgiven her for sleeping with Theo because he figured it would mean she owed him?

What if he has a secret life? A life I can't and don't want to imagine?

'Kitty!' Angus called, and she jumped. 'God, you were miles away. I was just saying that I have missed Soph. We should do something fun with her next weekend, a nice family day out?'

'Yes.' She smiled. Whatever else, he really was a wonderful dad.

'Christ, don't sound too enthusiastic!'

Kitty stared out of the window and cursed the tears that gathered. 'It will be lovely.'

'What is *wrong* with you? It was you that was keen to go to the bloody party, and now we have and you're miserable!' He slapped his thigh and she noticed he was using the loud voice that meant he was pissed.

'What is wrong with me?' She laughed. 'Oh, Angus.'

'What the hell does that mean?' he yelled, and they both heard the cough of the cab driver, a reminder that he was present.

'Can we talk about it when we get home?' she asked curtly.

'Oh good, we now have that to look forward to.' He made the 'T' sound and gave a brief, disingenuous laugh.

When they reached home, Angus paid the taxi driver and Kitty went ahead, switching on the lamp in the sitting room.

Angus slumped down onto the sofa with an audible sigh. 'So come on, let's have it!' He lifted his hands and let his palms fall loudly onto the cushions, as if already exasperated. 'What now?'

'I feel torn,' she whispered.

'What do you mean, "torn"?' He sounded impatient, irritated.

'I want to ask you something, but I feel sick about doing it and I'm scared of what you might or might not say, and I'm scared of how you'll react, but I have this gnawing feeling in my stomach that I've had for the last week, since the business-card incident, or actually longer, probably years, and I need to get it out.'

He shifted on the sofa, leant forward with his elbows on his knees. His head seemed larger than usual in the lamplight.

'I can do it, Angus. I can say what I am thinking if you promise me two things.' He looked up and she continued. 'I need you to promise to tell me the truth and I need you to promise not to get angry. I don't want to fight. I really don't. I just want to talk.'

'Okay.' He clamped his hands together and his foot jumped slightly against the floor.

Kitty took a deep breath and practised in her mind the many ways to phrase the question. It sounded ridiculous, laughable and distressing all at the same time. In the end her words were neither well planned nor dressed up but were simply the ones that leapt from her tongue.

'Are you gay?'

'Am I gay?' he repeated. 'For fuck's sake, Kitty! How could you even—'

'Don't lie to me!' Kitty raised her voice, thankful that Sophie was several miles away at Bonnie's house.

She waited for the little tell-tale 'T' that always preceded his derisive laughter. But he remained quiet. The moments ticked by, seconds that she expected would be loud with angry rebuttals and the row she'd been keen to avoid. But he didn't say anything. Which was almost worse.

Finally, he breathed out and then looked at her. There was a second of silent interaction that she knew was leading somewhere new, somewhere unchartered.

'I'm not gay,' he managed, 'but I am bisexual. At least I think I might be.'

The words punched her chest with force.

'Surely you know?' she whispered.

Angus twisted in the seat to face her, his face ashen. 'I don't know anything right now.' He pushed his thumbs into his eye sockets and sat like that for a minute or so.

'Have you...' She swallowed, not sure she wanted the knowledge she was seeking. 'Have you ever been unfaithful to me?'

'Yes,' he replied instantly, nodding, seemingly relieved to have been asked.

And what can you say, Kitty? You did it first, you slept with Theo. This is how it feels...

'Fucking hell!' She gasped. 'With... with men or women?'

'I don't want to talk about it.'

'Well, that's too bad! You don't get to choose! I need answers!' She tucked in her lips and bit down hard, cursing the lump in her throat that made her voice strained. 'How many times have you been unfaithful to me?'

He looked at her, his expression intense. 'Once, that's all.'

'Fucking hell!' She could only repeat her curse and place her shaking hands between her clamped knees.

Angus took a deep breath and looked skywards.

Kitty's desire to vomit intensified. 'With a man?' She tilted her chin in defiance.

He nodded.

'Fucking hell.'

'I wish you'd stop saying that,' he said with a flicker of disdain.

That was enough to fan her anger to fever pitch. 'Do you? Well, you know, Angus, there are lots of things that I wish. I wish I had never set eyes on you! I wish you had picked someone else's life to mess with, and I wish you hadn't fucked a bloke, how about that?'

'I know you're hurt—'

'You know nothing!' she yelled. Despite the beat of silence, the air crackled around them. 'And is that man Thomas?'

'Yes.' He nodded and took another deep breath.

'Oh my God!' Kitty gripped the arms of the chair and concentrated on not throwing up as the room spun. 'Did you sleep with him at uni? I remember that girl on your landing, the one with the boobs and hips – Mary...? Maxine! – I remember her being a bit shocked when I told her I was your girlfriend. Was that because you were seeing him then?'

'No! We were close friends, yes, and Thomas has always been... quite keen.' He gave a small smile. 'But it's only happened once.'

'When did you sleep with him?'

'Last year. I was... experimenting, that's all.' He looked at the floor.

'Really? After, what, ten years of friendship, all of a sudden you just fucked each other? How does that even happen?'

'Christ, Kitty, I don't know... We were drunk, you and I weren't getting on. Like I said, it was just the once.' He glanced up at her. 'You of all people should know how that goes.'

Kitty chose not to rise to that. She had other questions on her mind. 'Did you like it?' she shot back, and then immediately wished she hadn't.

Angus sighed. 'Let's not go there, Kitty. Please.'

She inhaled sharply and had a vivid flashback of her and Theo in bed together. Could that be how Angus felt about Thomas? 'Do you... do you love him?' she asked finally, through a mouth contorted with emotion.

'I love you! I love you and Sophie, you know I do!' He raised his voice, his fingers now balled into fists.

'But do you love him?'

'Yes,' he mumbled through his tears. 'Yes, I love him. Christ, it's so complicated. He's my friend, but you, you're my wife!'

'And it's not a new thing, this... this wondering if you might be attracted to men, to Thomas, is it?' Kitty said softly, connecting some of the dots, remembering Ruraigh's gentle hints.

Angus shook his head.

'God.' She shoved her hand over her mouth and gulped her tears. 'God, Angus, all this time, all the lies. All that crap you gave me about the Anvil only this week! I must be so stupid!'

'You're not stupid. I love you, I—'

'Just don't. Just don't say anything else.'

The two fell silent. Kitty's stomach swirled as if it was in the grip of a mini tornado. A hum was building inside her head; it built and built until all she could hear was an unbearable screeching. Angus started to ramble.

'I am sorry for any hurt, of course.' He shook his head again and placed his chin in his palm, as if they were discussing something naughty Sophie had done and were trying to work out a suitable punishment. 'And I'm sorry for being less than truthful, but—'

'Shut the fuck up, Angus! Just shut the fuck up!' she screamed as she stood. Her outburst shocked them both. 'How can you just sit there and calmly tell me my whole marriage is a bloody joke! You have had sex behind my back with a bloke who you love as a friend! What the hell am I supposed to do with that information? How do I begin to process that? How do I compete?' She continued to yell, loudly. 'And you were so benevolent about Theo, oh my God! I could see your halo glowing as you bestowed forgiveness, and all the time you were coercing me into a deal that I knew nothing about! I gave you the option of leaving, calling time on our relationship, but you did this to me when we were married, with Sophie!'

'You think I like this situation?' He spoke quietly, forcing her to calm down and listen. 'I am petrified, utterly petrified of losing you. It was a one-time thing, Kitty, and it won't happen again. Please, please give me a chance to make it up to you. We are a family, you and me and Soph. No matter how we got here, this is it! Please don't throw us away. Please!'

He tried to grab her hand, but she shook him off.

'And I'm shit scared of my parents finding out – they would die, they would cut me off, it would break them! You won't tell them, will you, Kitty?' He looked at her with an expression of abject fear.

'Christ, why would I do that? You think I'm worried about your parents' reaction? I have enough of my own shit to deal with!'

Kitty ran from the room and raced up the stairs. She managed to reach the bathroom before vomiting into the toilet bowl, ridding her gut of the alcohol she had consumed along with the belief that her future was set and that her marriage was built on a solid foundation of truth. And it tasted horrible.

Moving Home

Kitty finished emptying the downstairs cupboard and swept the dark space. It was as she scooped the sooty dust into the dustpan that she noticed the glint of something, a tiny flash of gold. Her heart leapt and she knew instantly what she'd found – her locket! It had been lost so long ago, she'd entirely given up on ever finding it, assuming it had snapped while she was walking on the heath or swimming in the public pool, and yet there it was.

She picked up the flat gold oval, minus its chain, and wiped it on the front of her T-shirt. Carefully, with her fingernail inside the join, she popped it open and stared at the tiny picture of her and Angus on their wedding day. The opposite side was engraved: *To my darling Kitty on our ten-year anniversary. I love you today and every day. Angus X*

'Oh gosh.' She scanned the words again. With the locket now on the tabletop, she went to the sink, stretched her arms over her head and let the cold tap run a little until it was cool. She took a long glass of water back to the table. Running her fingers over the locket, she thought back to the day he'd given it to her. She placed the little hunk of gold in her palm and pictured herself some twenty years ago, remembering the optimism of her thirty-one-year-old self, who thought she had outrun the storm.

'It's so beautiful! Thank you!' she'd enthused, beaming.

The months immediately after Angus's confession had been tough. There were tears and rows and further admissions – about secret nights out with Thomas, undeclared memberships of gay clubs, and a crowd of friends she knew nothing about – and all the while they had to put on a good show for Sophie, making sure that she felt as secure and loved as ever. Kitty struggled a lot, confiding in Tizzy but unable to open up to her dad or even her cousins. It took a long time before she could face sleeping with Angus again, and even then she often couldn't stop herself from picturing him and Thomas together, hating herself for wondering whether he got more pleasure from having sex with Thomas or her.

She opened the locket and gazed at Angus's face, trying to see whether, with hindsight, she could detect any confusion, any dissemblance back when they got married. But she couldn't. He looked genuinely happy. And perhaps he had been.

Kitty's first demand after that horrible night had been that Angus break off all contact with Thomas. He began making more effort to come home earlier and Kitty found him more attentive, more present. There were still moments when he was quiet and she wondered who he was thinking about, whether he was regretting the way things had turned out. But one year on and things between them seemed better than they'd ever been. Soon after that, he'd given her the locket. It had meant the world. A new beginning, in more ways than one. They'd decided to have a child, a sibling for Sophie, a symbol of their renewed togetherness and their commitment to being a family.

The locket represented all of that – the self-delusions, and the joy of new life growing inside her. Like many of the memories she'd unearthed already that day, it was bittersweet. Even so, Kitty was glad she'd found it again.

Nine

Kitty leant forward on the sofa and whispered so her daughter in the next room wouldn't hear.

'Sophie told me today she is looking forward to being a big sister, and all I could think was, pity the poor little one who will have her bossing them around!'

Angus sat back in the chair by the fire and laughed from behind his newspaper. 'It will make them resilient,' he replied softly.

'I guess, but I can't help but think of me growing up, trying so hard to be part of Ruraigh and Hamish's gang!'

'Oh, that's so sad! You can be in my gang.' He grinned at her.

'Thank you.' She smiled back at him. 'I spoke to Ruraigh earlier, actually. He and Tizz had a lovely time at Darraghfield, but Tizz said Mum was not so good. Poor Dad, it must be even harder on him now Marjorie has retired.' She sighed. 'I wish we could go up more, but it's so far and I can't really take Sophie out of school, and you're so busy at work.'

'Let's go up in the holidays, assuming you're okay to travel.'

'I will be, Angus. I'm pregnant, not ill.'

He chuckled. 'You say that now, but I remember with Sophie you got very cranky towards the end.'

'I was cranky! But I'm enjoying this pregnancy more. I certainly have less worry and it's probably my last time, so I'm trying to make the most of every second of it.' She cradled her bump. 'I spoke to Dad and he said it was wonderful to see Daisy-Belle. I can't believe she's one already! He commented on how lovely it was to see big tough Ruraigh completely smitten with his little girl. Mind you, she is scrumptious.'

'She is and I can't wait to meet my little one.'

He looked up sharply and she held his gaze, it was an accidental yet obvious reference to the fact that this was his first child when all was said and done. As ever, rather than let the statement turn into a discussion and possibly a row, she ignored it, aware of the eggshells on which she walked.

Kitty arched her back.

'Back aching?' Angus asked from over the top of the sports page.

'A bit.' She decided not to confess to loving every twinge, every reminder that she was nearly seven months pregnant. Her excitement at the imminent arrival of this baby was almost overwhelming.

'Can someone help me?' Sophie called from the dining table.

'What's the subject?' Angus called back.

'English.'

'Ah, that'll be your mum's department.' He smiled at her.

'Oh, cheers!' Kitty rose slowly from the comfy chair.

'It's only fair! I do sciences and maths and you take languages and history, like we agreed. Just think of the money we're saving by not sending her to Vaizey till upper school. Plus with us doing her prep, she's still getting the benefit of a Vaizey education but without the expense or having to board.'

'You sound like your mum. What next, Tupperware in

which to store our Tupperware?' She winked at him and he pulled a face.

'I want to go to boarding school! I can't wait!' Sophie yelled.

'Well, you've still got a while yet – not that we asked you anyway, miss,' Angus shouted across the room.

Kitty pulled out a chair at the dining table.

Sophie was on a roll. 'When I go to Vaizey College, Mum, I'm going to have midnight feasts every night with the girls in my dorm and I will be double-Vaizey, probably house captain, because my mum went there, and my uncles Ru and Hamish, and Daddy and my other dad, my biological dad.'

'That's right.' Kitty smoothed her daughter's dark curls. She glanced over at Angus and noticed the barely visible change in his demeanour; the slight cording to his arm muscles and a tension in his jawline. It was a source of pride to her, the ease with which Sophie accepted the situation. It had never been an issue, as it had never been a secret, but still, and despite all their best efforts, she knew that even the most matter-of-fact mention of it rankled with Angus. She hoped that this baby would be the ultimate unifier, the glue that bound them. Their baby.

'Right, so, what is it I can I help you with?' she asked, yawning loudly.

'I have to read this passage from *The Jungle Book* and talk about how the writer makes the animals seem like people and what we can learn about the hierarchy.'

'Goodness me, Soph! Don't think I knew about the word "hierarchy" until I left school!' Angus piped up from the chair and Kitty was glad that he was joining in, diffusing any potential awkwardness.

'Okay...' Kitty ran her fingers over the front cover of the book. '*The Jungle Book* by Mr Rudyard Kipling.' She felt a twinge in her heart, recalling the poem Theo had recited on that day, the day that would alter the course of their lives.

Morning waits at the end of the world,
And the world is all at our feet!

'Are you okay, Mum?' Sophie laid her hand on her arm. 'You went quiet.'

'I'm great, darling. Sorry, just a bit of indigestion.' She placed her hand on her chest.

'Naughty baby!' Sophie yelled and waggled her finger towards the bump that concealed her baby brother or sister.

'Poor little thing,' Angus called back. 'Maybe it should go straight to Vaizey when it pops out, to escape from this mad-house!'

The telephone rang in the hallway. Angus folded his news-paper and jumped up. 'Hello, Stephen. ... Yes, we're good, thanks! How are things north of the border? ... Keeping warm, I hope. Kitty was just telling me about Ruraigh's visit. I believe you were quite bowled over by little Daisy-Belle?'

'It's Grandad!' Sophie leapt from her seat. Abandoning her prep, she ran into the hallway and began jumping up and down on the spot impatiently, waiting to talk to her most favourite person on the planet.

Kitty picked up the book and began to read.

A few days later, she was at home, doing the morning chores. A regular day. She'd dropped Sophie at school and walked home with her bag of groceries. With *Wake Up to Wogan* on the radio, she stripped the beds, washed the sheets and pre-pared that evening's supper – chicken in red wine with shallots that would marinate all day. Perfect. It was as she emptied the bin in the kitchen that she spied Angus's work mobile phone on the countertop. It was unusual for him to forget it. Kitty picked it up and liked the feel of it in her palm; she didn't have a phone herself but loved the idea of the freedom it might give her, and the thought of being able to take calls from Sophie's school in an emergency was very appealing.

The screen flashed with an envelope sign: a message. Without thinking, she pressed the button to the side of it and read the three lines of text that popped up on the little screen.

Admiral Duncan Pub
Thursday
7.30

Kitty's legs went weak. She stumbled backwards until she felt the countertop beneath her hip and leant heavily against it, her breath coming in starts. She knew the Admiral Duncan pub in Soho. It had a particular reputation. Slowly she walked towards the dining table and sat down. With her head in her hands she sobbed, her heart hammering.

She waited until she had calmed a little before calling her friend. Ruraigh answered.

'Is... Is Tizz there, Ruraigh?'

'God, you sound awful. What's the matter?'

His concern was touching.

'I'm... I'm okay, I just need a word with Tizz.'

'Hang on, I'll go grab her. If you need us to come over, just say. Or if you want to come here... Whatever.'

'Thanks.' She closed her eyes, aware that Tizz kept him up-to-date on how things were between her and Angus. She was thankful for his offer, but she wasn't in the mood for company.

'Kitty! What's happened? Are you okay? Ruraigh's worried.' Tizz cut to the chase, as ever.

'I think Angus might be up to his old tricks. He left his phone and I saw a text about a meeting at a gay pub.' She closed her eyes as she spoke the words. 'I'm... I'm in a right state.'

'Shit!'

'Yes, shit.'

There was a moment of silence while both let the information sink in.

'So what do you think? What should I do?' Kitty curled the phone cord around her finger and waited for a response.

'I don't know what to think,' Tizz said. 'I mean, there could be an innocent explanation, and if you go flying off the handle or make a suggestion, it could cause friction that won't do either of you any good. Or...'

'Or what?'

'Or he could be, as you say, up to his old tricks. And you have a right to know and a right to make decisions based on the truth and not what he wants you to *think* is the truth.'

'I hate that I feel this suspicious. I just want us to be happy and in love. And as Angus always says, I either trust him or I don't; there's no halfway house. And it was only a one-off thing and he has no contact with Thomas now, hasn't had for two years.' Bloody Thomas Paderfield. She disliked even saying his name.

'In that case, I would say you don't trust him.' She heard Tizz sip at whatever she was drinking.

'But I do! God, I do!'

'Okay, so it's easy then. Ignore the message and put the phone back where you found it. No one will be any the wiser and you have nothing to worry about.'

'Shit!' Kitty sighed and ran her fingers through her hair. 'I don't trust him, do I?' The thought sent a chill through her bones.

'Look, I don't blame you. You can't feel guilty, Kitty – you've done nothing wrong.'

'So why does it feel like I have? It's been two years since it all blew up and I thought it was behind us. We've moved on. We're having a baby. But somehow, seeing that text message…'

Tizz sighed. 'You might be making a mountain out of a molehill, misreading the whole situation. And it's doing you no good, especially not when you're pregnant. You need a calm, happy mind.'

'God, then I am in trouble.'

'Look, if you want my advice—'

'I do.'

'Go and see for yourself. Go to the pub, hang out, go under-cover—'

'Undercover?' That brought a weak smile to her face. 'What do you suggest – fake moustache and glasses, a big hat?'

'No! But you could happen to be in the vicinity and watch to see who he meets, or if he goes in or whatever. Either that or, as I said, forget about the whole thing. And remember, Kitty, you have options.'

'God, you sound like your husband.' She laughed wryly. 'They do say you morph into your partner.'

'Urgh, don't say that! I'll be watching the rugby next and farting in bed.'

As Kitty ended the call, she thought about how different she and Angus were from her cousins and their partners. *Stop imagining warning signals where there are none, Kitty*, she told herself, and nipped to the loo before she had to leave to get Sophie.

*

That Thursday morning she woke with a headache. She observed her husband over the breakfast table. 'You look very dapper.' She nodded at his pale blue silk tie.

'Oh, work meetings and stuff,' he offered vaguely as he bit into his wholewheat toast and honey.

'Hope they're not working you too hard.'

He ignored her.

'What do you fancy for supper tonight?' she asked casually as she poured hot water onto the teabag in the bottom of her mug, her second cup of the morning.

'Oh, sorry, didn't I say?' He coughed. 'I won't be home for supper. Some of the lads are playing five-a-side and I said I'd go along for moral support. Some charity thing.' He rolled his hand in the air, as if to emphasise the lack of detail he had about the event, and made the little 'T' sound.

Kitty's stomach flipped. She concentrated on pouring the hot water into the cup despite the tremble to her fingers. 'Oh, no worries. What time will you be home?'

He took a deep breath through clenched teeth. 'Not sure. Might go for a curry after, so don't wait up. I could do without going, really.' He curled his lip.

'Well, don't then! They'll understand. Just write a cheque for the charity and come home.' *I am giving you a chance here, Angus, throwing you a rope...*

'I can't, more's the pity. I said I'd go, so...' He let this hang, and there it was: the spark that lit the flame of her mistrust, the words that were to prompt her next move, however out of character.

Kitty stood on the top step and waved her husband good-bye, accepting the slight brush of a kiss on her cheek as he swiftly made his way down the steps to the pavement. She closed the door and practised in her head the subtle ways she might apologise for doubting him if her suspicions were proved wrong, even though he would of course be unaware. She decided there and then to assuage her guilt by cooking a good supper and pampering him a little. She might even invite his very dull parents over, making sure not to flinch when his mother asked how much the leg of lamb had cost or his dad answered her in monosyllables as if they were having an interview not a chat. She also imagined what the conversation might be like if her suspicions were proved right. *'How could you do this to me? How could you lie to me?'* Even imagining the exchange caused her throat to sting with nervous acid reflux.

She took Sophie to school. The minutes of the day ticked by slowly. Kitty spent a large chunk of it staring into space and playing out in her mind what the evening might hold. She spoke calmly to her unborn child, taking comfort from her own soothing words of reassurance. And then, like a condemned man waiting for the cockerel to crow, suddenly it was time to collect her daughter. She was very nearly late. Time had inexplicably sped up and run away with her. Grabbing her coat from the hook, she slipped into it and ran as best she could, with her arm loosely supporting the swell of her belly.

At 7.25 Kitty stood rooted to the pavement on the corner of Old Compton Street and Dean Street with a clear view of the front of the pub. Sophie burbled away, pointing out the lights, and Kitty sent her into the nearby gelato shop to buy herself a double-scoop. The traffic was busy; an impatient cabbie beeped his horn and rain was in the air. Not that Kitty noticed. Her legs felt like jelly and she could scarcely take a breath.

A minute later she saw him. He looked flustered, clearly late, as he ran into the arms of Thomas Paderfield – the man he'd sworn he didn't see any more. And she'd believed him! Or rather, she'd chosen to believe him. Thomas tapped his watch face and placed his hand on her husband's lower back. Angus leant over and grazed his cheek with a kiss. The bile rose in Kitty's throat.

They stood there chatting easily until three more men joined them, also suited professionals. With her heart in her mouth she watched as Thomas tucked down the collar of her husband's shirt, the shirt she had washed and ironed with care so that, as always, he would look his best. It was a gesture so intimate, so familiar and Kitty knew it would be this that she'd see in her mind's eye when sleep was slow in coming. She wondered then how many hours she'd spent washing and ironing those shirts; shirts that his lover touched, peeled from his body.

With a burning pain in her chest and a tightness to her throat, she stood and stared at the group. They all greeted each other with a familiarity that made her want to throw up. Angus and Thomas looked just like any other couple meeting up with friends. It was unbearable. He had lied to her. He had lied to Sophie. And there she was, pregnant with his child, while he went for drinks with his man.

She replayed some of the dozens of conversations they'd had over the last two years: he casually sighing as he described his evening; she feeling like a nag for asking. That was what he did. She could hear him now:

'Oh God, Kitty, it was so dull!'

'Oh, Kitty, you really don't want to know.'

'Oh, Kitty, I'm damned if I can remember what we ate. I barely remember the name of the person I sat next to!'

But those lies sat on top of much bigger lies. He had built a pyramid of mistruths and at the heart of everything stood Thomas Paderfield. Thomas who tucked his shirt collar in.

'Is that okay, Mum?' Sophie asked.

She stared at her daughter, who'd popped up beside her. Thank God the pavement outside the Admiral Duncan was crowded. 'Is what okay, darling?'

'If I only give you a lick of the strawberry ice cream, not the chocolate?'

'Oh, Soph…' She squeezed her daughter's hand and fought her tears. 'I'm not really in the mood for ice cream. You have it.' And she led her daughter briskly away from the spot where a piece of her heart would forever lodge, shattered into tiny fragments on the pavement.

Darkness had crept up on them and Kitty gripped Sophie's hand as they stood at the bus stop. Her mind was in turmoil, racing through all the things she'd have to do, all the plans she'd have to remake, the upheavals, the new baby, the conversations… *I have options*, she reminded herself. *I'm a warrior, like my mum.*

Sophie danced in the rain and stomped on the wet pavement, sending droplets scattering into the kerb and over their shoes. She was snug inside her oversized duffle coat and her red and navy woolly hat. 'I liked our adventure, Mum! Can we do it again, walk around Theatreland? I liked the big lights and I like being out in the dark! Do you remember when you told me about riding out in the dark on your little pony called Flynn and you fell off and broke your arm and Grandad, Ruraigh and Hamish had to rescue you? And that's why you've got that wonky arm.'

Kitty nodded and feigned a smile. Speech was impossible; fear and anger stoppered her throat.

'I love getting the bus, Mummy! This is so great!' Sophie was still jumping and dancing as the number 53 bus pulled in. The two made their way up the stairs to the top deck. The windows had steamed up. Kitty felt quite dazed as she climbed into a seat and Sophie sat down next to her. There was a hollow sensation in her stomach and she felt like she was lost, running blind. She looked down at the people crowding the damp pavement as the bus made its way along the Strand.

'Can I have hot chocolate when we get home?'

'Yes.'

'I'm going to write about our late-night trip for our news at school! Can we do it again, Mum?'

'Yes.'

Sophie wriggled in the seat before kneeling up backwards so she could stare down the bus. Kitty reached her arm across the back of her coat to ensure that she wouldn't fall if the bus braked suddenly. The bus juddered and Kitty's grip slipped. One swerve and Sophie would take a tumble.

'Sit round now, please, Sophie.' Kitty spoke sternly, loudly, trying to get her to do as she was told but without taking the edge off their adventure.

'I'm waiting to go round a corner.' Sophie gripped the back of the seat and leant out towards the aisle, her tongue poking from the side of her mouth.

'You are not going to do that, you'll fall, so please sit round now!' Kitty sighed. *Please, Sophie, just sit down. I don't have the strength...*

She became aware that someone was looking at her. It might have been that she was drawn by his stare, or perhaps she sensed the shape of a face she'd known since she was fourteen. Either way, Kitty turned round slowly and found herself looking directly into the face of Theo Montgomery.

There was a moment of stunned silence while her breath stuttered in her throat and her pulse throbbed. She placed a shaking hand over her mouth and blinked furiously.

Oh, Theo! Theo, my friend! Of all the days, all the moments...

This was too much. Her heart couldn't take any more. She willed him not to say anything, not to acknowledge her, willed him to remember what she'd said in her letter – *if our paths should ever cross, please respect my wish for us to never mention this* – for Sophie's sake as much as her own. It just wasn't the right time for the two of them to meet. *Please, Theo, don't make this any harder than it needs to be. Please!*

Theo gazed back. They were both frozen in shock, anchored to the spot. He looked from her to Sophie and she did the same, their frantic stares joining the dots.

I am begging you, Theo – not a word! Not tonight.

She glanced down the aisle to the top of the stairs, trying to plan an exit route that would not involve walking past the man she'd put to the back of her mind for so long, but there wasn't one.

'Don't cry,' he whispered under his breath, shaking his head slightly. He mouthed his next words and she was able to make out most of them. 'Please don't cry. I won't cause any trouble. I didn't know she would be here.'

Kitty hadn't realised she was crying. She pulled a tissue from her sleeve and dotted her eyes and wiped her nose before popping the tissue into the pocket of her voluminous mac. Reaching down to the floor, she retrieved her handbag. Thankfully, Sophie was busy kicking at the seat in front and humming, lost in her own little world, quite oblivious for the second time that night of the drama unfolding only feet away from her.

Kitty and Theo continued to stare at each other. Then Kitty stretched up and rang the bell. The bus slowed.

'Come on, darling.' With false brightness and a sense of urgency, she ushered Sophie from the seat, following close behind.

'Why did you press the bell, Mummy?'

The two stopped at the top of the stairs, only inches from Theo now, both swaying a little, waiting for the bus to come to a halt. She looked at his hand as it gripped the rail of the seat in front and noted the gold band glistening on the third finger of his left hand.

You got married, Theo, to your Anna. And I'm glad, so glad. I want nothing but happiness for you. A part of me will always love you, Theo. Always, because you gave me Sophie. I hope Anna makes you happy.

She cursed the wobble to her bottom lip and tried to keep her expression blank. And there they stood, within touching distance, the three, who, in another life, if things had been different, might have been a family.

It was eleven years since she'd last seen Theo. She noted his tan, a sign of good living, and saw that his hairline had crept further up his forehead. Faint wrinkles now gathered at the edge of his eyes, but, if anything, he looked better for the advance in years, assured, somehow, as if he'd finally grown into the handsome face that had been lurking beneath his boyish lack of confidence all along. His dark lashes lowered and took in the baby bump protruding over the waistband of her jeans. She cradled her stomach protectively.

He gave a small, wry smile and she wondered if he had children other than Sophie.

'Where are we going, Mummy?' Sophie laughed. 'We aren't at Blackheath yet.'

Kitty pulled her head back on her shoulders and narrowed

her eyes at Theo, imploring him to keep quiet. All she wanted was to get home with her little girl and sort through the turmoil that raged in her brain. She again pictured Thomas reaching out and confidently tucking in the collar of her husband's shirt and she knew that if she'd been alone, she would have fallen into Theo's arms and sobbed. *My knight in shining armour...* But this was no time to ponder on what might have been, no time for self-indulgence. 'I want to get off now, darling.' She cursed the tremor in her voice. 'We can... We can get the next bus.'

'Why are we going to do that?' Sophie asked.

'Just because!' Flustered, she snapped at her daughter, instantly regretting it.

Theo made as if to rise, indicating he would get off instead, but with a single vigorous shake of her head she took another step towards the top of the stairs. She wished the bloody bus would hurry up and stop. As her tears pooled again, she cuffed them with the back of her hand.

Theo smiled at Sophie and Kitty felt so unbearably sad that she had to look away.

Finally, the brakes wheezed and she felt the cold rush of air up the stairs as the back doors sprang open. And there they were, on the dark, damp pavement, the air thick with the haze of rain.

'Why did we have to get off, Mum?'

'I... I thought we were on the wrong bus, but... but now I think it might in fact have been the right one, so we shall wait right here.'

'You should have asked someone!' Sophie curled her lip at her mum's stupidity.

'You're right.' She pulled her smart, smart girl towards her and kissed her face. 'I love you, Sophie.'

'Love you too.'

As the number 53 pulled away, Kitty looked up at the top deck and could vaguely make out the silhouette of a man craning his neck towards the window, peering out into the darkness.

With her night-light casting a soft golden glow over her bedroom and her duvet pulled up to her chin, Sophie snored lightly. She had fallen asleep recounting the best aspects of their adventure, namely that they had stayed out late on a school night and had even gone to McDonald's.

For Kitty, the most amazing thing about her daughter's evening was that she'd come face to face with the man who'd fathered her and yet was unaware. *I wonder if I will ever tell you about tonight, Sophie? I wonder if I could ever properly capture in words the beautiful way that Theo looked at you.*

She trod the stairs and made herself a cup of camomile tea, hoping that the calming, restorative effects the box described might just turn out to be true. It felt like a huge decision, choosing where to sit, where to be when Angus came home, and how to handle the confrontation that would inevitably follow. Kitty was tired. She yawned, but with her adrenalin pumping there was no chance of putting the exchange off until tomorrow, even though her thoughts and arguments might be a little more coherent after she'd had some sleep. The idea of lying next to him with the knowledge she now possessed swirling inside her head was inconceivable. Again, she pictured Thomas reaching out and lifting the corner of Angus's collar with his fingers, and a shiver ran down her spine.

She decided to sit on the sofa with the lamp on. She tucked her legs under her feet and propped her arm on two firm cushions. She sipped her tea and must have fallen into a slumber of sorts, as the sound of her husband's key in the door made her sit up with a start. She listened as he slipped off his shoes and heard the gentle thud, thud of them hitting the wooden floor. Next came the jangle of his keys as he placed them in the earthenware bowl on the hall table. All his actions sounded muted, duplicitous, trying for stealth. Her irritation grew.

She sat up straight and looked towards the door.

'Jesus Christ, Kitty!' Angus placed his hand on his chest and bent over briefly before righting himself with a smile. 'I didn't expect you to be sitting there! You scared me half to death!' He made the little 'T' sound and gave off the laugh of someone clearly relieved in the aftermath of a shock. 'What are you doing up? It's very late.'

'What time is it?' Her voice sounded calm even to her own ears. It was a genuine question; she was curious as to how he would build his lies around this one fact.

'It's late.' He tucked two fingers behind the knot of his pale blue silk tie and pulled it down. She stared at the collar of his shirt.

'How late?'

'Gosh, nearly one o'clock.' He grimaced. 'Couldn't you sleep? I told you not to wait up.'

'You did. And no, I couldn't sleep.'

'Well, what can I do? Make you a cup of hot milk?' he offered softly and she caught the slight slur on the word 'of', the one he had when he'd consumed too much wine.

'How was the five-a-side?'

'Oh, I hate football, as you know. It was in a cold, echoey gym with lots of shouting. But I clapped and hollered accordingly. I think it must have raised quite a lot of money. Sophie okay?'

'Yes, Sophie's fine. Where was the gym?' She untucked her legs.

'Err, near Clapham somewhere. I jumped in a cab from work with Leo and his gang. Nice bunch. Young. You know – keen.'

How easily the words slipped from his mouth, with just enough detail to give them the ring of truth. But she knew different. And Soho was nowhere near Clapham.

'I didn't realise you'd be this late,' she said neutrally, waiting to see how far he would go with his embellishments.

'Yes, well, all a bit of a cock-up really. We, err, watched the match and then the one after and then some bright spark decided the only place for a decent curry was Brick Lane and so cabs were called and whatnot and we all ended up in a curry house over there.'

'Till now?' She wrinkled her nose.

'Kitty, you must be getting old – the place was just hotting up, the restaurant was full. Great food though.'

'Mmm… what did you have?'

'Umm…' He looked up. 'Can't remember. My usual – chicken tikka masala, naan. Why, do you fancy a curry?' He chuckled.

'Do I fancy a curry?' Kitty pretended to consider this as she sat forward on the sofa and placed her hands on her stomach. Her next words were delivered coolly. 'I thought Thomas looked well. I like his hair shorter, it suits him, but I have to ask, does he dye it? It was a little dark around the temples.'

Angus turned and stared at her. The two high spots of colour drained from his face. 'What are you talking about?'

'Gosh, I almost admire your tenacity, the way you can carry on lying. What are you going to say next – that it wasn't you outside the Admiral Duncan but someone who simply looked a lot like you, with a man who looked a lot like Thomas Paderfield but with dyed hair?'

She watched with a measure of satisfaction as his legs swayed. He staggered to the armchair and sat down hard. Kitty held his gaze briefly, knowingly, challenging him to speak.

'You need to not panic, Kitty.'

'*I* need to not panic? *I* need to not fucking panic?' She let out a burst of nervous laughter. 'I remember you telling me in no uncertain terms, when you found out about Theo, that if it happened again, we would be divorced before I had finished mumbling a confession. You sounded so self-righteous and I felt like trash. Your tone... "I can give you the benefit of the doubt, Kitty, but I won't be made a fool of." That's what you said. You must have been chuckling over that, you and TP.'

'It wasn't like that,' he whispered.

'And you were right, Angus. Strangely, it's not about the sex as much as the lying, the deceit. I don't want to live like that. I won't live like that. I can't.'

Angus ran his hand through his fringe, once attractive but right now foppish, intended for whom? Her gut bunched with the urge to vomit.

'I...' He floundered, seemingly finding it a lot harder to speak when the truth was required. 'Did you follow me?'

'Yes! Because that's the issue here, Angus, the fact that I might have followed you, not that you've been shagging some bloke and lying to me!'

'I tried, I...'

'You tried? Well, thank you for trying!' She took a deep breath. 'I am equally as angry with myself as I am with you. I trusted you. I gave you the benefit of the doubt and all this time...' She shook her head. 'I believed you when you told me it was a one-time thing. I am so bloody stupid! How long did you wait before you started seeing him again?'

He stared at her.

'I'm asking you, Angus, how soon after promising me it was over did you go back to him?'

He looked at the floor and she gasped as the truth dawned.

'You didn't stop, did you? You never broke it off with him! You've been seeing him for all of this time!'

'You don't know what it's like for me, trying to—'

'Trying to disguise the fact that you live with the best of both worlds!'

Angus started to cry. 'It's not the best of both worlds, Kitty. It's the worst of both. I'm caught in the middle and I'm tired. I'm so tired.'

'Oh, poor you.' She was amazed by her tone; she sounded cool, even though her stomach churned and her thoughts were anything but.

'It doesn't mean I don't love you. I can't choose, Kitty. I can't—'

'You can't *choose?* You are my husband,' she cut in. 'You married me!' Her tears fell freely now.

'And I don't regret a thing!' he said levelly. His lack of hysteria suggested to her that he'd held this conversation in his head many times; she was probably just filling in the blanks of one of many scenarios he'd imagined.

'You don't regret a thing? Well, jolly good! Christ, you've been having sex with me since I was fifteen.' She shook her head, trying to make sense of the pictures that were forming in her head. She tried not to think of their rather dull, infrequent sex, wondering whether for him it was a chore. There was no need to sugar-coat anything now. 'I always felt you were… elsewhere.' She stumbled on the words. 'I trusted you.'

My dad trusted you, my lovely dad.

'Who gives this woman's hand in marriage?'

'I do...'

'I feel so cheated, and so bloody stupid.' Kitty ran her fingers over her forehead. 'You've been stringing me along and of course Thomas has always known about the situation, so that makes me the mug. I feel sick about it. All those bloody lies! I don't know what's true and what isn't. How much of our married life has been a lie? Some of it? All of it?'

'You can't think like that.'

'Can't I? I believed you, Angus. When you told me it was one night, an experiment, I felt in some way that it was like levelling the score. There was me and Theo and then there was you and Thomas. I accepted I would never fully understand your feelings towards men, didn't know whether it was a compulsion or whether Thomas had turned your head, and ridiculously I actually blamed him more than you! But we sorted it out, put it behind us – or so I thought. You promised to give him up and we moved on and... we made a baby together. A baby, Angus! Christ. I believed in us, and I thought you did too. I believed I was your number one, that our relationship was the main event and everything else was a diversion, a temptation. I really did.' Her voice wobbled, and she pulled unconsciously at the gold locket around her neck, but she was determined to finish. 'But when I saw you with Thomas, the way you were together...' The tears slipped down her cheeks now, as she spoke this unpalatable truth. 'You looked like a different person.' She held his gaze.

'Different how?' he asked softly.

'There was no stuffiness about you. You held yourself differently. You looked... comfortable, at ease. Happy. Happy in a way I haven't seen for a long, long time. And that's when

I realised that it's *me* that's the diversion. I am secondary, a smokescreen. And it doesn't feel good. If it were anyone other than you, my husband, who was leading this life of struggle, I'd feel sad that a man has to live so divided, but as it *is* you, Angus, the man I'm married to, the man I exchanged vows with, the father of my kids, that same thought leaves me cold. And you know why that is? Because of all the lies, Angus. Because of all the chances you had to come clean, to be honest – with me, with yourself, even with Thomas bloody Paderfield. But you didn't take them. You just made it all worse. Carried on with your affair. Piled lie upon lie, led me down the garden path and left me there. So I feel duped. I feel stupid and I feel angry.'

'And you have every right to feel angry,' he said. 'But you have other things to think about, Kitty. You need to concentrate on staying healthy and present for this baby and you need to keep things as normal as possible for Soph.'

'You think I don't know that?' She raised her voice. 'But you've made me doubt my life, made me doubt everything. You've pushed me into this dead end – ten years, more, of my life! – and now where? I wouldn't give up being mum to this new little one, not for anything, of course I wouldn't. My babies are my reward and my blessing. But oh, Angus, my God... The thought of you marrying me, becoming a dad, living our life *unwillingly*... It rips my heart.'

'I love being married to you. I do! I can't explain, but I love—'

'No, Angus!' She cut him short. 'No more pretending. Don't look so horrified. What's the problem now – afraid your mum and dad might find out? I mean, God knows, I'm not sure they would know what Tupperware box to store this merry mess in. You're a fraud and that for me is actually the worst thing.' She paused at the realisation of this truth. 'This isn't about sex or even your sexuality, it's about the fact that you're a liar.'

'That's not true!' He was getting upset now and she hated how glad she was to see it.

'It *is* true and you've dragged me and Sophie into the whole charade.'

At the mention of Sophie, Angus broke down. 'I love her. I'm her dad.'

'That's as maybe, but I can tell you now that you don't need to worry about choosing. I am choosing for us both. You are free to go and be with the man you love. We are done. That's it. We are over. You don't have to pretend any more.' Standing, Kitty pulled her wedding ring from her finger and placed it on the mantelpiece.

'But the baby…' He looked up at her, his eyes brimming with tears.

'What about the baby? What will you do – promise to give Thomas up so we can all play happy families?' She stared at the crumpled heap of him in the chair and felt strangely hollow. 'It's time for you to grow up and own up. As I said, Angus, we are done.'

Moving Home

Kitty answered her mobile phone.

'Sorry, Mum, first chance to call. Crazy busy today.'

'Darling, don't worry about calling! I know you've got a lot on your plate.' She smiled, delighted to hear from her son, whom she pictured in his scrubs in the busy A & E department where he was learning the ropes.

'You say that, but I thought I'd better check in to see if you'd fallen under that mountain of boxes?'

'Not yet. Progress is slow. I'm finding it harder than I thought. Lots of reminders, lots of memories.'

'Yep, I feel the same. Our home...'

'Oh, Olly, don't say that! It's difficult enough. I'm just about to tackle your school trunks in the spare room.'

'Oh God, who knows what lurks in there! Are you up to date on your tetanus?'

'Very funny.' She smiled; speaking to her kids always restored her spirits.

'Gotta go. Love you.'

Kitty held the phone and pictured her boy rushing off to do his thing.

'I love you too,' she whispered.

She had pulled their trunks into the middle of the room last week when the bed had been dismantled and disposed of and now they stood like sentinels, the keepers of secrets.

Kitty flipped the latch on Olly's trunk and pulled out his baby blanket. She brought it to her mouth and inhaled the glorious scent that had all but faded, picturing herself knitting of an evening in front of the fire up at Darraghfield. Kitty's eyes filled with tears. She remembered that particular trip back home in all its sad detail. She and Sophie had gone up there for the autumn half-term, just a couple of weeks after Angus moved out. They had both needed the change of scene, and Kitty was in desperate need of a shoulder to cry on. Heavily pregnant with Olly, she could think of nowhere she'd rather be than with her dad.

He was of course over the moon at having so much time with Sophie, and Sophie was as keen as mustard to go fishing with him. She looked adorable in Kitty's old waders and her grandad's fishing hat, and it turned out she was pretty good at tickling the salmon and even cleaning and gutting them.

Good old Soph, mature beyond her years, even at ten. No wonder she'd made such a good teacher. Kitty smiled proudly. Her kids were her lifeline. Always had been.

While her dad and her daughter were out on the river, Kitty nursed her hurt and rediscovered her favourite nooks and crannies at Darraghfield. The house always seemed even grander after any time away, another world from the narrow alleyways, terraced houses and twisty cobbled lanes of Blackheath. But there was a sadness about the place too, and it wasn't just her own. Her mum was frail, aloof, and Kitty found it hard to get through to her. She asked her one afternoon if she remembered Balla Boy and her mum simply looked away, as if that time and the woman she was then were almost too painful to remember.

There was one day, though, when her mum was in a quite different mood. Kitty had been resting in the library, trying to finish knitting the baby blanket for the new arrival. Her mum had walked in, composed and smiling. Seeing the little blanket, she took it from Kitty, saying, 'Oh, darling, that takes me back... I so loved being pregnant with you. It was such a special time.' And with a dexterity Kitty hadn't seen in her mum for years, Fenella deftly added on the final dozen rows, chatting away as she did so. 'I used to knit you a new wee jumper every year when you were little. I remember teaching myself how – it wasn't my natural forte, you know, but I was determined to do it!' She smiled dreamily. 'Every stitch was made with love. You were the centre of my universe, Kitty. Still are, darling.' Kitty was so choked up at this, she hadn't been able to reply. 'I can't wait to meet your new little one in a couple of months. I'll make them a wee jumper too – why not!' And with that, her mum had floated out of the library and back up to her room.

Kitty swam nearly every day, loving the chance to take the weight of her enormous belly off her feet. As she lay in the water, she would think about the day Angus had walked into her life. She'd been fourteen, a baby, as Tizz kept reminding her – lovely, loyal Tizz, who called up most afternoons while Kitty was at Darraghfield. 'Who wouldn't have fallen for Golden Boy?' Tizz said emphatically. 'He was gorgeous! Still is. You were fourteen, never been kissed, and the most handsome boy at Vaizey wanted to be your boyfriend? You didn't stand a chance!' Even Kitty had giggled at that.

Tizz was of the view that she and Angus had never really been right for each other; that Angus had confused friendship with love and had had neither the self-awareness nor the courage to think about what he really wanted. Kitty hated that she might be right. She wished she could run to her fourteen-year-old self in the pool and yank her from the water. She would take her in her wise, adult arms and rock her until the danger had passed, until the shape of the boy had slipped back through the gap in the hedge and the world had returned to a simple, sunny, ordinary day... And then, just maybe, she might have gone on to meet a different boy, a boy who really loved her, loved her for herself and wanted to lead a simple life together. A life where they both got to see the whole picture, without lies, without hiding.

Kitty placed the precious blanket back in the trunk and lifted out Olly's first Vaizey College blazer. That had been another decision reached during that half-term at Darraghfield. 'Send the kids to Vaizey early,' her dad had urged. 'Soph can start in the summer term. You'll miss her, of course you will. But you'll be so busy with the new baby, and she will love it there. I know she will.'

He'd been right, of course. He always was. Her lovely dad. He had so many challenges of his own to deal with, especially that year, but he was always there for her, even when his own world fell apart.

Ten

Kitty cursed under her breath as the telephone in the hallway rang and Olly, who had just slipped into a deep sleep, stirred and raised his tiny fists as if in protest. She smiled at her little boy, just eleven weeks old and a source of endless fascination to her.

Sophie ran down the stairs and grabbed the phone. 'Hi, Grandad! Guess what? I went to the Horniman Museum and I saw the most amazing butterfly—'

There was a pause in the chatter.

'Oh, okay, Grandad. I'll go get her. Love you.'

'Mum, Grandad wants to talk to you and he sounds a bit weird.' Sophie pulled a face.

'Okay, keep an eye on Olly for me.' She ran her hand over her daughter's scalp as they swapped places.

'Hi, Dad, is everything okay?' All she could hear at the other end was the tearful rattle of his breathing. 'Dad? What's wrong?' Her heartbeat quickened. She might have been a grown woman with kids of her own, but to hear her daddy cry was a painful thing, a reminder of his fallibility.

'It's Mum.'

'Oh no, what's wrong? Is she poorly?' She tried to locate the words that evaded her. 'Is she—'

'She's gone, Kitty. She's gone.'

'Gone?' She shook her head. 'What? Gone? Dad, is—'

'She's dead,' he managed, the words choked out between loud gasps. Kitty's heart heaved as she pictured him there, sobbing in his chair. 'She died, Kitty. Today. She died today.'

'Oh! Oh no!' The blood seemed to rush from her head and she swayed on the spot. Dropping down onto her knees, she stayed like that for a little while, holding the phone to her ear while her dad cried.

Oh, Mum! My mum, gone...

'Dad! How?'

'I found her...' He paused again. 'I found her up at Kilan Pasture. She looked beautiful, Kitty. She looked—'

'Oh Dad, I can't believe it. I'll come home, we'll be there by the morning. Just hang in there and we'll be with you as soon as we can.'

'You don't have to, Kitty, you—'

'Dad, of course. Of course I'm coming home. I'll speak to you on the way. Just hang in there, I'm on my way.'

She replaced the receiver and stood for a second, trying to order her thoughts.

I need to pack for the kids. I need to get fuel. I need to make some calls. Oh, Mum! I hope you're at peace. I hope you are fixed and happy. I love you. I love you so much.

'What's the matter, Mummy?' Sophie crept up behind her and placed her small hand on her waist.

'I've just had some sad news, but I'll be okay in a mo. Can you go and sit with Olly for me? And I promise I'll come straight in and talk to you, explain.' She swallowed. 'I think we might be going on a trip, but you can sleep in the car, okay?'

'Okay, Mum.' Sophie nodded and trundled off to mind her tiny brother.

Kitty picked up the phone and dialled Ruraigh's number.

'Your kids snore.' Hamish looked at the two children, fast asleep in the back seat of the car, their mouths slack and their heads tipped. He was wedged between Sophie and Olly's car seat.

'I told you I'd sit in the back with them,' Kitty reminded him.

'I think I'd still hear them in the front.' He pulled a face.

'It's way past their bedtime.' She looked at the clock on the dashboard of Ruraigh's Range Rover. It was ten thirty.

'It's past mine!' Ruraigh quipped.

'One hour down, only nine more to go if we stop for a quick loo break, coffee and refuel.' Hamish reached forward and patted his brother's shoulder. 'Let me know when you want to swap.'

'I can't believe you're both here – I can't believe you're driving, Ruraigh. I was preparing to fuel up the Golf.'

'Don't be daft. Of course we're coming with you.' He glanced sideways.

She felt the slip of tears down the back of her throat, finding their kindness, the kinship, a little overwhelming.

'I think I deserve more thanks than Ruraigh – he might be driving the main leg, but I am missing sex night,' Hamish stated matter-of-factly.

'You have sex night?' Ruraigh looked into the rearview mirror.

'Yes. We have to schedule it in or we find we can go for weeks without.'

'Too much information.' Ruraigh sighed.

'I think it's a good thing,' Hamish said. 'Flo and I are so busy, it means things like that slip.'

Ruraigh laughed. 'Speak for yourself.'

'You can't tell me that with two kids you and Tizz still manage to find time for passion?'

'No, I can't tell you that. I can't tell you anything because I, like most of the adult population, know that certain aspects of life should be kept private!' He raised his voice as much as he was able to without waking the kids. There was a beat of silence before Hamish spoke again.

'It's not the only thing we schedule – we have board-game night, cooking-from-scratch night, reading night, lazy-bath night…' Hamish looked out of the window.

'Do you ever get them mixed up, Hamish?' Ruraigh smiled. 'Do you ever think, oh God, we should be reading, but we are actually playing board games, or, oh shoot, here we are, having sex, but it's down as cooking-from-scratch night!'

'Sometimes.' Hamish nodded, unflustered. 'But we just go with it. That's how we roll.'

Kitty laughed despite the heavy yoke of sadness that was weighing everything down. It felt odd to be feeling even a pinprick of joy. Everything seemed a little dreamlike. 'This is surreal. One minute I'm at home and planning to have a bath and watch *Coronation Street*, and now here I am in the car with you two, driving home, and my mum's gone.'

'I can't believe it.' Hamish sighed.

And just like that, the easy banter of the car was replaced with the sound of Kitty's crying and the snores of her children in the back seat.

It was a little after seven thirty in the morning when Hamish navigated the car up the driveway to Darraghfield. The winter sun was rising over the stormy glen and the place was befittingly cloaked in bruised grey clouds. Olly gurgled winningly and Kitty felt another churn of deep sadness that her mum had never got to see him. *'I can't wait to meet your new little one in a couple of months. I'll make them a wee jumper too – why not!'* She'd made sure to bring the little blanket with him, at least. She could tell that Sophie wasn't really sure how she was supposed to behave, trying to find the right pitch between mourning the nana she only knew as a shadowy, withdrawn figure and her excitement at being surprisingly back at Darraghfield on what should have been a regular school day.

Kitty's dad opened the wide front door and she could see that he had slept in his clothes. He looked crumpled and bowed and his skin a little grey. She ran from the car and locked her arms around him and it was then that the grief hit her with full force; like a sharp thing, it landed squarely in her breast. The idea of her dad being there at Darraghfield without her mum was just unthinkable.

'Uncle Stephen...' Ruraigh laid his hands on his uncle's back. Hamish followed suit.

'Thank you, boys. Thank you for bringing her and thank you for coming home.' He nodded at them with bloodshot eyes.

The funeral was small and quick, the chapel cold. This suited all of them; a stuffy, lengthy service full of singing and lamentation would have felt incongruent with the way Fenella Montrose had lived and died. Kitty left Olly with Isla and her kids in the village but decided Sophie was old enough to attend. That was a good decision; staying brave for her daughter and monitoring her throughout proceedings was a helpful distraction. Tizz and Flo had come up on the train and Kitty took comfort from being surrounded by people who loved her and who had loved her mum. Ruraigh and Hamish wept openly and Kitty was glad that her mum's passing caused such heartfelt sadness; she could so easily have slipped away without making much of a dent in the world. She was to be laid to rest on a hill with a view of Loch Beag, one of her favourite places; Kitty hoped her mum's spirit would soar up and over the heather-filled glen, with Balla Boy cantering beneath her.

Angus, to his credit, had written to her dad and sent her a card. He had called a couple of times too, and in truth she hadn't expected him to travel all the way up on a work day for the funeral of his ex mother-in-law. Besides, emotions were still raw; it was only six months since the split, and her dad and her cousins were hurt, disappointed and angry at what they saw as Angus's abandonment of her. The fact that he had taken up with a man was neither here nor there. Kitty had decided not to tell them yet that Thomas had in fact dumped Angus within weeks of them being free to live openly as a couple. Angus had been distraught and Kitty wasn't proud of how little sympathy she'd shown. But no matter, for he'd since found someone else, apparently, a man called Nikolai, and they were now living together in Battersea. With her sight failing, Marjorie looked frail. Her once robust frame was now slight, swamped by the clothes she'd worn when she was a lot larger. She'd slipped down into the seat of her wheelchair and sat at an angle, a thick tartan blanket tucked around her legs. She pulled Kitty towards her with gnarled fingers and spoke directly to her. 'Never forget, you were her very best thing, Kitty. She loved you so much!'

Kitty nodded through her tears. Her heart ached with love for their loyal, long-suffering housekeeper, who chose not to recall the bitter snipes her poorly mother had cast in her direction over the years. Marjorie had often borne the brunt of her mother's suspicious and wandering mind.

'In fact you were everyone's very best thing, mine included. You still are.' The old woman wheezed her admission. 'Leaving you at that school was the hardest thing I ever did.' She broke off at the memory, wiping her eyes with her white cotton handkerchief.

Kitty bent low, laid her head on Marjorie's shoulder and reached around to hug her with her wonky arm.

After the service, everyone gathered in the kitchen at Darraghfield, downing the whisky in such liberal quantities that the wake was in danger of turning into a full-blown party. Kitty had no appetite for that and was glad to be out of the house. Wrapping her thick coat around herself, she sat on one of the steamer chairs by the edge of her beloved pool. Lit from the bottom, it sent an eerie glow into the murky, trout-coloured dusk. The wisps of steam that rose from the heated surface seemed to Kitty to be like the dreams and aspirations of her childhood floating into the ether and fading to nothing. The thought made her unbearably sad.

'There you are.' Her dad ducked through the laurel hedge and came to sit by her side. 'I thought I might find you here. Your special place.'

'Uh-huh.'

'Olly is still sound asleep and Sophie is earwigging in corners. She is so like you, taking it all in...' He smiled. 'How are you doing?'

'I don't really know, Dad.' She rubbed her face. 'It feels as if I've kept all my hurt inside for a long time and now Mum going has peeled the lid off and everything has come spilling out.'

'You have been through a lot, darling.' He sighed. 'He wrote to me, his lordship.'

She noted the sharp edge when he spoke of her former husband. 'Yes. He said.'

Her dad shook his head. 'I feel torn. Part of me wants to punch him on the nose for how he's hurt you and part of me feels sorry for him.'

'I agree. It's sad for us all, and sometimes I wish he'd picked someone else to drag into his whole pantomime. If only he'd had the courage to be honest – to himself, most of all. It would have saved so much heartache, changed the course of so many lives.'

'Are you thinking of that Theo chap – Sophie's dad?'

She smiled at her dad, loving how he had always been so accepting of the facts and had offered nothing but support, had never judged her. It was real and unconditional love. 'A bit... But we were never meant to be. We were friends. It was a one-time thing.' She smiled awkwardly at the frankness. 'But I don't regret it. He is lovely and Sophie is marvellous.'

'She really is. As for Angus...' There it was again, the sharp edge. 'Your mum always had her doubts about him.'

'She did?' Kitty turned to face him.

'Aye, she didn't like his lack of eye contact – bit shifty. I have asked the boys since and they both said there were rumours. I wish they'd told me.'

'I doubt it would have changed a thing. I've been emotionally invested in him since I was a girl, and I couldn't see a different life.'

'Your mum would have intervened, if she'd been well. She was plucky, and a good judge of character.'

'I can't believe she's not here, Dad.'

'She'll always be here, Kitty.' He sniffed and closed his eyes, unashamed at the tears that fell.

She took his hand into her own. 'I miss her and I feel guilty that I didn't get up to see her more often. There was always something going on with Angus or Sophie, and I thought I had all time in the world. I was always planning the next trip for the summer or Christmas.'

'She never expected you to come up more than you did, she knew you had a life. And, truth be told, Kitty…' He paused. 'It was probably easier for her when it was just the two of us. She struggled when it came to planning for an event or a visit, and the amount of effort she put in to make everyone welcome and paint that veneer of happiness and normality… well, it took it out of her.' He wiped his eyes with the back of his hand. 'It would set her back and she would close down for weeks afterwards. It was tough.'

'You never told me that.'

'Oh, darling, there's lots we just got on with.' He looked out over the pool. 'It's not been easy, Kitty, but I would not have changed a day, not a single day. I love her so much.'

'I know.' She squeezed his hand.

'Patrick and I found her.'

'Up at Kilan Pasture?'

'Aye, she…' He looked up and composed himself. 'She died of hypothermia. Officially. She must have slipped out in the night, and by the time we found her…'

Kitty already knew the details, her dad had gone over them more than once, but she understood his need to repeat them, to try and make them sink in.

'Do you think…' She paused, trying to figure out how best to phrase the question that had leapt into her mind the instant her dad had called to give her the dreadful news. 'Do you think that Mum—'

'I think your mother loved us all very much,' he said, interrupting her. 'I think she loved us from her first until her last and that any choices she made, like much of what happened over the last few years, were executed with the fog of mental illness as her filter. That wasn't the real Fenella, the Fenella who danced and laughed and sipped whisky from a hip flask as she rode her horse. No, that wasn't Fenella, it was the... the...'

'The monster who held her in his grip.'

He nodded as his chin fell to his chest and his body began to shake with sobs. 'When she first got diagnosed, I thought there'd be an ending, that she'd come back to me. I tried, Kitty. I tried every day to wrestle her from its grip, but I lost. I lost and now she is gone.'

Reaching up, she took him into her arms and let him cry as she stared out over the swimming pool. She remembered the night before her wedding when her mum had come out to the pool and, not far from where they now sat, had spoken with such emotion. 'No *matter what, I'll be there, darling, because I am here.*' She had touched her fingers to Kitty's chest. '*And it will be the same for you with your child. Whether I am stood by your side or miles away, I am always here.*'

Kitty cried too now, as she held onto her dad. 'You did everything you could, Dad. Everything.'

'Yes, but what do I do now? She was part of me and I was part of her and now I'm incomplete.' He gulped and stuttered out his words. 'I feel... halved.'

Kitty, too, was in danger of feeling halved. She wondered why she'd ever agreed to sending Sophie off to Vaizey early. But here they were, in the car, navigating the Dorset lanes, and she was putting on a brave face.

'Did you pack my tuck box, Mum?'

'I did.' Kitty smiled at her daughter, who was wriggling with excitement on the front seat of the Golf as they passed signs for Jackman's Cross and Muckleford.

'And have you written down all the telephone numbers I need?'

'I have, darling. Call me or Daddy or Grandad any time, any time at all, day or night.' She tried to hide the break in her voice.

'I will, Mum.'

'When I was at Vaizey, we didn't have access to phones and we only got one call a week. Every Thursday night we had to go to the matron's office and we were only allowed to speak for a few minutes and the matron would listen in, even though she made out she wasn't, and then she'd cough to let us know time was up and we had to get off the phone as quickly as possible and the next girl would come in for her call. Can you imagine that?'

Sophie humphed, and Kitty wondered if her daughter might not have minded only having one rushed call a week.

'And have you remembered my swimsuit? I'm going to swim every single day!'

'Oh...' Kitty sighed. 'I do envy you that. In my day, the Vaizey pool was less than inviting.'

'We've got a new pool and a new gym and an indoor football pitch and a tennis dome for all weathers.' Sophie recited from the brochure the tantalising facts she had learnt by heart about the school she couldn't wait to get to.

'And d'you think you might be able to fit in some studying while you're there? I mean, only if it doesn't interfere with your sport, of course.'

Sophie laughed. 'I might.'

'I'm going to miss you. Olly will too. He'll miss all those cuddles.'

'I'll be home for exeat.'

Kitty smiled at how easily her daughter used the lingo of her new environment.

'You will, and the next six weeks will fly by.' *Even if for me it might feel like a lifetime.*

'Daddy and Nikolai called to wish me luck this morning and Daddy has sent a card to my dorm. It'll be my first bit of mail.' Sophie grinned.

It had angered Kitty that Angus had declined the offer to babysit Olly that day – an important golf match, apparently – but Tizz, Ruraigh and their girls would no doubt be spoiling him rotten. She felt a pang of longing for her boy, as she did whenever he or indeed Sophie was away from her. She eyed her daughter and considered how calmly she'd adapted to their unusual family dynamics, taking it all in her stride. Nikolai had simply been made a member of their family and that was that. Kitty was happy to see Angus happy, but there was still the odd night when she sank a few glasses of wine and felt more than a little pissed off at how he had ended up with his new beau, all smiles and easy contentment, while she was the one surrounded by Lego and dirty clothes, alone on a winter's night.

'Is Olly staying at Tizz and Ruraigh's tonight?'

'Probably not. Depends what time I get back to London.' Kitty bent her head and looked up through the windscreen at the grand facade of her old school. 'We're here, Soph! It's beautiful, isn't it? I always forget.'

'Well, hurry up and park the car then! I want to unpack my stuff!' Sophie bounced impatiently on the seat.

Kitty laughed at her little girl, whose first day could not have been more different to her own. She recalled the sick swirl of nerves that had filled her up, even though she'd been several years older than Soph.

She accompanied her daughter up to her dorm, where girls now slept in cubicles that held only two pupils. They could use their own bed linen and were allowed to put posters up. It gave the place a more homely feel.

The matron smiled and said, 'Call me Jayne!'

Sophie smiled back. 'Hi, Jayne!'

It was all very different from the stiff formality of Kitty's day. 'I'll go get the rest of your bits and bobs from the car,' she said, unwilling to let Sophie see the tears that were pooling.

Kitty popped the boot of her Golf and rummaged inside, loading a pair of trainers, a cherished teddy bear and a hot-water bottle into the already bursting cardboard box. She placed her hands under the bottom and heaved it upwards.

A car beeped behind her. She looked up briefly at the silver Range Rover that had been blocked by a flashy Mercedes parked in the staff spaces. Two boys jumped out of the Range Rover in full games kit. She wondered if they would become Sophie's friends. She paused momentarily as she recalled her own attempts at trying to meet people; she had to remember that Sophie was an entirely different kettle of fish.

The cardboard box was unwieldy and it took all of her strength to hoist it from the boot of the car. As she levered it out, she straightened, looked up, blinked and squinted, then placed the box on the ground and looked again.

Oh my God! It can't be!

But it was.

Her heart leapt in her chest and her stomach flipped. Sitting in the flashy Mercedes was none other than Theodore Montgomery.

She walked over slowly, unsure if he was alone or what her reception might be. The last thing she wanted was a scene, especially there and on Sophie's special day.

He rolled down the window.

'Theo! Oh my God! Theo, it *is* you! I don't believe it!'

'Hello, you.' He beamed, studying her, and she was relieved and thankful for his smile, a smile of forgiveness, of friendship. 'I didn't want you to think…' He seemed to run out of words.

Kitty stared at him. He had aged, of course, but to her he looked… lovely. He climbed slowly from the car and smoothed his trousers with his hands, drawing attention to his slightly crumpled suit and the mud that clung to the soles of his shoes.

'So which is it – hell or high water?' she asked, her hands on her hips.

'What?' He looked confused and she was embarrassed that he hadn't picked up the thread.

'I seem to remember you saying that those were the only two things that would ever drag you back here to Vaizey.'

She took a step towards him, her face now only inches from his, as if this was the most natural thing in the world and exactly the right distance to have between them.

'Yes, I probably did say that.' He smiled and shoved his hands in his pockets. 'If you must know, I've been fishing and I'm about to gatecrash a funeral, if you can believe that.'

'Oh I believe it.' She grinned, her false smile hiding all the sadness that lurked inside her. The temptation to sob and fall into him and tell him that she had lost her mum was strong.

'And what about you?' He jerked his head towards the school.

'Just dropping off.' The significance of the situation almost overwhelmed her – she was dropping off *their* daughter! Her pulse throbbed insistently in her throat.

'Where's Angus?' he asked, looking over her shoulder towards the quad.

'How should I know? On a golf course probably.' She shrugged, hoping she'd struck the right note, trying to sound flippant and at the same time cool. 'Did you think we were still together?'

'Are you not?' He looked genuinely surprised. He never had been one for keeping up with other Old Vaizians.

'No, not for a while. But it works – we share the kids' care and we are quite good friends now, better friends in fact than we ever were when we were married.'

'So that's good?'

'Yes, it's good!' She laughed. 'Angus is… with a new partner and happy.' She nodded and gave a thin smile. This was neither the time nor the place for details. 'So it's all good!' she repeated with a flicker of nerves, embarrassed at the way she was overcompensating with awkward perkiness. 'So you're off to a funeral?' She pictured the hill with the view of Loch Beag.

'Yes. Mr Porter's, actually, who used to be the groundsman here.'

'Oh, I remember him! He had a lovely crinkly smile.' A stark memory flooded in, of the day she'd seen Theo get beaten up, and how Mr Porter had stepped in to help him. Her heart went out to him still. 'I must admit, I never had you down as the huntin' and fishin' type! What did you catch?'

'Nothing.' He raised his hands and let them fall as he looked skywards. 'Absolutely nothing. I actually went for the stillness, the quiet.'

'Stillness and quiet – that sounds like bliss. Sometimes I can hardly hear myself think.' It was true; the house was always abuzz with cartoons and music and chaos. 'Actually, that's not fair, I think I keep busy to stop from thinking.' She bit her bottom lip and silently cursed herself for giving too much away.

'Kitty, I've spent the last few years overthinking and it turns out it wasn't actually very good for me.' He nodded.

'Well, good for you, Theodore Montgomery.' Kitty leant a little further in, her voice now barely more than a whisper. 'It is *so* good to see you.' As she stood there, she willed him to understand her subtext. *Please hear my apology, Theo. I am so sorry for how I treated you. Angus and I made a bargain, and I stuck to my end of it...*

'It's good to see you too.'

'Are *you* still married, Theo?' She glanced down briefly, remembering the ring she'd seen when they'd bumped into each other on the bus last year, but his hand was hidden in his pocket.

'Yes, Anna's great – greater.' He looked at the ground, seemingly brim full of emotion. Kitty felt a flash of envy for what he and his Anna evidently shared.

'"Great – greater"? Gosh, you really didn't pay attention in Mr Reeves's class, did you! That is terrible English!' She threw back her head and laughed.

He laughed too. There was a beat of awkward silence and then, just like that, having wondered how she might steer the conversation, it felt like the moment was now. A hush seemed to come over the place.

'That letter I sent...' she began, taking a deep breath.

Theo nodded. His shoulders hunched and he looked down, as if the words she'd written all those years ago still hurt.

'It was a very difficult time for me.' She shoved her hands in her pockets and held his gaze.

'It became a very difficult time for me too,' he acknowledged quietly, and she felt the pain of his words.

'I never in a million years imagined... after that one time...' She pulled a face; it was almost physically painful to spit it out. 'I was about to get married... There was so much going on in my head.'

'You don't need to explain. I've spent a lot of hours thinking it through and I get it. I totally see why you didn't want anything to do with me, didn't want me in our… your child's life. Why would you? I'm hardly good father material. I had nothing to offer.'

'Oh my God, Theo, is that what you thought?' Tears filled her eyes. That this had been his assumption, so wide of the mark, was heartbreaking.

He nodded, avoiding eye contact; the boy who'd been called names at school; the boy who used to hide in the library for want of anywhere else to go.

Kitty shook her head, her mouth twisted as she tried to stop herself from crying. 'No! No, it wasn't that at all. I've never hidden the truth from Sophie – or Angus. Quite the opposite. You, Theodore, are the kindest, sweetest, gentlest friend I ever had. You are smart and funny and any child would be lucky to have you in their life, so lucky. It was never about you! It was only ever about me. I couldn't see any further than what I was going through. I robbed you.'

It was only as she said this out loud that she saw the truth of it. She'd robbed him of the chance to be the father of his little girl. That had simply not occurred to her at the time.

He exhaled and leant back on the car, looking for a second as if he might fall over. 'But… But then on the bus…'

Kitty shook her head. 'Angus and I were falling apart, I was pregnant with Oliver, and little Soph…' She smiled up at him. 'It would have been too much for Soph right then, and too much for me.' She sniffed at the memory of that night, the worst night, when her world had come crashing down. She pictured Thomas reaching up to tuck in her husband's wayward collar. 'I am so sorry, Theo. I was young and stupid and frightened when I wrote to you, and if I could—'

'Mum! Mum, have you got my hockey stick?'

Kitty whipped her head round and smiled through her tears at the confident girl striding towards them. She looked from Theo to her daughter; the likeness was undeniable.

'Why are you crying?' Sophie wrinkled her nose with embarrassment.

'I'm not.' Kitty swiped away her tears and pulled her daughter towards her. She took her face inside her hands and kissed her nose. 'Sophie, this man... This is...' Emotion stopped the words from forming. She had imagined so many times how this meeting might go and suddenly it seemed perfectly fitting that it was here and now, at Vaizey College, where it had all begun.

Theo stepped forward and held out his hand.

Her beautiful daughter with the clear skin, dark curly hair and brown eyes of her father placed her hand confidently in his palm. 'Hello.' She smiled. 'I'm Sophie. Sophie Montgomery Thompson.'

Kitty felt quite drained as she drove back to London. Theo had appeared similarly stunned. The only person who had seemingly taken the introduction in her stride was Sophie.

'Oh, so you are Theo!' She had beamed with a maturity that belied her years.

'I am.'

'Theo! That's really cool. I always wondered when I would meet you, and you look nothing like a rabbit,' she smiled at her mum. 'How cool is it that it's here!' She'd gestured towards the school.

'It is very cool.' Theo had nodded at her, gazing at her with a look of wonder that Kitty recognised; it was exactly how she'd felt when their baby girl had been placed in her arms nearly eleven years ago.

Their conversation had been general – her favourite subjects, which house she was in. Kitty wondered if either of them would right now be running over the things they wished they'd said or asked. She had taken Theo and Anna's address and number, hoping that this might turn out to be a wonderful beginning, but not presuming anything. After all, Theo had Anna, and goodness only knew how Anna felt about it all.

Moving Home

Kitty made her way downstairs with a folder stuffed with pictures and letters in her hand. She placed it on the table as her stomach rumbled; it was already past lunchtime. She opened the fridge and peered inside. 'What do I fancy?' She laughed because what she fancied was smoked salmon, brown bread spread thickly with unsalted butter and a big glass of plonk; what she was getting, however, were the remnants of a rather sorry-looking pot of hummus, half a packet of out-of-date carrot batons and a small square of pâté. Reaching up, she pulled the oatcakes from the tin on the larder shelf and settled back down at the table. She thought for the first time in a long time about lovely Marjorie, who had passed away a few years back, and her mouth watered at the memory of her hot home-baked loaves with the blackened crust.

She thumbed the papers that spilled from the folder in front of her, and rested her fingers on a letter from Anna to Sophie, her first, sent to her school dorm. Wiping the oatcake crumbs from her chest, she opened the sheet and scanned it.

Dear Sophie,
Hello! We've never met, but...

Kitty sat back in the chair, 'Oh! Oh my goodness.' She felt the swell of emotion in her throat and took a moment to catch her breath.

Eleven

2002

'How are you feeling?' Kitty looked across at her daughter, who was sitting calmly in the front seat. Her navy skirt and embroidered blouse had been carefully chosen and her dark, layered bob painstakingly styled.

'I'm okay.'

'You seem okay.' She kept her eyes on the road, trying to quash the nerves that bubbled in her gut.

'That's because I am, Mum.'

Kitty tapped her fingers on the steering wheel as they skirted Clapham Common on the South Circular. She loved having Sophie home from school for the holidays and she loved noticing all the small changes in her daughter. The past two years at Vaizey College had brought out some lovely qualities in her and she'd grown into a sparky but sensitive teenager. Somehow, she seemed to have inherited the best bits of each of her parents: she had her own sporty, warrior-like approach to things, but she also had Theo's sweetness and loyalty. Kitty didn't tell Sophie that, of course. 'I hope Dad and Nikolai do something fun with Olly today – I can always tell when he's been in front of the TV all day, he has too much energy.'

'I think Dad said they were going to do an Easter egg hunt around the house and in the garden.'

'Oh, that'll be lovely.' Kitty smiled. 'You're not nervous?'

Sophie shot her mum the sort of disdainful look that only a thirteen-year-old could manage. 'I think it's you who's nervous, Mum! But there's no need. I've already told you, think of it like any other Easter lunch, and if it's ghastly or we feel unwelcome or we change our minds, we do the signal. Which is...?'

'A cough followed by a fake sneeze.' Kitty laughed loudly at the very idea.

'Exactly. And the other one of us will say, "Do you need a tissue?" And if the answer is "Yes", we turn and run without looking back. We keep the car unlocked and we literally just leg it.'

Kitty giggled again. 'That's so funny, I can't imagine it, but it's good to have a plan.'

'Always good to have a plan, Mum.'

'You're so smart, Sophie. When I think of myself at thirteen, fourteen... I was a tomboy and a bit... lost, I suppose.'

'You had a lot going on with Grandma, and I guess Darraghfield must have been quite lonely if you didn't have a gang.'

Kitty gave a wry smile. 'I didn't have a gang, not really.' She pictured herself and Angus sneaking up to the bedroom for fast, unsatisfying sex. 'Any boys at school you like?'

'Plenty.' Sophie gave a small shrug, as though it were a ridiculous question.

'But any you *really* like?'

'None that I am prepared to tell you about.'

Kitty nodded. Point taken. 'I mean it – I do think you're smart, and cool. This trip today would throw a lot of people off-course, but you seem to be taking it all in your stride. I'm very proud of you.'

'I'm very proud of you too. There aren't many mums who'd be so lovely about stuff. You could have said I wasn't allowed to come or sent me on my own…'

'As if I'd do that! But I can't pretend I don't feel a bit weird about it all.' A blush began creeping across her face.

'In what way?'

Kitty took a deep breath and considered how best to couch her response. 'I've been kind of dreading today but looking forward to it too, if that makes any sense. I keep thinking about how I'll feel if Anna doesn't like you or is mean to you. I'd feel obliged to yank you out of there and it would make things very awkward between Theo and me, which would be a shame.' She glanced across at her child. 'And then, ridiculously, I think about what it might be like if Anna likes you a lot and you like her a lot, how that will feel for me, and I don't want to feel jealous, but you are my baby girl!' Her voice cracked.

'I get it.' Sophie nodded. 'Either way, you're in for a bad day.'

Kitty looked over at her, coughed and followed this with a fake sneeze.

'Mum! You can't deploy the signal in jest or I won't know if you really need help!'

They both laughed, and with the radio playing 'My Sweet Lord' they drove the rest of the way in companionable silence.

Kitty parked in front of the large Edwardian villa in Barnes, only a stone's throw from the river. There were already a couple of other cars on the verge.

'How do I look?' Sophie pulled her dark hair around her face and smoothed her skirt.

'You look perfect.' Kitty sent a silent prayer out into the ether, hoping that it was all going to be all right. Her little girl deserved nothing but love. 'Are you ready to do this?'

Sophie gave a stiff nod and Kitty knew her daughter's deep breathing, straight back and silent response were indeed the first sign of nerves.

They trod the path and Kitty stepped forward and rang the doorbell. She heard a dog bark and the yelps and shouts of what sounded like a crowd. It did nothing to alleviate her anxiety. One way or another, this day was going to change things.

There was no time to dwell on that: the front door opened and Kitty found herself staring at Theo and Anna standing side by side, arms touching.

Petite, dark-haired Anna smiled sweetly and lifted her joined hands to her chin, almost as if giving thanks. Kitty immediately warmed to her. Kindness radiated from her face and her whole manner was welcoming. Much of Kitty's fear melted away. Theo looked nervous and weepy all at once and it was in the silent seconds before anyone spoke that the enormity of the moment sank in. She couldn't imagine what it might be like for him, properly bringing his daughter into his life for the first time.

Kitty walked forward and tried to keep her voice steady. 'Hello, Theo! Good to see you. And Anna, so lovely to meet you.'

Anna reached out and took Kitty into her arms in a brief but sincere embrace.

'You too.' Anna smiled. 'I feel as if I know you already, I really do.' She spoke without malice, without any edge, as if addressing an old friend.

'Same.' Kitty nodded.

All three adults turned and stared at Sophie, hovering nervously on the doorstep. Kitty felt a swell of empathy for her girl. This was a big moment.

'And you must be Sophie.' Anna took a step forward, reached for Sophie's hand and guided her into their home.

Sophie nodded, embarrassed, her posture a little awkward; she was, unsurprisingly, overcome.

'This is quite a day for you, for us all,' Anna offered softly.

Theo looked at Anna with an expression of pure love, clearly overwhelmed at how wonderful she was being to his daughter, and Kitty knew that it was because of Anna that this day had happened at all. She could so easily have put a stop to it.

'Hello, Sophie.' Theo smiled and moved his arms awkwardly, as if unsure whether to hug their daughter or just shake her hand. Again, Kitty felt the pull of guilt that it was because of her that these two were strangers.

'Hi…' Sophie hesitated. 'I don't really know what to call you.' She looked over at Kitty, seeking reassurance, and Kitty was reminded that for all her poise, Sophie was still a little girl wary of doing or saying the wrong thing.

'Whatever you're comfy with, darling.' Kitty winked at her. It was permission of sorts; she wanted everything about this encounter at this early stage of the relationship to be as easy as possible for her child.

Theo beamed at her with thanks. 'Theo is fine,' he managed, his voice full of emotion.

'Or Dad-Theo,' Anna suggested without embarrassment. 'I know you already have a proper dad – Angus – but as someone who grew up with no one I could call Dad, I can only imagine how wonderful it might be to be able to say that to two people.'

Kitty looked at Theo's wife and could not imagine growing up without her beloved dad by her side. She was glad that Anna had found a good man like Theo.

Sophie beamed at Anna. 'Yes, you're right.' She looked at Theo and gave a small wave. 'Hi, Dad-Theo.'

'Hello, Sophie,' he repeated, grinning.

Anna placed her hands on Kitty and Sophie's backs and ushered them in. Kitty took in the grand, square hallway and the gorgeous Alsatian-cross who was scampering around in excitement.

'Don't mind Griff, he's very happy to see you. Now, I have to tell you, the house is bursting at the seams and we are an eclectic bunch, but everyone is very much looking forward to meeting you.'

Kitty held her breath as nerves bit again.

'I'm looking forward to meeting them.' Sophie spoke with confidence. 'And I'm used to eclectic bunches. My family… my… my other family, we're all really weird.'

Kitty laughed. *Yes, we are, darling. We are all weird!*

'Then I think you're going to fit in just fine.' Anna laughed too. She winked at Kitty, very much in the way she herself might have winked at Tizz. Kitty read it loud and clear. *It's okay. Between us, you and I have got this.*

Their home was welcoming. Chock full of antiques and neat, but still homely. The four walked into the spacious kitchen, where an Easter table was beautifully set with sparkling glass-ware and polished silver cutlery. The radio burbled away in the background and the sumptuous smell of roast lamb wafted from the range. Anna grabbed a pinny from the back of a chair and popped it on, before pulling a blue linen dish-cloth from the range door and wiping her dainty hands on it. Kitty felt an unwelcome spike of inadequacy: Anna was clearly a domestic goddess, a class apart from her own rather average skills in that department.

Kitty noticed the way Anna and Theo constantly looked at each other, touched hands or ran their palm along the other's arm. It was like a dance of reassurance, where the couple was so in tune, these gestures acted like a battery recharge. She and Angus had never shared anything like that and she felt a flash of longing in her stomach. It looked like a lovely way to live.

'Now, Theo, you grab drinks.' Anna smiled at him warmly and turned to Kitty and Sophie.

'He's been so nervous, excited. I told him it was all going to be fine – I promised, in fact. And now I've met you both, I can see that I was right.'

'It must have been horrible not having a dad,' Sophie said, leaning against the countertop with the sleeves of her blouse pulled over her hands.

'It was, Sophie. I missed him even though I never knew him. I had a big hole in my life.'

'But you had a mum?'

'I did have a wonderful mum until I was not much younger than you, but sadly she passed away and so then I had two big holes in my life!' Anna bent down and petted Griff. 'I think that's why it's so important we make the most of all the people we have in our lives who love us. It's everything, family.'

'It is,' Kitty agreed.

'She's so beautiful.' Anna spoke to Kitty as if Sophie weren't present. 'And you have a son, Oliver?'

'Yes! He's three and with his dad today – causing mayhem, no doubt.'

'Please bring him next time – I love the house with children in it. I spend a lot of time with my niece and my godsons when they're around. There's something about having little ones here, it makes the house seem alive! And actually, I don't know if Theo mentioned it, but we're on the path to adoption, and so one day, God willing, there might be the sound of our own little ones running around!'

'That would be so wonderful.' Kitty noted the flicker of sadness that crossed Anna's face and hoped that her dream would come true; she couldn't imagine a life without her babies.

Theo handed Kitty a glass of champagne and Sophie a thimbleful. 'Right, shall we get this over with and introduce you to the masses?'

'Yep.' Sophie pulled a face.

'You know, Sophie, if you ever feel nervous or your thoughts get too much, you should try this trick that my mum taught me.' Anna put her arm round Sophie's shoulders and planted a light kiss on the top of her head. 'It's called the alphabet game and you have to go round the room, or somewhere imaginary, and think of things for each letter in turn. You concentrate on it and suddenly you find the distraction's worked and your thoughts are more orderly and you're much calmer.'

'So, A for apple.' Sophie pointed at the fruit bowl. 'B for bowl.'

'Exactly. C for custard.' Anna gestured towards the pan on the range.

'D for Dad-Theo.' Kitty joined in.

They laughed. Theo lifted his elbow and Kitty and Anna watched as Sophie slipped her hand through her dad's arm and the two headed for the sitting room. The two women followed behind.

Anna put her arm around Kitty's waist. 'Bless her!'

'I know.' Kitty gazed lovingly at her little girl, walking forward with her dad. *Dad-Theo.*

The elegant sitting room did indeed seem jam-packed with people. Kitty felt the flutter of nerves and was once again quite taken by Sophie's maturity as Theo proudly walked her around the room, introducing her to Anna's friends from St Lucia and their twins, and another friend, Melissa, and her two kids. There were cousins all the way from the USA, and an older lady, Sylvie, who grabbed Sophie and kissed her affectionately, and of course Theo's mother, Stella, whom Kitty had heard a lot about when they were at school but had never met. She watched Stella look Sophie up and down from a distance. Kitty stepped forward to shake her hand. Stella was slender and chic, with killer cheekbones, a slick of red lipstick, and a large gin and tonic in her hand. Kitty remembered her being described back then as very pretty and dead trendy, and she was clearly still formidable, even now.

'You're an old Vaizian, I believe?' Stella said.

'Yes.' Kitty swallowed. 'The same year as Theo.'

'Of course, of course.' Stella nodded. 'Did you know Mr Beckett, Theobald's housemaster? He was our dear, dear friend, Becks. My husband was a Theobald's boy, you know, and his father, and many others in our family.'

'I know who Mr Beckett was, but I didn't really know him. My cousins were in Tatum's House.'

Stella had already lost interest and Kitty was struck by how unlike her son she was, in either looks or manner.

'Kitty, would you like to see my garden?' Anna asked.

Both women looked towards Sophie, who was standing close to her dad and being grilled by Anna's cousin Jordan. 'So, Sophie, I hear you're at boarding school – is it anything like Hogwarts?' he asked. 'Please tell me it is!'

'Yes, it's exactly like that.' Sophie nodded. 'We have owls deliver our mail and everything!'

'You don't?' Jordan's mouth fell open.

'No, of course we don't!'

Everyone laughed.

'I think she's fine.' Anna smiled and Kitty followed her back into the kitchen and out into the magnificent garden. She gasped to find herself in the beautiful oasis. It was a wonderland of planting, with dainty paths picked across well-kempt lawns, trees arching over ornate iron benches to provide secret shady spots, and terracotta pots bursting with brightly coloured blooms.

'Oh, Anna, this is so gorgeous!' She felt quite moved by the cottagey ambience. It was truly lovely. 'We have a little courtyard in Blackheath, no real garden, but this is something else!'

'It's my pride and joy. Here, come and sit down.' Anna perched on a bench beneath a willow and Kitty took up the space next to her.

'My family home has a lot of outside space, but it's much more rugged.' Kitty thought of the wide sweep of moorland that surrounded Darraghfield, wild and natural. 'This must be so much work.'

'It is, but it's a joy. I grew up without a garden in Honor Oak Park and my mum, oh my word, she loved her plants and she longed for some outside space. I sit out here and think about her a lot. How she would have loved it.'

'I lost my mum three years ago. It's hard, isn't it?' Thinking about her mum still made Kitty tearful; she suspected it always would.

'It really is.' Anna coughed to clear her throat and Kitty braced herself. Anna had obviously wanted to get her alone, had things that needed saying.

'I can't tell you how much it means to Theo, to us both, to have you bring Sophie here today.'

'It was about time.' Kitty picked at an invisible thread on her trousers.

'I was so worried about meeting you.' Anna lowered her eyes. 'Literally scared!'

'Oh, Anna, no!'

'Yes, I was! I've always been conscious of the fact that I went to a crappy school and wasn't part of the Vaizey set.'

'And I bet Theo's mum has never, ever mentioned that...!'

Anna laughed. 'Not once – never!'

It broke the ice. Kitty took a breath. 'Well, I was worried about meeting you too, partly in case you were off with me, but mostly on Sophie's behalf – she's had quite a time of it.'

Anna turned and placed her hand on Kitty's arm. 'I have held an image of you in my mind for years – the girl that got away.'

'Hardly!' Kitty giggled but was absurdly flattered.

'Yes, really! And when I found out about Sophie, especially with us going through our own struggles to become parents, it was hard for me.'

'I can imagine.' Kitty held her gaze and spoke softly.

'But then I thought about it and I realised that Sophie is a gift! Not just to Theo, but to me too. And I promise you, Kitty, that I will do my very best to make it work. I don't want to mess this up and I only want Theo to be happy.'

Kitty looked at the woman who had made her so welcome in her home, a woman who had every right to feel aggrieved at the world, which had taken her parents when she was so young and denied her the chance of motherhood, but that was clearly not Anna's way. She exuded goodness, like magic. 'You are quite remarkable, Anna, if you don't mind me saying. You are lovely.'

Anna reached over and held Kitty's hand. 'I will need your

help. Can I call on you for advice or if I don't know how to handle something? I'd hate to do or say the wrong thing.'

'Of course you can.' Kitty smiled at her. Her meaning was loud and clear: Anna would always make Sophie welcome, would make it as easy as possible for Theo and Sophie to spend time together, but she, Kitty, would always be her mum.

'I just want her to like us, to love us!' Anna bit her lip nervously.

'I think you're going to do just fine.'

Anna reached over and plucked a full-headed carnation from a plant. 'For you!' She smiled.

'Oh!' Kitty held the tender bloom in her fingertips. It was a long time since she'd been given a flower with so much love.

After that Easter lunch, a pattern was established, with Sophie meeting up with Theo and Anna once every school holidays, always the highlight of her break. It was a system that lasted right through until she left Vaizey. Anna was brilliant at finding things to do that Sophie would like, trips to the cinema, lunches in greasy spoons, and they even got Theo to go ice-skating with them one Christmas. Kitty was always invited, but never went. She told Sophie that it was because she wanted her and her dad to get to know each other on their own terms, without her in the middle. But if she was being totally honest, there was a tiny bit of Kitty that just couldn't quite face it, with Theo and Anna being so happy and she still a reluctant singleton. It wasn't that she was jealous, but rather that it was a sharp reminder of all that she was missing.

It was always Anna who called up and made the arrangements, and Kitty came to look forward to her calls. Once the pick-up and drop-off details had been decided, their conversation invariably moved on to other things – what was growing in Anna's beloved garden, gossip from Kitty's job in the art gallery in Blackheath, Olly's progress through nursery and kindergarten and on into primary school. On occasion they talked about Theo too, especially the ups and downs of his latest housing projects, but most of all they talked about Sophie. She was the glue that bound them, both were so very proud of all she achieved and the young woman she was becoming. They even, late one night, squealed with delight at the future possibility of Sophie's babies to whom they would both be 'Grandma.'

Kitty would quite often ask her advice about things. When Sophie phoned home from school and said she wanted to switch one of her A-level subjects and do art history instead of economics, it was Anna's thoughtful, helpful input that had persuaded Kitty. Angus, on the other hand, had immediately scoffed, making his annoying 'T' sound and acting like it was a ridiculous idea.

Sophie's next bombshell was that she wanted to learn to drive. Vaizey allowed them to learn in their last year, so long as they were over seventeen and had parental approval. Kitty immediately phoned Anna to see what she thought.

'I think it's a fantastic idea!' Anna had enthused.

'You do? I worry that she's a bit scatty with anything mechanical, not sure she's safe.'

'Yes exactly! I much prefer the idea of her being out on the road in Dorset rather than where we live – the girl is going to be a nightmare and the further from our streets the better!'

Kitty roared her laughter. 'I had not thought of it like that. You have a good point, Anna.'

Moving Home

Kitty slowly removed the pretty floral box file from the shelf on the dresser in the hallway. She sat on the sofa and balanced it on her knees, before slowly removing the lid. She ran her fingers over the faded layer of pink tissue paper, and stared at the shrivelled, dried carnation, once a vibrant lemon colour but now a pale khaki. Carefully, she lifted it from the box and laid it against her cheek.

This was how she sat for some minutes, allowing the memories to settle.

Twelve

2016

Kitty knocked on the front door and waited. She scanned the windows, but with the curtains closed and no obvious lights to be seen, it was hard to tell whether anyone was home or not. She banged the envelope against her palm and figured she'd give it a minute or so and then if no one answered, she'd pop the card through the letterbox.

It was almost a shock when the door opened rather suddenly and even more of a shock to see the state of the man who had opened it. His hair was dishevelled, he needed a shave and by the look of his shirt, he had been sleeping in it for some time. His eyes were bloodshot and swollen and he smelt less than fragrant. Theo Montgomery looked every one of his forty-nine years.

'Oh, Theo, you look terrible.' She stepped over the threshold as he stood back against the door.

'Good. I *feel* terrible,' he croaked. 'How did you hear?' His voice had the gravelly rasp of someone who hadn't slept.

Kitty had taken the phone call a couple of days earlier from a very distressed Sophie.

'Mum...' Sophie had fought to form words through her sobs. 'Mum, I can't believe it...'

'What is it, darling?' Kitty was at work, in the gallery. She quickly sat down on the stool behind the counter as her heart leapt in fear at what her daughter might be about to reveal.

'It's... it's Anna,' she began. 'Stella just called me.' An image of Theo's formidable mother came into Kitty's head. 'Anna passed away, Mum. She died! Very suddenly.' Sophie broke off to give in to her sobs and Kitty sat frozen in shock. 'Oh, Mum! I can't believe it. Theo is destroyed. Poor Dad. I can't believe it.'

'What happened? Do you know?' Kitty asked softly.

'Apparently it was her heart... Her mother died of the same thing, Stella said. I feel so sad, Mum. Really low. Anna was lovely. She loved me and I loved her, I really did.'

'I know darling, I know.' Her heart flexed in sadness for the loss of the lovely Anna, but also for the pain her daughter was in.

'She... she helped me so much, especially when me and Dad first got to know each other. All those trips to fun places in the school holidays... D'you remember?'

Kitty nodded vigorously. Of course she remembered. Her warm, funny phone chats with Anna had been a highlight during that time – almost every week, right up until Sophie had gone off to uni. After that, contact had dwindled a little. Kitty hadn't felt quite right about initiating phone calls, and news had mostly been passed to and fro via Sophie, with Christmas cards and occasional emails in between. She hadn't actually seen either Anna or Theo for about two years. And now it was too late. She felt like crying too.

'I can't think how different things might have been for Dad and me if we hadn't had Anna as our interpreter,' Sophie said.

'She was wonderful and I shall miss her so much, Mum.' Her voice cracked again.

'Oh, my darling. Please don't cry, Soph...'

A wave of sadness washed through her. Sophie was right. She had benefitted hugely from having Anna's influence in her life. Anna had been a woman without envy, without selfishness and with so much love to give.

'So how did you hear?' Theo asked again, drawing Kitty back into the now.

'Your mum called Sophie. And she told me.'

'Of course.' He nodded. 'Is Sophie okay?'

'Upset, naturally. Very upset. She sends you all her love.'

Again, he nodded and rubbed at eyes that were clearly sore. Kitty took in his bare feet, creased jeans and the faint aroma of booze. She remembered standing on that very doorstep with a nervous thirteen-year-old Sophie by her side. Fourteen years ago! It had taken only seconds after the door opened that day for her anxiety to slip away as Anna walked forward and wrapped her arms around her...

'I am so sorry, Theo. I have wept for you, wept for you both.' This she offered a little too matter-of-factly, trying to keep her emotions in check.

'Are you not going to ask me how I'm coping?' he shot back.

'No need, Theo.' She looked him up and down.

He smiled weakly. 'Everyone else seems to be using that special tone of voice around me – you know the one, softened, quiet. It reminds me of being a kid when an adult had some bad news to give. It always makes me feel worse somehow.'

'I understand that.' And she did. She recalled all too well the awkward pauses when people wanted to discuss Angus's departure from their marriage and were so wary of saying the wrong thing.

'I was going to send the card...' She placed it on the hall dresser. 'But then I thought I should come over and tell you how sorry I am. And I really am. Anna was wonderful, just wonderful and I know how much you loved her.' She cursed the catch in her throat as she pictured Anna's smiling, open face and the way the two of them used to look at each other with absolute devotion.

'I did, very much. I do.' He nodded and closed his eyes.

'Of course. She was so kind to me and to Soph.'

'She was kind to everyone. The letters I've had...' He ran his palm over his stubble. 'Shall we have a cup of tea?'

'Yes, that sounds like a good idea.'

She followed him into the kitchen, trying not to stare at the disarray on the countertops that she knew Anna had liked to keep pristine. She stopped herself from suggesting she could clear up a bit, aware that Theo probably needed to wallow a while in the mess of his own making; it would be horrific if he thought she was trying to take over any of Anna's tasks.

She sat at the kitchen table and watched as he filled the kettle and grabbed two clean mugs from the dishwasher.

'In case you're interested, I am doing very badly and I am *not* coping, not at all.'

She stared at him and remained quiet.

Theo spoke clearly and concisely, as he did when he had something of importance to say. 'She seemed so well.' He stared at the kettle. 'We knew she had this heart murmur, but it was diagnosed years ago and it hadn't troubled her since. She was fit. She'd taken Gunner for a run that day and then just an hour later...' He gripped the countertop. 'I don't know what I'm going to do without her!'

Kitty watched with a flush of unease as Theo cried loudly. She stood and walked over to him, placing her hand on his back, and hoped that the proximity of another human might help ease his pain. 'It's so hard, Theo. It is. And there are no magic words to make it better, so I won't try.'

Theo cried until he seemed to run out of tears. He straightened and stiffened, embarrassed by the display. Kitty made the tea and the two sat down at the kitchen table.

'We thought that if we were very lucky we might have decades left, thought we had all the time in the world to do all the things we wanted, and then just like that...' He clicked his fingers. 'She was gone. We were planning to revamp the garden and we had trips booked.' He looked at the window. 'This heart thing she had was genetic. Her mum died in her thirties and it was the reason Anna decided against adoption in the end – it was almost as if she knew, or was worried about it, at least. But we never really spoke about it. I suppose I assumed that because she'd gone way past the age her mum was, we were home and dry.' He scratched the stubble on his chin.

'I know it's not the same, but when I lost my mum, I could only think about all the things I hadn't done, the feeling that I should have made more effort.' Kitty sighed. 'Guilt is a natural part of grieving, I think, but as time went on, that faded. And now I think more about the times I did spend with her, and the happy things.'

'Please, Kitty, do not start with the touchy-feely stuff or the stages of grief! My wife has died and I didn't always treat her how I should have, not at the beginning. I became a better husband, a better person, because of her, but I can't stop thinking about those first years when she was hurting and I was closed down. I can't change that, but I wish I could and it feels terrible.'

'You're right, you can't change it. But that's what I'm saying, Theo – let it out, get mad and then move on, try and focus on the wonderful decades that you did have. You two were the envy of everyone who met you. You shared something very rare, something that most people don't ever come close to having, and so you should try and feel thankful—'

'Thankful?' He raised his voice. 'Christ, she has been snatched from me and she was everything! Forty-eight years old! I can't feel thankful, I am furious! Anna was sweet and kind and loving and all that despite having the worst start in life. We had so much left to do and say, how the fuck is that fair?' He sat back with his chest heaving and his breath coming in bursts, flexing his knuckles. 'I got home, put my key in the door and climbed the stairs, turned into the bedroom and there she was...'

'That's awful.' Kitty felt her heart leap in her chest at the image.

He took a deep, slow breath and stared at her. 'So maybe you are right. Maybe I do feel a little bit better for getting angry.'

She gave a brief smile, one of a thousand gestures to let him know that while she didn't see him often, she was invested in him. She cared about him.

'I'm a mess.' He sat forward.

'I would say so, yes.'

'Sweet Jesus, do you never sugar-coat anything?' He shook his head. 'When did you get so hardened?'

'I don't think I am, Theo, not really. But I do know that life can end in a blink.' She thought of her mum walking out onto Kilan Pasture in the freezing hours before dawn, and she also pictured Anna. 'And we don't really have time for the dance that goes with not being straight about how we feel and what we want.'

'You're talking about Angus?'

She gave a wry smile. 'A bit.'

The two sipped their tea in silence until Theo looked up at the clock. 'I think I might have a nap. I seem to be asleep more than I'm awake at the moment. It feels good to shut down, opt out for a bit. My head hurts from all the thinking.'

'I bet it does. Look, I'll push off.' She reached for her car keys. 'Listen to your body, Theo. If you need to sleep, sleep.'

He nodded. 'The funeral is next Thursday – I'll let Soph have the details.'

'Of course, and you know where I am if you need anything.'

'Thanks, Kitty.' He saw her to the front door and closed it firmly before she'd made it to the end of the path.

She sat in the car and looked up at the house with the curtains drawn and the cloud of sadness hanging over it. Even the plants seemed to droop forlornly, missing the hand of the person who loved and tended to them. Kitty was desperately worried about Theo and considered how best to proceed. She was tempted to hammer down the door, hold him fast and tell him she would be there for him no matter what; but this she knew would in part be fuelled by the feelings she had for him, inappropriate feelings when the man had just lost the love of his life, and inappropriate for her to confess, even to herself, as it would only mean further heartache for her, and that was the last thing she needed.

St. Mary's Church, Barnes was busy. Friends, relatives and neighbours crammed into the pews, shedding tears as they picked up the order of service with its picture of Anna on the front; she was holding her beloved Gunner and smiling into the camera.

Kitty and Sophie slotted into seats near the back. Kitty

reached for her daughter's hand. There was something about a funeral that seemed to pull the stopper from the bottle in which all the hurts lived. At twenty-eight, Sophie had still only been to one funeral before, her grandma's, and Kitty knew that when her daughter dabbed the tissue at her eye, it would be for Anna, of course, but also for Theo at his loss, and for all the other sadness that Sophie held, big and small.

Theo came in and kept his eyes resolutely on the front of the church. A taller, lanky man walked by his side. Kitty glanced briefly at Theo's sallow complexion. He looked utterly broken and just the sight of him was like a punch to the gut. It reminded her so much of how her dad had looked when her mum had died. She pictured him now, rattling around Darraghfield and keeping busy with the estate, still not fully restored to the person he was, but better; much, much better.

Hymns rang out. Jordan, Anna's cousin from New York, could barely get through his eulogy. His words were heart-felt as he clutched the sides of the lectern, reminiscing about their teenage year together in Birmingham, their shared love of music and silly theatricals, the regular phone calls across the Atlantic. Anna's friend Shania was next. 'Anna and I met when we were kids in care…' This reminder sent a jolt through Kitty. It was easy to forget the start Anna had had; her tough childhood could have made her bitter, could have sent her in a different direction, but Anna had pushed on through and become the loveliest of people, the most loyal of friends.

As Kitty sat listening, she imagined the kind words and fond memories dancing up above the rafters and then falling like stardust, settling on the congregation and making them all feel a little happier.

After the service, everyone drifted back to the home Anna had shared with Theo. It felt odd being there without

Anna present. She had always been a wonderful host and more than one person commented on how they half expected her to pop up and replenish glasses. Sombre-faced waitresses ferried platters of sandwiches and nibbles around the room. Kitty recognised some individuals she'd met at the house before. There was the very elderly Sylvie, who'd known Anna a long time. She cried loudly and without restraint, and was supported by a nice-looking man called Ned, whom Kitty assumed was her son; he kept crooking his finger into the collar of his shirt and pulling, as if he found it constricting. And Shania, of course, who'd spoken so eloquently in the church and who'd travelled all the way from St Lucia. She looked utterly bereft as she linked arms and chatted to another friend of Anna's, a heavyset American called Melanie. Anna's half-sister, Lisa, was there with her new husband, her cab-driver brother Micky, and her older daughter Kaylee, whom she knew Anna adored.

'It's Kitty, isn't it?'

She turned to see the tall, lanky man who'd escorted Theo into the church.

'Yes.' She nodded. 'I'm Sophie's mum,' she added nervously, for some reason feeling that she needed to explain her presence. Sophie herself was chatting to her gran, Stella.

'I know.' He gave a wry smile. 'I'm Spud, Theo's friend from university.' He tutted. 'I don't know why I said that – I've been his friend ever since university too. Can't seem to shake him off.'

'Yes, of course.' She'd heard the name mentioned by Sophie. Mostly in stories about Theo's misspent youth and usually featuring dingy student digs and a fondness for scampi no matter what the occasion.

'I'm worried about Theo.' He cut to the chase.

'Yes, me too.' She looked out towards the hallway, where

Theo was leaning against the bannister and sipping from his tumbler while Jordan seemed to be giving him detailed advice.

'He doesn't cope too well with major setbacks. He's not resilient.' Spud spoke in a fatherly fashion, caring and without sounding judgemental. She found it endearing.

'No.'

'I live in Washington, sadly, so I can't be here all the time, but he needs someone.'

She looked at him and wondered when he was going to get to the point.

'I think you need to keep an eye on him, Kitty.'

'Me?'

'Yes. He doesn't trust many people and no one knows him that well and it would be unfair to ask Sophie.'

'Yes, it would.' She looked at her girl, sitting on the floor and thumbing the skin on the back of her gran's hand as she listened to her chat. Sophie had only just taken up a new teaching post and needed to put all her efforts into her career.

'It feels weird me asking you.' He gave a snort of laughter.

Kitty was finding his manner a bit strange. 'How do you mean?'

'When Theo and I first met at uni, he told me you were kind of the one that got away, and we had a plan – "To erasing Kitty!"' He lifted his beer bottle in a mock toast. 'It basically involved heavy drinking and dating as many girls as possible. He was doing well, until you bumped into each other again.' He paused and they both looked again at Sophie. 'Sorry, this really is starting to sound weird.' He coughed.

'Just a bit.'

'What I mean is, he needs someone to look out for him and I think it should be you. He is totally lost without Anna.'

They both glanced up as Jordan now wrapped Theo in a warm embrace.

Kitty nodded. 'I will do my best, but I don't want to be pushy or stick my nose in where it's not wanted. I might have known Theo a long time, but we're only close via Soph. We don't know each other that well, not really.'

And I need to protect my own heart, I need to look after me. I am also not as resilient as others might think.

Spud swigged from his beer bottle. 'I don't know who else to ask.'

Kitty was moved by the genuine look of concern on his face. 'He's lucky to have a friend like you.'

'And I'm lucky to have him.' He straightened.

'So you are back off to Washington?'

'Yes, tomorrow. I hate flying, but I need to get back. I'm about to become a grandad for the first time.' He beamed. 'My wife would never forgive me if I missed the big event.'

'Oh, how lovely! Congratulations.'

'Yep, my daughter, Miyu. We don't know what she's having, it's a surprise.'

'I can't wait for that. But I better keep my voice down, don't want Sophie to feel any pressure. Mind you, when I was twenty-seven, I was well into motherhood. Soph was already six...' She beamed at the memory.

'Miyu's made an early start too. She's only twenty. But when the time's right, it's right, I guess. Motherhood has come knocking and she's happy. So's my wife, Kumi – just don't call her granny. I learnt that one the hard way.' He sucked air through his clenched teeth.

Kitty sipped her wine and both fell silent. She imagined Spud, like her, was thinking of Anna, who had so desperately wanted motherhood to come knocking.

'To Anna.' She lifted her glass and Spud clinked his beer bottle against it.

'To Anna.'

Kitty left it a week before picking up the phone. Spud's words rattled around her head. It was a fine line to walk: she wanted to be the best friend she could to Theo, but she didn't want to interfere, not at this horrible, sad time of reflection. She felt conflicted.

'Yes.' His voice was more of a growl and she suspected was tinged with booze.

'It's me. Kitty. I was wondering how you're doing?'

He sighed slowly. 'Not great.'

'What can I do to help you, Theo?'

'Nothing.'

'Do you have food in?'

'Yep.'

'Do you have someone to talk to?'

'Nope and that's just fine.'

It was her turn to sigh.

'Okay, well, I'll let you get on, but don't let things build up. I'm on the end of the line if you need someone to talk to, and I can be there in no time at all if you want someone to sit with you or you need anything at all. I am your friend. Okay?'

'Okay.' He sounded like he might be crying and this only put her at a further loss for words. 'Actually, Kitty, there is one thing.' He sniffed.

'Of course. What?'

'I have an estate agent coming to put the house on the market and I don't think I can face it on my own – could you come over?'

'You're putting the house on the market?' She couldn't help the surprise in her tone or the implication that this was the worst possible thing to do right now.

'Yes. I don't want to be here without her.'

'Well, if that's what you've decided, then of course, Theo, you just let me know when and I'll be there.'

She wasn't sure that moving so quickly was right for Theo. Time away, she understood; a change of scenery, yes; but ridding himself of the only place he and Anna had ever lived? She would have to think about how she might raise this when she saw him next.

A few days later she was in the car when her phone flashed on the passenger seat. She engaged the hands-free. 'Hey, Soph!'

'I just tried home and you aren't there. And I know it's not a gallery day.'

'That's right. I am allowed to leave the house occasionally!' She laughed.

'I didn't know where you were.' Her daughter's tone was almost accusatory.

'Well, I am sorry for not keeping you informed,' she offered sarcastically, actually rather liking the fact that her girl wanted to keep tabs on her. She had a fear of getting lost or ill and being unaccounted for, but with Sophie and Olly in regular contact, this was less likely to happen. 'If you must know, I'm popping over to Theo's.'

'*My* Theo's?'

Again, Kitty laughed, choosing not to point out that if he had not been *her* Theo first, he would never have been Sophie's Theo... 'Yes! He's thinking of selling the house and has an agent coming over. I'm going to sit with him.'

'That's a bit weird!'

'Not really. He's just lost his wife and he needs a bit of support.'

'I guess. I feel bad that I can't go, it's just that with my new job—'

'Soph, don't feel bad. No one expects you to take time off. We understand, and I bet he appreciates your calls, more than you know. Besides, I'm happy to go and see him. I've even got some beef bourguignon for his freezer.'

'Oh, thank you, Mum.'

Being thanked was another odd reminder of how Sophie and Theo shared a closeness that excluded her. Not that she was envious, not at all; they were father and daughter and she was glad, but it felt odd, nonetheless.

Sophie spoke softly. 'I think it might be a bit soon for him to be selling the house – it's where all of his memories of Anna live. I remember her telling me about the first time she ever went there and saw the garden and thought it was the most marvellous thing she had ever seen and that she couldn't imagine living anywhere so grand. She always loved the place.'

'Yes, she did. And I thought the same.' Kitty smiled at the shared insight. 'But Theo can only do what he thinks will help, and all we can do is be there for him.'

'Yep. Give him my love.'

'Will do, darling.'

The traffic in Barnes was exceptionally bad and Kitty had barely had time to take off her coat and step into Theo's kitchen before the front doorbell rang.

'Good afternoon!' The young man spoke with gusto and a grin, more reminiscent of a perky disc jockey hired to rouse listeners from their afternoon slump than a man of business. 'I'm Jason.'

Kitty looked at Theo over the top of Jason's head and stifled a laugh.

'Mr Montgomery.' Jason put his hand out, which Theo shook briefly, reluctantly.

'And Mrs Montgomery.' He did the same to her.

'Oh!' She felt her face colour. It was inappropriate and embarrassing on so many levels. 'No, I'm just a friend.'

'Righto.'

She couldn't be sure, but there might have been the vaguest suggestion of a wink from the young Jason. His cologne was strong and his hair neat. Kitty folded her arms across her chest in defence.

'Firstly, may I say what a pleasure it is to be invited into this wonderful home—'

'How does this work, Jason?' Theo cut him short, seemingly unwilling to go through the charade of giving a damn. He had told her before Jason arrived that he didn't have time for small talk or bullshit. He stood back and ushered him into the house. 'Do I follow you around pointing out that we are standing in the garden and so forth, which I am sure will be blindingly obvious, or do you wander about by yourself and take your measurements or whatever?'

'Whichever is easiest for you, Mr Montgomery.'

'What's easiest for me is that you get rid of the bloody place as quickly as possible.' Theo growled and clicked his fingers. Gunner, his springer spaniel, trotted to heel as he made his way to the kitchen, leaving Kitty alone with the chap in the hallway.

'I think maybe take a wander and then meet us in the kitchen?' she suggested.

'Righto,' Jason offered again, but this time with a lot less gusto.

'I just want the place gone, Kitty,' Theo said by way of justification. 'I see her everywhere I look and it's more than I can stand. I can see her now, standing by the lemon tree and if I look out of the kitchen window, I can see her kneeling by the flowerbed, taking cuttings. And I can't go into the bedroom, where I saw her for the last time...' He shut his eyes briefly. 'There she is, every time I switch on the light, lying as though asleep, with one hand under her head and her eyes closed. She looked beautiful...'

'Would it be okay if I started upstairs?' Jason called, a slight warble to his voice now that he knew he wasn't a welcome presence.

'Yes!' Theo bellowed and reached for the bottle of Glenfiddich.

'Would you like a cup of coffee?' Kitty hovered by the kettle.

'You mean in addition to or as well as?' He lifted the bottle.

'Whichever. What I *mean* is that I want one and as you have made no attempt to offer me one, it was the only way I could think to get one without being impolite.'

'I think we are way past worrying about politeness.'

She liked the small smile that played on his mouth, an indicator that beneath the gruff, grieving exterior, funny, smart Theo lurked somewhere inside.

'True.' Kitty filled the kettle and, like Theo, could only see Anna standing there, doing the very same thing within minutes of their arrival, staring adoringly at Sophie and asking her question after question:

'So, who is this new man? Is he tall? Short? Are you keen?'

'Have you seen Angus? What are he and Nikolai up to?'

'Olly must have exams looming, is he studying?'

'Have you been eating, Soph? You look a little too slim – how about some of my Victoria sponge, homemade of course!'

Theo poured a generous slug of whisky over cubes of ice that were still in his glass, unmelted, from his previous serving; he was clearly knocking his drinks back in quick succession.

'I know you know this, but getting sloshed all day isn't going to help and it isn't going to change anything.' She poured hot water onto the coffee grains that sat in a tiny heap in the bottom of the mug.

'Actually you are wrong, it changes me from sober to pissed and I quite like that.'

She shook her head. 'You can do whatever you want, Theo, but being pissed won't help you make a decision. Any decision.' She gestured upwards to where Jason the estate agent rattled around overhead.

Theo stared at his tumbler. 'I miss her. And I can't accept she isn't going to walk though the door.'

'I know.' Kitty adopted the tone she used when the kids needed reassuring.

The front doorbell rang.

'Can you get it?'

'Sure.' Kitty placed her coffee mug on the countertop and went to open the front door. She was met by the steely gaze of Theo's mother, Stella. The sprightly octogenarian was as ever immaculately turned out, with her red lipstick sitting askew on her thinned lips and a teal and grey Hermès silk scarf tied stylishly at her slender neck.

'Oh good, is Sophie here?' This was her greeting as she gripped the doorframe and trod with great deliberation over the brass-lipped top step.

'No, just me, I'm afraid, Stella.' She smiled and held the door open.

'Oh, what a shame!' Stella shouted, as if it were others whose hearing was on the wane.

'None taken…' Kitty mumbled under her breath.

Stella turned into the sitting room and took up a seat by the fireplace. 'Can you tell Theo I'm here,' she instructed and Kitty felt the flicker of hysterics. This woman treated her like the housekeeper.

'Theo…' She grabbed her coffee and took a swig. 'Your mother's in the sitting room.'

'Oh God! Can't you get rid of her?'

'Look…' Kitty placed her free hand on her hip. 'I came to support you, not act as go-between or referee between you and the estate agent and you and your mother. Come and sit through here, otherwise I shall have to hover in the hallway passing messages like a bloody telephone exchange!'

Theo huffed and reluctantly made his way into the sitting room. He sat on the sofa. Kitty sat on the other chair, beneath the window.

'I was saying it's a shame Sophie isn't here.' Stella eyed Kitty with suspicion. 'I do like that girl. Good head on her shoulders!'

'She has,' Theo said, and Kitty wondered if she was invisible.

'I see you're drinking.' Stella nodded at his glass of whisky.

'Well, it's good that there's nothing wrong with your eyesight.' He raised the glass and took a sip.

'Drinking is so jolly predictable at a time like this and it makes you so very dull.'

'My mother was always big on compliments.' This he addressed to Kitty and she again felt like an interloper.

'Now, Theodore,' his mother began, removing her gloves and placing them neatly in her lap. 'I shall get to the reason for my visit. I have spoken to Mrs Philpott who lives next door but one – you know, the family who moved in seven or so years ago; new money, husband a banker – do you know the people I mean? Ghastly curtains and too many children.'

'Yes, I know them.' He took a slug of his drink.

'Good. Well, I told her about your situation…'

Kitty wondered why Stella couldn't use her name? *Anna!
Her name was Anna and she was your daughter-in-law, not
'a situation'.*

'And she told me about a friend of hers who lost his wife
and took up dancing, if you can believe that. He joined a class
locally and literally rhumbaed the evenings away, too exhausted to think. He lost a stone, which, let's be honest, darling,
wouldn't do you any harm, and as if that weren't benefit
enough, he met a lovely girl, Lithuanian, I think, no, wait a
minute, Albanian. Anyhow—'

Theo sat forward on the sofa. 'I am so sorry, Mum, but I
can't listen to this today. I am going to assume that you mean
well, but right now I am not too fond of waking up, let alone
going dancing.'

A head appeared in the doorway. 'Is it okay if I go outside
and get the measure of the garden?'

Stella looked Jason up and down. 'And who might you be?'

'I'm Jason.' He lifted his hand from his clipboard and gave
a small wave.

'Jason is an estate agent. I'm selling the house.'

'Don't be so ridiculous. Of course you're not selling the
house! What a thing to say. This is your home!'

'It's not my home. Not any more.'

Kitty felt very sorry for Jason, who was switching restlessly
from one foot to the other.

'I think going out to the garden is probably a good idea.'
Kitty shot him a look and he made a speedy exit.

'It's complete madness,' Stella continued. 'You don't sell
the house because of one bad memory. Not when it contains
a million good ones. That's ludicrous and it's typical of you,

Theo. It's very indulgent and dramatic. You can grieve – in fact you *must* grieve. But to sell your home… Don't be so bloody stupid!' She gathered her gloves from her lap and put them on.

'What do you think, Kitty?' Theo looked at her from beneath heavy lids.

'I agree with your mum to a certain extent.'

'Well, there we have it!' Stella sniffed.

'Not about the drama or the self-indulgence, but you're distraught, Theo, and I understand why. You've lost your Anna.' She let this sink in. 'I think you need to not add any more pressure to your thoughts right now, and moving at any time is a big deal, let alone with everything else you have going on.'

Stella stood to leave; clearly she had only come to say her piece. She made her way to the front door.

'Do you think I should tell Jason to come back another day?' Theo asked a little sheepishly.

Kitty nodded. 'I do. Maybe selling up is the right thing for you, but I think you need to slow things down.'

He nodded. 'I think you might be right. I just don't know what to do.' He looked unbearably sad and it ripped her heart.

'That's the thing, Theo, you don't have to do anything.'

Again he nodded.

'And if you don't want to stay here, come and stay with me. I've got a spare room.' The words slid out as easily as if she were offering a cup of tea or a lift, and once they were out there was no way to pop them back in.

'Can I? Really?'

She was taken aback by his immediate interest, feeling an instant spike of concern at what this might mean for her mental health and their friendship.

'Of course you can.' She hoped she spoke with more certainty and benevolence than she felt. She reminded herself of her discussions with Spud and with Sophie, that the most important thing was to keep an eye on Theo and help him right now when he needed it the most.

Gunner loped into the room and yawned. 'Can I bring Gunner?'

'Sure.' She smiled and just like that she acquired two lodgers, one with two legs and one with four.

Moving Home

Kitty carefully placed the flower back into the safety of the box and nipped to the loo. It was as she made her way back to the kitchen that the telephone on the wall rang.

'Mum? Me again, bit more time now. Sorry about before, an emergency.'

'They all are, aren't they?'

'Yep, pretty much and I have to watch as much as I can, it's how I learn best.'

'I get that, darling. Where are you, Olly, still at work?'

'I hate how you ask that question, it's always with an air of hope, as if you think I might be outside or up the road to surprise you, and I know you will be planning what to feed me!'

'That's not true at all!' She laughed, mentally erasing her plan to whip up an omelette and salad for her boy. 'So I take it you are not close by and popping in?'

'No. I'm working a double-shift.'

She heard him yawn. 'Poor darling. Are you tired?'

'I'm always tired! But it's my own fault this week, lectures, studying, rounds at the hospital and I've been burning the candle at both ends, big time.'

'Well, don't! You can't do good studying and partying, they don't mix!'

'All right, Mum, you win. I shall give up studying and concentrate on good partying.'

She laughed. 'Yes, that's exactly what I was driving at.'

'Soph texted to say she feared you were stalling in the packing department and were being far too airy-fairy about the whole thing.'

'Guilty as charged! I'm flitting from box to drawer and getting lost in some lovely memories, and some not so lovely ones. But it feels a lot like saying goodbye. I'm really very happy.'

'It's exciting.'

'It is. It'll be weird though. As I say, so many memories here, the place where you were a baby.' She swallowed the lump that rose unexpectedly in her throat.

'Have you spoken to Dad?'

'No, why? Everything okay?'

'I think so. Well, last I heard they've had a fight.'

'Again?'

Olly laughed down the phone. 'I know, right? Anyway, Mum, got to go. I've got a lecture. See you soon.'

'Hope so. Take care, Olly. Love you.'

'Love you too.'

A burst of happiness filled her chest at his sign-off.

Kitty sent out a silent prayer that Olly would settle down soon. It was at times like this that she especially missed Anna. They would have had a good old natter about Olly's love life, and, knowing Anna, she would have come up with a hare-brained scheme for finding him the perfect girl. She could picture her drawing up a list of their friends' daughters and inviting everyone round for an introductory tea. It was one of Kitty's many sadnesses that Anna had never got to meet Sophie's Greg. She would have loved the man.

Kitty smiled, remembering the day Sophie had been due to bring Greg home for the first time. She could tell that this was different.

Every other boyfriend of Sophie's had suddenly appeared at the kitchen table without fanfare and it was always obvious from her daughter's casual behaviour that she was rather indifferent. But this one...! Kitty laughed at the memory of the telephone conversation prior to their arrival, the semi-formal plan for dinner.

'Make sure Olly is there too, Mum.'

'Will do.'

'And don't mention Angus and Nikolai. Or Theo and Anna. Or your views on veganism.'

'God, Soph, you are making me nervous! You can't hide your family away!'

'And I wouldn't want to. It's not that they'll always be off-limits, but I'm trying to ease him in gently...'

This told Kitty two things. Firstly, that Sophie envisaged spending time with him in the future, and secondly, that she was bothered about what he thought of her.

This for Sophie was a first.

Kitty had felt nervous and excited all at once. All she knew was that the young man in question was a lecturer in modern languages at King's College, was originally from Belfast and that his name was Greg.

Please, God, may we like him.

Please, God, may he like us.

Please, God, may he be kind to Sophie.

Please, God, may any feelings she has for this Belfast man be reciprocated. Don't let her get hurt.

That's all!

Thinking about it now, she should have added an extra prayer: Please, God, make him a good cook, but on no account make him an experimental one.

Thirteen

Kitty hovered in the kitchen. It had been a busy day in the gallery. The new owner was making sweeping changes and she'd had to bite her tongue. The dishwasher whirred and the supper was cleared away. Not really a supper – there'd been no cooking, more of a quick ferret around the fridge for the remaining half of a gala pie and the coleslaw left over from the weekend, which she and Theo had eaten with pickles, all washed down with a large glass of red. She was glad to see him with some appetite; by his own admission, his calorie intake since Anna's passing had been mostly in liquid form.

In truth, she was now idling in the kitchen, finding jobs to keep her out of the sitting room. There was something rather awkward about having Theo under her roof without Sophie present to take up the slack in the silent moments. Also, it had been decades since she'd had a man other than Olly or Sophie's various boyfriends under her roof and she wasn't sure she liked it. She tended to spend longer in the bath and the loo just to have some alone time.

'Anything I can do?' Theo called.

'No, just clearing up.' She ran the cloth under the hot tap again and wrung it out, before reaching into the larder for another bottle of plonk.

Kitty took up her favourite seat at the end of the sofa and curled her feet under her. She had to admit it was nice to have Gunner loping around the place; his presence was comforting and her brisk walk with him over the heath before supper had been invigorating. He too had an aura of sadness about him. His ears drooped and his eyes were a little watery, as if he missed his mamma. He sat down hard on Theo's feet and let out an almost human sigh, which made them both smile.

'It's funny, I consider you one of my oldest friends, you *are* one of my oldest friends and yet I feel a little awkward. We haven't spent much time alone together, have we?' Theo sipped at his glass of wine. 'Yesterday, when you were in the bath, I felt I should hide in my room, give you some privacy. It felt like spying on a stranger and yet we've known each other for most of our lives.'

'Yep, I suppose our situation is a little odd.' Kitty tried to look a little surprised, as if she hadn't just been having very similar thoughts.

'Apart from picking Sophie up and dropping her off, this week is the first time I've properly been inside this house. And the first time I've eaten with you, just the two of us.'

'Yes, probably. If you don't count cake.' Kitty silently cursed the words the moment they left her mouth. They were embarrassing, drawing attention to that long-ago afternoon when he had seen her naked, when they had made Sophie. She glanced down at where her wine glass rested against her thickened middle and considered the various other bits of padding she'd acquired; she reached up and touched the space beneath her chin, aware of the loss of definition to her jaw. Theo's physique had fared well, better than hers, she thought, looking at his slightly weathered face and his dark curly hair. It had thinned, certainly, but was still striking. Age had mellowed his shyness too.

'I told Sophie about our cake-sharing a while ago. She was intrigued!' Theo arched an eyebrow. 'I think she can only see us as her middle-aged parents and not the young things we once were.'

'Mmm. And because we've never been together, she's probably keen for any glimpse of that. It must make her feel more secure.'

'I think she is secure, Kitty, despite our best efforts to cock up her childhood.' He raised his glass to her. 'You did a good job, you and Angus.'

'Thank you, Theo. That means the world.'

There was a pause. They both took several sips of their drinks.

'Have you forgiven Angus?' Theo reached down and stroked Gunner's silky ears. 'I mean, I know it's a long time ago now, and Sophie and Olly are obviously very much at ease with the whole situation, but I don't know…' He paused. 'It must be tough.'

'It was, but not so much now. I was angry for a long time. Angus became scarily good at leading a double life… He was like a photographer who clicked his fingers trying to get my attention, and I was so busy looking at that hand, I didn't see what the other was doing. But I wasn't exactly blameless either…'

She looked up at Theo. He held her gaze and gave a reassuring little nod.

They'd had a big conversation two nights earlier, Theo asking sweet, gently probing questions about Angus's reaction to her pregnancy with Sophie, listening intently as she'd tried to make it clear how Angus had held all the cards, how her being so grateful to him for not rejecting her had made her blind to what was really going on.

She coughed. 'I should never have cheated on him, no matter that it was spur of the moment and we were sloshed.' She swirled her glass. 'That's no excuse, I know, and I sometimes wonder if it was me trying to find a way out, you know, as if my subconscious was kicking me, acting on something that had lain dormant in me for a number of years.' She felt bold admitting this.

Theo returned his attention to Gunner.

'But now, if anything, I feel sorry for Angus. He felt he couldn't be himself, denied his sexuality and we all suffered because of it. His parents are very odd, narrow-minded and a bit mean, and he was confused, fighting against nature, which is tough, impossible. It was very different for me than if he'd cheated on me with a woman. I knew I could never compete. I had nothing that he wanted and that made me feel...'

'Rejected. Useless.'

'Yes.' She nodded, wondering if Theo, like her, was thinking of the letter she'd written him.

She took a deep breath. 'But you know what, Theo, we're all in our fifties nearly, not kids any more, and life feels settled. I don't care about the things I used to care about, and the things I didn't use to care about now feel terribly important. It seems to me that life is like a constantly moving see-saw and once you get past middle-age you stop worrying about which way it tilts and start just enjoying the ride.'

'I can't say I'm enjoying much at the moment.' He sniffed.

'I know, but you will, Theo.'

To her horror, he placed his hand over his eyes and started to sob once again. 'I miss her so much. I can't stand it!'

And just like that, she was reminded of her friend's very raw grief and the reason he was there.

By the time Theo had been there a full fortnight, the two had fallen into a routine of sorts. It was now Thursday evening and Kitty was listening to the rain hitting the windows post-supper. Theo sat down at the kitchen table and opened the newspaper.

'Has Gunner been out for his run?' Kitty bent down to pet the dog's beautiful ears.

'Yes, I took him earlier. Thankfully before the deluge.'

'Cup of tea, Theo?'

'Yes, please.'

His telephone buzzed on the tabletop. She tried not to listen in to his conversation, but it was hard not to.

'No, not at all, just about to have a cup of tea.' He paused. 'Yes. Yes, I know.'

Kitty left him to it and went into the sitting room to plump the cushions, gather the dirty mugs that lurked by the sides of the chairs and swoosh her hand over the dusty mantelpiece. She heard Theo laugh softly and felt a flash of joy at the lovely sound, which rippled through the house.

She bit her lip and tried to remember the Serenity Prayer she'd learnt in school. Truth was, it was doing her no good living in such close proximity to this man. It unsettled her, how quickly she'd got used to his presence at the breakfast table, the sound of him visiting the bathroom at night, the scent of him lingering on a towel. It was a reminder of a life she couldn't have. She tried to remember all the pluses of living a solitary life: being able to swig straight from the juice carton, wander around in her knickers, break into spontaneous song if the mood took her, eat nothing but heavily buttered crackers for supper and fart on the sofa at will. She walked now towards the dishwasher, gripping the dirty mugs tightly.

'That was Spud.' He nodded at the phone on the table.

'How's he doing?'

'Good. I'm surprised you couldn't hear him – his voice carries.'

'He calls a lot. He's a good friend to you, Theo.' She remembered their conversation at Anna's funeral.

'He is. He promised to call every day and he has. I've told him there is absolutely no need, but he says it puts his mind at rest.'

She knew how that felt. It was the same for her with the kids.

'He says he's checking in, but I think "checking up" would be more accurate. He and Kumi have invited me to go and stay...' He sighed. 'They have the space, but there's a new grandchild, a little boy, and... It's such a happy time, I think in my present mood I might only take the joy out of the moment. Plus it's such a long way.'

'Ah, a little boy! Spud said his daughter was expecting. How lovely. What's his name?'

'Kento.'

'Kento... I haven't heard that before, it's nice.' *Kento, Kento...* She practised the sound in her head.

'Miyu becoming a mum makes me feel very old.'

'You are very old.'

'There you go again with your sugary compliments.' They both chuckled. 'But it's a privilege, isn't it, getting older? I never really thought of it like that until recently, but I know I would have been thankful for every extra year Anna got. It's made me think of my friend, Mr Porter – you remember the groundsman?'

'I do indeed.' She looked at him wistfully as he ran his finger over the fishing fly pinned inside his shirt pocket. He did that quite a lot.

'He and his wife only got weeks together after the war. That feels especially cruel, doesn't it? To be separated by conflict only to be denied a life together afterwards. I didn't overly consider the tragedy of it until I lost Anna.'

'That is sad.'

'I'm not going to go to Washington.' He rallied. 'The thought of being fussed over by Spud's neurotic wife is more than I can stand. It's kind of them to offer though,' he added.

'It is kind.' She poured the water from the reboiled kettle onto the teabags.

'Shall we watch our next episode of *MasterChef*?' he asked.

'Ooh yes, what time?'

He looked at his phone. 'On in twenty minutes.'

She smiled, thinking how nice it was to share this small thing with him, watching the programme they loved with a cup of tea. She looked at Theo and he held her eye and something seemed to stir, a realisation, an awakening that was both unexpected and disturbing.

Theo cleared his throat and folded his newspaper. 'I guess I should start thinking about going home. I can't stay here forever, getting under your feet.'

Kitty turned to face him. 'You are not under my feet. You go when you're ready, Theo. No rush. But you *do* need to go home. You need to get back on track, and being here, as welcome as you are, both of you...' She looked at Gunner with fondness. '... it feels a bit like hiding out, and that won't take you forward, not in the long run.'

'No. At least I've stopped trying to seek oblivion in the bottom of a whisky bottle.'

'Yes! And I am glad about that. Anna wouldn't want you permanently pissed or moping around.'

'I know. I do feel a bit better.' He cleared his throat again. 'I can't imagine my heart hurting any less than it does and I can't imagine not seeing her behind my eyelids every time I blink, but I don't feel like I'm falling any more, so that's good. Solid ground beneath my feet and all that.'

'Maybe your heart won't ever hurt any less, maybe how it is now is your new normal and you have to find a way to build a life around it.'

I have had to do that, Theo, more than once, and it's possible, if not easy...

He nodded. 'Thank you for having me here, Kitty. It has meant more to me than you will ever know.'

'Any time, my old friend.' She placed the mug of tea in front of him. *And to me too, my dear old friend, my Theo. I shall miss your presence more than I could ever say, but I know it's the right thing, for us both. Time to move on. We mustn't dwell on what might have been.* 'I will always be a short cab ride away or on the end of a phone, okay?'

'Okay.' Theo forced a smile and stared up at her and just for an instant he looked like the boy who had sat opposite her in the booth, the one with whom she had shared a slice of dry Victoria sponge. 'I'll go and put the telly on.'

'Righto!' She beamed as he and Gunner lumbered from the kitchen. 'I'll be in in just a mo.' She took a second to brace her arms on the countertop and close her eyes to stop the maddening flow of tears.

'So Theo has gone back to Barnes?' Kitty could tell that Tizz was eating as she spoke into the receiver.

'Yes, the day before yesterday. The house feels very quiet. What is it you are eating so noisily?'

'Chocolates, left over from Daisy-Belle's birthday party.'

'Aren't they Daisy-Belle's?'

'Not any more.' Tizz laughed. 'Are you missing him – Theo?'

'No! Not at all. It was good to help him out, the right thing to do, but I need my space.'

'Oh God, yes! Above all you need your space, Kitty!' Tizz laughed.

'What do you mean by that? What are you insinuating?'

'Nothing! I'm just saying that you have this hot guy under your roof who you have been intimate with in the past and all you can think about is when you can get the sofa to yourself! You could have had some fun!'

'Christ, Tizz! He is grieving the loss of his wife. He is about as far from wanting to have fun as it's possible to be.' She tutted loudly to emphasise her dislike of the topic.

'Ah, I notice you aren't saying you're against it, but rather that he's not ready. Very interesting...'

'You are putting words into my mouth!'

'If you say so. I'm not sure I ever asked, but what was sex like with Theo?'

'For God's sake, that was thirty years ago, Tizz! I am not talking about it now!'

'Why not? I'm just curious. I mean, you don't have to say, but it's good to chat like this.'

'Good for who? Not me. You are just so nosey!' Kitty giggled.

'Only because I care.'

'It was lovely.'

'Lovely? Is that all I'm getting?'

'Yes.' Kitty smiled, not only at the memory but also at the use of the word. 'It was lovely.'

'So if you had to give both him and Angus a score out of—'

'Oh for God's sake! I am not prepared to talk about this with you any more. It's bloody nuts.'

'I know when you're holding back.' Tizz wasn't giving up.

Kitty was as surprised as her friend by the sudden, noisy onset of tears.

'Oh God, Kitty, I am so sorry, darling, I wouldn't upset you for the world. I was only teasing! I feel terrible. I thought it was funny, trying to make you talk about sexy stuff!'

'It's not your fault.' Kitty took a breath. 'Sex with Theo was beautiful, just beautiful, and having him here has been so nice, like letting me look through a little window at a world that I can never live in. I will be okay, I will,' she said determinedly. 'But I'm not okay right now.'

'You don't know what's around the corner, Kitty. You—'

'I do. I do know, and it's not that, so the sooner I stop thinking those thoughts, the better. Anyway…' She sat up straight and pulled herself together. 'The reason for my call was to tell you I'm taking a little bit of time away from the gallery and going up to stay with Dad for a week or so. If there are any problems with the house, you have your key, right?'

'I do. Are you going alone?'

Kitty caught the suggestive tone to her question.

'Yes, I am going alone. Now sod off.' She laughed, wiping away the last of her tears. 'I'll call you when I'm back.'

'Love you! Safe travels!'

'Love you too.' Kitty ended the call and looked at the open suitcase on her bed. She listened to the quiet of the house and pictured Theo sitting in the chair by the fireplace with Gunner by his feet. Maybe Tizz was right. It *had* been nice to have company…

'Oh don't be ridiculous, Kitty. You are a grown bloody

woman, not a teenager.' She slammed the lid of her suitcase and zipped it up with more force than was necessary.

It was as she programmed the satnav and placed her handbag on the front seat of her Golf that she decided to give Theo a quick ring.

'How are you doing? Settled back home okay?'

'Yes.' He took a breath. 'I still don't like it here, but I feel able to cope, which is progress, I guess.'

'It is! Massive progress. Be kind to yourself, Theo. Be patient. You've been through a lot, you have to give yourself time.'

'Yup. I was thinking I wish I hadn't taken early retirement. It seemed like a good idea when I wanted to spend my days at home, but now...'

'You need a project.'

'Yes, I do.' He sniffed. 'A project.'

'Anyway, I shan't keep you.' She glanced at the clock. She needed to leave soon to avoid the London rush hour. 'Just wanted to let you know I'm going up to Scotland to stay with my dad for a week or so.'

'Oh, how are you getting up there?'

'I'm driving.'

'Driving? That's some road trip. Well, be careful, won't you. Take it steady.'

She liked the note of concern in his reaction. 'I will. I've done it a million times and I stop in the same three places for coffee, the loo and a nap.'

'Sounds like you have it down to a fine art.'

'I do.' She nodded. 'Call any time, Theo, if things get you down or you just want to talk. I know Sophie's around, but it can't do any harm to have me as a back-up to her and Spud.'

'Thanks, Kitty. I think I might set a fire. It's chilly tonight.'

'Yes. Well, night-night, Theo. And, look, if you get lonely, come up to Darraghfield. Come to Scotland!' She felt the sting of embarrassment on her cheeks, as if she had overstepped a mark. She bit her thumb, silently cursing Tizz for her stupid and fanciful suggestions that had undoubtedly influenced her offer. *Idiot.*

'Thank you,' he replied coolly.

What was I thinking? As she indicated out of her street and onto the Hare and Billet Road, she turned up the radio and sang loudly, 'If I could turn back time...'

Kitty pulled the shoulder of lamb from the Aga and placed it on the stained cork tablemat in the centre of the kitchen table. She stood still and looked at her dad, who sat at the head of the table, his beard thinner and now peppered with grey, his face a little gaunt, but his demeanour calm.

'God, Dad, after all this time, I was counting in my head three plates, three sets of cutlery...'

'I know.' He looked skywards. 'I still do it. I chat to her during the day, just the odd thing here and there, telling her what I might have for breakfast or if Patrick's called with any of his news. And I talk about the photos that Ruraigh and Hamish send of the kids and of course I keep her up to date with all that Soph and Olly get up to.' He smiled at her, his wonderful crinkly eyes almost closing, as if giving thanks, his look confirming that his grandchildren, indeed his family, were still his greatest joy. 'These chats I have with her are so real, so relevant that when I pop the kettle on, I often grab two mugs...'

'Has it not got any easier, Dad? Do you miss her as much

now as you always did? I ask because my friend Theo has just lost his Anna.'

'Sophie's Theo?'

'Yes.'

Again, she felt the desire to say that had he not been *her* Theo to start with then there would not have been a Sophie! She was unsure why this bothered her so much.

Her dad dipped the big spoon into the peas and sage-buttered carrots, loading a healthy heap onto his plate. 'A terrible business. Sophie sounded so upset when I spoke to her. She loved Anna.' He used the big spoon to dive into the crispy tatties; she'd cooked them in goose fat, just as Marjorie had shown her more years ago than she cared to remember.

'We all did. She was a wonderful woman.'

Her dad nodded. He watched her intently as she placed two thick slices of soft lamb onto his plate. She added another and another and it was only then, with the mountain of food in front of him, that he raised his palm to indicate 'when'. He smothered the food with dark, glossy gravy from the white gravy boat.

'It has got easier.' He piled up his fork. 'And at first I felt guilty that it had, as though I should stay in some permanent state of mourning to show how devoted I was to her.' He put the food into his mouth and chewed with slow appreciation.

'And then?'

'And then...' He swallowed. 'I realised that I could still love her, still miss her, but I could also carry on with life. That's it. It was that simple for me.'

'I miss Mum too.'

'I know, hen.' He smiled at her and then turned his attention back to the lamb. 'I've never met Theo. That's strange for me, being that he's Sophie's dad.'

'I guess it is strange. It's a funny old relationship really. I've known him since my first day at Vaizey and yet I feel as if I'm only just getting to know him now. He came to stay with me in Blackheath—'

'Yes, Olly told me.'

'It was nice, odd in a way, because we've never spent that much time alone, but nice.'

'And what's his Lordship up to?'

'Oh, you know, Dad, had a falling out with Nikolai by all accounts, but I think that's just how it is. They seem happy, volatile – maybe that's passion, who knows?'

'Hmmmf.' He forked more food into his mouth. 'I wish I'd had the confidence to voice what my instincts were telling me.'

'Oh, Dad, not that again.' She'd lost count of the times they'd raked over this.

Stephen rested his knife and fork on the edge of the plate and finished his mouthful. 'The thing that makes me so mad, Kitty, is that you didn't get the life you deserved. Who knows where you might have ended up or with whom?'

'I can't think like that, Dad, or I'd drive myself crazy! I have to think about what I do have – the kids, my lovely home, my friends, my job in the gallery…'

'Yes, but what I wanted for you was all that and more. I wanted you to move up here and take over Darraghfield. I wanted you to know a love like the one your mother and I shared! God, she made every day worth waking for, even the bad ones. I never lost the wonder of how someone like her could love someone like me! Never.'

He placed his hand on his chest as if heartburn had bitten. And just like that, Kitty's appetite flew out of the window and whistled down the glen. She looked at his expression and knew that despite his words, living without the woman he had so loved was anything but simple.

Four days in and there was something about waking in her childhood bedroom that made her feel happy, encased in the soft surroundings that had nurtured her. She might have more years behind her than ahead, but when at Darraghfield she shrugged off many of her worries, slept soundly, put the minutiae of life out of her mind and reverted to her carefree childhood self, treading barefoot over the wooden floors and dusty flagstones.

She stretched and looked out of the window at the rising sun, an idea forming.

'Where are you off to?' her dad asked as he cut the loaf on the breadboard ready for toast. The jam pot, marmalade and butter dish were already on the breakfast table.

'I'm off for a swim!'

'I hope it's warm enough.'

'It'll be great.' Gathering her bathrobe around her and with her towel in one hand, she pulled on some old tennis shoes she found in the boot room and trotted down the gravel path, over the shrub border, across the patch of grass and through the narrow gap in the laurel hedge. Even at her age, this narrow gap still felt like a secret. Throwing her towel onto one of the wicker steamer chairs, she paused, taking in the perfect vista as she stood on the edge with her long, pale toes curled around the curved lip of the tiles. The sunlight danced on the surface as it shifted in the breeze and the Roman steps at the far end wobbled, distorted in their watery home.

Kitty bent her knees and angled her back slowly, ignoring the creak to her limbs, and just as her dad had shown her when she was no more than a girl, with her head tucked, arms level with her ears and hands reaching out, she leapt and pushed herself forward, feeling the immediate thrill of breaking the surface as the water rippled from her form. Working quickly, she propelled herself forward, hands slightly cupped, waggling her feet, moving at speed until her fingertips touched the opposite wall. She flipped around awkwardly and headed back, feeling the delicious pull of her ageing, aching muscles against the resistance of the water.

Eight, maybe ten lengths later and her breath came fast. She trod water and wriggled her finger first in one ear and then the other, then smoothed the droplets from her face with her wrinkled palm. She felt both peaceful and very much alive. The sun warmed her freckled skin and all was right with her world.

She lay on her back in a semi-doze as the water lapped at her ears. Lying like this turned the world into a quiet place, a refuge of sorts. Her stomach groaned and she pictured the breakfast she would eat: crispy bacon, shiny fried eggs peppered with sea salt, thickly buttered toast, maybe a roasted tomato or two...

She had no idea how long she stayed like that – minutes, an hour? Her hold on time was skewed, so lost was she to the water. But then, quite unexpectedly, she sensed a change to the shape of her world.

A dark shadow loomed between Kitty and the sunshine.

Slowly she opened her eyes to see a man standing on the poolside. He stood with his hands in his pockets, shirtsleeves rolled above the elbow. She blinked. Embarrassment made her right herself in the water. Ashamed that he'd seen her in a state of complete abandonment, her blush flared.

She stared at the man, who smiled at her, and felt the

unmistakable twist of joy in her heart at the very sight of him. She quite forgot she was wearing her swimming costume that was unflattering and bobbly in places. Truth was, she could barely think straight.

'Theo!' she called out, astonished and delighted in equal measure. 'Oh my God! Theo! You came!'

'It would appear so.' He smiled at her. 'It was only as the cab was dropping me off at the bottom of the drive that I considered the possibility that you might have only been being polite in inviting me. But here I am!' He raised his arms and let them fall.

'Not at all, it's lovely to see you!' she said with enthusiasm. 'Who's got Gunner?' She looked to his side, half expecting the lovely boy to come bounding through the hedge.

'Our niece, Kaylee. She has two young kids who just adore him, so he'll be spoilt rotten.'

'Lovely!' Kitty trod water and looked at the towel on the back of the steamer chair, wondering how she might retrieve it without revealing too much of her body.

'Can you grab my towel?' She nodded towards it and watched as he walked round to gather it into his hands.

'This is really some place!' His gaze swept the roofline of Darraghfield and then took in the enclosed area around the pool. He handed her the towel and continued to look up, out towards the garden, ever the gentleman.

Kitty hauled herself up out of the water and dried herself off before pulling her bathrobe on with relief. She ran her fingers through her hair, spraying water droplets around her in an arc.

'It is, isn't it? I never get sick of it. It's where I feel most at home.'

'I remember you saying as much when we were kids.' He

kicked the flat, warm stone of the pool edge. 'So this is where you tried to earn your gills?'

'Yes!' She laughed, remembering their conversations over the years. 'I love it here. This little spot right here, it's my favourite place on earth…' She smiled, displacing any potentially melancholic reflections. 'I was just thinking about breakfast. Are you hungry?'

'I am. I got the sleeper train but didn't do much sleeping!' He took in a full lung of fresh air.

The two walked back through the hedge, side by side.

'Dad!' she called out as she made her way through the wood-panelled corridors and across the hallway back to the kitchen, Theo now walking behind her. 'Dad, we have a guest!'

'Oh?' Stephen looked up from the breakfast table and stood quickly with his hand outstretched.

'Dad…' She paused. 'This is Theo. Theo Montgomery.'

'Well, I never did! Sophie's Theo?' He took Theo's hand warmly inside his and held the top of his arm with his left hand.

'Yes, Sophie's Theo.' Theo answered with something that sounded like relief, but his expression was one of pure pride. He clearly loved being Sophie's Theo, and Kitty felt none of the irritation from before.

'Well, I never did!' her dad repeated. 'And here you are! Sit down, sit down.' He pulled out a chair while Kitty filled the dented black enamel kettle and popped it onto the top of the Aga.

'That takes me back.' Theo stared at the kettle. 'When I was a kid, I used to hang around with the groundsman at school.' He smiled at Kitty's dad. 'He was to have a massive influence on my life, actually. And he had a kettle just like that. I've not thought about it for years until now.'

'Ours is as old as the hills, but I'd rather patch it up than fetch a new one. I think every celebration and commiseration over the last few decades has been marked by the setting of that very kettle on the stove. It contains all of our history.'

The two men stared at the Aga, as if both lost in their memories.

'Do you know Scotland?' Kitty's dad leant on the tabletop and Kitty was reminded how he came alive with company.

'My father used to come up every year to shoot. We'd stay up at Arbereekie.'

'Oh, I know it well!' Her dad spoke fondly, clearly delighted at the connection.

'I can't say I was a good shot; in fact I never got that far. The first time I saw the bird in the gundog's mouth, I cried – it seemed unfair. I was only a child, but I think I rather embarrassed the old man.' Theo laughed softly.

'Nothing to be embarrassed about there.' Her dad sat up straight. 'You have compassion and an affinity for nature, a love for it, well, that's important for anyone who wants to live close to the land. The respect, it's not something you can teach. Do you know my boys, my nephews, Ruraigh and Hamish?'

'I do indeed. They were a year or two above me at Vaizey. And of course those two years were like a lifetime when we were younger, but I see them from time to time, usually with Sophie, and that couple of years' difference was erased a long time ago.'

'It happens! We all end up the same age, we all end up old!' Stephen laughed and banged the table.

'Speak for yourself!' Kitty joined in, feeling, for the first time in an age, anything but old.

A quietness washed over them, as if they were all thinking of Anna, who had not had the chance to get old.

'I was very sorry to hear about the passing of your wife,' Stephen offered sincerely.

'Thank you.' Theo swallowed. 'I have days when I'm doing well and then others when it feels like it happened only yesterday.'

'Yes, well, I don't know if this helps or not, but I still feel that way, and my wife died many years ago now.'

'I remember Kitty talking about you both at school; she said you were like her best friends and I had never heard anything like it. Parents like friends…?' He shook his head. 'It was another world to me.'

'You weren't close to your own parents, Theo?'

'It was difficult. Or rather my dad was difficult. I don't think I was ever going to live up to his expectations or meet his high demands.' He looked at the floor.

'Well, goodness me, what a foolish man, if you don't mind me saying. And from the way my family talk about you, having the gift of a fellow like you for a son…?' Stephen shook his head. 'That's a thing most men can only dream of.'

Theo's face coloured at the compliment.

'It's good to finally meet you, Theo. Did you know his Lordship?'

'Dad!' Kitty rolled her eyes at Theo. 'He is referring to Angus, who, as you might have gathered, is still a sensitive subject.' She cracked eggs into the skillet, where a nub of lard had melted.

'I did. Again, not as friends, but our paths have crossed.'

'He was never straightforward, Theo. My wife used to say it.'

'Dad, please don't start with the shifty-eyed thing!'

Theo laughed. 'It can't have been easy for him.' He spoke softly. 'And Sophie loves him and that's everything, I guess.'

Stephen looked at Theo with fondness. 'As I said, you have compassion, Theo. That's no bad thing. And you look a chap straight in the eye!'

'Bacon?' Kitty yelled, wary of the conversation straying into areas that might make some or all of them uncomfortable. 'Who wants bacon?'

It was a happy few days. Kitty tried and failed to interest Theo in the clay-pigeon shoot in the lower paddock and he made a ham-fisted attempt at catching a trout for the grill. Luckily, she and her dad were on hand to scoop up three fat examples, and these were sizzled on the barbecue until the beautiful skin was blackened and the flesh had turned a comforting shade of pale pink. Adding a squeeze of lemon, a chunk of soda bread, rips of lettuce and a large spoonful of buttered new potatoes, the trio feasted on them as the sun began to sink, eating from plates resting on their laps as they sat on the front patio with the glen stretching out below them as far as the eye could see.

'Can I get you another beer, Theo?' Stephen reached down into the slightly battered cooler by his side and plucked a pale bottle from the iced water.

'Thank you.' Theo stretched across and took the beer eagerly.

They all enjoyed each other's company and Kitty was pleased. It was good to see Theo becoming a little less tense and she found a new lightness in herself that made the world a happier place.

'I'm getting a tad chilly.' Stephen rubbed his arms. 'Think I might call it a night.'

Kitty stretched up to receive his kiss on her cheek as he left. She watched him walk slowly back into the house before pulling the tartan rug over her legs and zipping up her long-sleeved fleece. With the dropping sun, the temperature was indeed a little cool.

'You warm enough there, Theo?'

'Yep.' He pulled on his jersey before taking the other rug and tucking it over his lap.

'I feel a bit woozy.' She sipped her fourth glass of white and gave a little laugh.

'Can't think why.' He eyed her glass. 'Maybe that trout was a bit off?'

They both chuckled.

'Nothing wrong with the trout.' She sighed.

The two enjoyed a comfortable silence between topics. It was a nice state of being.

'I remember you telling me you'd been fishing before, the day Soph and I saw you at Vaizey. You said you'd hated it.'

He reached up and ran his hand under the collar of his shirt. 'I still wear this fishing fly that Mr Porter gave me. It reminds me of him and all he taught me.' He swallowed. 'But yes, you're right. I'm sorry to say that the actual fishing was not for me.'

'You were fond of him.'

'I was, very. I know it was different for you, but school was a tough time for me. It shaped me, and a lot of the hurt was so ingrained, I couldn't let it go—'

'There's something I want to tell you, Theo,' she interrupted.

'Oh?'

'I was there the day of the big fight in the quad.' A look of surprise and embarrassment crept over his face. 'I was behind one of the pillars – I'd just arrived back after the summer break.' She drew breath. 'I didn't know what to do, didn't know how to help. It was horrible.'

'It was. Horrible.'

'I've never known how to mention it, but... I understand

what you went through and I'm sorry. How did you put it behind you, that whole horrible time?' She sat forward, sincere.

Theo took a deep breath. 'Anna taught me how. Also, I eventually faced up to my tormentor and, weirdly enough, we became quite good friends—'

'Wilson?' She cut in again, disbelieving.

'Yes, Wilson. Magnus. I gave him a job.'

'You did?'

'Yes. We worked well together for years. We actually had quite a lot in common.'

She let the gentle breeze flow over her, lifting her hair from her face. 'I am glad you came up.'

'Me too.'

'It's weird, isn't it...'

'What's weird?' He took a swig from the bottle.

'Us. Here I am with this guy who was my friend at school, no more, who ended up being the dad to my precious girl – *our* precious girl,' she corrected. 'We've been in each other's lives for a long time – we just kind of fell in together, didn't we?'

'I guess we did.'

'I always felt okay if you were around, Theo, especially at school.'

'I can relate to that.' He smiled. 'I was pretty smitten with you for a long time – until Anna, really.'

'I think I probably knew that, and that day when we met, the Sophie day, when we went for coffee and then the pub, I was so happy to see you. It was the first time I had the tiniest flicker of doubt over marrying Angus. And I know how bad that sounds, but it's true. I had this little sliver of reflection, a "what if" moment. But I buried it. And the rest, as they say, is history.'

'I guess we all have those regrets, those "what if" moments.

Since losing Anna, I've often wished I could go back to the start of our marriage and do things differently.'

'In what way?'

His gaze dropped. 'I wasn't always as emotionally present as I could have been, not in the beginning.'

'Emotionally present? Is this your ex therapist speaking?'

'Yes.' He laughed and she liked his honesty.

He looked out at the big Highlands sky. 'We had a rough start. Anna was terribly keen for us to have kids, I denied her that and… and that will haunt me forever. Then she found out about Sophie in a way that was very hurtful to her, and… we spent some time apart.' His voice got wobbly, but he collected himself and continued. 'But then we came to our senses and kind of settled into each other. We had everything we wanted – a simple life with our dog Griff, and then Molly, who was a lovely puppy, and then Gunner. Everything except kids.'

Kitty finished her glass and reached for the bottle of wine by her side. 'It's sad you didn't get to adopt in the end.'

'It is, but Anna came to dearly love being part of Sophie's life. Her role as second mum was one of her most cherished.'

Kitty smiled; she knew this.

'And she had our niece, Kaylee, who's now a mum herself. And her godsons, the twins from St Lucia, now both grown-up, of course, both lawyers with their own practice in New York. Lovely boys. Who I think you might have met?'

'Yes.'

'They all flocked to her, all of them. And it was enough, as the years went by. It satisfied her craving for motherhood. And we liked our time alone.'

'I don't think Angus and I ever liked our time alone. He was always a little on edge, as if he needed to be elsewhere, and that unease was quite infectious. He made me jumpy.'

'Your dad is still mad with him and I understand that. If someone led Sophie along like that…'

'I get it too.' There was really nothing more Kitty wanted to say on the topic.

'I could never have cheated on Anna. My dad was a serial philanderer and it still punches me in the gut if I think about his behaviour.'

'Because you are a good man, Theo.'

'So people tell me. I don't know about that, but I know that when Anna and I started out I was selfish, so selfish.' He shook his head.

'You can't keep beating yourself up, Theo. Not forever.'

'And yet you still reflect on how Angus was dishonest or, at the very least, selfish. I think we both agree that you owe it to your spouse to be open about the grand plan, about what you're hoping for out of the marriage. Otherwise it's not fair: one leads and the other gets dragged along, hoping they can stay upright on the path that only one of you can see…'

'I guess so. And yes, if that's how it is, then it's bloody selfish!' she said frostily.

There was an awkward silence.

'Sorry, Theo, I shouldn't have said that. I just get angry when I remember what it felt like to know I'd been "dragged along", as you put it.'

He looked over at her. 'Do you think less of me, if that's what I did to Anna?'

'Yes, a little bit. She was so wonderful, open, kind.'

He sighed and gave a small nod. 'I hate myself for having done those things. I hate my weakness, my deceit and most of all I hate the hurt I caused.'

Kitty stayed quiet.

'I was afraid, so afraid. Cowardly, really. I should have listened to her.'

'But you didn't.'

'No, I didn't. Her constant attempts at reassurance just messed with my head and I know she... she deserved better, much better.'

'We all do.' Kitty wrapped her arms around her trunk, trying to ward off the chill that was creeping into her bones. The sob that left her chest was quite unexpected, and it was followed by a steady torrent of tears that were one part sadness, two parts Chardonnay.

'Oh, Kitty, don't cry.' He reached over and took her hand.

She liked the feeling of her hand curled in his warm palm. She liked it very much. It was rare to feel the joy of human contact. Slipping from her chair, she came to kneel in front of him and laid her head on the tartan blanket that covered his knees.

'Sometimes, if I let myself think about everything, it all feels too much,' she whispered hoarsely.

He leant forward and she felt the touch of his palm against her scalp. Her tears continued to fall, her sadness anchoring them to the spot.

'Don't cry,' he whispered. 'Please don't cry. I hate to see you so sad. Talk to me.'

She shook her head. It was too hard to put into words the real reason for her tears. *Lost moments, wasted years, and love... The love I have had, the love I have been denied and the love I have lost.*

'Theo?' she said softly.

'Yes?'

'Would you mind if we didn't talk? Would it be okay if we just sat like this for a minute?'

His hand resting on her made her feel peaceful, in the way that a sincere human touch often did.

'Sure we can.' He ran his thumb up under her sleeve and over the kink in her left arm.

After a while, she sat back on her haunches and looked up at him. She stared at her lifelong friend and one-time lover and wondered if he, like her, felt ripples of longing pulsing through him.

'I like being with you, Theo. I have always liked being with you and I have this feeling that is scary and yet wonderful. And it's because of you.'

Theo looked up sharply, then focused his gaze on the horizon, which shimmered in the moonlight. To Kitty it seemed like an age before he answered.

'I... I never thought you might feel that way about me, Kitty.' There was another unnervingly long pause. 'Lord knows, I wished for it long enough throughout school and long after, but...'

'But?' There was a hard edge to her voice and she could sense her tears building.

'I think...' The slow nature of his delivery was maddening to her. 'I think I am so bound up in Anna, my love for Anna, my loss of Anna... It's all I can see.' He shrugged, as if it were that simple, and she could see that for him, of course, it was.

He rose suddenly, as if stung, and she recoiled in horror.

'Theo! I'm sorry, I didn't—'

He raised his palm, halting her mid sentence, dropped the tartan blanket onto the chair and strode purposefully across the lawn, disappearing inside Darraghfield.

Moving Home

Kitty grabbed three chocolate digestives, a most inadequate yet delicious afternoon snack, and made her way up the stairs. She decided to tackle the books on the shelves on the top landing. With the empty box by her feet, she began to pack volumes into the base. She knew she had way too many books, but the idea of throwing them away was utterly ridiculous. She'd find space for them one way or another.

She lifted three Anita Shreve novels, which she'd read time and time again, and out fell a birthday card she'd secreted inside one of them. It was handmade, with a large heart on the front. She recognised Oliver's handiwork. Opening it up, she read: *happy birday mummy I love you.* It made her smile, this precious thing. She decided to put it to one side to show him; his spelling wasn't that much better now.

Someone had once said to her that life was like a whirlpool, that the older you got, the faster it spun, until finally you were sucked into the central abyss and disappeared for good. Kitty laughed as she recalled this now; despite how melancholic and dramatic it sounded, it also felt true! She sat down on the carpet with her back against the wall and thought about the year just passed.

Angus was doing well after having had a cancerous growth removed from his throat. It had been a terrible shock, a terrible worry of course. But the chemo seemed to have done the trick and everyone was mightily thankful that he was on the mend. It amused her that his biggest concern was the rather unsightly scar on his neck, which he was convinced spoilt his profile. It didn't – he was as handsome as ever.

It was a strange thing, but out of the bad had come some good. Angus seemed to have lightened up a bit and Kitty felt a new fondness for him. His illness had reminded her that no matter what had occurred between them, he'd been a major part of her life since she was fourteen and that was to be treasured. It had also shone a spotlight on Angus's relationship with Nikolai and they had finally called it a day. Kitty didn't have anything against Nikolai, but she really, really liked Richard. He seemed good for Angus, a sensible head on young shoulders who was teaching Angus to stick two fingers up to the world and to go about life with confidence. She resumed her book packing and chuckled to herself, trying to imagine what it must have been like when Richard was introduced to Mr and Mrs Tupperware; now for that, she wished she could have been a fly on the wall.

Fourteen

'Can you believe it – Sophie engaged!'

'I can, and we do love Greg,' Tizz cooed.

'Oh, we do!' Kitty beamed.

Tizz fanned her chest with a placemat she had grabbed from the table. 'Is it me or is it hot in here?' She exhaled through full cheeks.

'It's you, honey.' Kitty smiled at her. The function room of the Crown and Sceptre pub was pleasantly warm.

'God, Kitty, it's driving me crazy! Ru is freezing at home. I only have two temperature settings: Arctic chilly or the burning fires of Hades. I have to have all the windows open or I literally feel like I am going to boil. He is constantly closing them and I go nuts and reopen them immediately. I fling the duvet off about fifty times a night and then grab it back. The neighbours must think we're crackers, shrieking at each other about the bloody temperature! I mean, the man could commit adultery, sell my jewels (if I had any), buy a Porsche, and I'd be like, meh, but he puts the heating up and I turn into the Hulk!'

Kitty bent over laughing and decided not to confess that she seemed to be escaping quite lightly by comparison.

'It'll get better, honestly.'

'So people tell me, but when? Daisy-Belle and Verity call my outbursts a mumapause moment. Good God, Kitty, my rages even have a name!' She tutted. 'I am considering going to live in Antarctica or somewhere equally as cold. Norway!'

'Oh, don't do that.' Kitty ran her eye over the buffet table in the corner of the room and arranged the breadsticks in the glass vase, which made the perfect holder. 'I've heard Oslo is glorious, but I would really miss you!'

'I'd miss you too. Flo said you've cut your hours at the gallery?'

'Yes, it's not the same with the new owners. I mentioned the other day that I saw a big print I rather liked in Ikea – oh my word, you should have seen the look of disdain that John, the husband, gave me! It was too funny. I'm going to buy it for him for Christmas, for sure!'

'Oh, you must.' Tizz paused. 'So how do you feel about seeing Theo?'

Kitty felt the jump in her chest as her heart skipped. It had been a year since the evening up at Darraghfield when things had got a little out of hand, with her words slipping off a wine-gilded tongue and him letting his guard down. She shivered with regret, as she did every time she thought about that night. The prospect of seeing him tonight petrified and thrilled her in equal measure.

'I don't know how I feel really. I'm nervous, of course. I mean, we have had some contact – Soph has sent messages of hello and the usual health enquiries back and forth between us, but it all feels a little awkward.' She smoothed her hair from her face. 'Anyway, this is not about me, and it's not about Theo. It's about our girl.'

They both looked towards Sophie, who was standing by the door in her pale green silk wrap-dress and grown-up shoes, her arm resting against her beau, greeting their guests with a sweet smile and a welcome hug.

'Is she pregnant?'

'No!' Kitty tutted. 'Not that I would mind if she was, quite the opposite, but why would you think that?'

'Just wondered why now? I mean, she's glowy and her and Greg have been together for centuries.'

'She's glowy, Tizz, because she's happy. They've been saving up and busy with the house and all that, and I guess now feels like the right time.' She felt a little flutter of happiness at the prospect of a baby, but it was highly unlikely. Sophie had career plans and a baby was a few years away yet, if ever.

'Here come the boys.' Tizz turned away from the door and pulled a face.

Kitty looked up in time to see Angus and Richard make a grand entrance. It was strange to her that her family continued to harbour animosity towards her ex. She understood it was them being protective, but she disliked the fact that Angus as 'a target' had become a thing. She let her eyes sweep over him and noted that he was as ever, his usual fastidious and attractive self, handsome no matter that the years advanced. He looked dapper in a new suit probably bought for the occasion.

Out of the corner of her eye she saw Hamish lean in and speak to Ruraigh from behind his cupped palm and guessed that he might be making an unfavourable comment about Angus. She wasn't having that. Rushing across the room, she walked forward and swept her ex into a hug, kissing him on the cheek before doing the same to Richard.

'Engaged! Can you believe it?' She linked arms with both men and steered them towards the buffet.

'I know! I feel so old.' Angus grimaced. 'I still think of her as a baby.'

'Angus, you will never be old, not to me. You will always be that gorgeous floppy-haired boy who was as smart as he was gorgeous. Don't you think so, Richard?'

'I do.' He nodded. Looking at Angus with such affection it again sent a flare of loneliness through her core.

They made small talk, marvelling at Sophie's poise and commenting on how fond they were of Greg. It was a relief that they all liked her man. Kitty could only imagine what it must have been like for her parents, watching her hitch her wagon to someone they instinctively knew fell short in the devotion stakes. She felt the inevitable twinge of guilt that when her mum had had more than enough to deal with, she'd had to cope with that too.

'I don't know why, but I was just thinking about Marjorie's wedding cake!' She laughed.

Angus turned to Richard and placed a hand on his arm, affectionately. 'I'll have to try and dig out a photo. Marjorie was already getting on when she made our wedding cake. And, well, let's just say it was less than magazine perfect.'

'It was positively wonky!' Kitty giggled. 'With great blobs of mismatched icing shoved on to cover the gaps, but she was oh so proud of it!'

'We did the full cake-cutting thing with a sword, no less.' He nodded at her. 'And we thanked Marjorie and she beamed.'

'Oh, she did.' Kitty smiled fondly at the memory of the woman she had so loved. 'I wish she could see Sophie today, grown-up and so gorgeous. My mum, too, of course. Are your parents coming?'

'No.' Angus rolled his eyes. 'I think Mum felt the journey was a bit much just for an evening and of course there was the expense.'

'Of course,' she said with a wry smile. 'It is a long way for them. Plus I seem to remember that Friday night is Tupperware-sorting night.'

'For the love of God, let it go, Kitty!' They both laughed.

Busying herself at the buffet, handing out plates and napkins, Kitty heard Theo's unmistakeable voice before she saw him. In an instant she was transported back to that beautiful bright Highlands morning a year ago.

It was the morning after the night before, and she'd sat up slowly in her bed, rubbing her eyes and cursing her throbbing headache. She'd made her way downstairs. Her dad was at the table, already demolishing his fried eggs on toast.

'He's gone.' He spoke without looking up, his tone almost angry, as if he in some way blamed her and was not in the least bit happy about whatever had caused this.

'Gone?' Her voice was gravelly, tiny rocks of regret in her throat.

'Aye, taxi first thing. Away back to London.'

She had sunk down into the chair at the top of the table and laid her head on her raised knees as her tears fell, her loss all-consuming.

But this was not the time to dwell; this was Sophie and Greg's party. Tousling her roots with her fingertips, she sucked in her tummy and painted on a smile, turning slowly. At the sight of him, her smile became genuine. He looked… he looked fresher, younger and very much as if the weight of grief that had bowed him so completely had gone. Her joy turned to embarrassment, as, rather than acknowledge her, he turned and headed straight for the bar.

What did you expect, Kitty? You made a fool of yourself and you embarrassed him. You blew it!

'Where are you sneaking off to?' Tizz called after her as she opened the French windows at the back of the room.

'I'm not sneaking off! Just going for a bit of fresh air. You of all people should understand the desire to cool down!' She spoke with a joviality she certainly didn't feel; she needed to put some distance between herself and Sophie's party in case she was unable to stem her tears.

She leant her arms on the brick wall and looked out over the rooftops of East Dulwich. There was something quite beautiful about the dark silhouette of chimneys, aerials and treetops sitting against the inky south London twilight. She felt like this sometimes, like everyone in the world was clinking a glass and snuggling up with someone they loved, and it made her feel so alone. Not that she *needed* anyone – she didn't, and she wasn't even sure she *wanted* someone – but on occasion the loneliness bit regardless.

'I thought I'd grab you a drink. You look like you're miles away.'

She turned round in surprise.

Theo stepped out onto the small terrace and pushed the door closed with his foot, before handing her a glass of fizz.

'I was.' She took the drink from him.

'Where were you – somewhere nice, I hope?'

'Timbuktu.' She laughed, annoyed at the tearful wobble in her voice.

'It's a big day.' He gave her the justification for her tears. 'Sophie seems happy.'

'She really is. Greg's lovely, isn't he?'

'Yep. He's cooking supper at my place next week, his famous grapefruit, orange and fish surprise, which sounds intriguing – you have to come.'

'I'd like that very much.' It felt odd to her that Sophie and

Greg had a relationship with Theo that excluded her, but to be invited to join them was a welcome thing. 'Are you not drinking?' She was embarrassed at how glad she was of the Dutch courage she'd so swiftly knocked back.

'No, I'm driving. I didn't know if I might need to make a hasty exit. Truth is, it's been a while and I was worried about seeing you again, Kitty.' He walked forward and stood next to her, looking out over the city in the dying embers of the day.

'Me too.'

'A lot has gone on since Darraghfield and I'm not sure I was the most polite houseguest. I left rather hurriedly and would hate to have offended Stephen. How's he doing?'

Kitty shook her head and pictured her lovely dad, now with a permanent nurse/housekeeper in residence, who wasn't a patch on Marjorie, as he regularly reminded her. 'He's okay, and you didn't. I think it's me who should apologise. I never meant to offend you. Not for the world! And I'm sorry if I did. I have cringed over my actions a thousand times since. Call it a moment of madness.'

He inhaled slowly. 'It was nothing you did or said. It was me. My head was all over the place, still is really, but much less so.'

'That's kind of you to say, but I know...' She ran out of words, feeling the blush on her cheeks at the memory of how he had almost literally run from her.

'I felt...' He turned to face her. 'I felt so guilty because for a second, just for a split second, I forgot about Anna and I thought about you. And I never want to forget about her.'

Kitty's breath caught in her throat. The two stood in silence as the significance of his words sank in.

'Of course! Oh my God, Theo, of course!' She covered her face with her hands, 'God, I can't bear to have this conversation with you. It's horrible. You don't have to say that – I know it. Darling Anna, I know it...'

'Hey, you two!'

Kitty whipped around to look at Sophie, who was calling to them from the doorway.

'We're thinking about doing a speech or two and we don't want to start without you both there to listen.'

'We'll be right in, darling!' There it was again, the false brightness she could summon in an instant.

'I don't want you to feel that way, Kitty. As I said, it wasn't you—'

'Can we talk about it later, please?' She headed for the door, her tone a little curt.

She found a spot in the middle of the crowd, and watched with pride as her daughter spoke with great composure. An arm snaked around her waist and she was delighted to see that Olly had arrived and had chosen to stand by her side.

'You're late!' she whispered.

'Yep.' He nodded and supped his pint, as if it was to be expected.

Everyone's attention was on Sophie as she continued. 'I always thought that you get the people in your life that you are meant to have, particularly as you get older.' She paused and looked from face to face. 'I've been very lucky to have the most incredibly supportive family: Mum, Dad-Angus, Dad-Theo, Anna, Olly, my uncles Ruraigh and Hamish, Tizz and Flo, the whole gang...' She smiled. 'And I thought I had all the people I needed, thought I had enough. And then I met Greg.'

There was a collective murmur of 'Aaah' and 'How lovely!', along with the odd sniff. 'I met him and I liked him and I loved him and I know I always will. And I couldn't be more excited about spending the rest of my life with him. We wanted to get everyone together tonight to celebrate our engagement, and also something else.'

Kitty looked at Angus, then Theo and all looked equally perplexed.

Greg took the floor. 'Yes. Do we have any knitters in the room?'

A hush came over them all as Sophie beamed at the crowd in front of her. 'I'm having a baby!' She jumped up and down on the spot.

'Oh my God!' Kitty kissed Olly before rushing forward, almost blinded by the fog of tears. 'Soph!' She took her girl into her arms. 'This is just wonderful! Wonderful!' She turned to Theo and Angus, who, along with the rest of the laughing, crying crowd, were raising a toast.

Tizz grinned at Kitty. 'Told you!' she mouthed. 'Glowy!' She whirled circles on her cheek with her fingertip and laughed.

It was a wonderful evening and Kitty knew she would not forget it. *A baby!* It was the best thing imaginable. Her excitement came in waves and she couldn't wait to call her dad and give him the news.

'How are you getting home?' Theo asked as he slipped his arms into his linen jacket, interrupting her thoughts.

'Oh, I'll grab a cab.'

'Let me drive you.'

'No! It's out of your way. Plus Olly might be coming home, so it'll be two of us.'

'That's fine. I have more than two seats.' He smiled. 'Olly, are you coming back to Blackheath? I've said I'll drive your mum.'

'Oh, cheers, Theo, but no, early start for me tomorrow, plus I said I might pop in on a friend.' He coughed.

'Oh! A *friend*!' Kitty giggled.

'She's called Victoria and I like her. I like her a lot.'

'Well, that's wonderful! I am happy, Olly!' She beamed at her boy as she grabbed her bag. They spent an age saying their goodbyes.

Kitty had to admit it felt nice to be driven. Driven by Theo. His fancy-pants car purred through Dulwich as she reclined in the leather seat that cocooned her. 'Our baby is having a baby!'

'She is.'

'Theo, we're going to be grandparents!' She howled her laughter. 'Oh my word... Grandpa Theo!'

'I don't know what to do with a baby. They absolutely terrify me.'

It was a stark reminder that his daughter had only arrived in his life in her early teens.

'You'll be a natural.' She studied his profile. 'I wonder what it'll be, a little boy or girl...'

'It's exciting, isn't it?' He smiled at her.

'It really is. Do you think we should put their name down for Vaizey the moment they're born? Sixth generation on your side, is that right?'

'Something like that.' He sat up straight and gripped the wheel. 'I think we should let the little thing go somewhere it can flourish.'

'Sophie loved it. Olly too. And I did, really. I mean, I was lonely at times, of course, but it shaped my whole life. I met you. I met Angus. And it was always such a big part of Ruraigh and Hamish's life.'

'It shaped me too, but not in a good way.' He blinked rapidly. 'I'm going to tell you something that I don't tell many people.'

She sat up and twisted in her seat to look at him.

'Do you remember Alexander Beaufort? Xander. A prefect in Theobald's.'

She closed her eyes and pictured the boy. 'Yes, I do. Tall, quite nice-looking, went out with Johanna van Stroother who was in my house. That's really funny, I haven't thought about either of them for years and I didn't know I remembered them until you said their names.'

'Well, he's my brother.'

Kitty laughed. 'He's your *brother*? What do you mean?' She looked at him quizzically.

'My father was his father – different mums. I was the only one who didn't know about the situation, they kept me in the dark until I was in my thirties, but apparently Xander knew, even at school. Never said a word.'

'That's insane!' She tried and failed to imagine her parents keeping news like this from her. It would feel devastating.

'I know.' He sucked his lip.

'Do you… do you ever see him?'

Theo shook his head. 'No. No contact ever. I half expected him to come to my father's funeral, but he didn't. I sometimes wish he had, a chance to clear the air and all that.'

'Why don't you contact him?'

'For what purpose?' He glanced at her, then back at the road.

'I don't know! To clear the air, as you put it? It just seems weird that you know he's your brother and yet you don't know him.'

'Christ, Kitty, there was so much weird about my upbringing, this pales into insignificance.'

'We all have them, you know—'

'What?'

'Those dark corners of our life which we choose not to illuminate, things that we bury.' She cleared her throat. 'My mum, my lovely mum... She suffered with mental illness all her life, and I'm not entirely certain, but I think she took her own life. My dad thinks he's shielding me by keeping the details vague and I don't want to distress him by bringing it up. It's complicated.'

'Oh, Kitty! That must have been so tough on you.'

'I kept my mum's illness a secret at school because my dad did at home, at least for a while. It wasn't a shame thing, it was more that he thought if he didn't talk about it, then it wouldn't be real, we could all pretend. And he didn't want Mum to hear the words, the diagnosis, in case it made her feel afraid or diminished her. He loved her so much.'

'I can't imagine how hard that must have been for him.' He spoke softly as the car idled at traffic lights. 'I remember you coming back to school with tales of things you'd got up to with your parents. I was always very envious. Mine were so remote.'

'Often it was just me and my dad, and that was fine. He's always been wonderful, but Mum hiding away in her room or, worse, coming downstairs and floating around like a ghost, it was a pressure and a sadness all in one. We were all pretending and it was exhausting.'

'I guess everyone pretends some of the time. I used to sit and watch you in class, laughing at the things you said, trying to show an interest when you spoke about Angus, but it killed me inside. I used to lie awake in Theobald's thinking about all the things you'd said, feeling sick to my stomach.'

She stared at his handsome profile and felt a punch of sadness for the teenage Theo. 'I wasn't aware of that – not really.' She wished she had understood, hoped she'd been kind.

'I know. I don't blame you, of course not, but it wasn't easy.'

They continued the rest of the journey in silence, alone with the ghosts of their secrets. Theo eventually pulled up outside her house.

'Are you coming in for a coffee?'

'Bit late for coffee.' They both looked at the digital display on the dashboard.

'I have herbal tea?'

Kitty put the key in the front door and scanned the hallway and sitting room, regretting not having run the vacuum cleaner over the floorboards and tidied away the newspapers that littered the rug.

Theo walked into the lounge and turned to her. 'It feels a like a lifetime ago that I came to stay here with Gunner.'

She placed her keys in the china bowl on the table and shrugged her arms free of her coat.

The sitting room was dark but for the golden glow coming through the plantation blinds and casting its stripey light on the floor and furnishings.

It would have been hard to say, with hindsight, exactly who moved first. How it happened. Who initiated and who followed. Not that those details would matter. The fact was, the two came together. Theo and Kitty, kissing with the ferocity of those who had known abstinence and loneliness, their arms wound tightly around each other, separating only to remove outer layers of clothing, running palms over skin that was warm and known to them yet still excitingly unfamiliar.

'Oh my God, Theo,' she whispered as she kissed him, as her heart thudded and her pulse raced, 'here we go again.'

He laughed as he lifted her and the two fell onto the sofa.

⋆

Kitty woke and for a split second wondered why she was on the sofa and not upstairs in her room. This was followed by the realisation that her head was resting on Theo's chest.

'Is this where you jump up, tell me you have to be somewhere and disappear for a decade or two?' He smiled, still with his eyes closed. 'I mean, you do have form.'

'You are not funny!' She scowled at him.

'I am a bit funny,' he countered.

'Actually, I was going to jump up and make a pot of coffee and heat up some stale croissants, but you can forget it.' She pulled the throw that usually lived on the back of the sofa over her bare legs.

'Oh, stale croissants sound wonderful.'

She liked the feel of his slightly rough palm running over her back. Her skin still aglow with the feeling he elicited in her, which she could only liken to electricity that sparked desire in her unfelt since that glorious afternoon all that time ago...

'Or...' He sighed. 'We could walk into Blackheath and have a forage for *not*-stale croissants and fancy fruit for a salad, and we could come back and have a proper breakfast?'

'Okay.' She answered with measured nonchalance, smiling at him.

My Theo...

'Try not to overwhelm me with your enthusiasm – you don't want me feeling confident or anything like that.'

'It's not that, Theo. I'm... I'm scared.' She sat up, pulling the throw with her to cover her chest.

He placed his arm behind his head and looked at her. 'I'm scared too. It took me a lot of years to erase the hurt I felt, to cope with the rejection after what happened between us, and this feels risky. My heart and my ego are both fragile. Life has messed me up, Kitty.'

Kitty thought of the moment she saw Thomas Paderfield reach up to adjust Angus's collar and how her whole life, her marriage, her future and her past, had seemed to disappear down a large black hole. 'Me too.'

'So what's the answer? Do you want to run? Because if you do, I'll understand. And I can be in my car within minutes and gone – all the way back to Barnes.'

'All the way back to Barnes?' She laughed. 'And then what? Set a date for thirty years' time so we can have sex again, as part of our thirty-year ritual?'

Theo laughed too. 'I hate to think about it, hate saying it even more, but in thirty years' time I'll be eighty! I might still be able to rustle up croissants and a fancy fruit salad, but sex might be off the menu.'

'Well, in that case, I suppose I'd better get it while I can. What are you grinning at?' She grabbed his arm.

Theo shook his head. 'I was just thinking that if my fourteen-, fifteen-year-old self had known that this was going to happen, well, I might have exploded.'

'In a good way?'

'Yes, Kitty, in a good way.'

Kitty felt bold, leaning forward to kiss his handsome face, as she lay back down next to him on the sofa. She felt alive! But most of all she felt happy. She hugged the man who was her knight in shining armour. It felt a lot like coming home.

Moving Home

Kitty pulled the cork from the bottle and poured a glass. She flopped down on the sofa and rested her feet on the coffee table. The walls were bare except for the boxes piled high against them, and the rug was propped in the corner; all of her belongings waiting to be shipped.

She lifted the glass in the air, raising a toast to the memories and ghosts which lurked in the very fabric. 'To new beginnings!' She took a sip.

She thought back to a night at Darraghfield shortly after Theo had left, sitting with her dad around the table in the kitchen warming themselves by the Aga. They had finished supper and now nursed cups of tea and buttered slices of fruit loaf.

He leant across the table and said, 'When I have seen you happy, Kitty, truly happy then I will go and join your mum.'

Kitty had become upset. 'Please don't say that, Dad, I can't bear to think about it. I can't imagine a world without my mum or my dad. No matter that I'm a grown-up, I don't always feel like one.'

'Ah that's the thing, darlin', none of us do.' He placed his hand over the back of hers. 'Never doubt that being your dad has been my greatest privilege.'

She sniffed the tears that gathered.

'But I miss her, you know, and I am tired, I think I am hanging on to see you settled.'

'I am settled, Dad. I'm fine.'

'Fine...' he smiled, 'that magic word that seems to calm a thousand worries. But I know you Kitty Dalkeith Montrose. I know there is more than "fine" and I know it is waiting for you.'

She raised her dad's hand and kissed the back of his palm.

She had travelled back to Blackheath and less than a week later, a crate of vintage red wine had arrived on her doorstep with the note that read, 'For my Kitty and new beginnings. Drink it when the time is right. Your Dad X.'

She took a sip and thought about him now, unable to stop the tears that fell.

Fifteen

Tizz nursed her crowded glass of Pimm's and stared at Kitty across the table in her back garden. Ruraigh was at work on the patio, his tongue poking from the side of his mouth as he tried to assemble the bedside cabinets they'd bought from Ikea. 'There must be bits missing!' he yelled, scratching his head. 'These instructions make no bloody sense.'

'Ignore him.' Tizz waved in his direction. 'He's busy and we can chat – and we *do* need to chat.'

'Why do I feel like I'm about to get grilled or told off?' Kitty sat with her hands clasped between her thighs.

'Because you are. Now, just to get this straight, you're telling me that you and Theo, Sophie's Theo...'

'My Theo, technically,' she whispered.

Tizz ignored her. '... you and Theo have been snogging the face off each other for the last six months, since that night at the Crown and Sceptre, and you are only telling me now?'

'Yes. We didn't want to tell anyone in case it was just a thing and not a proper thing.'

Tizz curled her top lip. 'So it's a proper thing now?'

'Uh-huh.' Kitty felt the swirl of teenage angst in her gut.

'And you're doing proper grown-up sex and everything?'

'Yep.' She nodded. 'And it's wonderful. When I'm with him, I feel like everything is okay. And I like how that feels. This relationship is like a gift that I had no right to expect. It's companionship, friendship... it's love! I didn't know it was waiting for me and I didn't know I was capable.' She looked up at her friend. 'As you know, I'd sort of assumed that I had this flaw when it came to giving and receiving love, and I figured that was why Angus picked me. Turns out I'm not flawed. I'm good at loving and being loved – in fact I'm great at it!'

Tizz gave her a long, hard stare. 'Oh, that'll wear off. Do the kids know?'

'Not yet.' She sighed. 'Please don't tell anyone. I don't want anyone to know until *they* do. Although I have told my dad,' she smiled recalling his joyful reaction, 'and he is absolutely over the moon. But with the kids, I can't seem to find the right time to tell them, but I know I need to. It's getting ridiculous. The other day, Olly called to see if I wanted to go to a fundraiser at the hospital with him and Victoria and I was reading on the sofa next to Theo. I ended the call and Theo's phone rang and it was Olly to ask him the exact same thing. I felt guilty he was having to pay for two calls.' She sipped her Pimm's.

'Yes, because *that* is what you need to feel guilty about, the cost of your son's mobile phone bill and not the fact that you are shagging his sister's dad, someone he knows and loves, and you are doing so in secret!' Tizz banged the table.

'Who's shagging who?' Ruraigh called from the patio.

'No one. Are those cabinets finished yet?' Tizz hollered back.

'No! I told you, I think there are bits missing. Bloody things.' He sounded quite exasperated.

'Useless.' Tizz tutted. 'So, you *are* going to tell the kids?'

'Yes, of course!' Kitty ran her fingers through her hair. 'And I need to tell them soon. Theo is thinking of selling his house in Barnes—'

'And moving in with you?' Tizz said loudly.

'Who's moving in with who?' Ruraigh called out.

Tizz rolled her eyes. 'Ignore him.'

'Yes. I mean, we're only talking about it, but we aren't getting any younger and the fact we're talking about it means I need to tell the kids.'

'Oh, you think? Or you could just make him hide in the wardrobe every time they come home. Leave a bottle of pop in there and some crisps so he is comfy. Christmas might be a bit of an issue though – the kids tend to stay for days and he can only sit in the dark for so long.'

'You are not funny!' Kitty laughed.

'You look great. You look happy.'

'I am.' She beamed at the admission. 'Properly happy.'

'I am glad for you, for you both. You deserve it.' Tizz squeezed her arm.

'Who deserves what?' Ruraigh came over to the table.

'Kitty and Theo are in love, they are doing sex and everything, and he is thinking of moving in with her.'

'I told you not to tell anyone!' Kitty shouted.

'I won't! But Ruraigh doesn't count!' Tizz flapped her hand.

'Thanks a bunch!' Ruraigh swigged from the beer bottle on the tabletop. 'I am not surprised, Kitty, and for what it's worth, I really like Theo, and so does Uncle Stephen, we all do.'

'Thank you, Ruraigh. That means a lot. And it will to him too.'

'So what do the kids think?' he asked casually.

She pulled a face. 'I haven't told them yet.'

'That's what we were talking about before you interrupted us,' Tizz said. 'And we need those cabinets, Ruraigh!' She banged the table top. 'You can't be out here building them in the dark!'

He lumbered back to the job in hand, scratching his head and turning the instruction sheet this way and that.

'I think he's struggling.' Kitty nodded in his direction.

'Well, he will without these.' Tizz pulled four large bolts from her pocket and placed them on the table.

'You are a terrible person!' Kitty chuckled.

'Who's a terrible person?' Ruraigh called, just out of earshot.

'No one!' they yelled in unison.

It was the following weekend and Kitty and Theo had made a plan of sorts. She was going to tell the kids and he would arrive a bit later to mop up any emotional spills, provide support and help navigate the aftermath. It had all felt perfectly reasonable when they were discussing it; now, however, as Kitty sat at the dining room table with the double doors thrown open, she felt more than a little nauseous, and it was nothing to do with the prospect of Greg cooking her supper.

She chuckled at the sound of squabbling coming from her small courtyard garden. Sophie, who looked beautiful with her enormous bump, was barking instructions at Greg and Olly, who seemed to be taking an age to light the barbecue.

'Let me do it. I'm training to be a doctor!'

'Really? You're training to be a doctor? Gosh, Olly, thank God you said that, because I hadn't heard you mention for five minutes the fact that you are studying medicine – and I had almost forgotten!' Sophie clicked her tongue. 'And yes, you are training to be a *doctor*, not a chef or a barbecue-pit master, so sod off! Greg can do it.'

'Greg's not a chef or a pit master either, he's a lecturer, in modern languages!' Olly yelled.

'Again, thank you for your valuable insight. Dork.'

Olly pulled a face and mimicked her stance.

Kitty always found it quite remarkable that no matter how old her kids got, how impressive their achievements or even the fact that one was about to become a parent, after mere minutes of trying to complete any chore together, they reverted to being toddlers.

Greg grabbed the matches but appeared to be quite clueless as to how to get the flames to jump and light the coals. Sophie now looked bored by the intense, almost scientific discussion about the best point at which to start cooking, should they ever get that far, and had started to pull tiny weeds from the crevices in the wall.

Kitty smiled at them from the dining table as she sat back and sipped her chilled glass of white wine, admiring the honey-suckle around the French windows, its slender tendrils taking the opportunity to snake into the room like a nosy creature. Her pulse quickened as Sophie came inside.

'Don't sit in here all on your own, come outside! We have sunshine, I ordered it especially for you.' Sophie stood behind her and placed her hands on her shoulders.

Kitty turned her head to the left and kissed the back of her daughter's hand. 'Thank you, Soph, that was kind. If you could summon up some rain for later on, it'll save me having to water my tubs.'

'I'm on it!' She laughed. 'You look miles away. Plus you've got your booze glow on.'

'Have I?' She touched her cheek and felt the warmth.

'Yep.'

Kitty smiled at her girl. 'Well, touché, and you have your baby glow on, as Tizz would say. I'm quite happy here, having a good old think.'

Sophie pulled out a chair and sat down. 'What are you thinking about?'

She noted the crease of concern above her daughter's nose and felt a spike of love for her.

Now, Kitty! This is the time. This is the moment...

'I'm thinking about your dad, actually.'

'Dad-Angus or Dad-Theo?'

Kitty laughed at the somewhat ridiculous need to clarify. 'Dad-Theo.' She took another glug of the cold, dry wine whose citrussy tang was just what she needed on this hot day to help ease the words from their hiding place.

'Theo is one of those people who has always just been there,' she began.

'Because you met at school.'

'Yes, but more than that. The day I met him, I felt...' She exhaled, trying to find the right words. 'I felt connected to him. I must have met dozens of people on that first day at Vaizey, but there was something about him and me... As I say, a connection.'

'It's good to be such old friends, nice to have that shared history. It's lovely for me. And it will be lovely for this little one too.' She cradled her bump. 'You will both be its grand-parents, after all.'

'Yes, we will. And that's the thing – I love him, Sophie,' she whispered.

'Aww, bless you, Mum! I know you do. He loves you too.' She smiled.

Kitty shook her head. 'No, Soph. I *love him* love him. Like proper love.'

The smile slipped from Sophie's face and she laid her hands flat on the tabletop. 'What do you mean?'

'I mean things have changed for me. For us. You know that moment when you cross the line in your mind and someone goes from being just a friend to the possibility of something more? It happened to me.'

Sophie's breath quickened. 'Did it happen for Dad?'

'It did.'

Sophie ran her fingers over her mouth. 'So I'm not sure what you're saying – do you, like, want to have a *relationship* with him?' She said this with a chuckle that carried the faint echo of disbelief.

'I *am* having a relationship with him.' She levelled with her girl and felt relief and fear in equal measure.

'Shit, Mum!'

'Is that "Shit, Mum, good!" or "Shit, Mum, bad!"?'

Sophie shook her head. 'I'm not really sure.'

Kitty stared at her, waiting for the words that would give her a clue as to how this was going.

'How long has it… have you…' She rolled her hand in the air.

'Erm, about six months, since the night of your engagement and baby announcement at the pub. But if I'm being honest…' She ignored the little humph noise her daughter made, suggesting she had been anything but. '… I think it was probably in the background for a lot longer than that.'

Sophie exhaled. 'This is… it's weird for me.'

'What, the fact that your mum might have fallen for your dad?' She tried to lighten the mood.

'Yes! Because you have always been Dad-Angus's wife, ex-wife, despite everything, and you and Theo were friends.

I know I was made in love, I get that, but it was hardly from a stable, long-term thing, and Theo and I are really close and it feels strange for me that you and he might—'

'Might what?'

'I don't know… It sounds ridiculous even to me, but I feel a bit odd about you going behind my back.'

Kitty let out a small burst of nervous laughter.

'I told you it sounded ridiculous.' Sophie looked down.

'No, it doesn't, darling. I understand. I think it might be a case of old-fashioned jealousy and I understand that completely, more than you know, but I can absolutely assure you that no matter what happens between Theo and me, you are our focus, you and Olly and Greg and the new baby. Nothing changes.' She looked out into the garden at her boy, who was now fanning the barbecue coals with the lip torn from a cardboard box.

'But that's not possible. It changes everything! It changes the whole dynamic of how we function as a family, and if it all goes tits up, it changes it even more!'

'I am hoping it doesn't all go tits up.'

'Well, of course, as I am sure you did with Dad-Angus, and he did with Nikolai, and every couple does with every other bloody relationship that hits the rocks and disintegrates! No one plans for failure, but *we* kind of have to, because we're all linked.'

Kitty considered this. 'I don't think that's any different from any family the world over. If things go wrong, the ripples are felt far and wide, of course. But we're not entering into this to fail and we are not doing it lightly.'

'I don't want you or Theo to get hurt. And it would be doubly hard if it was the both of you hurting each other. How would we deal with that?'

Kitty stared at her daughter. 'So do you think it's safer not to try? Do you think we should nip this happiness in the bud and go back to being lonely and alone? That can't be right, can it?'

'We need help out here, Soph!' Greg called through the French windows.

Sophie stood slowly and spoke softly. 'No, but I have hated being in the middle of you and Angus, and Angus and Nikolai, and you and Angus and Richard. Even though you all kind of get on, it's not been easy, for me or Olly, and the relationship I have with Theo, despite the rather odd beginning, is one of the most straightforward. I can talk to him, just talk without first having to filter my words in case I say the wrong thing, mention the wrong event, pick off a scab of hurt about something that might have happened a long time ago. He and I can just chat and I like how easy it is.' She sighed. 'I'm scared of losing that.'

'You won't lose that. What you and Theo have is very special. He's your Theo,' she admitted, and smiled.

'I don't want things to become difficult or complicated. I've had enough of that – we all have.'

Haven't we just.

'I want you both to be happy, Mum, I do, but there's something else…'

'What, darling?'

'I don't know if I should say.'

'Go on, Soph, you know you can say anything to me.'

Sophie looked skywards, as if mentally selecting the right words. 'I can only think of Theo and Anna. Anna and Theo. They were a great love story, and they worked.' She shrugged. 'And I don't want you to be a poor second. That's not fair on either of you.'

Kitty felt the force of her daughter's words like a punch to the chest, hitting her precisely where she was most vulnerable. 'A poor second... The great love story.... Theo and Anna. Anna and Theo.' It left her winded. She could only nod at Sophie, who headed back outside.

Kitty stood and made her way on wobbly legs up the stairs to her bedroom. She slipped onto the bed and turned her face into the soft down pillow. *You fool, Kitty. You bloody fool. How could you be so blind? Blind all over again.* Her tears were muffled and her heart ached. *Sophie's right, of course she is. Anna and Theo – two people, one love...*

She must have fallen asleep, because when she woke, the sky had darkened and the smell of barbecued meat permeated the air. She sat up and looked at the clock: an hour had passed. She heard the sound of conversation in the courtyard and then the boom of Theo's laugh. *Shit!* She had quite forgotten that he was coming over. And he would already have spent time with Sophie, whom she'd told, and she would surely have mentioned it to the boys... Kitty buried her face in her hands. The situation was already a knotty mess. She lay back on the pillow and wished again for the sweet oblivion of sleep. She closed her eyes for a few minutes.

'There you are, sleepy head!' Theo burst in and sat down hard on the side of the bed where his cufflinks, cologne and *Classic Cars* magazine nestled secretly in the bedside drawer. 'I came up earlier, but you were dead to the world.' He leant over and kissed her. 'Sophie and the guys are happy! I'm happy!' He lay down next to her. 'I'm giving you fair warning, but act surprised – they've put a bottle of bubbly on ice and are planning a bit of a toast.'

Kitty couldn't stifle the sob that left her throat.

'Oh no!' He propped himself up on one elbow and looked at her face. 'Why are you crying? It went well – we can relax! The cat is out of the bag and we can relax, finally! It's a good, good day.'

Kitty shook her head, sat up against the pillows and grabbed a tissue from the box on her night stand, which she balled and dabbed at her eyes and under her nose.

'What on earth's the matter?' He held her hand.

'I didn't plan on having these feelings for you, Theo.'

'I don't think feelings like this can be planned,' he replied, clearly confused about where this might be heading.

'There has always been a strong link, a friendship…'

'Yes, always.' He squeezed her hand inside his.

Sitting up even straighter, she rested against the headboard and shrugged her hand free of his grip before wrapping her cotton cardigan around her middle. 'I love you, Theo. I do.'

'I know. And I love you.' He kissed her hand.

Kitty recalled the way Angus could never comfortably say those words to her, and this made her sob even harder.

'I love you very much,' he repeated, 'which is why I am finding it hard to fathom the tears!' He stared at her and it was difficult to read his expression.

Kitty swallowed, dry mouthed, hating the feeling of vulnerability and something approaching shame that pulsed through her. Her cheeks flushed. 'Sophie said something that has made me think. It made sense.'

He looked concerned. 'What did she say?'

'She said that you and Anna were the great love story – Theo and Anna, Anna and Theo – and she's right! Anna was your one, and you had something perfect.' Her tone was purposefully neutral, to deflect her embarrassment. 'And I don't know *why* I thought there could be anything between us other than the friendship we have shared for all these years – and Sophie, of course. But we need to forget everything, we need to go back to how it was because I don't want to be anyone's poor second choice.'

'What on earth are you talking about? Where has this come from?'

'I told you, it was something Sophie said and she's right. It's Anna and Theo, that's the way the universe intended it, not Kitty and Theo!' She let her tears fall.

Theo took her into his arms and the two sat in silence until her breathing had found its natural rhythm and her tears had ceased.

'We shouldn't waste this life, Kitty. This one short blip of a life, it goes so fast.'

'It does.' She pictured her once lively mum ensconced in the prison of her choosing with one eye on the window and her fingers clutching the sheet, white-knuckled with fear.

'We shouldn't waste us,' he said. 'That would be a tragedy.'

'Do you think so?' she whispered.

'I know so.' He kissed her scalp. 'I did love Anna. I *do* love Anna, and I always will. I do feel that sometimes we don't mention her when it would be appropriate to do so and that's a shame as she was a big part of my life and a part of yours. She loved your daughter, very, very much.'

'Yes, she did. But I want to be honest, Theo.'

'I need you to be.' He held her tight.

She hesitated. 'The thing is, and I am just shooting from the hip here, so please feel free to pick out the bits that resonate, and I'm nervous, so it might be garbled.'

'Okay.'

She had his attention. 'I have never been anyone's first choice.'

'What do you mean?'

'Quite rightly my dad adored my mum first and foremost and I slotted in where I could, happily, and then with Angus, I was his consolation, his alternative, but Thomas was his number one. Sophie has found her wonderful Greg, and Olly has Victoria, and for you it's Anna. Anna is and will always be your great love, and that makes me the runner-up again.'

Theo looked up, seeming to consider this. 'Life doesn't work that way.' He pulled her even closer. 'You are right, Anna and I were the greatest love story and I will always treasure that, but that doesn't mean that's it! My life doesn't end because hers did. I get to go on, and believe me, I didn't want to for a while, but you are not and never have been my consolation prize. You are my now, my present. And I love you now, right now, with all my heart, like I love no other. Anna taught me that was possible. She gave me the foundations of how to love and I loved her and I love you. I do, Kitty. I love you!' His voice caught.

'I guess I'm worried that I can't compete with someone who's no longer here.'

'Don't go there – you'll drive yourself nuts. Anna is forever forty-eight. You, God willing, will get old, wrinkly and cranky and I will love you just as much then as I do now. It's not second place, not for either of us; it's the world settling so that everyone is in their rightful place right now! And our rightful place right now is together. What we share can't diminish what Anna and I shared, and if anything happened to me and you went on to find someone else, it wouldn't diminish what we have. It's all we can work with – today, the present, this moment! And I'm not prepared to waste a second of it lamenting the past. I have done that for far too long and for too much of my youth. Okay, Montrose?'

'Okay, Montgomery.' She reached up and kissed the mouth of the man she loved and who loved her right now, this very moment, in the present.

'We should get married.'

'What?' She stared at him, open-mouthed, as happiness filled her up. 'Is that a proposal?'

'Yes. If Olly and Soph are okay with it.'

She held his gaze. 'I think we should keep it to ourselves for the time being. It might be more than anyone can cope with! I love you, Theo.'

'I love you too.'

It was as they kissed that they heard the light tap on the bedroom door. Sophie walked in with two glasses, Greg held the bottle of bubbly and Olly was bearing a cupcake with a candle in it.

'This was all we could find – consider it a congratulations cake!' Olly walked towards the bed and Kitty and Theo blew out the tiny candle.

'Yes, congratulations!' Greg fiddled with the cork until it fired from the bottle and hit the ceiling.

'Jesus, Greg!' Sophie yelled. 'I would like to propose a toast.' She lifted her glass of orange juice. 'I would like to officially say how wonderful it is to know that two of the people I love most in the whole wide world…'

'None taken.' Greg high-fived Olly.

Sophie continued. '… are in love. I wish you both all the happiness in the whole wide world!'

Greg passed around the glasses and everyone sipped. Kitty felt a flutter of joy in her heart, knowing she would never forget this night or her daughter's beautiful words.

'Thank you, darling.' Theo spoke for them both.

'Okay, my turn!' Olly cleared his throat.

'Can I just—' Sophie tried to interrupt.

'No, Soph, this is my turn.' Olly shot her down. 'I would like to say—'

'Olly, please!' Sophie tried again.

'Christ, you've had your five minutes – you always do this. It's my turn now! I just want to say how absolutely—'

'Olly, for God's sake, I need you to stop talking!' Sophie shouted. 'I need everyone to stop talking.' She placed her hand on her stomach and her glass of orange juice on the window-sill. 'My waters have broken! This is it – the baby is coming!'

'Oh shit! Oh shit! Oh God, Soph! Oh my God, no!' Olly walked in a circle, seemingly unable to decide where to put the cupcake and with a look close to panic on his face.

Greg looked at his soon-to-be brother-in-law and spoke calmly. 'That's it, Olly, you turn around in circles. I've got this. Me, a lecturer in modern languages.'

The kirk was packed to the rafters. It felt like the whole of the Highlands had turned out and it made Kitty smile. It was proof of her dad's kindness. It was still unreal to her that he had gone.

Patrick, resting on the arm of his son, stopped at the end of the pew and held Kitty's hand. 'Stephen was a fine man. My dearest friend. And I shall miss him greatly.'

'Thank you, Patrick. I know he loved you.'

The old man walked away with tears in his eyes.

Theo reached for her hand. It was the show of support she needed on this sad day. All stood in silence as the single piper slowly made his way down the centre of the kirk; the sweet sound of the pipes filled the space and reverberated in their chests. Ruraigh and Hamish wept loudly, tears cried in earnest for the man who'd been like a father to them. Kitty wiped her eyes and looked up. The piper played louder, as if to ensure the sound would break through the roof, glance off the water in the burn and twist away along the glen like mist on the morn. Heaven would be in no doubt that today they were receiving the soul of a proud son of Scotland. She pictured Marjorie and her mum and smiled at the thought of them putting the kettle on.

It was good to see the house busy. The rooms, usually empty and a little flat, were alive with the dance of fires in the grates and the echo of chatter. A drink or two was taken and Isla and her daughter Rhona, who now ran the village pub, had done them proud with the catering.

Tizz came and stood by Kitty's side with the sleeping Roseanna in her arms. 'I am stealing your granddaughter,' she whispered. 'I love her. I can't give her back, and you can't make me.'

'I think her mum might have something to say about that.' Kitty ran her fingertip over the sweet, rounded cheek of the six-month-old baby who had brought them all so much joy.

'I love the photos of your dad holding her.' Tizz closed her eyes briefly. 'I am glad he knew and loved her.'

'Me too.' Kitty swiped at her tears that were never very far away.

Ruraigh, Hamish and Theo had taken root on the sofa in the library.

'What are you three plotting?' She sat on the chair by the fire and pushed off her shoes with her heel and then her toes.

'We were just talking about Darraghfield, wondering what will happen to it.' Hamish took a sip of his whisky.

Kitty looked into the fire and remembered them burning things as kids, anything they could get hold of – paper, wood, wrappers and junk. It had been a major preoccupation. She liked how every sight, every room held so many happy memories. 'Well, either of you could come up and stay here. You know the life. Or both of you, in fact – it's big enough!'

'What about you two?' Ruraigh looked at Theo. 'I mean, it's yours, Kitty, by rights. It's your home.'

'I wouldn't do that to Theo.'

'Do what to Theo?' He sat forward in his chair.

'Take you away from London and all you've ever known, the bright lights of the big city. I couldn't ask you to swap that for a life of dark, icy mornings, temperamental weather, and an estate that will bleed you dry!'

Theo stood up, straightened his jacket and looked at them one by one. 'I know you all remember Mr Porter, the groundsman at Vaizey, my friend. What you may not know is that he gave me this...' He turned over his lapel to reveal the little gold safety pin with its fishing fly of delicate green and blue feathers and a square red bead. 'He told me to wear it somewhere discreet and to use it as a reminder to seek out the stillness. He told me that's where I'd find peace, and he was right. I *have* found peace – with you, Kitty, and here at Darraghfield.' He fixed his gaze on her. 'It's something I've been thinking about for a while now... I think we should sell our houses in London and move here. New beginnings and all that. I know it's what Stephen wanted. I always thought it would be lovely for you to be able to swim every day, Kitty, weather permitting, and here you can. You might get your gills after all!'

Kitty stared at him; she had never loved him more.

'Not a bad speech for a Theobald's boy.' Ruraigh chuckled. 'But if you'd been in Tatum's you'd have done it with a bit more flourish!'

'Tatum's!'

'Tatum's!' Ruraigh and Hamish made the toast.

'You Tatum's boys were always the same, boasting about your bloody cricket shield!'

'Ah, did I hear mention of the Tatum's cricket shield?' Angus walked into the library with Roseanna, still asleep, in his arms. He had evidently managed to wrangle her from Tizz. 'Might I remind you that *I* was captain of that very team for the whole four years we were unbeaten!'

'No one cared about your shield!' Theo shook his head and sat down.

'Oh Theobald's sour grapes!' Angus, Ruraigh and Hamish laughed.

'Do you think Roseanna will go to Vaizey?' Angus asked casually.

'No!'

'Yes!'

'Yes!'

Theo, Ruraigh and Hamish answered in unison.

Sophie put Roseanna down for the night while Greg stacked the dishwasher and Olly and Victoria gathered discarded plates and glasses from around the house. Kitty and Theo finished clingfilming the leftover food before making their way back to the library. They sank down onto the sofa and gazed at the orange glow from the fire.

'How are you feeling?' he asked as he placed the blanket from the arm of the sofa over her lap.

'It's been a funny old day. Sad, of course, but so lovely too. It was great to have everyone together and it's been good reminiscing with the boys.'

Theo gave a soft laugh; she knew he had enjoyed it too.

'Bless you for saying that earlier.'

'What?'

'About moving up here. I know we never could, but it meant the world that you didn't dismiss it immediately. This place is part of me. My heritage, my history.'

'I wasn't joking, Kitty. I meant every word! We should pack up, sell our houses and relocate. Let's just do it!'

'What would your mum say?'

'I can still visit her, poor old thing. She loves it at Hill View, bossing everyone around.'

Kitty smiled at the image of Theo's cantankerous mother holding court. 'Are we really going to do it, Theo? Are we going to come up here to live?'

'Yes. We are.'

Kitty laid her head on his shoulder and closed her eyes. She too had found peace at Darraghfield, she felt settled, sitting on the sofa with her toes curled against her man in front of the fire. And her dad was right, it was so much more than fine. She glanced down at the ancient Indian pouffe and saw herself as a little girl, looking up at her mum and dad sitting just where she was right now.

Moving Home

Kitty yawned and lay back on the sofa. Night was closing in. There was still plenty of packing to do, but she was struggling to find the energy. It felt strange to have spent the day reliving so much of her past. It was still surreal that she was moving back to Darraghfield, going home, and with Theo by her side.

'I hope I can make him happy. I love him so much!' she whispered into the ether.

Making her way wearily into the kitchen, she took a deep breath; the air was filled with the unmistakeable scent of lemons. It was heady, intoxicating and quite delicious. She gripped the lemon in the fruit bowl and inhaled the aroma, much fainter now.

She heard a key in the door; a quick glance at the clock told her it was nearly 9 p.m.

'Only me!' Theo called out.

'What are you doing here?' Kitty smiled, reaching up on tiptoes to kiss her man. 'You're supposed to be staying in Barnes tonight – we only have two more days of packing and that's it, we're off!'

'I couldn't stay away.'

'Poor Theo.' She wrapped him in a hug. 'Did you hear? Roseanna has a new tooth.'

'I did.' He grinned. The shared joy of grandparenthood had not diminished.

'I am so excited!' she whispered. 'We are about to take on this whole big adventure, but I don't feel in the least bit afraid – I'm just happy.'

Theo pulled away and stared at her face. 'I do love you, Kitty Montrose. And you're right, it is a whole big adventure.

> 'The wild hawk to the wind-swept sky,
> The deer to the wholesome wold,
> And the heart of a man to the heart of a maid,
> As it was in the days of old.

> 'The heart of a man to the heart of a maid –
> Light of my tents, be fleet.
> Morning waits at the end of the world,
> And the world is all at our feet!'

Epilogue

It was a warm, sunny day at Darraghfield with only the mildest breeze to ruffle the leaves; even the birds seemed to be lying low. Kitty popped on her sunglasses and looked out over the sweep of the glen. She was waiting to see Morgan and Missy, Olly and Victoria's little ones, as they came across the slope on their ponies. They'd promised to stop and wave.

'I hope they go easy on that ridge, it can be dangerous if the weather changes.' Almost instinctively she rubbed the kink in her arm, a reminder of the night she had absolutely refused to do as she was told. Now that she was in her late sixties, her bones seemed to ache no matter what, her arm more so.

Theo placed the teacup back in its saucer and held up the postcard. 'From Spud and Kumi!'

'Yes, you've already read it to me!' She tutted, knowing that this would not stop him doing so again. She kept a lookout for Morgan and Missy as he read aloud:

'India! Who'd have thought it! It's a whole new world of sights and sounds and I am savouring every one. Hotel grand. Weather hot. Only downside, not a plate of breaded scampi to be found anywhere, old friend, and you know how I love my scampi!'

He wheezed his laughter – 'Scampi!' – and flipped over

the card to study the vast golden dome shining in the sun of Lucknow. 'It seems that India is the place to be. Angus and his friend Rex are currently trekking in the foothills of the Himalayas. I don't know how he does it. My creaking bloody hip means it's a struggle to get up and down the stairs, let alone going trekking!'

'And we now know your mum was born in India,' Kitty reminded him.

'Yes, she was.' Theo smiled, and she knew he remembered her fondly.

'Grampy, can we go and look in the hedge?' a small voice called from behind him. He turned to find Sophie's four-year-old daughter Amelie standing behind him in her jeans and pink sparkly T-shirt.

'Of course we can!' Placing his arms on the table, he pushed himself up and took a second to let the twinge in his hip settle.

Amelie rushed forward and placed her tiny hand inside his. 'You come too, Grandma!'

'Oh, righto!' Kitty stood, as ever doing the bidding of her adorable baby granddaughter.

The three strolled slowly to the end of the lawn and came to a stop at the spiky hedgerow.

'I can't see any birdies!' Amelie whispered, peering into the dark space, having been taught to only whisper so as not to alarm any chicks.

'They might be asleep or not hatched yet?' Theo suggested.

'Shall we make them something for their nests?' Amelie asked enthusiastically.

'That's a great idea.' Theo kissed the top of his granddaughter's head. 'What do you think we should make, Grandma?'

'Ooh, I don't know, how about we put a few berries in to

make them lunch?' She straightened and looked out again over the glen. Still no sign of the kids on their ponies.

'I know!' Amelie gasped. 'A cushion! Let's make them a tiny cushion! So they don't scratch their heads on the branches when they go to sleep!' She clasped her little hands in excitement.

'That is a very good idea. I might have some fabric and a bit of stuffing in the workshop, shall we go and see?' Theo grasped his wife's hand and they strolled back up towards the house.

'Yes!' Amelie skipped and ran ahead up the wide sweep of the front lawn.

Theo pushed on the stable door of his workshop and Kitty was surprised to find Elliott sitting reading in an old winged-back chair in the corner.

'Hey, Elliot! It's a lovely sunny day, you don't want to be cooped up in here alone.' She smiled at the handsome, book-ish boy, Sophie's middle child, a couple of years younger than Roseanna.

'I'm not alone.' He pointed to the floor, where Twitcher the grouchy bulldog dozed by his feet.

'Ah, just so. You can help us if you like. Amelie, Grampy and I are going to make tiny cushions to go inside birds' nests, so the birds don't scratch their heads on the branches.'

Elliot rolled his eyes, reminding her that in a couple of years he would be reaching full-blown teenagehood.

'Elliot was crying in the car,' Amelie said.

'Shut up, Amelie!' Elliot slammed the book shut and jumped up.

'Steady now, Elliot, Amelie is only worried for you.' Theo ruffled the little girl's hair. 'Tell you what, Ami, can you go and have one more look in that hedge, we need you to count any nests you can see to make sure we make the right number of cushions. But remember, we mustn't touch them or disturb them in any way, we can only look.'

'Okay!' She raced out of the workshop and back down the lawn. Kitty stood by the open door so she could watch her.

'What's going on, Elliot? What's making you angry? It's not like you to snap at your sister like that,' Theo said gently.

'Nothing.' Elliot kicked the concrete floor.

'Well, trust me when I tell you that a problem shared is a problem halved.' Theo walked forward and leant on the workbench.

'Grampy is right,' Kitty said.

'I just hate school. I don't want to be a Vaizey boy!' He briefly caught her eye.

'You hate school or the people in it?' Theo asked.

'I just don't want to go.'

'I'm afraid it's one of life's necessary evils, but there are things you can do to get through it and make it easier.'

Elliot looked up at his grampy with such hope that Kitty's heart flexed. 'It's okay for you, Grampy, you don't have to go there every day.'

Theo smiled. 'Trust me, I wasn't that fond of school either.'

'Everyone tells me how much everybody loved it, and I know that's where you met Gran!'

'Yes, I did and that was the one good thing. And I made a good friend, other than your gran.' He closed his eyes briefly and Kitty knew he was picturing Mr Porter. 'Is someone being mean to you?'

'Not really. One or two of the sporty boys are horrible to me, they laugh at me because I'm rubbish at catching, but it's not just me, they're mean to everyone.'

'Can you tell your housemaster?' Kitty suggested.

Elliot shrugged as if that would be futile.

'The thing is, Elliot, when people are mean, it's usually not because they are bad people but probably because they are a bit sad inside. I used to have a boy be mean to me, his name was Wilson. And yet in the end we became quite good friends. It's important to remember that you never know anyone's story by looking at them; you never know what's going on. They might be sad but making out to be happy, or angry or mean because they don't know how to explain how sad they're feeling.'

'I suppose so.'

'And you are so lucky, you have all of us, who love you very much and who will always fight your corner.' Kitty walked forward and embraced the boy she loved. 'And you know, Elliot, you can talk to Mum and Dad any time.' She decided to tell Sophie.

'Have you heard about the alphabet game, Elliot?' Theo asked.

The boy shook his head.

'Well, here's a neat trick that someone wonderful once told me all about, and I think it might help you.'

'What is it?' Elliot looked up at him.

'If your thoughts are too loud, or you feel afraid or you just want to pass the time, you go through the alphabet and find things to match the letters and by the time you get to Z, things have usually calmed a little and you will have taken time to breathe.'

Kitty could see Elliot was confused. 'So for example in here we could have A... armchair, B... bench.'

'C... chisel,' Theo chimed in.

'D... dog!' Elliot pointed at Twitcher.

'Now you've got it!' Theo beamed. 'It might help.'

Elliot nodded. 'I love you, Grampy, and I love you, Grandma.'

The boy nestled in, laying his small head on Kitty's bony chest and linking his hands around her waist. She inhaled the scent of the boy, evocative of summer meadows, and she smiled. This contact, this love was the very essence of joy. She felt the usual flutter of happiness in her chest at hearing those words. 'And I love you. Now then, how about we go and see if there's any more tea in the pot?'

'Okay.' Elliot smiled. 'Come on, Twitcher! E… easel. F… frame. G… golf club!'

Kitty winked at her husband.

Sophie had taken a seat at the table on the patio and was sipping tea while watching Amelie by the hedgerow.

'My friend said you were very rich,' Elliot announced as he sat on his mum's lap and spoke to his grampy.

'Did he now?' Theo half chuckled and sat in his favourite chair.

'He said you were in a magazine article about people who had zillions of pounds and his mum saw it.'

'Sounds about right – I know the mother.' Sophie pulled a face behind her son's back.

'Here's the thing, Elliot. I don't quite have zillions of pounds, but more importantly, I would swap every penny of it to spend days like this with you and your grandma. Waking up with her by my side makes me the richest man in the world.'

Kitty looked over at Theo and smiled at him from the wicker chair in which she reclined. The sight of him still sent a bolt of joy racing through her. It made her think of dear old Tizz, who had lost her battle with breast cancer only the year before and whom she still missed dearly. Ruraigh was still hiding away. Hamish and Flo were with him. She remembered Tizz telling her that she might have unrealistic notions about sex and that bodice-ripping and romance were overrated. Kitty had discovered that on this point Tizz was wrong.

'Ignore your grampy, he's an old fool.' Kitty began cutting the Victoria sponge that sat on the tray in the centre of the table.

'I might be an old fool, but I am your old fool.'

Kitty beamed at him.

'Oh, please, you two!' Sophie tutted.

'Darling, I only hope that you and Greg get to laugh and love every day, even when you are old fools like us.' She refilled Theo's cup from the teapot and handed it to him.

'Because it's the small things that count, Soph.' Theo nodded. 'Small things, shared with the person you love. It's all you need.' He took a sip and waved to his granddaughter, who waved back from the hedgerow. 'That's happiness. At least it is for me.'

Me too, my darling man. Me too.

Kitty stood and shielded her eyes as she looked out over the deep glen and beyond to the rolling hills. 'Where are those kids?' She was getting anxious. It was late afternoon and the sky had begun to turn mackerel-coloured.

'There they are!' Theo called out, pointing to the distant hill opposite.

Kitty watched Missy weave her way across the slope with her two red plaits bouncing up and down. Morgan followed close behind, walking his pony across the field, where clumps of tall thistles and lichen-covered rocks littered the grass.

'Go easy!' she urged under her breath, knowing the terrain made the going a little tough along the sharp incline. Missy bent forward and patted her pony's flank with the flat of her palm. At the top of the field, they both broke into a canter and cleared the ridge; it was now only a matter of time before they would make it round to the main bridleway and back home. She felt a wave of relief.

'Well, I don't know about anyone else, but I think I fancy a swim.' Theo placed his teacup on the table and went off to change.

'I'll come with you,' Kitty called, never able to resist a dip.

The two flung their towels on the back of the faded steamer chair and trod the Roman steps cautiously as they slipped into the warm water.

Kitty swam lengths, pulling through the water until she was out of breath, then floating on her back. This pool was still her most treasured spot on the planet. She bit her lip and felt an unexpected wave of emotion. It happened on occasion, this jolt to her senses, as if time had been erased. It seemed like mere months since she was a young girl, swimming and lost to her watery world while Marjorie prepared food in the kitchen, her mum languished upstairs and her dad roamed the estate with Patrick and Champ by his side. Yet it wasn't months; decades and decades had passed and she had to concentrate, wrinkling her nose, to figure out where all the time had gone.

Theo swam over and placed his arms under her back. 'You look a little thoughtful, my love.'

She relaxed against him and let the water lap over her shoulders and ears. She didn't know how long they stayed like that – minutes, an hour? Her hold on time was skewed, so lost was she to the water, the sunlight, and the sensation of being held, carried, weightless and fragile, in the arms of the man she loved, her Theo.

'I used to think a lot about the girl who swam here, the girl Angus courted, the little girl who didn't know how to help her mum or support her daddy. I wanted to go back in time and take her in my wise arms and rock her until the sadness had passed, until the shape of that boy had slipped back through the gap in the hedge and the world had returned to a simple, sunny, ordinary day...'

'And now?' Theo leant forward and kissed her cheek.

She smiled. 'Now I want to go back and tell her to hang in there, that everything will turn out all right. That she will go on to meet a boy and she will like the look of him and he will like the look of her and they will fall in love and lead a simple life surrounded by the family they create.'

'That sounds like a lovely way to live, Montrose.' He spun her around in the water.

'Oh it is, Montgomery. It really is.'

THE END